Veil of Shadows

A novel of *The Seven Deadly Veils*, Book One

Diana Marik

Veil of Shadows ~ Seven Deadly Veils, Book One
Copyright © 2016, Diana Marika Preston
Cover Art by Kris Norris

Published by Diana Marik
Released June 2016

The Seven Deadly Veils

Available Now
Veil of Shadows, Book One
The Blue Veil, a novella
Veil of Mists, Book Two
Veil of Darkness, Book Three
Veil of Secrets, Book Four

Coming Soon ~ March 2019
Veil of Destiny, Book Five

Praise for Diana Marik's Veilverse

"This is one series not to be missed!" —*RT Book Reviews*

Veil of Shadows

"The suspense is as dramatic and intense as the action, and paired with Marik's steamy sex scenes, will leave readers satisfied on many levels."

—*RT Book Reviews*

"Ms. Marik has made this new Paranormal World come alive and leave me begging for more."

—*Sik Reviews*

"The characters are edgy, sexy, and intriguing; the suspense kept me on the edge waiting to see what would happen next. I highly recommend this book to fans of paranormal romance and romantic urban fantasy."

—*Comfy Chair Books*

"Completely captivated me; I absolutely LOVED it! With so many awesome characters, I simply couldn't put it down until the last page."

—*Paranormal/Urban Fantasy Book Lover's Haven*

The Blue Veil

"Marik's compelling delivery commands readers' attention; the easy, seamless passion and intensity between characters is a welcome companion to a perfect balance of action and suspense."

—*RT Book Reviews*

"The characters are edgy and intriguing; the plot is suspenseful and sexy. I'm drawn into this series and fascinated by the world that Ms. Marik has created."

—*L. M. Reigel Reviews*

"I am so Team Remare. This novella just keeps us hooked to the story."

—*Sik Reviews*

"Just one word...REMARE! Love that dark and dangerous vampire."

Veil of Mists

"Danger and deception know no bounds in this riveting installment of the Seven Deadly Veils series. Marik continues the spellbinding tale of Miranda Crescent, weaving an edgy tale of romance and reconnaissance."

"I am obsessed with this series. Diana Marik has created a high intensity series that grabs you and doesn't let go."

"Completely captivating; I LOVE this series...deception at its finest! One hell of a ride."

Veil of Darkness

"The chemistry between Miranda and Remare is extraordinary. Marik holds nothing back in this action-packed romance, which delivers all of the danger, darkness and sensuality that readers crave; this is one series not to be missed."

"Smoking hot chemistry! A wonderful suspense and action novel complete with a sizzling romance. Very addicting!"

"Another fantastic read in this series. An amazing journey. The characters come to life on the pages pulling you into their world."

Veil of Secrets

"The characters are well-developed and fascinating. The series plot is growing and expanding; the action, suspense and romance are woven perfectly together!"

"Ms. Marik has created an interesting, intricate vampire world, with other paranormal elements.

"All paranormal fans need to read this series filled with strong, sophisticated, fun, sexy characters."

—Amazon Reviewer

"A fantastic installment in this intriguing series. Superb! A delicious plot! Once again all her richly developed characters pop in the spotlight teasing with juicy clues to all the secrets behind the veil. When it's pulled back be prepared for some shocking revelations."

—Goodreads Reviewer

Dedication

This book is lovingly dedicated to the real Lizandra, who knew better than anyone else how to lift the veil of shadows.

Acknowledgments

I think every author feels a great deal of gratitude toward the people who make her dreams come true. I want to thank my editor, Jessica Bimberg, for all the work and encouragement she has given me, my cover artist, Kris Norris, for her amazing work. Also, fond thanks to the original members of "Marik's Mortals" fan club: Joanne, Jane, Marlene, Lorraine, Barbara, Matisse, Kathy, Lori, Celia, Jennifer, Laurie, Theresa, Nil, Loren and the amazing Bridget. Last, but not least thanks to the wonderful people of the Book Obsessed Chicks Book Club. A special thanks to Kim and Janet. You rock!

Chapter One

"He's a dumbass vampire," Miranda Crescent snarked into her iPhone as she ran down the stairs of the New York City Museum Annex. "He has hundreds of people working for him! Any one of them could've brought my handbag to me, but does he even think of that? No!" She flagged down a cab on Seventh Avenue to go to the Financial District to meet with Lord Valadon in his corporate fortress, ValCorp. "I bust my ass to get his credentials done on his painting so he can have his board meeting, and does he even think to thank me? No!"

"Miranda, *dahling*, he's da leader of da VN—the entire freakin' Vampire Nation. He can do whatever he wants," Lizandra Wells purred with a hint of her Caribbean accent. "And did he make you forget your bag? Is he responsible that you left it behind, again?"

Miranda stifled the growl in her throat. "No," she reluctantly admitted.

"Perhaps he just wants to spend more time with you. You know—after-hours stuff."

"Oh, get real! With the supermodels he hangs out with, I don't think so." Miranda laughed at her best friend, who was always trying to fix her up with someone. Vampires now, she muttered. As she got into the cab, she gave the driver the address. "I mean, *really!* The museum is on an austerity budget. We don't have the resources ValCorp has to afford couriers, and he has millions, no—billions! He could have sent someone. This was damned rude if you ask me." Miranda inhaled a deep, calming breath and admired the sights of the city. Lowering the window to let the night air in, she breathed in New York's more intriguing scents: the Hudson River, various ethnic foods from the street vendors, restaurant refuse, as well as car exhaust fumes. "Anyway, I'm going to be late tonight. Save me a seat at Nightshade."

"Will do," Lizandra said, "But, if you want to spend a couple of hours chatting up da sexy vampire, feel free. I'm sure Cyra and I can find plenty ta do."

"Not happening. I'm getting my purse, and then, I'm getting the hell out of there. Dumbass vampire," Miranda muttered again. "I'll let you know when I'm on my way."

"No worries. And give da vampire king my greetings."

"Funny!" Miranda ended her call and tried not to think about Valadon. As queen of the Black Star werewolf clan, Lizandra had been in meetings with the ruling vampire and deeply respected him. Valadon was fabulously wealthy, handsome, and the paparazzi went nuts wherever he went, but he was also a very old and powerful vampire. *A vampire, for Christ's sake, and a dangerous one at that!* True, he was attractive with his dark brown hair, penetrating green eyes, sculptured cheekbones, and he dressed to kill. *Though with his fangs he didn't have to.*

Miranda closed her eyes and thought back to earlier in the day when she'd been in Valadon's conference room examining the Matisse painting. She'd felt her skin going cold and slowly scanned the room sensing...someone else was present, watching her; but when she turned, no one was there. Shrugging off the disturbing feeling, she finished her analysis of pigment hues and brush techniques. After staring so long at the figures in the painting, she decided to get up closer. Impulsively, she toed off her heels and climbed up on the leather couch.

Matisse was a master of shading, and Miranda loved eyeballing the variations up close. Unexpectedly, she'd felt something icy crawling up her spine and lost her footing. She'd been about to fall on her ass when two powerful arms caught her. The combined scents of vampire and night ocean breezes permeated the air.

"Professor Crescent, if you require a ladder, I'm sure I can arrange to have one made available." Valadon's baritone voice made the hairs on her arms stand up as he slowly lowered her to the floor. It was impossible not to be affected by his presence. His scent was too powerful—like the man himself. And his eyes, my God, of all his striking features, his emerald eyes were the most captivating.

Damn, what a way to meet the enigmatic vampire leader. She righted her glasses and smoothed her dress. Valadon was far more handsome in person than he was in any of the magazines. Pictures could never capture the essence of the man; no image would ever be able to define his presence or his power. With his tantalizing half smile, Lord Valadon had seemed amused, but Miranda thought she saw something deeper, darker in his penetrating gaze as if he could see through to her very soul.

Vampires had an otherworldly aspect: Something that spoke to the differences between humans and vampires—an ethereal intensity she couldn't fathom, and she was *very* good at reading people. To Miranda, an empath, the various races of the world had unique frequencies that identified vampire and Were as *different* from human. And Miranda was especially sensitive to that pitch.

Shaking off her reveries, Miranda watched the skyscrapers of the Financial District pass by. There was construction going on to repair the damage caused by the war nearly twenty years ago, when some lunatic in a foreign country decided to send air strikes to America. Retribution had been swift and complete. The city was almost completely rebuilt with the help of the Vampire Nation, even though there were still dead zones with abandoned buildings.

The cab pulled up to ValCorp, the black steel and glass edifice stood eloquently against the night sky. After paying the driver, Miranda quickly sped up the stairs and went through the circular doors. Since it was a Friday night, the building was nearly deserted and had an eerie feel to it. *Silent as the grave.* She stifled a shudder. The black and gold marble floor had columns supporting the high ceiling and were polished to such a sheen it gave the impression shadows were following her.

A young man in uniform behind the console said, "Valadon is waiting for you in his office. He said for you to go right up." The guard motioned to the elevator that went directly to Valadon's penthouse offices. She nodded and wondered where Valadon's *real* security force was located; she was sure her every step was being monitored somewhere in the building.

She smirked as the doors of the elevator closed. Whoever said vampires had an aversion to mirrors had never been inside ValCorp, she thought sardonically. She checked her reflection in the darkly tinted mirrors and held her stomach at the silent speed of the elevator.

When the doors opened to the penthouse suite, where Valadon employed only his most trusted vampires, Miranda glanced again at her watch and grimaced. "Dumbass vampire could have sent my bag down to me." She walked quietly down the hall.

Gazing out the windows at the NYC skyline, she was mesmerized by the view—a view she never tired of seeing. No other city in the world could compare. The lights glowed brightly in the office buildings against the darkness. She shook her head in awe and shuddered. Vampires, coldblooded creatures, didn't need heat the way humans did and kept the thermostat turned down low. Miranda paused to catch a whiff of perfume and smiled; it was the same fragrance Cyra had given her as a present.

As she approached the sunken conference area, she saw the partially opened door to Valadon's darkened office. Slowly, she pushed the door open and spotted her bag on the couch. Searching the shadows, she heard a shuffling sound and inhaled Valadon's seductive scent.

"I believe I'm the dumbass vampire you were referring to."

Miranda gasped as she heard the deep, evocative voice of New York's premier vampire. Valadon appeared out of the shadows. He stepped closer to the windows; she could make out his form, but not his face. "Lord Valadon." She steadied her breathing. "I didn't see you. I thought everyone would have gone home by now."

"Almost everyone." His voice hinted at humor. "Please do not call me lord. That is a term only very old and familiar vampires use. The media likes to play up that idiom whenever they write about me."

The city was under a veil of shadows behind him, and Miranda could only see his face by the light of his computer screen. She knew she was in the presence of a predator. This vampire didn't have to use his allure to hold anyone in a state of mesmerism; all he had to do was walk into a room. His presence alone could capture an audience. Valadon's power was permeating the room, and Miranda's skin prickled. Her ire resurfaced at the unnecessary trip she'd been forced to make. "You could have sent a courier to deliver my bag."

"I know. I could have." Valadon smirked. "But then, I would have missed the opportunity to talk with you." He walked closer to his desk so she could see him better. "You've been in my offices several times now; yet, neither one of us has taken the time to get to know the other." Valadon inhaled her scent of orange blossoms, intrigued he didn't frighten her as he did other humans. Earlier, he'd been transfixed by her sense of serenity, which most women couldn't hope to possess—her kind or his. When she had stood back in rapture and studied his painting, his fangs ached. He'd watched her before, been appreciative of her intelligence and perceptive nature.

He motioned to turn on the lights. "No, don't. I prefer the dim light. After staring at a computer screen all day, the bright light hurts my eyes."

"You almost sound like a vampire saying that." The amusement was back in Valadon's voice. He pointed the remote at a low light over a Greek statue, giving the room a little more illumination.

"I've been like this since I was a child." Miranda came farther into the room. "My night vision doesn't compare with yours, of course, but it's still very good. I can see you fine now, thanks." Placing her hands on his desk, she spoke directly to him. "Why did you really have me come here when you could have simply sent my bag to the museum?"

Charmed by her courage, Valadon paused for a moment. "You've worked for me for some time. I simply wanted the opportunity to meet you. I like knowing the people who work for me." Valadon appreciated her evening look with the black shimmering top and the black jeans caressing her legs. She wore makeup accentuating her sharp, whiskey-colored eyes and nicely defined lips. Her long chestnut hair made a man want to run his fingers through it, wrap his fist around it as he drank her in. But it was her perceptive eyes that held his attention, and a hunger, long dormant, awakened deep inside him.

Miranda knew Valadon was studying her just as she was him. The smart thing would be to grab her purse, make some sort of excuse, and then beat feet out of there. But she stood transfixed. Valadon had a mysterious essence that made people want to know him, discover what lay beyond his penetrating gaze and explore forbidden realms. Therein lay his true appeal, the elusive charm that challenged the curiosity in others: To know the unknowable.

For Miranda, the attraction wasn't just physical appeal, but the intelligence behind those keen eyes. What knowledge he must have accumulated over his centuries of existence, almost enough for her to offer a little neck. Almost, she smiled.

It was the movement in the shadows behind him that suddenly broke into her thoughts. Helicopters weren't unusual in this section of New York as the helipad was merely blocks away. But unlike the tourist helicopters, this one was silent. That was her first clue something was off; her second was the figure in black with the sniper rifle. Miranda screamed, *"Get down!"* She flew over the desk and pushed Valadon to the floor as a blaze of gunfire shattered the windows. The thunderous sounds of rapid gunshots were deafening.

She heard the glass spraying all over the office as Valadon held her tight, burying her face in his chest as they lay on the floor. She felt something sharp piercing her hip, but dared not move until the gunfire subsided.

What occurred next happened so fast she hardly had time to process it. The door swung open, and men poured in. She heard one angry voice above the others giving orders. The next thing she knew she was being lifted and thrown across to the other side of the room.

Suddenly, someone was on top of her, pinning her down, and the burning sensation in her hip lessened as she pulled the bullet-shaped dart out of her hip.

"Get off of her! She had nothing to do with this," Valadon bellowed as he stood over her and the vampire pinning her to the floor.

"There were bullets fired, you're bleeding, and she's holding a weapon. You want to explain to me how she's *not* involved?" Remare, the deadliest of Lord Valadon's Torian Guard, snarled.

Chapter Two

Miranda quickly remembered what Lizandra told her about vampires. If Valadon was the poster boy for the VN—their eloquent spokesperson and diplomat, professional and debonair in front of the cameras—Remare, his second in command, was the opposite.

Unlike the other Torians, Remare flaunted his vampire nature, especially when in the public eye. He kept his long raven-black hair and his goatee neatly trimmed and lived a notorious lifestyle, frequenting many New York clubs that catered to vampires. If Valadon was the VN's epitome of political correctness, Remare was the VN's bad boy. He was the only vampire at Valadon House who openly defied Valadon's mandate of social integration—the only one who could get away with it.

Remare's face was made up of harsh angles and dark brown eyes almost as black as his pupils. Where Valadon could easily win over people with his calm and confident demeanor, Remare had people on guard and distrustful of his intentions. His distaste of humans was legendary. There were all types of rumors concerning him. Not the least was his penchant for many bed partners.

Lizandra had once told her she thought it was all PR hype to foster support for Valadon. His way of saying either accept me as leader of the VN or deal with my successor.

No one wanted Remare to rule New York City, especially after Valadon had written into law vampires weren't allowed to use their mental powers on unsuspecting humans, thereby winning over those fearful humans who believed vampires were evil bloodsucking creatures. The Vampire Nation's public relations department had fostered a positive image of vampires as a separate race of beings who had lived alongside humans for centuries and simply had larger incisors, an allergy to sunlight and lived longer than humans. *A lot longer.*

Better to keep Valadon the political diplomat and Remare as his enforcer and leader of the Torians. There was no telling what Remare would do with the political power Valadon wielded. Better the devil you know.

Valadon's Torian Guard, aptly named after Caesar's Praetorians, consisted of his elite force of trained soldiers. They vowed to protect Valadon with their lives; there were no deadlier creatures on the planet as far as Miranda knew, and the deadliest Torian was currently on top of her, gripping her wrist until she dropped the bullet-like dart.

"Get off me! In case you haven't noticed, I'm the one who's bleeding." Miranda tried to buck him off, but Remare held her down with muscular arms. Searching the faces of the men who surrounded Valadon, she realized fear does strange things to people: Most people would have retreated from the dangerous vampire, but when pushed to her limits, Miranda's darker side evolved, and instead of fear, anger surfaced. Turning to see the hostility in Remare's face, she saw his red rims around his irises glowing. She gripped his forearms, digging in with her nails to push him off, but he only pinned her tighter to the floor.

Miranda breathed in Remare's woodsy, earthy scent and could swear she saw steam coming from his ears; his enmity was palpable. She was sure he would've killed her if Valadon hadn't pulled him off her and then helped her stand as Remare reluctantly released her, never once taking his dark eyes off her.

In the depths of those sinister orbs, Miranda could see her death.

Snatching the dart, Remare sniffed it and then became contemplative. Keeping her in sight, he seemed to calm then brushed himself off. "It seems our old friends have decided to make an appearance. Their calling card." He handed the dart to Valadon, who sniffed it then handed it to one of his guards.

Miranda glared at them as she straightened up. "If you had sent my purse to me, I wouldn't have gotten shot." She tried to walk off the pain, but her leg folded in on itself. Valadon caught her before she hit the floor.

"But then, I'd be the one lying injured on the floor, Professor Crescent." Valadon smiled as he lifted her into his arms. "Let's get her to the infirmary. Remare, have your men report in, then join me in the medical suite."

Remare slowly backed away and nodded suspiciously as Valadon left with his guards and the woman who had returned his defiant stare. His nostrils flared. *Intriguing scent.* Exhaling slowly, he then turned and surveyed the damage. Whoever dared this attack on Valadon would soon learn the true definition of retribution.

An evil smirk lit up his face; Remare could hardly wait.

***

ValCorp's infirmary was already prepped as they entered. Like everything else in the building, their equipment was state of the art. The long, rectangular room consisted of four hospital beds set up like an emergency room with curtains separating each area. "Who's in the lab tonight?" Valadon demanded.

Amory, a physician's assistant whose dark complexion was in sharp contrast to his hospital whites, carefully accepted Miranda from Valadon and placed her on the second bed. "Your son, Gabriel."

"Get him in here."

A tall, handsome man of slender build with light brown hair and golden-brown eyes exited the lab and came closer to the bed. "What's wrong with her?"

"I was shot with a dart." Miranda glared up at him and noticed his blond highlights. *Must be a trick of the light.* Vampires didn't get sun streaks. "You can ask me. I was actually there." Her sarcasm rose as she stroked her left hip. "It went numb then started throbbing."

Gabriel's eyes lighted then he offered her a crooked smile. "My apologies."

"Professor Crescent was in my office when the assassins attacked. They missed me but hit Miranda. I presume you didn't hear the alarms?" Valadon crossed his arms over his chest as Gabriel smirked and pulled on a pair of latex gloves.

The tension rose significantly in the room as the two vampires stared at each other.

Finally, Gabriel's shoulders relaxed, and he nodded in acquiescence. "I sometimes wear my ear phones when I'm working. Josh Groban was singing loudly tonight." Then, his face sobered. "Were you wounded?"

"No, but here's the dart that injured Miranda." Valadon motioned for his guard to give the projectile to Gabriel.

Gabriel sniffed it then handed it to Amory. "Run a diagnostic. We'll soon find out what new toys your friends have been playing with." He turned to Miranda. "Now, let me see your wound."

Miranda looked pointedly at Valadon, who nodded and stepped away. She focused on the handsome, but moody doctor. There was something different about him. A vampire, for sure, but something was off. Humans tended to have a moderate frequency; Weres had a higher, faster pitch. But vampires had a different frequency altogether that made her skin tingle.

The older the vampire, the more intense the prickling sensation.

Lizandra couldn't explain how Miranda had this talent, other than to say she was a *sensitive*—someone capable of reading people, *all* peoples. Miranda thought it was one more thing that made her a freak.

She removed her boots, unzipped her pants and kept her eyes on the doctor, curious about the tension between the two vampires and why his current flowed unlike the others. "You're different from the others." She reclined on her side. There was no way she was taking off her thong. It left more than enough room for the examination. If she'd known she was going to be on display tonight, she might not have worn the little red silk panties.

Gabriel applied antiseptic to a gauze pad. "Figured that out, did you?"

Miranda narrowed her eyes at him as she raised her body up on one elbow. "Are you having a bad night, or do you not get out enough to know how to have a pleasant conversation?"

"I've had better." Gabriel rubbed his neck and glanced at Miranda. "And I get out plenty." He softened his tone. "Be quiet now while I examine your wound."

Miranda hadn't been hushed since childhood, so she did what she'd always done when she was young: She ignored him. "You're not a practicing medical doctor, are you?" She ventured an educated guess: "Researcher?"

"I have my medical degrees, professor and I've been a doctor for longer than you've been alive. What exactly is it you're a professor of, anyway?"

"Art history. I authenticate Valadon's paintings for the insurance company."

"Ah, that explains it." He prepared an inoculation. "This topical is going to numb you, but it will only affect the area around the lesion. You're probably going to need a few stitches."

"That explains what, and how many?" Miranda twisted on the bed and tried to get a better look at the needle. She had to be the only woman in NYC who didn't have her ears pierced. Lizandra had laughingly threatened her with piercing them and even went so far as to bring back beautiful dangling earrings from the Caribbean islands as an incentive. Never worked, though.

"How many what?"

"Stitches. I sort of like knowing these things." He really needed to get out more.

Gabriel grinned. "Four or five and...as for your other question." He pierced her skin with the needle. "You don't seem like Valadon's type."

"Ouch!" So *not* gentle there, she turned to face him. "Exactly what is Valadon's type?"

"Vampire, of course." He looked directly at her. "A bit sensitive there, are you? Now that didn't hurt at all." He shook his head and softened his tone. "Just relax. I'll be done in a few minutes."

"It's not your freakin hip that got hurt."

Gabriel's face seemed to heat as he placed his hands on her ass. Miranda's opinion of the doctor improved when she saw his disconcerted look and was inwardly impressed with his shyness.

"There seems to be some viscous fluid. I'm going to suction it out." He smiled as he went to the medical cart and retrieved a length of tubing that looked like an aspirator. "Don't go anywhere."

"Oh, yes, so in the mood to do laps around Central Park, right now. *Not!*" She smirked up at him. She clutched the pillow beneath her. "What do you use the tubing for?"

"Oh, all sorts of *nasty* things," Gabriel teased as he concentrated on his task. "Now be still for just a moment longer."

Miranda wasn't sure what to make of Gabriel. Here she was lying half naked, and all the doctor could think of was doing a procedure on her—a potentially painful procedure. And why was she even thinking about the handsome doctor?

"You shouldn't be able to feel anything. The shot I gave you should've numbed you, but if you're in pain, let me know."

"Nah, I'm tougher than I look or so I've been told."

Gabriel briefly glanced at her then concentrated on his task. "I've suctioned out the fluid. I'm going to clean it then you'll only need a couple of stitches and a dressing. You'll need to keep that dry for a few days. I can take the stitches out then or your personal physician can."

"I don't have a doctor." When Gabriel appeared surprised, she said, "I don't usually get sick, but I have a friend who's a PA. She'll take them out." Miranda reached for her pants the same time Gabriel handed them to her. She immediately felt the low electrical current go through her as their hands touched and from Gabriel's reaction, so did he. "Rubber soled shoes?" she chided as she pulled her pants on and tried to stand, but wobbled instead.

Gabriel steadied her, liking the way she felt in his arms. It had been a while since he'd held a woman, especially one as attractive as Miranda. He belatedly realized being caught in the crossfire of an attempt on Valadon's life couldn't have been easy. Gabriel wished he could get to know her better. Maybe she was right. He didn't get out of his lab often, his work too important.

"I'm sorry you were hurt. We usually don't get that sort of thing happening here." He smiled. "ValCorp is pretty safe." He let her go when he saw she could walk on her own.

"Thanks for patching me up." Miranda turned back to him. "Any chance I can get a copy of the toxicology report?

"Sure." Gabriel shrugged. "But why would you want it?"

"I want to know what was in me." She rubbed her hip and tilted her head. "Wouldn't you want to know, doc?"

Gabriel nodded. Yes, he would. For nearly a century, he'd tried to figure out what was inside him that made him vampire and how it could be reversed. But his latest batch of results was far less promising than he'd expected. "I'll see you get a copy of the results." He was reluctant to say goodbye.

"Thanks." Miranda returned his smile and hesitated for a moment before she turned to leave, then gingerly walked down to where Valadon was waiting.

Another attempt on Valadon! Gabriel removed and disposed of his gloves. *How many did this make?* Although Valadon and he had argued many times, he still considered Valadon a good leader for his people.

But could he ever call Valadon father? *Not in another hundred years!*

He'd had one human father—only one. However, he could call Valadon his monarch; he could do that much. But nothing was going to prevent him from taking the grant to study genetics and finding a way to turn himself back to human. What Valadon had taken from him, science would give it back: his humanity.

As for the assassination attempt, Valadon and Remare would deal with it.

They always did.

Chapter Three

"She needs to be interrogated." Remare steamed as calculation glared in his eyes.

"It's not necessary." Valadon shook his head. "She's innocent in this."

"Is she now? And you know this how?" Leaning against the door frame, Remare raised an eyebrow as he stood with one foot crossed over the other and his arms folded across his chest.

To others, Remare's form might seem casual, but Valadon knew his second was coiled tight as a snake. "Christ, Remare, she took a bullet for me. Isn't that enough?" Temper surged in Valadon's voice—rage for the enemies who would dare to target him in his own territory and frustration for the beguiling woman who'd been caught in the crossfire.

Remare eyed his closest friend. "What *exactly* do we know about her?"

As if on cue, Aiden, one of Remare's best Torians and an ace at IT, strode down the hall and handed Remare a file. After a few whispered words, Aiden nodded then departed. "She's been to our offices several times over the last few years. An art authenticator, works for the NYC Museum." He paused for a moment as he sped through the file. "Also, professor of Art History at NYU. Works part time in the evenings." He glanced up at Valadon. "No *known* political affiliations... Known being the key word."

"She had nothing to do with the attempt. It was a simple coincidence she happened to be in my office when the shots were fired." Valadon dismissed the idea with a wave of his hand. "Let it go, Remare." Valadon paced a few steps; he had much on his mind, not just the attempt on his life, but Gabriel's upcoming independence and his responsibility for jeopardizing one of his employee's lives—one he'd been interested in for some time.

"Coincidence...never quite sits well with me," Remare remarked, as he stroked his tongue against his fang. "How many times has something *seemed* trivial and then turned out to be quite complex?" He walked closer to Valadon. "She *needs* to be questioned."

"No! It's *not* necessary!" Valadon said with absolute finality and then exhaled with a pained expression. "Better you focus your men on who was behind the helicopter. After I speak with Miranda, I want to meet with you and the others. I want to view the videos of our outside perimeters, as well as our internal feeds. I also want lists of who was in our building at the time: vampire and other. Get me data, Remare. We'll take it from there. If our enemies are up to their old tricks, I want to know who."

Remare nodded as Valadon stalked back into the treatment wing. He was so convinced the young professor was not involved in the attack he wasn't thinking straight. Remare wondered if Valadon wasn't becoming soft on yet another human female. Christ, the last time Valadon was involved with a human, he'd become dangerously detached and disinterested in the affairs of the VN. Remare was going to see to it that never happened again.

He'd order an investigation into the art historian's background and then they'd see *exactly* with whom she was connected. It was too convenient for him that she just happened to be there at the precise time the shots were fired. *A distraction, perhaps? To lure Valadon into striking position?* His eyes narrowed pensively as he stroked his goatee and the thin line of his beard along his jaw with his thumbnail.

There was something about her that didn't sit well. Her scent was different from most human females.

And to him, different was potentially dangerous.

Remare didn't trust her or the defiant look in her eyes. She should have been terror struck, not rebellious of his authority. *Whatever do you know, professor? What are you hiding? Could it be as Valadon suspected: a coincidence? Not likely.* Remare tapped the folder against his thigh; he didn't believe in coincidences. The attempt was close—closer than the others, but Remare would be damned if it happened again on his watch. Valadon didn't think she needed to be questioned. Well, he'd see about that. His Torians were experts at information retrieval. And he knew exactly who to assign to her.

He smiled with lethal anticipation.

***

Valadon escorted Miranda out of the treatment area toward the elevator. "How are you feeling?"

Grinning, she snarked, "Like I've been shot."

"Will you allow me to make this up to you?"

"You don't have anything to make up for." She glimpsed the restrained emotion blazing in his eyes. "But I think you should find out who's trying to kill you."

"Be assured, we will." Valadon's voice held a terrifying depth of darkness. "In no uncertain terms will I, or the vampires under me, rest until we find out who orchestrated the assassination attempt."

Miranda regarded him, not in fear, but in awe. "If you really want to do something for me," she rubbed her hip, "find out what was in that dart. Dr. Gabriel assured me he suctioned it all out, but I still would like to know what was inside me." She lifted her chin. "It's important to me."

"As it is to me, Miranda." Valadon studied her with eyes that held a profundity of knowledge. "Surely, there's something else I can do for you." He seemed to compel her to ask something of him.

"Forget it." She managed a pained smile as she stared into his eyes. "It was you they were after, not me."

Valadon's gaze peered deep into her. *Oh hell no! Not after I took a bullet for you!* She broke eye contact. "Valadon, you're not going to scrub my memories, are you? By your own laws, you can't do that to me."

When he tried to reassure her by putting his hand on her shoulder, she recoiled. "No. I will not touch your memories. You never have to fear me, Miranda. I give you my word on this."

"Thank you," she said, knowing suspicion laced her words.

Valadon waited with her by the elevator. "There's going to be an ongoing investigation. Please refrain from discussing what happened here tonight...or what nearly happened with your associates."

"My *associates* know I came here to collect my purse." She looked around for her handbag.

"Ahhh, yes, Lizandra." Valadon grinned. "It's delightful to know two of my key people, Morel and his wife, Cyra, are friends with you, as well as the Were Queen. All right. You may confer with Lizandra, but no one else. It will make the investigation go more smoothly. Your purse will be waiting for you at the security desk."

"All right then. I'm considerably late to meet her down at Nightshade—one of your clubs, I think." She smiled, almost hesitant to leave him. There were so many questions she wanted to ask. She exhaled slowly and lamented she'd never get the opportunity again.

"There will be a car waiting for you. The driver will take you anywhere you want to go." He lifted her hand and brushed a kiss along her knuckles. This time, she didn't draw back from his touch. "Thank you for saving my life."

"Remember to duck quicker next time." Miranda grinned as she stepped into the elevator. Of all the articles she'd read in the media reports, nothing, absolutely nothing, had prepared her for meeting the vampire lord of NYC.

There was much more to him than the reports hinted at, more than she ever imagined. She'd seen beneath the façade, glimpsed the man behind the enigma, but knew it was ludicrous to consider becoming involved with a vampire. Wasn't getting shot once bad enough? As with any human, she had dozens of questions about vampires, their histories and powers. She'd read all the public relations stuff the VN had issued: Carefully worded discourses about vampires being no threat to our well-being— after all, they'd been amongst us since time began.

But she was more curious about what was *not* in those speeches. She was hardly in a position to ask, even if Valadon was feeling indebted to her. The price would be too high. Another woman would have milked this for all she could, but Miranda wasn't another woman. She would do her own research. And knew exactly who to go to for help.

When the doors of the elevator opened, she was about to step out—then nearly hissed as her body backed up a step before she could stop—her instincts on full alert. The air around her had become electrically charged.

Dangerously so.

"Your purse, professor." With an arched brow, Remare dangled her handbag from his fingers. Perverse delight danced in his eyes at her obvious discomfort at being alone with him.

Her heart pounding, Miranda wouldn't allow herself to be bullied. Straightening her spine, she met his stare, refusing to be the first to look away. A stupid thing to do with a vampire who could easily glamour her, but she didn't sense that particular power stirring. He silently stepped aside. His movements mirrored those of a dancer: graceful, elegant, and carefully controlled. *How could anyone move like that without making a sound?*

"You seem to be in the habit of forgetting it."

"Thanks." She practically ripped it from his fingers, wanting to get as far from him as fast as possible. He was one vampire she had absolutely no interest in whatsoever. Dangerous males, no matter how handsome or sexy, didn't appeal to her. The allure, the rush and excitement of experiencing something risky didn't interest her. Miranda no longer felt the need to explore the hidden corners of her psyche. She'd seen the depth of darkness, had nearly drowned in it except for one powerful Were's intervention. The abyss could stare back at her all it wanted.

She quickly brushed past him and headed for the exit.

"Professor Crescent."

Damn! She cocked her head, how very distinctly and seductively he said her name.

"A moment of your time."

Again, that woodsy, earthy scent of his suffused her nostrils. *Temptation or damnation!* Of all the vampires in Valadon House, the one she didn't want to find herself alone with was Remare. Miranda briefly shut her eyes and shook her head. She would not give him the satisfaction of knowing he got to her.

"What is it?" she asked, meeting his eyes, refusing to show any fear, then added with an impatient exhale, "I'm already running late."

"What a coincidence you just happened to be in Valadon's office when the attack occurred." He slithered closer, never taking his dark, penetrating gaze from her.

"Valadon's collection of Greek statues is superb. Don't you think so? He's been collecting them for some time now." Like a predator sighting prey, he moved stealthily toward her. "Every time he goes to the Greek Isles, he brings one back." Remare crossed his arms over his chest. His breath was close enough to brush her hair back from her face. "Did you ask him to turn the light on so that you could see them better?"

His eyes focused solely on her as her breaths intensified. Remare obviously wanted a neck to strangle over the attempt on Valadon's life, and the neck he currently was scrutinizing was hers. She wouldn't let him intimidate her. "I'm not your villain here, Remare." She narrowed her own eyes at him. "You need to look elsewhere." Staring at his cold, dark gaze the tension heated between them. He stood perfectly still but looked coiled enough to attack. The frequency she could detect in vampires hummed loudly in her ears.

Vampires could mute their powers, and it was considered impolite to direct their level of power at a human. Remare was doing nothing to mute himself, and it was beginning to piss her off. "I didn't tell him anything, Remare." She held her ground, feeling the muscles in her legs tighten in readiness. "It was his idea to turn on the light. Besides, he wanted to turn on the overhead lights. I told him not to."

"I wonder, why is that?" Remare began to circle her, trying to intimidate her.

It wasn't working. "I was only there to retrieve my purse, Remare. I'm sure Valadon has already updated you." She shook her handbag for emphasis and met the vampire face to face. "If you're so hell bent on finding out who attempted the assassination, why don't you spend your time looking for the responsible party?" She slung her bag over her shoulder. "It's not me."

Remare smiled in a manner that would've made the Grinch proud—if the Grinch had long, sharp fangs. "Oh, don't worry, Mir-r-anda." He said her name as if it were spelled with two or three r's instead of the one, betraying his European roots. "I assure you we *will* find who was behind the attack." His voice darkened and held an edge of danger as he stared pointedly at her. "And any persons found to be in consort with the attackers will be punished. Harshly."

He said the last with a hiss, like the snake he was.

She quickly turned and left the building. Where the hell was *he* when Valadon was nearly killed?

Chapter Four

"But the poison was tested, was it not?" Mulciber didn't turn his attention from his task of cutting the thorns off the roses in his solarium, a place he could only frequent during evening hours. Gardening was the one thing that soothed him. An ancient, he couldn't tolerate the sun's rays, but he could at least find some semblance of satisfaction in the fruits of the sun's labors.

"Yes. It should've done what it was designed to do, but it seems the other person in the room, a woman, a human, was injured, instead."

"A human." Mulciber said the words with distaste as if he was talking about insects. "The drug will have no harmful effects on her."

"She's already been released from the infirmary."

"How fortunate for her. She's of no concern to me. Who has the dart now?" *The attempt and not the deed confounds us,* he thought bitterly of Lady Macbeth's line.

"Gabriel."

Mulciber smiled. *Valadon's fledgling.* "He'll have to be dealt with, won't he?"

"Yes, my lord. I will see to it."

Mulciber took pleasure in his spy's hesitancy. Ancients possessed a speed unmatched by other vampires, and he had been known to rip out the throats of those who displeased him. Mulciber glowered at his confederate with a face that would frighten any human who'd never seen what damage sunlight inflicted on a vampire. Over the millennia, certain vampires had evolved enough to develop a natural immunity to the sun's harmful rays, while others possessed only partial protection. But the old ones never developed that ability. They'd lived too long far beneath the earth's surface. Vampire medicine had tried to develop a vaccine for the ancients, but was met with disastrous results—especially in his case.

"Will that be all, my lord?"

"No. I require another blood source. See that it's delivered before sunrise and make this one...pretty." Mulciber sneered as his spy left. He did not do well when deprived, and his hunger was growing. He'd refused the bagged blood most vampires used and would not consider the synthetic blood ValCorp manufactured. *Let the lesser vampires drink that offal.* He would not.

"You let him live?"

"He has his uses." Mulciber slyly smiled at his daughter, Persephone. "For now." He finished placing his roses in the vase. "Now tell me. What brings you here?"

"You have a message from the council. They wait on your reply."

As an ambassador of the Euro-Council, the governing body of vampires worldwide, one of his responsibilities was to oversee how the vampires in America were accruing wealth and monitor their progress. "Did you complete the task I assigned you?"

"Yes, the folder's on your desk in your study."

Mulciber appraised his only living offspring and thought of her mother: The one woman he had loved...before he'd killed her for her betrayal. Persephone was beginning to resemble her more and more. With her soft, angelic features, long blonde hair and blue eyes, people often underestimated her cunning and craftiness. She knew well how to use her looks to acquire what she wanted. He knew because he'd been the one to teach her. "I want you to start socializing more with Valadon's Torians. Learn what you can about Valadon's movements."

"As you wish, Father." Persephone turned to leave. "There's one who may be accommodating."

He walked down the hall to his study and read the message on his computer. "Well, that's interesting." The council would be sending another agent. "Ah, the possibilities." He relaxed back into his chair. It seemed someone else among their ruling members had his own plans where Valadon was concerned.

He approved of their choice. Passionately.

Mulciber felt like celebrating and mentally summoned his favorite acolytes to attend him: Jeremy entered his study, dressed only in a short wrap around his hips. Mulciber remembered years ago when he'd first come to New York from...wherever the hell it was he'd come from. One of his lieutenants had brought Jeremy to the overlord's home under the pretense of a modeling job where he resided ever since with Mulciber's other child bride, Kaylee—who followed Jeremy in dressed in a similar wrap that hung low on her hips. She'd been only twelve when another of his people had lured her to his home. Brave thing had fought him in the beginning. But over the years, Jeremy and he had taught her the pleasures of the flesh until she'd forgotten her past life. Mulciber had been gracious enough to addict them to his blood, which would keep them young and strong for as long as they pleased him.

And they were both pleasing him now as they began fondling each other. Mulciber liked that they were near mirror copies of each other with their dark blond hair and hazel eyes. They could have been siblings for all their similarities. Each was disrobing now for his viewing pleasure. He encouraged them to continue and watched with glee as they began to fuck in earnest. When Jeremy began to climax, Mulciber would enter him from behind and ride them both to ecstasy.

Chapter Five

Nightshade was crowded as usual with vampires, Weres and humans amicably socializing. The seductive, elegant ambience was only part of its allure. The drop-dead gorgeous vampires who frequented the establishment were a main attraction as was the sensual music. Adding to the mystique were the reflecting lights of the mirror ball making it appear as if shadows were dancing on the smoked mirrors decorating the walls.

The topical Gabriel gave her was wearing off, and Miranda could feel the throbbing in her hip as she slowly walked. Lizandra and her other friends were in their usual corner in the back of the club.

"And look what the cat just dragged in," Lizandra bellowed to her entourage, who were leisurely sitting and drinking around her as befitting the queen she was. She rose from the leather sofa with her long braids flaring out. Her shimmering, sleeveless gold top accentuated her well-proportioned breasts and showed off her muscular form. Black leather pants caressed her long, shapely legs. No one had a better statuesque physique than the Were Queen. "You're late...and this time, more than usual." They exchanged hugs and kisses to each cheek—no girly-girl near-kisses for Lizandra; the Were Queen liked to show and receive affection. She held Miranda at arms' length and knew something was wrong. "What the hell happened to you?"

"I stepped on some broken glass." She didn't want to lie to her friends so she kept it as close to the truth as possible. "It's all good now, just a little sensitive." She eyed the remains of Buffalo wings, nachos and veggie platters and sighed as her stomach growled.

Gavin, the red wolf, Liz's bodyguard and latest lover, stood and hugged Miranda tightly, then let her sit on the couch near Lizandra. "Don't worry. I'll get you something to eat." He grinned at her. "What's your poison?"

Miranda had a warm spot in her heart for Gavin. He was tall, gorgeous, with the most amazing reddish-brown hair. His eyes twinkled with humor, but it was his quick grin that she found most striking. When he walked, his muscles rippled. She tried hard not to stare at his butt—but, as Liz would say, *"Dang! That is one fine ass!"*

The Were Queen was a fitness guru who led exercise classes for her pack mates in Central Park. She'd make any drill sergeant proud. Several times, Miranda had nearly passed out from exertion, but damn, if her body didn't develop the way Liz promised.

"C and V, the usual." Miranda winked back at him. She'd been drinking cranberry juice and vodka for years now.

"How've you been?" Cyra, the third in the girlfriend love-fest, asked. Her long red hair and amazing green eyes accented her elfin face. She had a pale complexion that had nothing to do with her vampirism, but her Irish/English heritage did. She was happily married to another vampire, Morel—who was noticeably absent tonight.

"Pretty good." Evasively, Miranda smiled at her. "So, what's everyone been up to?"

"Orion has a new gig at Oasis, he's gonna start next week, and we're all invited to hear him play." Maxine, the newest member of Lizandra's Black Star Clan, was bouncing in her seat. She was young, vibrant and quickly becoming a clan favorite. Max didn't believe one hair color was enough and often had at least two different shades. She got teased a lot about being the runt of the litter at only five-foot two, but the clan would fight to the death to protect her.

That's what family was all about. And Black Star was family.

"Give me some time to get used to the sound system there, then you're all welcome." Orion was a very handsome Were with long black hair, and when he looked at you with his baby blue eyes, it was as if he could see your most intimate thoughts. His smile was one of the most welcoming Miranda had ever seen, but it was his scintillating voice that made people swoon. It was no wonder women flocked from all over to hear him sing. And he played a mean guitar. One that was currently residing in Miranda's home.

Coming home late from work one night, Miranda had found Orion a block away; he'd been badly assaulted and bleeding from multiple claw wounds. After she'd called Lizandra, they'd managed to get him into her home and nursed him back to health. Liz had warned her it was dangerous to take a wounded Were into new surroundings, but as it turned out okay. Miranda got a new roommate, one who was rarely home because several months out of the year he was on the road touring. And Orion found a safe place to stash his prized guitars.

"Now, sorry to leave you guys, but I promised Max I'd show her how the recording studio works."

"I gotta leave, too." Cyra chimed as she pocketed her phone. "Morel texted he was called back to work."

When they were finally alone, Lizandra shifted forward in her seat, keeping her eyes on the club's patrons in the nearest vicinity. "Your foot's not injured, is it?"

"No...it's not." Miranda also scanned the crowd as she started to play with the flame on the candle in the glass holder on the coffee table. She held the flame in one hand, closed her fist, transferred it to her other hand and then back to the candle holder. As an *Elemental*, Miranda had some control over the elements—but especially with fire, a power she hid from everyone, except Lizandra.

Miranda knew Liz would notice she was favoring one hip from the way she was leaning. The Were Queen could see through a lie faster than anyone.

"Gonna tell me what's going on?"

"Yup." Miranda mirrored the way Liz was sitting and moved forward with her elbows on her knees. She began rubbing the palms of her hands together the way she often did when she was thinking. "Just not here."

"Anything I need to be concerned about?" Liz eyed her people who were scattered throughout the club.

"Not in the immediate scheme of things. But soon."

Gavin returned with a steaming plate of nachos rancheros, chicken fingers and her drink.

"Oh, thank you. I'm starving." Miranda bit into the nachos and almost drooled. When she took a sip of her drink, she frowned. The C was missing the V.

Gavin grinned. "Painkillers and booze don't mix well."

Miranda shook her head; she'd forgotten how sharp a Were's sense of smell was. "Could the others detect it as well?"

"Probably, that's why they left." Liz smiled knowingly. "Finish eating. We'll go back to Werehaven."

***

Werehaven was Black Star's underground stronghold in Central Park across from the Museum of Natural History; the hidden entrance was under one of the many overpasses in the park. More vivacious and exhilarating than Nightshade, Werehaven started out as a cave where Weres socialized without having to hide their true natures, but with the clan working laboriously, it was turned into a sanctuary. Besides the dance club, which rivaled any NYC club, though the type of dancing that went on around the full moon was not to be found in any human club, there were two long bars located along the sides of the sunken dance floor.

Werehaven was Miranda's home away from home.

Besides being a powerful leader, Lizandra was a good businesswoman and used the money from Werehaven to invest for the clan. She only required two things from her clan: Every member had to tithe a percentage of their income and get a tattoo of a black star. Lizandra inspired loyalty because she ruled in a democratic manner; her decisions, though fair were final.

They walked past the dance floor, through the shadows of the curved bar and then passed the Were Queen's VIP lounge at the back of the club, which many Weres simply referred to as *The Throne Room.* Gavin grabbed Liz and kissed the hell out of her; Miranda admired the heat between them and felt the magnetic energy of the Weres tingling on her skin.

Perhaps her news could wait until tomorrow.

As if he heard her thoughts, Gavin stopped kissing Liz, winked at Miranda and went to the bar.

The Were Queen purred. They continued down the hall to her rooms, which were decorated with paintings and figurines from the Caribbean islands where Liz's family originated from. African masks lined the walls as did tapestries from South America. Native American pottery adorned the shelves, along with several pictures of her family. Her brothers had the same aquamarine eyes and mocha complexion Liz possessed. Liz's apartment was where her close friends hung out to watch old DVDs. Many of the clan's informal meetings were conducted here.

Liz strode over to the fridge and took out two Coronas. The Amazonian strength her friend exuded when she walked amazed Miranda. How a nearly six-foot woman could walk with the grace of a ballerina was beyond her. *Must be a Were thing.*

Lizandra sat on the sofa next to Miranda and handed her a beer. As usual, they tapped bottles and took one long swallow. "Now, tell me. What kept you so late?"

Since Liz was the closest thing to a sister Miranda had, she turned and faced her. "Why would anyone want to assassinate a vampire lord?"

Liz nearly choked on her beer. "Several reasons... Take your pick." She relaxed into her sofa cushions. "Why do you ask?"

After Miranda relayed the earlier events of the evening, Lizandra paced with her hands on her hips, her long nails digging in. "So, they're starting this business up again."

"What do you mean, *they?*" Her eyes narrowed. "You know something." There was much about the paranormal community humans didn't know—never would. Although Miranda knew more than the average human ever would. "You paranormal types hang out together. What do you know that I don't?"

"It's probably better you don't know." Lizandra prowled back and forth. "Men that powerful, that wealthy have many enemies."

Miranda knew her friend well enough to know when she was conflicted about wanting to tell her something vital, but having to adhere to the codes of the preternatural alliance. "This isn't the first attempt, is it?" She sat up straight, tapping the tips of her fingers together.

Liz turned back to her. "What makes you say that?"

"Just a feeling I had when all the vampires rushed into the room—like they weren't all that surprised." Miranda placed the empty beer bottles in with the recyclables, then turned to face her friend, arms crossed over chest. "Now why would that be?

Liz paused from her pacing and ran a finger slowly over a picture of Grandpa Wells. She smiled as she glanced back at Miranda. "Sometimes, I forget you were only a child when the vampires decided on '*The Grand Reveal.*'"

"I was eight years old," Miranda said. "I remember that day clearly. I was home sick from school, lying on the couch, flipping through the channels. When the announcement was made about the existence of vampires, I thought I was on the friggen Syfy channel." Miranda recalled the world leaders had tried to alleviate the fears of the public by saying vampires had always been here and had evolved just as we had, but for political reasons, the vampires had kept their identities secret. *Political reasons?*

"Valadon came on screen, shaking hands with the president in a strong show of support." Miranda remembered thinking he didn't look any different from a human grown-up. "Then, a famous blonde actress came on screen to reveal her fangs, and the nation had a collective sigh; after her, others in the arts and entertainment industries also revealed themselves. The Vampire Nation made assurances they were more like distant cousins, rather than the monsters of pop literature. After the last war, Valadon promised the vampires would help in the rebuilding of hospitals, schools, and businesses. And they did."

"You remember well." Liz continued pacing. "But there was much the media never reported. There was a lot of controversy whether or not to make the announcement. The conservative vampires said they had remained hidden for centuries and wanted to stay that way. They feared they'd become targeted and deeply resented Valadon's decision."

"There were riots with injuries and fatalities on both sides." Miranda reminisced. "When the human authorities failed to contain the mobs, many innocent vampires perished in fires."

Liz continued, "The progressives stated with all the technology, surveillances around the world, it was impossible to keep their existence secret anymore, and that if they didn't make the decision to come out, someone else would...and it wouldn't be handled as properly. Eventually, the progressives won, and the rest they say is ..."

"History." Miranda decided she needed to learn more.

"After the vamps revealed themselves and the world didn't stop, we decided to do the same," Liz added. "Several clan leaders got together and decided to make the announcement as well. We didn't cause quite a start as the vampires did, though."

"So, do you have any idea who might want Valadon dead?"

Liz closed her eyes. "There were several human hate groups who called for their eradication. Their fears, their hatred of vampires couldn't be assuaged."

"But it's been twenty years now; surely those extremists are long gone?"

"Are they?" Liz raised an eyebrow. "Do you think racism dies in only one generation?"

Miranda shook her head. History showed the ignorance of the few caused the pain and suffering of the many. "You think those hate groups are still around?"

"Wanna find out?" Liz arched her brow and smiled. "Just what kind of effect did da handsome vampire king have on you? Sex'eh beast, ain't he?"

Liz and Miranda made their way into the kitchen where Liz got out the chocolate mocha cake from the fridge: The seven-layer cake with the rich, thick, creamy, chocolate frosting. Orgasmic cake.

"You made that yourself, didn't you?" Drool began gathering in her mouth as Liz sliced the decadent dessert. "You're going to make me pay for this, aren't you?"

"You bet your round, white ass I am. Which, by the way, Gran says looks far more like a black woman's ass than a white woman's." Liz snickered as she handed Miranda her slice.

Miranda nonchalantly ran a hand over her backside. *Chocolate,* she moaned, *it had to be chocolate mocha!* Liz would use any means necessary to get what info she wanted.

"Mmmmmm, it's so good. Better than sex." Liz taunted her with sounds of intense orgasms as she swallowed a piece and smiled the most satisfied, evil smile Miranda had ever seen.

"Give me the goddamned fork! You *so* don't play fair. You won't put on an ounce, and I'm gonna have to run up three flights of stairs for a week to lose it."

"So, tell me now what da very hot vampire lord told you not to tell me."

"You're so sure he did?" Miranda paused to savor the silky smoothness of the cake, agreeing with Liz that chocolate was the next best thing to orgasms.

"Of course. Vampires are the most secretive of us all. Tell me, what did ya tink of Valadon?" Liz laughed as she got out the skim milk. Seven-layer cake and skim milk: Made perfect sense.

Miranda thought back to the way Valadon had stood in the shadows and the look on his face as he'd watched the city below. There'd been a wealth of emotion in that one look. "He's not what the media says about him. There's more to him." Valadon had some elusive quality she couldn't identify. "There's something sensitive. I get the feeling he doesn't often show that to others."

"How can he? Valadon can't afford to. He has to maintain a certain image." Liz gulped down some milk. "Hell, even I have to maintain a certain decorum with my own people."

"He asked me not to discuss the assassination attempt...except with you."

"He knows we're friends." Liz rinsed out their glasses.

"Think so?"

"You enter his territory. You work in his building on a consistent basis. Baby, he knows all about you and some things you probably didn't."

"Really?" Miranda shuddered. "I haven't said more than half a dozen words to him before tonight. Why would he know me?"

"Have you looked in the mirror lately?"

Miranda narrowed her eyes. "What are your impressions of him?"

"He's a fair ruler and has done right by the city. Especially after the war. His corporation, ValCorp, gave millions to the hospitals, schools, your museums and others in the rebuilding process." Liz seemed reflective. "His people love him, would die for him. From what I hear, he is well-respected in the business world, even his competitors admire him."

"Tell me something I don't know." Miranda read the financial reports; she thought it important to have some knowledge of the business world when socializing with museum patrons at fundraisers. "What do you really think of him...personally?"

Liz had that twinkle in her eye that often meant trouble. "I think, if someone is trying to kill the vampire king, we should find out who."

"*We?* What do you mean *we*? He has an army of soldiers to protect him and investigate. He doesn't need us."

"Aren't you curious?" Liz laughed. "After all, it was your ass that got shot."

"Not *that* curious." Miranda flexed her fingers on her hip. "Okay, a little curious, but I'm sure he has people to look into it." She shivered at the thought of Valadon's second and the extent Remare would go to find the truth. "I met some of Valadon's Torians tonight. One of them was Remare."

Lizandra fell back into her favorite recliner. "Ah, da other sex-eh vampire. I know him. He's been here a few times on business from Valadon."

"He's been here? At Werehaven?" Miranda was surprised. "When? I've never seen him. I thought Werehaven was for Weres only." She was aghast the intimidating vampire was even allowed in Werehaven. Werehaven was *her* haven.

Liz noted her reaction to Remare. "On occasion, we entertain *others*." She slowly smiled as she swiveled in the recliner. "Especially those we consider friends."

Miranda rolled her eyes. "He scared the bloody hell out of me. He thinks *I* had something to do with the plot." *Lizandra considered him a friend of the clan? How was that even possible?* Lizandra was no fool; she was a great judge of character. But still...*Remare?*

"You should be scared." Liz narrowed her green eyes. "He's a highly-trained assassin and *fiercely* loyal to Valadon. I'm sure he's already deep into his investigation and probably has more answers than you or I will find." Her brow rose at the way Miranda became unsettled at the mention of Remare's name. "Relax, Mira, he'll soon find out you had nothing to do with it. If he's not aware you're a friend of Morel's and Cyra's, he will soon enough, and they will vouch for you."

Miranda's breath evened out. "Okay...it's late, and I'm tired. I'm going to crash here tonight."

"No, you're not. You're going to hit the computers as soon as you leave, *Pan-dor-a*."

"Funny!" But Liz was right. She wouldn't sleep until she downloaded what she could. Like Liz said, it was her ass that got shot.

"Your room is always available, whenever you want. I'll send one of my best computer geeks your way."

"Who?"

"Dane just got back from Chicago. I'll send him to you."

Miranda's face lit up at the mention of the attractive blond Were who kept his hair in a long braid. Dane wasn't as big as some of the other Weres; he was only about five-foot ten, had an average build, stunning brown eyes and an easy, sexy smile.

And at one time or another, Miranda had woken up next to him. Naked.

"Liz, don't pimp for me." She sighed.

"Someone should. If I don't, you'd never get laid."

"I get laid enough. I don't need you to keep setting me up."

"Really? When was the last time you got some?"

Miranda squinted her eyes, trying to remember.

Liz snickered. "Um-hmm! My point exactly!"

Chapter Six

Bitch was right! She was Pandora! Miranda sped read through everything concerning vampires twenty years ago. Immersed in her online sources, she barely heard the quiet knock and the door opening to reveal a handsome blond Were.

"My God, you're here!" She jumped from the chair and sprang into Dane's arms, locking her ankles around his hips. After reading so much disturbing news about hate groups, seeing Dane's smiling face was a welcome reprieve. She breathed in deep his masculine scent.

"Hello, gorgeous." Dane laughed as he gave her a bear hug and a kiss hot enough to melt her bones. "How's my favorite girl doing?" He nipped her bottom lip. "I'd ask if you missed me," he glanced down at her thighs, "but I kind of have the impression you did."

Miranda's legs slid to the floor. "Oh, sorry. I was just happy to see you. I'm glad you're back. How was Chicago?" California Boy was looking good, but then, he always did. With his long blond hair, tanned skin and enchanting brown eyes, Dane was a looker.

"The consultations went okay, and the project is complete. Enough business talk. Lizandra said you needed help with something?" His radiant smile warmed her heart.

Dane was one of the most unassuming men Miranda ever met. He was brilliant, but never made anyone feel like an idiot because they didn't have his tech skills. She needed to stare at him a minute longer just to take him in. The guy generated positive karma, and after her night, she could do with a good dose. "Yeah, but if you just got back, you probably want to get some sleep."

"Got some on the plane." He tilted his head to the side and cracked his neck. "Whacha need?"

"What did Lizandra tell you?

"Not much. Just that you were doing research on some project."

Miranda frowned. She wasn't supposed to share what happened at ValCorp.

"Relax, princess," he laughed. "She told me you were shot protecting the vamp king."

She grimaced. "Liz wasn't supposed to tell anyone."

"Jay-sus, Miranda. Bad timing or what?" He kissed her forehead. "Well, we can pretend she didn't." He grinned sexily. "What happens at Werehaven—*stays at Werehaven*."

"God's truth." She gently kissed him, then recounted a much condensed version of events. "So...I'm looking at known hate groups, competitors, anyone who might have a grudge against him."

"I see." Dane flipped his ponytail over his back and cracked his knuckles. "Let's see how far you got." He checked her sites with lightning quick strokes over the keyboard and then looked up at her with his lips curving. "So...did the vamp king bite you?"

"I think he had *other* things on his mind." Miranda rolled her eyes. "I found information on a bunch of different groups. But mostly, it looks like press releases, some court documents, charges that were filed, counter-charges processed, but then dropped. Every now and then, I hit a wall that says '*access denied*'. I'm wondering what's behind those walls. Can you get through...without causing red flags?"

"You doubt my comp skills?" Dane wagged his eyebrows at her. "Or *any* other skills?" His fingers flew over the keyboard. "Hmmm, a few minor challenges." Several files and links opened then something shut him down. The encrypted files and firewalls got his attention. "That's interesting."

"What is?"

"This information should be public record, but it's been sealed. I'll check more with my equipment at work." Stretching, his stomach growled. "Got anything to munch on?" He smiled seductively.

"Sure, in the fridge." Miranda read the files as he went to the mini-fridge.

Drinking a bottle of chocolate milk, Dane watched her work then took off his shirt and reclined on the bed. "Did you find what you wanted?" he asked in a sleepy, throaty voice.

"Huh? Oh, yes, and then some." She yawned loud enough her jaw cracked. "God, what time is it?"

"Late. Mind if I crash here tonight? Don't have the energy to make it back to my room. Liz said if she sees me leave before dawn, she's gonna feed me the family jewels." Grinning, he emitted a low, sensual sound. "I'm rather attached to them."

Amused, Miranda asked, "Did you just growl?"

"Maybe. So, do I get a reward for sharing my expert comp skills?"

"Depends. What did you have in mind?"

Dane sat up, discarded his boots, and then removed the rest of his clothes. Giving Miranda an eyeful of his slim but nicely shaped butt, he walked the short distance to the dresser and undid his watch.

Nudity wasn't an issue for the Weres. To them, skin was the same as fur, natural. And she was admiring his natural form. How slender men could have such distinct muscles intrigued her. Dane never seemed to lose his tan, and his golden skin gleamed over the taut muscles of his back.

"Come keep me warm, woman." Dane playfully sprawled out on the bed in all his glory.

"You're a Were; you're warmer than I am." She grinned. Damn, he was hot. What was it about a man's butt that got her going?

"Maybe, but now, I'm tired, and I want to sleep." He turned on the Bose music system to a song by Coldplay called *White Shadows*. "And I want my favorite cuddle bear." He pulled the sheet over him and growled whimsically.

Smiling, Miranda stretched the muscles in her neck and back. Dane's lazy, sensual grin got her every time.

He howled his approval as she undressed.

She laughed. "Move over." After shutting the lamp, she slid under the sheet and heard more growling as Dane pulled her back against his front. His warmth quickly enveloped her, and his chest hairs tickling her back aroused her. "Am I really your favorite cuddle bear?"

He whispered, "For tonight, you are." Then, he sang along with Chris Martin's song.

Miranda smiled as Dane nuzzled her neck and stroked her arm. Weres liked to touch and be touched. Sleeping naked didn't always imply sex—sometimes, it was just for affection or comfort. Sex with Weres was very different than sex with humans. It was simple, natural. Humans complicated the hell out of it. However, making love with a Were was a little tricky. They were built bigger than the average human male, and under no circumstances were humans allowed near Werehaven the nights before, during, or after the full moon. When Weres went into heat, they turned feral. In their werewolf form, they were larger and more dangerous.

Sex at that time would be painful, if not impossible, for a human.

Sliding his hand down her hip, Dane found the bandage covering her wound and snarled. "This where you got stuck?"

"It's healed," she murmured as she turned to face him. "The doc went in, cleaned it out, and then stitched me up. It's okay now."

Concern in his eyes, Dane asked, "It still hurts?"

"Not really. I just get this weird zinger every now and then." She kissed his bicep. "Get some sleep. And thanks again for helping me."

"My pleasure, princess." Dane continued singing to her as she drifted. The last few haunting lines of Chris Martin's song echoed in her mind, and she knew it would always remind her of Dane.

Chapter Seven

Waiting for the last arrival, Valadon considered his most trusted Torians seated in his conference room. His elite circle of guards had been his loyal friends and advisors for centuries; each had proven themselves under crucial circumstances. All were strikingly handsome, acutely intelligent, and each had sworn blood oaths to him—the most sacred bond between vampires.

"We caught a shadow on one of the feeds," Aiden, the calming voice within the group and computer genius, offered. "But we haven't been able to make out a face." With his fallen-angel looks, Aiden assisted Valadon in many diplomatic missions. Tonight, tension was etched into his dark blue eyes.

"Keep working on it," Valadon whispered back.

Across from Aiden sat Tristan, the youngest of the Torians, known for his demented sense of humor. "Bastien and Gregori are still canvassing the neighborhood." As his weapons master, Tristan's aim was perfect. "They're due to report in shortly."

"Good."

Next to Tristan sat Valadon's beloved nephew. A student at NYU, Nick wasn't a Torian; he was a Blueblood, the only surviving son of his sister, Bianca. Nick's parents had been killed when their private jet crashed in the South of France. Valadon had hoped Nick would one day take his place as leader of the Vampire Nation, but much to Valadon's regret, Nick had shown little interest in finance or the affairs of the VN.

Morel, the only fair-haired male and the tallest of his elite force, was being briefed about the assassination attempt. He and his wife, Cyra, were communication specialists. "Cyra's in the communications room and reports no unauthorized transmissions were detected within ValCorp."

Gabriel, glued to his laptop, was also in attendance. Although not a Torian, his knowledge of medicine and science was crucial. His golden-brown eyes had the same red rims all vampires possessed—whether born or made. *"Amory is sending the reports now,"* he communicated silently to Valadon through their blood bond.

"Let me know when they come in."

"Will do."

Irina and Katya were at the far end of the table. Katya, an intelligence strategist, was more reserved with her dark features. Irina, *The Ice Queen,* was a beauty with her long, platinum blond hair and tall, svelte figure; she was lethal in the art of seduction. Her piercing blue eyes were always frosty, betraying her Russian-Siberian heritage. His Torians said the look in her cold eyes was matched only by her cold heart.

Finally, the current leader of his personal guard and second in command entered: Remare, his most trusted advisor and loyal Torian, the oldest and most powerful of them all. Remare was his closest friend throughout the centuries and his ambassador to the other courts and, when needed, his war commander. Because of his long tenures in the European courts, Remare still retained his Roman accent, especially noticeable when he was agitated.

Lately, that seemed more often than not.

After Remare assumed his usual seat on his right, Valadon immediately took charge of the meeting. "All of you know the situation that occurred earlier tonight; Gabriel will now inform us about the chemicals used by our enemies."

Gabriel nodded as he clicked on the large overhead screen. "As you can see, the breakdown shows they are adjusting their composition of chemicals and have now added cadmium and mercury, and to a lesser degree, these other compounds."

Tristan was the first to question the findings. "How lethal is it? Could this fatally harm us?"

"Just about any chemical compound, especially those with metal bases in excessive doses, could be potentially lethal." Gabriel perused the group. "For a human, given enough of the compound, there could be adverse effects: nerve damage, organ failure, disruption to the respiratory and circulation systems enough to cause cardiac arrest. However, this did not severely injure the woman who was shot tonight. It appears the needle was bent before penetration, therefore, it prohibited the substance from entering the blood system." Gabriel locked eyes with Valadon. "She was lucky."

"And for a vampire?" Remare's voice sounded deadly calm. "How much damage could have been inflicted?"

"Difficult to say." Gabriel sat back in his chair. "The other samples contain variables." He rubbed his temple. "I think they're experimenting. I'd wager they're trying to determine what slows down our systems and what is potentially lethal. To be frank, I don't know how much damage the compound could do. Every vampire has different strengths. Age would be a factor, as would distinctions in immune systems. For a younger vampire, yes, this compound could be potentially dangerous." Gabriel rubbed his neck. "Fatal? I don't know. The older the vampire," he glanced at Valadon, "the stronger the resistance to the compound. These are only the preliminary reports. We'll be conducting more tests in the interim."

Valadon knew what Remare was thinking: Gabriel was a turned vampire, not born. He knew many aspects of vampirism, but not all.

"If that's all, I'd like to get back to the lab."

"Does anyone have any other questions for Gabriel?"

The Torians shook their heads.

"Thank you for your time, Gabriel." Valadon nodded his farewell.

"How is the human woman fairing?" Aiden asked quietly.

"Professor Crescent was not significantly harmed." Valadon smiled at the thought of the feisty human. "She is healthy."

"Professor Crescent was the woman who was hit? You didn't tell me it was Miranda! My God! She's my professor!" Nick, who had remained silent during the meeting, suddenly found his voice. "Why didn't anyone tell me?" He peered around the room, his eyes going from Tristan, his closest friend, who shrugged as if to say, *I didn't know she was your instructor*, to Remare, who gazed indifferently at the tips of his fingers, as if annoyed at his question, to Valadon, where they rested waiting for an answer.

"You were out when the attack occurred. Had you been present, you would have been informed. In any event, the professor is fine. She was treated by Gabriel, who assured me she suffered no lasting effects."

"And exactly how much do we know of this human who just happened to be in your office when the attack occurred?" Remare snarked with lethal impatience.

Morel's voice resonated in the room. "She's a friend of Cyra's and mine, and we've socialized often over the years. She's not a threat. I'd bet my life on it." He looked pointedly at Remare, who coldly stared back at him.

Nick appeared incredulous that Remare would even consider his favorite professor would be involved. "No. You're wrong. Professor Crescent wouldn't have anything to do with the attack." He shook his head. "No way!"

Remare responded, "And how much would you know of your college professor, Nick? Enough to guarantee the life of your uncle?"

"She had nothing to do with it." Nick jutted out his chin, refusing to back down to Valadon's most elite enforcer.

"I'd guarantee it," Morel stated. "She had nothing to do with the attack, Remare. As I said before, Cyra and I have known her for years. She's not politically motivated."

"And you know this how? Have you considered the people she works for? Who she does her authentications for?" Remare kept his voice even, though his eyes pulsed with controlled rage.

"As a matter of fact, we've already done a thorough investigation. She's clean." Morel smirked. "Do you think I would allow my wife to socialize with a potential enemy?"

Valadon interceded. "About a year ago, when I watched Miranda work on one of my paintings, I was curious about her so I ordered a full investigation. She has no political affiliations."

Remare looked exasperated as he faced Valadon. "And you didn't tell *me*?"

"You were out of the country at the time." Valadon swiveled in his chair. "I assure you the report is quite complete. And I agree with Nick, Morel; she is not involved. It was a mere coincidence she happened to be in the room with me." Valadon grimaced. "I was the one who insisted on her coming to my office tonight. She was quite irritated with me about that." He offered a sly smile to his oldest friend. "You should be happy she took the dart for me."

When Remare narrowed his eyes and opened his mouth to say something, Valadon raised his hand, indicating the discussion was over. "Now, Tristan, what do we know about the helicopter?"

"There were no reports of privately-licensed helicopters flying in this area. The tourist helicopters were all on the ground at the Downtown Heliport. Detective Vetti informs us there were no accounts of any 'borrowed' or stolen choppers." Tristan continued, "We're waiting on intel of any government or army copters in the area."

Valadon knew his other two elite Torians, Gregori and Bastien, were in the field. He already had his people well-placed in certain organizations to keep an eye on his former enemies. Something didn't sit well about this attack—something Gabriel had mentioned to him in private, which he wasn't ready to share with his Torians. "All right then, you all know your tasks." Valadon directed, "If anything breaks, report in immediately."

As everyone left the conference room, Valadon motioned for Morel to join him in his private quarters.

Remare stayed behind and signaled to Irina. He whispered quietly in her ear, and she nodded as she left the room.

***

Hurrying across Madison Avenue, William Tolliver shivered as a late night breeze chilled him. He climbed the steps to one of the toniest homes in a wealthy neighborhood on New York's Upper East Side. The people waiting for him were not known for their patience, and he was already running late. *What the hell had gone wrong?* They had planned the assassination with the finest attention to detail—it should have gone off like clockwork. But like the previous attempt, there'd been some variable that couldn't be envisioned.

He rode in the elevator up to the penthouse suite of Peter Lundquist, a nephew of one of the original leaders of the HOL, and was led to the private study where his associates were waiting. There were eight of them now, eight key people who had vowed to see the eradication of the vampires. It would just be a matter of time now before they went through with the venture known as the *DOL Project.*

"For God's sake, William, come in and close the door behind you. We have much to discuss," the figure behind the desk said in his impatient, cultured voice. Of all the members of the HOL, he was the one who Tolliver feared the most. His icy stare went right through Tolliver and chilled his bones. *Regent* was the name he went by; no one knew his true identity. The man had an icy, soulless look in his eyes and was assiduously methodical in his plans. From the way he carried himself, Tolliver was sure he was a member of the regency in Europe.

And William knew to the depths of his soul the man had murdered before...and derived pleasure from it.

Chapter Eight

Valadon admired the speed in which his people had cleaned his office. With the new window installed, it hardly resembled the atrocity it had been hours before. He walked silently into his dark room and examined every corner, resting his hand lightly on his collection of Greek statues. *Well, if Apollo wasn't broken before, he certainly was now.*

As a Blueblood, the purest bloodline of vampires, his vision was the sharpest of all vampires, as were his many other talents. Talents the human world would never learn about, as they would frighten the weak-minded individuals who thought them to be the monsters fiction often portrayed them to be. Although there were vampires who resembled the creatures made popular in movies—they kept to the shadow world, and when they didn't, his enforcers dealt with them.

Valadon gazed out at the city and wondered which of his human enemies were sleeping well tonight and who would be furious that their plans had failed, yet again. Sensing Remare's presence, he turned toward his second.

"Do you think that wise?" Remare leaned against the doorframe with both arms crossed over his chest. "They might come back."

"They might," Valadon smirked, "but not tonight. I'm sure the news of their failure has already reached their employers. Have you learned anything new?"

"Bastien and Gregori are on their way to meet with Stryder. They will report in soon...as will the others." Remare joined Valadon in the shadows near the window. "Preparations are being made to replace all the windows in this suite with tinted bulletproof glass. Had I known they would make an attempt at this height, I would have had them installed long ago."

"Do not blame yourself, old friend. No one could have predicted they would strike this high up. They usually try for me when I'm out in public."

"Yes, I know." Remare smiled sarcastically. "That is why I often accompany you to your social events."

Valadon peered up into the night sky. "Tonight, someone will pay for their failure."

"Of that, I am very certain. The others are apprehensive about the chemical warfare our enemies seem to have grown fond of. I've read the report Gabriel prepared, and I'm concerned, too, though for different reasons." He faced his friend. "Have you considered the possibility that the poison was not designed to kill you, but to render you vulnerable?"

Valadon frowned. Remare had reached the same conclusion he'd been trying to avoid. "For what purpose?" He glared at Remare with a hint of sadness in his eyes. "So that one of my own could finish the job? Yes, the thought did occur to me."

Remare nodded. "Ingratitude is a merciless bitch. We'll know something within twenty-four hours. If there is a traitor at ValCorp, we'll find him, or her."

"I know you will." He glanced one last time at his office. "Come with me to my apartment. Morel is already there. You need to hear his report and his perspective on the intriguing Professor Crescent."

Valadon laughed at the sound Remare made deep in his throat. His private elevator would take them to the subterranean levels that housed his Torians. The above ground floors of ValCorp were for public display; below the surface levels, there was a whole world down there the humans would never learn of—House Valadon, where his closest vampire friends gathered to socialize...and when necessary, plan strategies in their seemingly never-ending war with the HOL.

Chapter Nine

"She's human, all right." Bastien bent down and examined the wounds on the young female's throat. He knew, if he inspected the insides of her thighs, he'd find more bite marks as the scent of sex was mixed with blood and death. "No more than fourteen," Bastien relayed to his partner, Gregori, who was busy searching the alley. Brave thing had fought back, but it had been too late. The thought that she'd been used by more than one vampire made his stomach recoil.

Valadon had long ago outlawed the public drinking of mortals, preferring the blood banks at ValCorp. For those who desired to drink from the flesh, there were designated vampire clubs, where privacy rooms were established for just that reason. It was all very clean and well-organized to avoid situations like this one.

Bastien brushed her dark hair from her angelic face. Definitely vampire or...the possibility it had been made to appear as a vampire attack. It wouldn't be the first time some extremist group sacrificed one of their own to foster hatred and fear toward vampires. But in this case, he didn't think so. "Most likely Rogues."

Rogue vampires lived nomadic lifestyles without declaring their allegiance to a house lord. Bastien shook his head in disgust. Rogues were what gave vampires a bad rep. The Torians spent much time hunting them down and dispensing justice. Depending on the severity of the crime, a Rogue was either incarcerated in one of the underground vaults or executed. He'd once escorted a prisoner to the vaults and never wanted to repeat the experience.

"Better contact Vetti. This girl is one of his." Bastien straightened, wiping the dirt from his pants. "How many does this make?"

"Four, no three—the last one was a Were." Gregori rose from the far end of the alley as he finished his search. "There's nothing here. I'm calling Vetti now. Contact Remare; he'll want to know."

"What do you make of the scent traces on her body?" Bastien frowned. The scent clearly distinguished one of their own. A very old and powerful vampire.

Gregori looked pained and held up four fingers. "Vetti. Bad news. Yeah, we found another one." He closed his phone as Bastien related the same information to ValCorp. "Perhaps it's time to pay a visit to Rogue territory."

Bastien smirked. "Nightworld. I can hardly wait."

***

Nick's leg was casually draped over hers as Cerise lay on her stomach. He reached over with one slender, but muscular arm and stroked her curls. "You have the most amazing hair. You can see all the golds, reds—even some black strands. Are you sure you don't use highlights?"

Cerise playfully hit him with one of the pillows. "Of course not, I told you some Weres retain the colors of both parents. Everything you see on this body is *au natural*." Wanting Nick to worship her body, she stood gloriously nude, the throw from the sofa carelessly falling to the floor. There were few women in the Red Claw Clan who could match her muscle tone. What she lacked in height, she more than made up for with cunning and sexual skills that merited what she most desired: status in the clan.

Her uncle, Edgar Renworth, was pack master, and when the opportunity presented itself that a vampire, a Blueblood, lusted for her, Cerise spared no effort in planning his seduction. Nick once mentioned female vampires were too aggressive with their fangs on his cock, so she was careful with her canines. But, oh, how she wanted to torment him, often giving him little scrapes just to watch his quick healing. "So, tell me about your week. You said there was trouble over at ValCorp."

"I'm not supposed to talk about it. You know how it is. Vampire business." Nick gathered up their leftover pizza and beer bottles and carried them into her kitchen. He put his arms around her as she washed the plates. Wetting his hands, Nick made sure the water was cold and then caressed her ample breasts.

"Still don't trust me?" She pouted as he played with her nipples, moaning in appreciation of his touch. Having been taught since puberty to use her body as a tool, Cerise turned the faucet off and arched into him. Any trouble over at ValCorp was worth repeating to her clan chief. She turned and stroked Nick's cock. Knowing it sent tremors through him, she exhaled by his ear. "I told you, whatever you tell me is just between us. Always."

Nick's breath grew labored as she continued to stroke him. "You better stop," he said raggedly, "or I'm going to come again."

"That's all right. I want you to...come." She stroked him faster, watching as his panting intensified. Nick tossed her over his shoulder and, with the strength and speed of a Blueblood vampire, ran back into the living room and tossed her on the couch. Within seconds, he was inside her.

Cerise laughed as she came. Oh, yes! A couple of more times and she'd know everything that went on at ValCorp.

Chapter Ten

"Waiting to see you again—V." Miranda admired the beautiful bouquet of flowers Valadon had sent her: Crystal roses and white orchids with pink inside. She stroked the card. *"At the restaurant of your choice."* She swiveled in her chair, remembering his deep sea green eyes and considered replying. Then decided against it. Too much potential for danger; getting shot once was enough. The last thing she needed was to get involved with the most powerful vampire in NYC. No matter how handsome he was.

Dr. Felicity Walcott texted her back, *"Will meet you @ library."* The thought of seeing her former professor at NYU made Miranda smile. Pondering the flowers, she inhaled their magnificent scent, then wondered what Valadon was doing tonight. Probably leading the investigation into his attack. She hoped he ran *Remare the Rude* into the ground. Serve him right, she snickered as she grabbed her purse and headed out.

The New York Public Library was one of Miranda's treasures. Besides the myriad of books, the architecture and the artwork were truly remarkable. The arched high ceilings, all the marble and the chandeliers adorning the library fascinated her. After the deaths of her parents and sister, she used to bury herself studying here. The map room had been a favorite of her father's. Carl Crescent had also liked the rare books division, but tonight, she chose the map room to do her research.

When Felicity walked in, Miranda's face brightened. Even with her diminutive stature, when Walcott walked into a room, all heads turned in her direction. Tonight, she was dressed in loose fitting trousers, a beige turtleneck and matching scarf; her low heeled boots completed the outfit. Miranda loved her dangling earrings and bangle bracelets—Walcott's signature jewelry.

Felicity hugged Miranda and stepped back to study her. "You look smashing, but overworked...as usual." She sighed as she set down her backpack and bags. "What does dear old Jordan have you working on now?"

"I'm doing research on an obscure Berthe Morisot."

"What concerns you the most?" Walcott adjusted her gold rimmed glasses and scanned her reference books.

"Aside from the fact there is no record anywhere of this painting, no working title, no reference of it in any of her letters or those of whom she was most acquainted, oh...just about everything."

"I take it you checked the Art Index and the Directory?"

"Of course. The style, composition, shading variations and pigment analysis all seem to match. I just can't find any historical references."

"I'm glad you remembered something from my classes." Walcott smiled one of her trademark smiles that reminded Miranda of the cat that swallowed the canary.

"I remember *everything* you taught me." Miranda's stomach began to grumble, reminding her she only had a KitKat bar for lunch.

"There's a private dining room a few floors below. We'll go there." Walcott seemed amused at Miranda's confused expression.

"We're going down below? In the stacks? Is that legal?"

"Still drawing inside the lines?" Walcott arched a brow. "Didn't I teach you to think outside the box? Besides, there's someone I'd like you to meet."

"Who?" Miranda gathered up their possessions.

"You'll see." Walcott beamed as they walked down the hall, then took out a key for a private elevator Miranda didn't know existed at the end of the marble hallway.

"How far down does this thing go?"

"Well, I'm sure you know there are two levels below housing the books. But actually, there are more than that."

As the elevator doors closed, Miranda knew she was being baited, but asked anyway, "How many more?"

Felicity answered nonchalantly. "A few."

Miranda had the queasy feeling they went farther down than she anticipated. As an *Elemental*, she could sense the planet's natural vibration and the deeper into the earth she went, the pitch grew stronger. Her gut clenched, but given the events of the week, she decided it was just a bad case of nerves.

When the elevator doors opened, they stepped out and walked down a hallway, passing stacks of books scented with age. Miranda was in awe of the magnitude of books kept this far down. Walcott unlocked a door at the end of the hall and flicked the lights on.

Miranda marveled at a vast, but quaint, sitting room fashioned out of the eighteen-hundreds with antiques. The décor included two sets of French doors to the side of the room with cerulean drapes tied back, an ebony grand piano in the far corner, large oak bookcases with leather bound books and a few objects d'art on both sides of the enormous, hand carved mahogany fireplace. On the left was a dining room table with place settings and a decorated basket containing pine cones—Felicity's favorite.

"How much does someone have to contribute to get access to a room like this?" Miranda quipped as she eyed the room's many antiques.

"It's not the how much that matters, as...the who knows who." Walcott grinned as she lifted one of her bags to the table and unwrapped sandwiches.

Miranda smelled corned beef and almost drooled.

"Come, let's eat, and then, you can tell me why you *really* called me."

Miranda bit into one of NY's best sandwiches. There was no other state in the country that made corned beef sandwiches on rye bread with deli mustard that tasted this good.

When they were done eating and had cleaned up, Walcott went over and turned on the gas fireplace. "So, tell me what you wouldn't say on the phone."

Miranda debated whether or not to confide in her friend. But she trusted Felicity as she trusted only a few people. "How well do you know vampires?"

Walcott tossed her head back, shaking her dangling earrings, and heartily laughed. "*Mon cuer,* is that what you wanted to ask me?"

Miranda felt chagrined at Walcott's laughter and decided to give her a short version of the events at ValCorp as Walcott sat on one of the leather chairs with one leg crossed over the other. When Miranda finished, she noted Walcott's expression. "You're not surprised by any of this, are you?" A sinking feeling began to gnaw in the pit of her stomach.

"The fact that there was another attempt on Lord Valadon's life? No, I'm not surprised. Men—vampires such as he are rife with enemies." She carefully scrutinized Miranda. "But I'm glad you were able to walk away from the situation relatively unscathed. You could have been killed."

"Yes, I know," Miranda murmured as she rubbed her arms. "Which brings me back to my initial question: How much do you know about vampires?"

Walcott's eyes shifted to the back of the room, and a chill shot up Miranda's spine as the temperature in the room dropped dramatically. The prickling of her skin was more intense than she'd ever felt before.

"I should think she knows quite a bit about vampires." A deep, male voice with a cultured accent resonated around the room behind Miranda as she heard the door close.

And then lock.

Chapter Eleven

Nightworld, the underground Rogue hangout, aka *The Devil's Den, Paradise Lost* or *The Last Exit* was located in the bowels of an abandoned subway station. The gossip was if you couldn't find what you were searching for in Nightworld, it didn't exist. The aroma of opium, mixed with a special blend, permeated the air as Stryder, nicknamed after a character from *The Lord of the Rings* movies, relaxed in the privacy of his office. The Rogue leader inhaled deeply. "Exquisite," he murmured, knowing the high would only last minutes because vampire physicality expelled most toxins. Stryder wanted one moment of peace before dealing with the two problems that just walked into his territory.

Arliss, one of his lieutenants, knocked before entering. "Boss, you won't believe who just walked in." The tall, but lanky vampire was dressed in black jeans and shirt with a knife sheath attached to his thigh.

"Would that be two of Valadon's flunkies?" Grinning, Stryder nodded to the monitors above the doorway. Although not enemies, they weren't exactly allies either; Valadon had established a truce between the Rogues and his Torians, and neither side wanted to see it fall. *Not yet,* Stryder mused as the remnants of the drug dissipated. Nightworld catered to all; but mainly it was a refuge for vampires and others who'd grown jaded with the above clubs. His was a world that existed outside of the law; Stryder intended to keep it that way. Of course, if Valadon ever found out about the blood clubs he had on the side, he'd be *"ended"*.

That's why he'd chosen this locale: It had hidden tunnels no one knew about except him and his bodyguards.

"What do you suppose they want? I've never seen them here before. They're not regulars like the others."

"We're about to find out."

Zoe, his other bodyguard, had already approached them. His warrior woman with Asian ancestry and diamond tattoos on the left side of her face, Zoe had dark, almond-shaped eyes with finely arched brows, high cheekbones and scarlet lips. Her straight, jet black hair was pulled back in a long ponytail.

Dressed in black leather from her deadly spiked boots to her long black leather gloves, Zoe exuded the image of a death-dealer.

Stryder watched as Zoe led the two Torians through his club, passing the main bar, gambling section, billiards room, a gaming room, and rooms that specialized in assorted drugs. But the rooms that generated the most income were for pleasure—of all types.

"Enter," he said as Zoe knocked and Arliss took his place by his side.

Bastien pretended to choke at the fading smell of opium. "You'd think dealers would know not to touch their products."

Zoe closed the door, shutting out the noise of the club, and leaned against the wall.

Gregori chose the seat closest to Stryder.

"Valadon's Torians. I'm impressed." Stryder scrutinized them, quickly identifying where their weapons were concealed. "Whatever brings you to Nightworld? Valadon not paying you enough and you seek employment here?"

"Can it, Stryder." Bastien grunted. "You couldn't pay us enough to work in this dump."

Stryder ignored the expected insult. "Perhaps then I can offer you something to drink." He lifted an eyebrow. "We have many vintages and blends here, perhaps something more exotic than what you're used to?"

"No, thanks." Gregori appeared older and the more patient of the two. "Word is you deal in information, among your many interests."

"Perhaps. But nothing comes for free." The corner of Stryder's mouth rose slightly. "What kind of information were you seeking?" He relaxed as he swiveled in his chair.

Bastien snarked, "It would be in your best interest to cooperate. Don't try to shake us down, Stryder. Valadon would shut you down so fast your head would spin and you wouldn't need your product for the rush."

More even tempered, Gregori maintained an even tone. "We hear someone's been trying to develop a poison potentially dangerous to vampires, your kind and ours."

Stryder sat up straight. He was not a purebred vampire—unpolluted with human ancestry—but a mixed-blood vampire. If the Bluebloods were concerned about this drug, it would be far more dangerous to the Rogues, whose blood wasn't nearly as powerful as the purebreds. "What kind of poison? What else have you heard?"

"We were hoping you could tell us. You get all types passing through here." Bastien questioned, "Surely, you've heard something?"

Stryder leaned back in his chair. To possess that kind of knowledge might be worthwhile. If Valadon was so hot to obtain that information, he'd be in Stryder's debt. He smiled at the possibilities. "At the moment, I've heard of no poison affecting a vampire adversely. Nothing the humans have produced has any enduring effects." He waved his hand at the fading scent of opium. He assessed the stoic expressions of the two Torians and wondered if he might be wrong.

Gregori glanced at Bastien and then rose, reaching in his pocket for a card he slid across the desk to Stryder. "If you should hear anything worthy of our attention, you will contact us."

That wasn't a request, but an order from an elite Torian. Stryder knew if Valadon ever desired it, he could wipe out his entire organization with just one command. Better to appear compliant. "But of course. However, next time you come here, be prepared to trade something of equal value." He nodded as the two left.

Arliss waited until the door closed then asked, "Do you really think that's the reason they were here, boss?"

"I'm not sure." He rose and circled the desk to lean against the front as he watched them on the monitors exit his club. "But I think it's something we need to find out. Zoe?"

"Yes?"

"Your impressions."

"The younger one was barely containing his disgust. The older one was more reserved, determined to get answers. Both were not forthcoming with any details and each knew more than they were offering."

"That's what I thought." He admired her ability to sense when others were lying or withholding a truth. Of course, her skill with a blade was why he'd hired her in the first place; her other abilities had been a bonus. "I want you to contact your former employer. See if there's any truth in that supposed rumor."

Zoe left without a backward glance. She didn't relish tracking down any of her former employers, but she knew who to turn to for information. If someone was experimenting with chemicals that could harm vampires, she'd make it a point to discover who. Perhaps then a door long shut would open.

She just had to make one quick stop before setting out.

***

Bastien waited until they were a block away. "Think he was telling the truth?"

Gregori retrieved his keys and rested his arms on the hood of his Range Rover. "No reason to lie. He didn't flinch at any of our questions, but he's old enough to guard his emotions." Gregori scanned the street, checking out the rooftops and the cars along the curb. "What did you think about his lieutenants?"

"Obedient, aren't they? Like two guard dogs." Bas smirked as he mirrored his partner and placed his hands on the hood, tapping out a tune as he raised both eyebrows. "The female looks like she'd be fun in bed, though."

"Stop thinking with your dick. I asked for an opinion."

"I gave you one." Bastien laughed. "I think she might be mag in bed."

"More like deadly. Did you see the claws on her; they were peeking through her gloves."

Bastien growled sexily in his throat. "Wouldn't mind having them rake my back."

"Could be painful; she'd draw blood." Gregori quirked a smile as he jangled his keys.

"So would I." Bas grinned and let his fangs glimmer in the light of the street lamp; then his voice got serious. "What were your impressions?"

"You don't remember Zoe, do you?" Gregori clicked the remote and entered the car.

"Should I?" Bas got in and closed his door.

"She used to be a Torian." At Bastien's incredulous face, Gregori recounted her past and how she lost her status at House Valadon.

Bas let out a low whistle. "Shit. That explains some things."

"Yeah," Gregori exhaled.

"Should we tell him she's working here?"

"He knows." Gregori sat back and tried to replay something that had been bothering him since they first entered Nightworld. "Something was... I don't know. That place..." He ran a hand over his head and frowned. "It's rank."

"Those people who go there... Some are walking diseases." Bas stated, "They know what the deal is, that's why they go. Stryder's no fool. He keeps his various enterprises low-key enough to fly under the radar. If he didn't, he knows Valadon would end him."

Fools! Gregori rubbed the back of his neck. They were trying to prevent the production of a poison, and these people willingly consumed them. He narrowed his eyes in concentration. "Something was off tonight. It was one of the scents in the place... I can't place it." He shook his head and blew out a long breath in frustration. "Something seemed familiar...for just a moment...yet it was gone before I could identify it."

"Your instincts are the best of all the Torians. Come on, let's get back to ValCorp and report in. Maybe they have more news, by now."

Gregori started the car. "Did you see the scar on the left side of Stryder's jaw?"

"Yeah, he must have gotten it before he was turned or it would've healed." Bas adjusted the music system until he found a song by the vampire, Tiseira.

"Not necessarily." Gregori tapped the wheel, thinking. "Some newly-turned vampires don't recuperate as quickly as more mature vampires. Depends who's doing the turning. Also, half-breeds don't heal up as well as full-blooded vampires." He regarded Bastien. "He received that wound when he was a vampire, not human...from the point of a sword."

"How do you know?" Bastien faced him as Gregori drove down the deserted street.

"Because I was there when he received it." Gregori rubbed his chin, remembering an old memory.

"Yeah? Who gave it to him?"

Gregori smiled as he turned his head sideways. "Remare."

Bastien whistled softly. "Must've pissed him off royally."

"I'd say so," Gregori agreed. Cutting the face was considered a major insult, and he knew the wound wasn't an accident. Remare didn't make mistakes in sword fighting. It was given as a warning.

"Why'd he do it?"

"You'd have to ask him." Gregori smirked as he drove to their compound. "But I'd wait until he's in a good mood."

"No shit." Bas laughed, turned the music up and hummed along with the song as he tapped his fingers on the dash. "He hasn't been in a good mood for some time."

"He has a lot on his mind." Gregori wondered if the others noticed how remote Remare had become. "But I'll tell you this," he grinned, "I bet he gets in a real good mood when he finds out who's behind the attacks."

Chapter Twelve

Remare stared at the ceiling while his fingers tapped lightly on his chest, too restless to sleep. He had much on his mind with the attempt on Valadon, but there had been attempts before, and Remare always managed to get a few hours' sleep. Lately, however, Morpheus—the god of dreams, was avoiding him, and Remare could not figure out why. He checked his phone again as he stroked the woman's arm draped across his abdomen. Katya was sound asleep, as well as the woman next to her, Irina. Their usual bout of sex games should have ensured sleep, but he still couldn't shake this feeling of unease.

If he thought back long enough, he should've realized this vague sense of vexation had been evolving for some time. Both women were beautiful, sexually adventurous and attentive to him. Neither was coy in their bed play; both showed a fantastic lack of restraint. Irina, as always, was the more daring. Each desired to pleasure him and he them.

Still, there was a haunting feeling that something was lacking.

Remare rolled to his side and sat up, careful not to wake Katya. Tenderly, he brushed the hair from her face and admired her beauty. He'd never had a favorite between them. It was because there were two that he'd kept them as his lovers for this long. Of the two, Irina was the one more given to jealousy. But he'd learned long ago how to assuage the feelings of the weaker sex. *Weaker?* He snorted. Irina was one of the world's best assassins.

Katya was more reasonable when it came to their arrangement. He wondered if he'd have become involved with either one on a solo basis, then dismissed the thought. Two women were preferred because neither one formed a possessive attachment he found disturbing. Naked, he rose and walked down the two steps of his raised platform bed to get a drink.

Remare surveyed his apartment with its Oriental décor that he'd always found comforting and relaxing. During his years in Asia, under the tutelage of Qui Ti Huay, he had acquired a fondness for all things Asian. Especially the two samurai swords mounted on his bedroom wall—a gift from Master Huay when

Remare left Japan to return to the European council and Valadon's service. He eyed his other favorite piece on his dresser, a palm-sized gold dragon with ruby eyes, and walked around the silk screen partition separating his bedroom from his living room. He grabbed a robe and strode down the two steps to the bar in the corner and poured himself a glass of blood wine.

Sipping his wine, he relaxed into his black leather couch. Valadon had been wise in constructing rooms for his Torians in ValCorp's subterranean levels. There were other levels below, but hardly anyone went down there anymore. Studying his rooms, he realized there was only one drawback: No windows—unlike his town house in Sutton Place that overlooked the Queensboro Bridge. On nights when he couldn't sleep, he'd look out over the East River and admire the lights on the bridge. Remare exhaled and let his eyes close. Until this nasty business with their adversaries was resolved, it was wiser to stay here.

"Remare?" Katya's soft voice roused him from his reveries. She tied the belt to her short robe and descended the steps to join him.

"What is it?" Remare smiled as she kneeled before him and rested her chin on his knee. "I'm sorry to have woken you." He met her concerned look.

"You've not been sleeping well for some time now," she said tenderly. "What is it that has you so preoccupied?"

"Nothing." He shook his head. "Nothing you need to be worried about." He stroked the strands of her hair. "You should go back to sleep."

"It's something if you cannot sleep. Tell me, maybe I can help."

Remare tried to put into words exactly what it was that had him on edge. He often thought he should cut Katya loose—allow her to find a lover who would give her more than he ever could, give her what she deserved. But he knew she'd never leave if Irina stayed, and Irina would not leave him. And that was something he would soon have to address. Her possessiveness was just one of the things on his mind. Had she not been lovers with Katya he'd have asked her to leave him years ago.

Irina, too, deserved someone who could give her what he could not.

Oh, he still enjoyed the sex the three of them shared, but he feared he was growing disinterested and the residual implications of that boredom. He gazed down at Katya. "I'm just tired; we'll talk about it another time. Come here." He drew her on the couch beside him, her head in his lap. He stretched out one leg and pretended to sleep while so much was on his mind.

However, the rest did not last long when the text he'd been waiting for finally came through.

Chapter Thirteen

"Are you ever going to answer any of his messages?"

Miranda glowered at her friend and emitted a low growl as she completed her workout in Cyra's training room.

"You've been spending too much time with the Weres; you're beginning to sound like them." Cyra's laughter earned her another glare. "You can work out like that for the next ten years, and you still won't have a body like Lizandra's."

"Or yours." Miranda admired Cyra's vampire form and agility. "I'm not trying to be. I just like feeling good—healthy, strong." She sipped her water bottle, then smiled slyly. "Did Valadon ask you to check up on me?"

"He has tried to reach you several times now." Cyra handed Miranda a small towel. "It would be polite if you answered him."

Miranda loved Cyra as a sister. Even though she had many questions about vampires—especially after meeting Felicity's beau, who Miranda was not allowed to mention *"under any circumstances,"* she wouldn't risk putting Cyra in a compromising position.

She was still in shock at having met an *ancient*. In her mind, an ancient would be someone resembling Dumbledore or Yoda— *not* a handsome dark blond grad student who dressed in navy T-shirts and blue jeans, whom she had promptly nicknamed Blu.

"Miranda, it's a pleasure to have finally met you." The ancient extended his hand. *"Felicity's told me so much about you."*

When Miranda could actually form words, she said, *"Unfortunately, you have the advantage there."* She glanced at Felicity. As soon as Miranda shook his hand, she immediately felt the rush of power up her arm. Then, when she met his perceptive eyes, he dampened his power.

"Miranda." Felicity stroked her shoulder. *"This is Guy de Montglat—my companion."*

"Why is it you and Liz are always trying to set me up?" Miranda gulped more water. "I'll have you know I'm quite capable of finding someone on my own. Besides, I have no desire to be some vampire's tasty treat."

"*Some* vampire?" Offended, Cyra said, "Valadon is our leader, and he doesn't need you to feed on. We *do* have our own blood bank."

Miranda knew that, but the thought of having dinner with Valadon was overwhelming. "I didn't mean it like that." She knew she sounded pissy. "I just don't want to become involved in something I can't...I can't..."

"Control?"

Miranda raised an eyebrow. "Walk away from something that doesn't work out." She walked over to the mirrored wall. "And we both know, eventually, it would go south." Miranda examined her reflection, not sure she liked what she saw. "Valadon is a complication I don't need." She swallowed more water. "Besides, I like my life the way it is now: uncomplicated."

Cyra playfully brushed her shoulder against Miranda's. "Haven't you ever wanted more?" Seeing Miranda's raised eyebrow, she amended her approach. "I mean, don't you ever get tired of the Weres? You know you can never mate one. You deserve more."

"I get your concern, but maybe I don't want more." Miranda removed her hair tie and massaged the tension in her scalp. "You and Morel have a great relationship, and Liz has Gavin—for however long that will last. But I really do like my life the way it is."

"Are you afraid?"

"Of a vampire lord? *Yeah!* Who wouldn't be? Besides being the most powerful man I've ever met," ...*well almost!* "I've seen pictures of the models he's dated." Miranda shook her head. "I don't look *anything* like them and have no wish to be. Besides, I doubt we have much in common."

Amusement shone in Cyra's face. "Most women at ValCorp would give their right fang for a chance with Valadon. It's just dinner, Miranda. He's genuinely sorry you were injured and wants to make it up to you." Cyra rested her hand on Miranda's shoulder. "Won't you let him?"

Miranda grunted and knew if she'd been a Were, it would have sounded more like a growl. "The flowers were plenty. He really doesn't have to give me jewelry."

Cyra laughed. "Yes, I heard you returned the necklace. He was going to buy you a car, but he wasn't sure if you drove or not. Do you?" she asked innocently.

"He *did* send you to spy on me!" Miranda was playfully insulted. "I *knew* it!"

"Not really. He just asked if I would talk to you, reassure you there's no reason to fear him."

Miranda exhaled deeply and considered her options. "Just one date?"

Cyra crossed her heart and laughed. "Absolutely. If I'm lying, I'm dying."

"And what happens if another one of his enemies decides to take a shot at him and misses and hits me instead, again?"

"He'll have his guards with him this time. You'll be perfectly safe, I promise."

Miranda wasn't so certain. All right then, she decided. She was eager to try that elegant restaurant on Barrow Street in Greenwich Village her boss raved about. "Fine, tell him I accept, but no more gifts."

Cyra could hardly contain her glee and hugged her. "It'll be fun. I swear, you'll see." She smiled at Miranda's grimace. "Stop looking like we're dragging you off for a root canal."

Both of them burst out laughing. *God, friends. Gotta love 'em—though, at times, you want to strangle them.*

"I thought I heard you two in here. What's up?" Morel walked in, put his workout bag down and kissed his wife.

"Miranda's finally agreed to see Valadon."

"Ah, trading a little fur for fang?" he teased as he hugged Cyra.

"Ha, funny!" Miranda snarled at him. But admired the carefree affection between the two and smiled warmly instead. *Sometimes, people actually got it right.* Rare in her world.

"Well, that should put him in a good mood. He's been a little short-tempered since the night of the attack."

"Who wouldn't be?" Cyra hugged him back.

Miranda could feel the sexual heat building between her friends. "And...I think it's time I left. I'll call Valadon when I get home."

"Something I said?" Morel smirked as he caressed his wife.

"You never answered my question."

Miranda turned to Cyra, "What question?"

"Do you drive?"

"I know how." She rolled her eyes. "But I don't need a car, so tell him no. I meant what I said. No more gifts." She was halfway to the door, shook her head, and then turned back. "Okay, you got me. What was he going to get me?"

Cyra grinned and shrugged; Morel had a smile on his face a mile wide.

Neither said a word.

Chapter Fourteen

Miranda exited the subway before her usual destination because she needed time to think and walking always helped clear her mind. This had to be one of the craziest weeks she could remember. As she climbed the stairs to street level, she gazed up to see if it was a full moon, but with all the buildings, it was impossible to see. It had to be getting close. She debated stopping at the corner deli when the aroma of cooked meat hit her, but decided to keep walking.

She still couldn't believe she'd met an ancient. Earlier, when she'd observed Felicity and the youthful-looking Blu as he put his arm around her—the affection between them obvious—it had taken a minute for the image to compute. Felicity had looked radiant. But then again, for some time, she'd been looking younger. *Love could do that to a person.*

When Miranda crossed the street, she realized for a city that never slept, it was unusually quiet; no taxis or pedestrians were out. *Off night!* She pulled her jacket tighter as a cold breeze blew across her back.

As for Blu, she smiled at her surprise in having met him. The stories were seriously wrong about ancients looking old. Blu had the most beguiling hazel eyes that appeared green when the light shone on them and brown when he was in shadows. Appearances aside, he had to be one of the most astute men she'd ever met, and between universities and the museum, she'd met some of the best intellectuals.

He'd told her while exploring the stacks underneath the library, he'd discovered an abandoned wing and made it his home. *"Court life in Europe became tedious so I traveled around the world...several times over."* He'd even gone into the golden slumber, vampire sleep: *"A form of hibernation that could last as long as a century, though mine had lasted much longer."*

The only thing he'd requested was to keep his presence in New York secret. He had no interest in Valadon or the VN, preferring the life of a recluse. *"The intrigues of being a courtier bored me. I lived that life once, long ago, and have no desire to revisit it."*

Miranda was so lost in her thoughts she didn't notice the sight up ahead, until the stench of death hit her. Reaching down into the back of her boot, she slowly pulled out one of her knives Liz had taught her how to handle. She'd debated taking them, but remembered Lizandra saying, *"Better safe than sorry, and with your curvy ass, you're more likely to be sorry."*

Staying in the shadows, she crept quietly along the street. She spotted the body of a young girl whose throat had been torn out; her blood saturated the air. Rogues often orchestrated scenes like this to lure some Good Samaritan into a trap, so she texted Detective Mike Vetti, the city's liaison with the VN.

Miranda silently stepped the way Weres and vampires did, not quite as adept as either race; she moved furtively. She placed the tip of her blade behind the murderer's ear and said authoritatively, "Ease up, slowly. Hands where I can see them." Too late Miranda realized the killer was a vampire. Usually vampires had a scent or a vibe she could sense; this one had neither. The vampire slowly turned to her, and then, she understood why she hadn't made him. "Well, good evening...Dr. Death."

"Professor Crescent, you can put away your knives. I didn't kill her. I was merely collecting evidence and measuring the bite radius," Gabriel explained as she eyed him, the body on the ground and their surroundings. "Surely, you can't believe I'm capable of murder."

"Next, you'll be telling me you were out for a stroll and just happened to find her body." Miranda's sarcasm bled through her voice as she scrutinized Gabriel's eyes for any tells he'd attack. She felt repulsed that this vampire she'd met less than a week ago, a vampire she'd found attractive, was a murderer.

It was a sight right out of one of the old movies Lizandra liked. She remembered the villain's name: Jack the Ripper. "Wait, don't tell me, that slight accent you take such care to hide, White Chapel?"

Gabriel rocked back on his feet as if she'd slapped him and tossed his instruments into his bag. "Don't you think you should put your blades down before you hurt yourself? If I wanted to harm you, I'd have taken them from you by now. I *didn't* do this!" He pointed to the body. "There was a call to ValCorp, and I was sent to investigate. Our people will be here shortly. It would be better if you weren't here when they arrive."

"I'll bet!" Miranda inched around him to get a better look at the body. In addition to the mauled throat, the girl's short leather skirt revealed bite marks on her inner thighs. She regarded Gabriel with disgust. "I already called the NYPD. They're on their way. Does Valadon know your dirty little secret?" Her anger always incited her sarcasm. "Blood banks running a little low on B positive?"

"I told you," Gabriel said indignantly, "I didn't do this! I was already out for the evening when Valadon ordered me to investigate." He removed his latex gloves and placed them in a plastic bag. "I'm a doctor; I save lives, not end them. Why on earth would you think I could do this?"

"Oh, I don't know," Miranda said caustically. "There's blood on your clothes. Looks like the same blood on the girl. I come walking down the street, and you're bending over her." She glanced around the alley. "No one else is around, so yeah, I kinda think you had a hand, or should I say, a fang, in her death."

Gabriel exhaled in frustration. "I'm telling you now. You should leave while you can."

"Oh, really? Or else what?" Miranda said mockingly sweet, wishing Vetti would get there already. A sick feeling began to develop in her stomach, the same feeling she got when she realized something was terribly off. She gazed at Gabriel and noticed for the first time he had no blood on his mouth or anywhere on his face.

Gabriel dropped his shoulders and shook his head. He rubbed his neck and peered up at the roof of the building behind him. "They're here now. I can sense them."

Miranda watched Gabriel's movements, half expecting him to rush her. She slowly followed his eyes up, thinking it was some sort of ruse to distract her. But the voice inside her head negated the thought. "Oh, bloody hell!"

"I told you to leave." Gabriel glanced her way. "Now do you believe I didn't do this?"

"How about them?" Miranda eyed the three, no, four vampires staring down on them.

A dark figure with a billowing coat appeared before them. "Well, what do we have here?"

Miranda and Gabriel were so distracted by the above vampires they didn't see Rogues had entered the alley behind them, their fangs already extended. One was dressed in a black leather jacket; the other was taller and sported a cruel grin. Both regarded Miranda and Gabriel as though they would be easy victims, then the taller one spotted the dead girl and the blades in Miranda's hands. "Your handiwork, pretty girl?"

"Maybe she went out to get dinner for her boyfriend," snarked the shorter vampire who laughed at his own joke.

The tall one eyed the backpack then Gabriel. "You bag any blood?"

"No. And we were just leaving. I suggest you do the same. The authorities have already been alerted."

"We don't take orders from your kind," the dark-haired vampire grunted.

Miranda rolled her eyes at the standoff. "Listen to what he says. The police are on their way, so if you don't want to wind up in a cell facing East, I suggest—*owww!*" The taller one grabbed her so fast she hardly had time to react, effectively cutting off her use of the blades by pinning her arms against the building.

"No marks on your neck, pretty girl. I guess no one's claimed you yet." His fangs lengthened as he bent to taste her.

"Get away from her!" Gabriel tackled the tall vampire and left her to deal with the shorter one.

Miranda briefly glanced at Gabriel, who was keeping his own with his opponent, and faced off against her vampire, who had picked up one of her daggers. *Let's see how good you trained me, Liz.* "I guess it was a boring night for you that you just had to return for the body you dumped."

"Not my kill. Besides draining to the point of death is *illegal.*" He sneered. "Not that your kind follows all the rules." He smiled callously.

Then lunged for her.

***

"Perhaps we should offer some assistance," Remare suggested as he stood above the apartment complex, watching the fight below. "Gabriel hasn't been to training for some time; he might not be able to fight the two of them."

"Not yet. Give him a moment. I want to see how well he handles himself." Valadon wasn't being cruel; his Torians had already eliminated the other Rogues. If either Gabriel or Miranda were in real trouble, he and his Torians had the speed to destroy the Rogues. He was curious to see how well his progeny would fare in a fight.

***

After racking her vampire, Miranda circled him and felt the adrenaline pumping in her veins as he bent over in pain from her kick to his groin. Even though he was quickly recovering from his injury, his movements were still sluggish, probably due to an over-indulgence of blood. She knew she could take him. After all, she was an *Elemental* and could use her powers to defend herself. Just to shake him up, Miranda decided to create a fireball in her hand.

The Rogue's eyes widened. "So, you're a witch," he snorted, "I've never had a witch before." He charged as she pitched the fireball at him.

"Damn it!" Miranda grunted, as he swiftly batted it away and rammed her, crushing her back against the building. She ripped the lid off one of the nearby garbage cans and used her power to wrap it around her assailant's arm, tightening it to the point of pain. Her assailant tried in vain to peel it from his arm. Miranda had a dark side she kept concealed—except in moments like this. "Fire or ice?" She sneered at him. "Either way, I will make you burn."

Idiots like this always got off on hurting those weaker than themselves, but once they figured out their opponent was stronger, the coward in them always surfaced. God, she hated bullies.

"When my master hears about you, you'll be in so much pain you'll beg for death."

"Yeah, yeah, that's what all the bad vampires say. But you're missing a key point here."

"Yeah, what's that, bitch?"

"You won't be around to tell him." Miranda used her power to fling the chain attached to the lid around the vampire's neck and mentally yanked both ends. When his eyes rolled back and she was sure he was unconscious, she watched his body slink to the ground.

"And what do all the *good* vampires say?" Gabriel smirked as he joined Miranda, who was hunched over, panting. The cut above his brow was still bleeding.

As his wound closed, she was amazed how fast vampires healed. Even knowing they had that ability, it never ceased to boggle her mind.

"You okay? With those blades of yours, I hoped you knew how to use them." He reached down and picked up the blade she had dropped and handed it to her.

"I'm fine. Not sure about the jerk on the ground, though." She slipped her knives inside her boots.

For vampires, a severed spinal cord resulted in death. Gabriel pointed his thumb back at the vampire who laid at an impossible angle farther down the alley. "He won't be bothering anyone else. I was able to read his mind before he died. They were Rogues out of an underground club called Nightworld. One of their masters got a little sloppy, and they were sent to clean up the mess."

The sirens finally sounded to alert them to the arrival of the police. "Let me talk to them," Gabriel exhaled, concern in his eyes. "Then, I'm taking you someplace safe to check you out."

"I'm fine." Miranda nearly growled, except she really was a little lightheaded.

"Really? Your head's bleeding." Gabriel used his thumb to gently brush Miranda's hair away from her face. "That bastard probably cut you when your head hit the wall. Give me one minute." He turned to talk to Detective Vetti.

As they talked near the unmarked car. Miranda averted her gaze. She didn't want to see Vetti—someone she'd once known. He always had questions in his eyes she didn't want to answer. Not tonight.

Not ever.

***

"Did you just see what I saw?" Remare remarked inquisitively as he uncrossed his arms and stood above the fracas below, silently impressed with how well the mortal woman had defended herself.

Valadon's smile widened, pleased by what had just transpired. "Yes, I did. It seems there's more to Miranda than she lets on. Come." He turned to leave. "Gabriel will see to her. We have other business to attend to: Brandon is arriving home."

Remare frowned at the mention of Valadon's younger brother. If Brandon hadn't been in Europe at the time of the attack, he would've had questions for the Blueblood. But Valadon loved his brother and refused to believe Brandon harbored any feelings of jealousy or resentment. Remare wasn't so sure. But he'd reserve his judgment. For now. "What about the girl's body?"

"Let Vetti handle it." Valadon paused for a moment. "She's human and should be returned to her family."

"And if the girl has no family?"

"We'll take care of it." Valadon sighed deeply as he briefly closed his eyes then continued walking. "Like we did the others."

Remare hesitated as he watched Gabriel escort Miranda from the alley; a smile tugged at his lips, then he turned to join the others.

Chapter Fifteen

Hearing the engine of his motorcycle, Zoe knew her former lover was approaching.

She chose the Upper East Side for a meet because it was far enough from ValCorp. Staying in the shadows, she watched as he threw his long, muscular leg over the Bugatti and removed his helmet. Her breath caught when his face was illuminated by the streetlight. He was as handsome as ever with his raven hair and piercing blue eyes. And one of the best fighters she'd ever known. She had loved sparring with him when she was a Torian. "I wasn't sure you'd come."

"Zoe, you know better than this!" Tristan's voice was heated with anger. "If Valadon found out about me meeting you, he'd have my head!"

After his lord abjured her, she'd left Valadon House and worked as a freelance bodyguard until she'd hooked up with Stryder, who'd given her a home in Nightworld, when no one else would.

"I needed to see you." Zoe stared at his dark eyes and remembered how brightly they'd shown with passion. She'd been a fool believing she could convince Valadon she had good reasons for her betrayal and had been horrified at his lack of mercy. But she should've known better: Once Valadon issued a proclamation, he never went back on his word.

Not ever.

"Why did you call me?" Eyeing all the focal points in the alley, Tristan grabbed her arm and pushed her farther into the shadows. "Are you trying to get me killed?"

She brushed a lock of hair off his face. "Of course not. There was a time when you would never have asked me such a question."

Tristan backed away. "That time has passed, Zoe." He ran a hand through his hair, then stared down at her. "You took care of that when you betrayed Valadon."

"They had my brother. I would've done anything to save him. What I did wasn't for me; it was for Kai. If your precious Valadon would have seen the condition he was in, he'd have understood." She fought to rein in her own temper fueled by her own frustration. Everything she had done, every sacrifice she had made had been for naught: Kai had died, anyway.

"You were damned lucky Valadon didn't kill you with his own hands. Damn it, Zoe. You broke his Prime Directive. You knew there was no coming back from that, yet you did it, anyway."

"I see you've cast me out of your heart as Valadon did out of his house." Zoe fought back the tears she swore she'd never shed. She'd known her decision would cost her. She just hadn't realized how high a price it would be.

Tristan managed a ragged breath. Exasperated, he turned to face her. "Why am I here?"

Resigned there'd never be a chance for them again, she hoped to make amends for the past. "Is it true what they are saying about the poison?"

Impatience laced Tristan's voice. "What do you know, Zoe?"

"Gregori and Bastien came to Nightworld asking questions. They informed us there's a poison out there harmful to vampires. But I think there's more than they were willing to share."

"A goddamned fishing expedition! You're using me to get information." He shook his head in disgust then pinned her against the brick wall. "I ask *again,* Zoe; what do you know?"

"Such distrust in your eyes." It hurt, but he didn't owe her anything. "I know someone who specializes in substances. If anyone is buying lethal chemicals, he'd know. I'm going to meet with him."

"Who?"

"I can't give you his name, but I'll let you know any information I acquire. Take it to Valadon. It may help soften his heart toward me."

Shaking his head, Tristan looked at her with regret. "Nothing will, Zoe."

And it was true; once someone betrayed Valadon, he never forgave. The vampires in his house understood and accepted this. Few people betrayed Valadon and lived; Zoe was lucky Valadon hadn't cut her to pieces. She grieved as Tristan got back on his motorcycle without looking back. A single tear fell from her eye. Even if she did discover who was behind the poison, Valadon would never accept her back into his house.

***

"C'mon Nick, it's not that late." Cerise laughed as she jaunted through Central Park to the carousel. "It'll be fun, like when we were kids. Surely your uncle let you play in the park. Everyone's ridden the carousel at least once."

"Not everyone," Nick muttered, as he jogged to keep up with her. "Wait up." *This is so not a good idea.* But he loved the way her face lit up like a child's, and found it hard to refuse her. The Weres owned the park after sunset, and humans weren't allowed in after dusk. It was too dangerous, especially this close to the full moon. But he wasn't a human and, after all, he was with a Were, so what harm would one ride on the carousel hurt?

Chapter Sixteen

Gabriel searched his bathroom for supplies. "Make yourself at home. I'll be right out."

"Okay." Cuddling Gabriel's black cat, Miranda strolled around the basement apartment. Several medical journals were left on the coffee table between the two brown leather couches facing the large flat screen TV. *Man cave.* Whether human, Were or vampire, men had to have their toys, and from the amount of remotes on the table, Gabriel had plenty.

She guessed his age to be about a hundred-twenty, but knew better than to ask. Cyra once told her asking a vampire's age was considered rude. Vampires detested nothing more than ignorant humans commenting about how good they looked for their age.

Miranda turned to see Gabriel watching her, and warmth suddenly flared in her stomach. "I see you met Rexi. Sit down on the sofa, and I'll take a look at your head."

"I think it's pretty much healed." She put the cat down and tested the side of her head. "I've been called hardheaded before."

"So have I." He grinned. "Let's take a look, anyway." Gabriel ushered her to his couch and sat on the coffee table, facing her. He placed the bandages and bottle of peroxide by his side.

Miranda smiled when Gabriel averted his eyes as she looked at him. *Shy?* His voice was softer now, as was his touch. Away from ValCorp, he was more relaxed. Even his face seemed more attractive. She admired his hands with the long, tapered fingers as he cleaned her minor wound with the gauze. Miranda kept her head bent, trying not to stare at the place between his thighs. When the cat made a disapproving purr, she thought, hey, I'm trying. No, she was not looking there. Nope! Not happening.

Lefty, she sighed.

Gabriel muttered, "Sorry," when he touched a particularly tender spot. "Well, you were lucky. You don't need any more stitches."

She met his soft brown eyes and finally asked the question that had been niggling at the edge of her mind since she met him. "What's between you and Valadon?"

"What makes you think there's anything?

"Got eyes." She pointed to them. "Not blind here. The tension in the infirmary was pretty crystal. Or did you think you were hiding it?"

Gabriel narrowed his eyes. "Why weren't you surprised at finding the girl's body in the alley? Sure, you were out for my neck when you thought I killed that girl." He sat on the opposite couch. "But you didn't act all that surprised. Why not?"

"I wasn't." She refused to be diverted. "What's between you two? You were communicating silently with him."

"Why do you care?"

Miranda knew she was hitting a nerve and should probably back off. But that just wasn't who she was. "Well, for one thing, I'm having dinner with your boss tomorrow. I'd just like to know. All his other Torians seemed tightly wound." *Especially Remare.* She considered Gabriel. "You didn't look all that concerned." Her face lit up as a sliver of understanding crept into her consciousness. "It wasn't the first time an attempt was made on Valadon's life, was it?"

He returned her inquisitive look. "Intuitive much? That wasn't the first body you've seen in an alley, was it?"

She slowly smiled. "No, it wasn't." Instinct more than anything triggered her thoughts. Something about the apartment hinted at its occupant being more human than vampire. "You're not a *born* vampire, are you?"

Gabriel appeared stunned by her perception. "You guessed as much in the infirmary when you said I was different. How can you tell?"

"I'm not sure." Miranda shrugged. "Lizandra says I'm a *'sensitive'*, that I pick up on things other humans don't."

"Lizandra?"

"Boy, you really don't get out much, do you? Lizandra Wells is Were Queen of the Black Star Clan." At his blank look, she continued, "Your boss' ally. The clan that hangs out in Werehaven, the sanctuary beneath Central Park." Still puzzled by her responses, she added, "What kind of vampire are you?"

"A reluctant one," he murmured as he went into his kitchen. "Want a drink? You probably could use one after tonight."

"Sure." Miranda wasn't sure if she should follow him or not, so she stood in the alcove, and thought when instinct kicked in, it really kicked hard. "Valadon's your maker."

"Don't use that expression." He handed her a beer and marched back into the living room and flopped on his couch, his eyes on fire. "I was *made* a long time ago, by both my parents and the grace of God." He seemed to deflate just a fraction, his eyes never leaving hers. "Valadon turned me. I had no choice in

the matter as I was unconscious at the time." He sucked back some of his beer. "Given a choice, this is not something I'd have chosen."

Miranda didn't need her empath skills to sense his pain; it was there in his eyes. She wondered why Valadon had turned him since he was the one who prohibited the creating of new vampires. She knew, in some rare cases, such as a marriage between a human and a vampire, the vampire was allowed to turn the human spouse, but *only* if the spouse was willing. Because of certain blood anomalies, not all humans could be turned, and sometimes, the attempt ended in the death of the potential vampire.

She'd heard stories of turned vampires who had to be put down because of their adverse reaction. The enhanced vision, hearing and other heightened senses drove some humans insane with their inability to cope with all the sensory bombardments. Over time, some humans adapted, others never did. "What would you have chosen?"

Gabriel measured the sensitivity in her eyes. "One mortal lifetime. Just one would've been enough. For me, my wife and my children."

"What happened to them?"

"I don't want to talk about it. It was a long time ago." Gabriel sipped his beer and slumped back on the couch. "Your head is fine." He exhaled slowly. "You should go now. It's late."

Miranda considered leaving. "When I was eleven, my family was taken from me." She sat across from him and crossed both arms over her knees and leaned forward. When he didn't demand she leave, she continued, "We were vacationing in France. My dad had rented a car, and we were doing all the touristy destinations. We had vacations before, but this one," she rubbed her hands together remembering, "this one was the best vacation of my life—so many sights to see, museums to visit, castles to get lost in. So much history to take in."

She checked to make sure Gabriel was listening and noticed the gold flecks in his soft brown eyes. "One night, on our way back from a day trip, a drunk driver ran us off the road, and my dad lost control of the car, and we went over a steep incline. I was the only one not wearing a seat belt, so I was thrown clear of the wreck or I would've been killed like they were."

"It wasn't until two days later that hikers found the wreck. They kept me in the hospital for weeks with a concussion and some broken bones, said I was suffering from shock. I couldn't even go to their funeral. My Aunt Meg had them buried on a little piece of land we owned in France. I think that's why I went to grad school in Paris, so I could occasionally put down flowers. They never did find my sister's body. They said wild animals must have carried it off."

She gave him a pointed look. "You either heal or you die." She realized he'd never really healed. Not completely. "You're not the only one who knows loss, Gabriel. And I don't think Valadon made the decision to turn you lightly." She reached for her jacket and bag and turned for the door.

Gabriel's heart sped up, not knowing what to say. He didn't want to open old wounds, didn't need to go there. The memories were still bitterly painful, even though it had been nearly a century. He thought he had buried them, thought he'd let go. He hadn't.

But there was one thing he did know: He didn't want Miranda to leave. "Wait."

Chapter Seventeen

As Brandon's helicopter made its way to ValCorp's roof, Remare admired ValCorp's logo with the *l* in Val connecting to the *p* in Corp underneath to form a staff with a blazing flame on top. *A suitable emblem for a king.* Remare gazed out over the city. The night was clear, and even without his vampiric ability, he could see the approaching chopper. He wondered what news Brandon was harboring and couldn't refute his own wish that Brandon had stayed in Europe.

The helicopter's blades ruffled Remare's clothes as it set down, and Brandon disembarked. Except for the ebony hair and slighter build, Brandon was a near-perfect copy of Valadon. An impeccable dresser, the beauty of a fallen angel, it was no wonder the media loved him. Remare couldn't think of a more handsome vampire—except one, he smirked. Brandon always had a quick smile for the cameras. But Remare had always thought there was something cruel to his lips. Brandon wore his hair long as Remare did, but unlike his own dark brown eyes, Brandon had the same emerald green eyes as Valadon.

But there the similarities ended: Valadon had a perspicacity for politics and the acumen for détente and business negotiations; Brandon enjoyed the life of the younger playboy brother, benefiting from the prestige of Valadon House. But Valadon loved him and could find no fault with his younger brother.

Remare did not share Valadon's trust and made sure Brandon was watched.

"Welcome home, Brandon." Remare shook hands with Brandon and led him inside. "I take it you had a satisfying trip?"

"I'll fill you in when I speak with Valadon."

"We missed you." Remare smiled beneficently. "We've had a bit of excitement while you were gone."

"Oh?"

Brandon's face betrayed no guile. But then again, he'd always been good at conveying an air of boyish innocence—whether it was legitimate or not. "Valadon will fill you in." They rode the elevator down to Valadon's subterranean rooms. Then walked silently down the hall to Valadon's office. Remare knocked twice and entered to find Valadon behind his desk. This office was a near replica of his penthouse office except for the color scheme; here, there were more tans and golds. As the brothers exchanged greetings, he went to the bar in the corner.

"How was Europe?" Valadon asked. "Are our esteemed elders satisfied with the financials?"

All vampire lords tithed to Council of Elders, and Valadon paid an enormous amount of money to the COE. Remare often thought the council members left Valadon alone because he made them wealthy. As long as the proceeds poured in, they kept their distance. Unfortunately, there'd always be at least one...who wanted more.

Greed never went out of fashion, especially among old-world vampires.

"The usual grumblings, brother, but no major questions or finger pointing." Brandon reclined on the couch. "They had their accountants go over the figures while I was present, a bit insulting if you ask me. Although most seemed pleased with the tithe, there was some talk of them coming for a visit."

"Why would they come now? They were just here a year ago." Valadon eyed his brother as he casually crossed his legs. "They never visit the outside territories that often."

Remare knew the last thing Valadon wanted was another visit from the COE. For the most part, they were on good terms, but there were those who would love a stake in ValCorp. Something Valadon took great pains to prevent.

"What else did you hear?"

"You tell me, brother. You have more spies than I do." Brandon sarcastically smirked as he leaned back into the couch.

Each knew Valadon had contacts in every court in Europe as well as the other territories.

"Ah, but you were there. Surely, your agents have kept you informed."

"Truly, brother, that's about it. Though I did hear one *other* piece of information you might find particularly interesting."

"Such as?" Valadon raised a pointed eyebrow.

"A certain lady has been quietly inquiring about you, one you know very well. Care to guess who?"

Valadon made quick eye contact with him. Remare knew only one female associated with the COE who'd been interested in Valadon. Though it had been centuries, she was the last person Valadon would ever invite into his territory. Although one of the most beautiful women in the world, with her mane of dark hair and lavender eyes, she had a heart as cold as forged steel and was just as dangerous: Vivienna.

"And what does the raven-tressed beauty want?"

"To visit, of course." Brandon laughed and then turned serious. "Enough of court intrigues. We can speak more about it at my welcome home party." At Valadon's arched brow, he added, "We *are* having a party to celebrate my return, *aren't we?*" He glanced at Remare with rakish charm. "Remare tells me you had some excitement while I was away?" he queried, the picture of perfect innocence.

"There was another attempt. Obviously, they failed. Sniper rifle blew out my window in the penthouse office." Valadon relaxed back into his chair. "All the windows on that floor have now been replaced with bulletproof glass."

Remare nodded once in agreement.

"Were you there?" Brandon asked with the right amount of concern in his voice.

"Yes, but whoever they're hiring these days was a terrible shot and missed me and hit my statue of Apollo."

Brandon quickly sat up straight. "Good God! Do we know who?"

"The investigation is ongoing, but we'll know soon enough who the would-be assassins are." Remare raked Brandon with a scathing look. "And then...they will pay for their transgression."

"I should hope so." Turning to Valadon, he said, "Brother, do you need help with the investigation?"

"It's being handled. Don't worry about it. They always miss." Rising from his chair, he added with a mock grin, "Besides, I believe we have a party to plan: traditional or modern?"

"You have to ask?"

Valadon grinned as he circled his arm around his brother. "You must be tired from your trip. Go, get some rest. We'll discuss this tomorrow."

"All right. I am fatigued. But don't think you're getting rid of me that easily. I want to hear all the details." As Valadon steered him to the door, Brandon turned to Remare. "If you need my assistance, all you need do is ask."

Remare smiled evenly. "I'll remember that."

After the door closed and a moment had passed, Remare leaned against the couch, crossing his arms over his chest and one foot over the other. He would not ask the question that burned inside him. Once before, he'd accused Brandon of disloyalty and had been royally rebuked. Remare was not in any rush to repeat the mistake, even though he knew he'd been right at the time. He just couldn't prove it.

"You're unusually quiet, Remare." Valadon walked back to the side of his desk and remained standing with his hands on his hips. "Impressions?"

"None that you want to hear," Remare muttered.

Valadon slanted him a look, then crossed his arms over his chest. "Try me."

Even though it was considered an insult to question a Blueblood such as Brandon, Remare didn't trust Brandon. Sibling rivalry was one thing, and there'd been much good-hearted banter between the two, but at times, Remare sensed something underlying Brandon's cool façade—something not quite so innocuous. "He didn't ask if you'd been hurt."

"He didn't have to. Obviously, I'm uninjured." Valadon glared at his oldest friend. "Stop seeing shadows where there aren't any. He was thousands of miles away when the attempt occurred."

Remare didn't want to point out the first question Brandon asked was if they knew who was responsible. Valadon's usual razor-sharp perception wasn't as precise when it came to Brandon. Remare thought it interesting Brandon didn't bother to ask if anyone else had been harmed. Curious. Even more interesting: Valadon hadn't mentioned the young professor.

How cunning of Brandon to bring up Vivienna.

It was no secret in the European courts Remare had once been foolish enough to become romantically involved with the cold-hearted seductress. Even though it had been centuries, he could still hear her shrill laughter in his mind. Brandon knew it would disturb him, and that was precisely why he had mentioned Vivienna. If he thought that would distract him from the case, he had entirely underestimated him. "Are we really going to have a party in his honor?"

"Why not? We could use some distraction around here, and we haven't had something to celebrate in some time."

"I didn't think you liked the traditional parties."

"Not usually, no. But he is my brother."

"All right then." Remare dismissed the matter, for now, and walked around the couch and sat down. "We have something else to discuss. You will not be pleased."

"What now?"

"Tristan has met with Zoe." At the hostility in Valadon's eyes, he added, "Hear me out."

"I gave a direct order that no one in my house was to have any contact with her. Zoe is abjured." Valadon tried to even his breaths. "She will *not* be allowed to use one of my best Torians to worm her way back into my domain."

"Tristan knows this," Remare said quietly. "He won't disobey you."

"He already has."

"Tristan only did so after contacting me first and letting me know his intent. He did not defy you."

"Tell me this much: Did he at least take back up with him?"

Remare shook his head.

"That's twice now. He's going to get himself killed one of these days." Valadon motioned with his hand. "Continue."

"He immediately came to me when she contacted him. Zoe said she had information about the poison," he said calmly. "That was the only reason he met with her. The *only* reason."

"How did she know about it in the first place?"

"Gregori and Bastien paid Stryder a visit. They were careful not to mention your name in connection with the poison. According to their report, Stryder seemed genuinely surprised, as well. He had no information; that's why he set Zoe on the trail."

"And what has she found out?"

"Nothing...as yet, but she was going to contact her former employer. Tristan planted the tracking device in her jacket. Aiden has been monitoring her location ever since."

"I see." Valadon sat and swiveled in his chair as he tapped the tips of his fingers together.

"Tristan thinks she is doing this to win favor with you."

"And you?"

Remare stood and paced the room. "Perhaps she is. I'm sure she has long regretted her decision." He glanced back at Valadon. "But she was Tristan's lover for some time. Perhaps it is his heart she is trying to seduce."

"I want you to go to her location. Interrogate the bastard yourself. Find out what he knows." Valadon rose from his seat and accompanied his friend to the door.

"I planned to." Remare was reluctant to bring up another matter he knew would also displease Valadon. "There's one other thing you should be aware of."

They walked down the hall in companionable solidarity, and Valadon muttered, "This should be interesting."

Remare pressed the button and waited for the elevator. "Oh, it is." He smiled knowingly. "It concerns Nick."

Chapter Eighteen

"Tell me more about Columbia Medical School," Miranda said as Gabriel lit the gas fireplace. Ever since he'd apologized for his abruptness, they seemed to forge a truce of sorts, and she was grateful for it. She liked the sound of his voice and wanted to hear more about his past.

Gabriel smiled warmly. "Why do you want to know about Columbia?"

"Because you seemed the happiest, then." She stretched out on his couch.

"After Valadon and I reached an accord over his having turned me *without* my permission, Valadon provided the necessary funds and connections for me to attend Columbia. His only stipulation: I live in the mansion we had near Washington Square Park. At first, I didn't want to." He glanced at her as he reclined on the other couch. "Bad memories."

Suddenly, the cat jumped into his lap and made herself comfortable. Miranda had the oddest sensation Rexi was purring, "*Mine.*"

"My turning was not my finest hour. The sensory overload nearly drove me insane, and they kept me in the basement until I learned to cope. It took weeks before my eyes and ears adjusted to the new sensations. Becoming vampire has its allure for certain individuals." Gabriel shook his head. "But it was never what I wanted. I was glad when he built ValCorp, and we moved there."

Miranda had many questions but decided she'd hold on to them. After they finished off a six-pack and a bottle of wine, she was beginning to feel the effects of the alcohol. "Tell me more about Professor Wexler."

"Ol' Wexler." Gabriel beamed as he rubbed Rexi behind the ears and stroked her fur. "He kept giving me grief about getting a research paper to him during daylight hours. When I tried to explain I could only get it to him after his posted hours because I worked during the day—I still couldn't tolerate sunlight back then—Wexler finally relented. Back then, we hadn't perfected the formula for the sunblock many vampires use now, and as a fairly young vampire, I had no immunity to the sun. Valadon had ordered me a coat made of certain fabrics treated with chemicals that helped keep the sun out. But, I looked like the invisible man with the fedora and my face wrapped in bandages. Summers were a bitch, I can tell you that, but I got my degree...again."

"What was he like?" Miranda felt soothed by the sound of his voice.

"Wexler was awesome. I learned more in one day of his classes than I did in entire courses with other professors. He was way ahead of his time—a true progressive." Gabriel's expression turned solemn. "He died a few decades ago."

She tried to stifle a yawn.

"You still with me there?" Gabriel smiled as he caught her eyes slowly closing.

"I haven't left you, yet." She grinned up at him as she turned on her stomach, folding her arms under the pillow she laid her head on. "I was just thinking of someone."

"Your professor at NYU?"

"Yes. Not sure how I'm going to handle her passing," Miranda reflected, not allowing herself to become too morbid. "One thing's for certain. I don't take her for granted and spend time with her whenever I can."

"Your turn, tell me more about that art forgery. I can't imagine your client was too keen on that."

Miranda nearly hissed out the name, "Simmons. He actually offered me a bribe." She narrowed her eyes. "It served him right. I always tell my clients to make sure they have their prospective buys authenticated *before* purchasing. There'd been a bunch of thefts in Europe, at the time, and the thief had substituted good forgeries." *Excellent* forgeries, the best she'd ever seen, and a quick memory of a student she'd known in Paris, *Calisto,* came to mind. "The thief was never captured, but Interpol was pretty sure it was a woman. The warning was out. But Simmons was in such a rush for the Vermeer, he was suckered in."

"Don't say suck to a vampire." Gabriel grinned with a hint of fang.

"Pardon moi." She laughed. "If Liz was here, she'd say something entirely different."

"I'd like to meet her, someday."

Miranda's voice sounded husky. "Maybe you will." She smiled and told herself she'd only close her eyes for a few minutes.

Relaxing into the couch, Gabriel felt more content than he had in a long time. Miranda didn't know it, but she'd helped him clarify a few things that had been niggling at the back of his mind. "What do you say, Rexi? Ready for bed?" The cat purred in agreement. Gabriel studied Miranda's sleeping form and considered picking her up and tucking her into his bed, but when morning came, she might be pissed at finding herself in his bed. He smiled, then got up and retrieved a spare blanket from the closet and covered her, letting his hand tenderly drift over her back. She felt warmer than most humans, and he wondered what it would feel like to wake up surrounded by all that heat.

As Gabriel regarded her serene face, he was reminded of an angel. He pushed a lock of hair off her cheek as he bent down and kissed her temple. "Sleep tight, angel," he whispered. "C'mon, Rexi, let Miranda sleep in peace." When the cat jumped on his shoulder, he slowly retreated to his room, knowing his dreams would be filled with images of Miranda's naked body enveloping his own.

Chapter Nineteen

"Come in and have a seat. You must be tired after your trip." Mulciber didn't glance up, rapt in his work of twisting flowers into a striking arrangement. Over the long stretch of centuries, he'd had many hobbies, but horticulture offered him a sense of peace he didn't find elsewhere.

"I didn't want to disturb you." Brandon moved farther into the atrium where many of Mulciber's creations were gracefully displayed. "But if you insist."

"Did you enjoy your time in the European court?"

"As a matter of fact, I did." Brandon casually strolled around the greenery. "Always a pleasure to meet with our old friends and play catch up."

"Have you something for me?"

Brandon slid the leather messenger bag, containing documents from a council member, slip from his shoulder. He laid the pouch on the worktable, careful not to disturb Mulciber's work. Others on the council didn't trust the Internet, especially with the recent hack attacks. When it came to sensitive material, he too, preferred the old vellum and hot wax. "Thank you." Mulciber wouldn't open the correspondence in his presence. "What else have you learned?"

"Funny you should ask. It seems our esteemed elders will be paying us a visit sometime in the foreseeable future."

Mulciber's eyes betrayed nothing. As ambassador to the American courts, he was in contact with his underlings in Europe and had expected as much. "Yes, they seem to have taken an interest in Valadon and his business pursuits," Mulciber looked up and smirked, "among other matters." He wondered how much Brandon had discovered and knew Valadon's brother enjoyed the machinations of court life: Everyone trying to curry favor and jockeying for position, and the parties—so unlike Valadon's restrained ones.

"You're not surprised?"

"Why would I be? Of course, I'd be kept informed of their movements; did you think I wouldn't be?" Mulciber continued with his task, barely glancing at Brandon.

"I heard there was another attempt on Valadon's life."

"As if you didn't already know." Mulciber sneered. "His people have been diligently running around, trying to find the responsible parties." He blinked once in recognition of his daughter's arrival. "My darling, how good of you to join us."

Brandon turned to see Persephone.

She was as lovely as she was dangerous, and from the glint in her eye, she'd been up to something deliciously nefarious. Mulciber watched as she slithered up to Brandon.

"Welcome home, Brandon." Persephone purred sexily. "We've missed you. It's been boring without you."

"It's good to be home." He took her hand and barely brushed his lips over her knuckles.

"Why don't you escort Brandon to his rooms, Persephone? He's had a rather long flight."

"It will be my pleasure." She smiled wickedly, then took Brandon's arm and led him from the atrium.

Mulciber had hoped for a marriage between Persephone and Valadon. But when Valadon politely refused her advances, Mulciber began to make other plans. He'd considered Remare as a suitable alternative, but he, too, had shown little interest. *Oh, well.* Brandon was probably the best choice, after all. When the time came, he'd be the most malleable of the three. *Bed him well, Persephone. Teach him patience. He's going to need it when the elders arrive.*

Then, life would finally become interesting. Mulciber missed the old rituals, the old traditions. Valadon had become too modern, too reserved in his years in America. Perhaps that was why certain council members wanted to visit: To remind Valadon, that although a business tycoon, he was still a vampire. A Blueblood. One with responsibilities.

Mulciber walked silently to his room and flicked a light on in his private bath. One thing he had always insisted on was comfort, and his bathroom was luxurious. But the huge, sunken marble tub didn't entice him tonight. He turned and studied his reflection in the mirror. He'd been named after the Roman god of the forge, the only ugly one. As if the fates had known. He'd once been a handsome vampire. Until he'd let others persuade him to take in the sun. The scientists had been *certain* their formula worked and had convinced him to try it. But something in his metabolism had absorbed and expelled the ingredients far too quickly.

He stared at his face as he slowly peeled off the latex mask he wore in public. One side of his face had been untouched by the sun's harmful rays, but oh, the left side was not as fortunate. He considered the scars that had refused to heal and the monster he'd been turned into. Mulciber remembered too well the excruciating, painful screams of horror as the sun cooked his flesh before he could take shelter. But it had been too late. The damage had been done. Somehow, the fact that half of his handsome face retained its vigor and beauty was even more of an atrocity. A constant reminder of what he so dearly lost.

Mulciber shrieked in fury and banged his fist into the mirror, shattering it to pieces. It had been Valadon's company that had manufactured the sunblock and Valadon's scientists who had assured him the lotion would work.

Soon, Valadon would know the suffering and despair Mulciber had endured. He would taste the cold hell of pain and torment.

And know exactly who had caused it.

Chapter Twenty

Miranda checked the office clock again, doubting it had moved at all in the last five minutes. Last night had been enlightening. Before leaving, she'd checked on Gabriel. Damn, if the vampire hadn't been tempting with his hair all rumpled and the sheets barely covering his butt. She'd been wondering all day what he looked like under those sheets.

Finally, it was four, and she was so out of there. If she was lucky, she'd be able to grab a couple of hours sleep and then get ready for her dinner with Valadon.

As soon as she rushed through the door of her home, she stripped and slid into the comfort of her own bed. She wasn't asleep for more than a few minutes when she heard the sound of knocking. *It's the neighbor's door*, she told herself and turned over and went back to sleep. More knocking. Miranda covered her head with a pillow to stop the noise from invading her skull. The rapping grew louder.

She grabbed a robe off the chair and went to answer the door. What she found made her heart quicken: Two faces peering at her with the dissatisfaction a teacher would have at a child who spilled a bottle of glue on her desk and was rubbing circles in it.

"I don't know." Lizandra gave her the once over and frowned. "I'll take the hair. You do the nails." Both were carrying bundles in their arms.

Cyra grinned up at her. "Okay, I've got Scarlet Red, Ruby Red or...," her eyebrows flexed up and down, "Passionate Peach."

"Oh, c'mon, guys! I can get dressed by myself. I was hoping to catch a couple of hours sleep." Miranda rubbed her tired eyes. "I worked late last night."

"Yes, we know, we tried to reach you." Liz raised a pointed eyebrow. "Don't you ever check your messages, girlfriend?"

Miranda groaned, not sure if she should mention the dead girl or the night with Gabriel.

"Um-hmm. And what time is Mr. Tall, Dark and Sexy coming to pick you up?"

"He's not. He called and left a message he was sending his limo at seven." Miranda glanced at the clock. "That can't *possibly* be the right time." It was nearly six.

"That gives us one hour to make you presentable. Quick, get in the shower and make sure your legs are shaved." Lizandra turned and marched her friend into the bathroom. "When was the last time you waxed?"

Miranda growled. "None of your business. Besides, Valadon doesn't have a need to know." She stripped out of the robe and went into the hot spray and moaned at how blissful the warm water felt. When Cyra popped her head in to tell her to hurry, Miranda yelped.

"Don't worry, she's waxed," Cyra called out.

After the shower, she barely had time to wrap a towel around her when Lizandra grabbed her and sat her down in a chair and started fumbling with her hair. "You ever think of getting more highlights in your hair?"

"No," Miranda grumbled.

"Passionate Peach coming right up." Cyra was shaking the bottle as she came to the table where they were situated. "So, where's Valadon taking you for dinner?"

"Seventeen Barrow Street, it's a converted carriage house in the village. I figured I'd go historic with him."

"Nice, very elegant." Cyra smiled. "We brought over a few dresses for you to choose from."

"I already picked something out. I do have a wardrobe, you know. Jordan makes me attend all those fundraisers so I have several black formals."

"Not those ugly black dresses you wear?" Lizandra grunted. "You're going out with one of the hottest bachelors in the city and you were going to wear *one of those?*"

"Yes." Miranda loved her friends dearly, but really, give her some credit. "It's tasteful and understated."

"You mean boring and ugly. Cyra, show her what we brought." Lizandra continued brushing Miranda's long locks.

"I don't know why you bothered. Cyra is way thinner than I am, and you're about six inches taller. There's no way anything you guys brought will fit me."

"Oh, these aren't our dresses." Cyra looked up at Lizandra and grinned. "We felt you should have something new and knowing how much you like to shop..." Cyra unveiled the first dress: A stunning red outfit with cleavage low enough to put Miranda's assets clearly on display.

"*So* not my style." Miranda shook her head at both of them. "You really think I'd wear what has to be a vampire's idea of a wet dream?"

With laughter in their eyes, both of them nodded enthusiastically. "We kind of hoped you would. But didn't really think you'd go for it." Cyra then pulled out a black number with sleeves that went off the shoulder and was made of a thin, clingy material. Again, not Miranda's style. She'd have to lose another ten pounds before the dress would look good on her. She shook her head at Cyra.

Lizandra moved to the last bag and took out a midnight blue dress that was chic and sophisticated. The neckline wasn't too low and the hem not too short. Miranda sighed her approval when she stroked the silky material. Liz smiled at Cyra and bumped hips. "And I think we have a winner. You owe me twenty."

Cyra laughed. "You'll get it." She turned to Miranda and cocked her head. "She bet me twenty you'd pick the blue. I said you'd go for the black since that's your usual color."

Lizandra reached for one more bag and removed a box. "Consider it your birthday present, early."

Miranda opened the box, and her eyes widened as she took out one elegant indigo shoe. The stiletto heel had to be five inches long. She glared accusingly at them. "These are *come fuck me heels.*"

"And I bet they'll look great on you." Lizandra grinned. "Now, let's get you ready."

Liz did up the zipper as Miranda stepped into the heels. Surprisingly, they were comfortable. Miranda gazed in the mirror and adjusted her gold necklace. Liz had done a fantastic job styling her hair, and Cyra had made up her face like a professional. Her hands looked long and elegant with the nail polish. The last touch was a gold bracelet that had been her mother's: a cuff with Celtic designs.

Miranda turned to face her friends. "Well?"

They just stared at her. For a moment, Miranda thought she had overestimated her looks.

"Jay-sus, girlfriend, you look hot!" Lizandra whistled and fanned herself in appreciation. "My girl's got it going *on!*"

"You're going to really impress him." Cyra smiled as she stood beside Liz.

"Thanks, guys. You're the best." She hugged them as a limo pulled up in front of her house.

"Yes, we are. Now, go blow Mr. T. D. & S's socks off." Liz snickered. "And anything else you might..."

Miranda smirked and grabbed her purse. "*Not* happening." She closed the door behind her as Liz and Cyra were giving her the thumbs up.

***

In the ride to ValCorp, Miranda felt butterflies fluttering in her stomach and thought about what she was doing. Valadon wasn't just a vampire. He was *the* vampire lord of NYC. Not only that, he was also a billionaire who held board meetings. She hung out with her friends at Werehaven. What could they possibly have in common? All right, she'd have just one dinner with Mr. T. D. & S., and that would be it. She exhaled and felt better.

During the elevator ride to Valadon's level, Miranda felt the butterflies returning. She really should've canceled, but it was too late, now. Besides, it was only one date. She could get through it with her neck intact, couldn't she?

When the elevator doors opened, she was stunned to see Valadon standing in his dark three-piece suit and pale gold shirt, his hair perfectly styled. He was breathtaking. His emerald eyes were mesmerizing as he stared at her, and she felt herself being pulled in by them. Whatever scent he was wearing was intoxicating; she dubbed it, "*Eau de Valadon*". If Liz was here, she'd probably call it, "*I'd do Valadon*".

Miranda was the first to speak, breaking the eye contact between them. "They told me to come straight up." She cocked her head. "That was the plan, right?"

Valadon blinked then kissed her hand in greeting. "You look beautiful. Thank you for coming," he said in a deeply masculine voice. "I'm sorry I couldn't personally pick you up, but there were things here I needed to tend to."

She smiled effortlessly. "It's all right. I got here in one piece."

Miranda heard a low whistle and spotted Morel entering the room. He was dressed in a sharp dark gray suit. "Miranda, you look stunning." He walked over and gave her a kiss on her temple. She always liked Morel and his affable manner; he made her feel welcome whenever she and Cyra got together. She relaxed at his touch.

Then Remare appeared and stood unmoving, watching her with eyes that missed nothing. In her mind, he was *Remare the Dark*, a vampire who carried himself in a manner that said *don't fuck with me. Ever!* Miranda would never think to do so. He was dressed in a dark blue suit, and she was certain from the bulges he had weapons under his jacket. The way he stared at her disturbed her; it was as if he looked at her long enough, he could see *all* her secrets. As he came closer, he met her eyes, smiled pleasantly and said, "Some women are just born with it," and then, as he passed her, whispered, "and some aren't."

Miranda would have flipped him the bird, but wouldn't give him the satisfaction. *Human hater!* She watched him go to the bar. Jerks came in all kinds, she mused and then had a terrible thought. "Are they dining with us, too?" she asked Valadon.

"Morel, along with a few of my other people, will be a short distance from us. In light of what has happened this week, it's prudent I have some of my guards with me. However, Remare has other plans tonight."

She glanced at Remare. One corner of his mouth slowly curved up, and then, he saluted her with his drink. *Well, that's a plus.*

***

After dinner, during the ride back to ValCorp, Miranda noticed it was in the privacy of his limo and at ValCorp where Valadon seemed most relaxed. Dinner at Seventeen Barrow Street, a.k.a. *One if By Land*—a centuries old carriage house that had been renovated into an elegant restaurant had been marvelous. But the paparazzi must have gotten wind Valadon was dining there and snapped their picture as they had exited the limo. With the license plate *ValCorp 1*, it was a pretty good guess who was inside. Valadon had been gracious to them as his guards kept the reporters a safe distance away.

Valadon had an easy manner that made her feel comfortable, despite their many differences. He'd arranged to book the entire upstairs in the restaurant with his guards placed at a discreet distance. "*No windows up here,*" Valadon had joked. The only windows were in the front and rear of the downstairs.

Later on, when people would ask what they'd talked about, she wouldn't be able to remember much because she'd been captivated by his presence and enjoyed watching him as he spoke. His deep melodious voice was seductive.

"I believe I promised you a tour of my building." Taking her hand as they exited the limo, he escorted her to ValCorp's underground garage elevator.

"That you did."

"What did you think of the fresco in the lobby of my building?"

"It's magnificent, but a sun god as your central piece?" She arched a brow and smiled at the irony of having Apollo in his lobby.

"I know. It was a bit of indulgence on my part, but I couldn't resist," he said with a glint in his eye. "I've always had a fondness for ancient Greek art." He stopped the elevator at the lobby and led her to a room that housed an exact replica of ValCorp in diminutive size. He was like a young boy showing off his latest toy, but ValCorp was his baby and she understood his desire.

"When I envisioned what my headquarters would look like, I didn't want just a place of business; I wanted the people who worked for me to feel comfortable." His eyes held a wealth of warmth. "All my people. Are you up for this, or would you like to rest?"

He'd noticed her walking slowly on the mammoth heels. "No, not at all." Miranda was fascinated with his building and wanted to see more.

"All right." Holding her hand, he guided her to where the shops were located. "These boutiques contain many of the products we manufacture. Those over there," he pointed down the hall, "include many of the fashions our designers create."

"Valadon Creations. Yes, I've seen them in magazines. Very chic." Cesare, their head designer, had incredibly artistic designs. Valadon showed her various boutiques, two coffee shops, a florist, hair/nail salon and a child care area. It was like a mini-city in the heart of the Financial District. Only one thing was missing. "Gee, Valadon, ever think of opening up a chocolatier?"

"We could," he narrowed his gaze and seemed to actually ponder the thought, "but we were thinking more in the way of opening a restaurant on one of the higher levels. But the public relations department said their research showed many people wouldn't patronize a vampire restaurant." Valadon grinned, showing a bit of his fangs. "I guess they were afraid we would snack on them."

Miranda burst out laughing. Nothing had prepared her for his sense of humor. "Your company is wonderful. I can easily see how you inspire corporate loyalty."

"We try. The floors above are all pretty much laid out the same." Valadon stood closer to her and moved a lock of her hair back. His face immediately sobered. "But there is something else I would like to show you." He paused for a moment. "However, I have to tell you, we don't usually show it to humans."

Miranda was both curious and taken back by his reserve. "You don't trust us?"

"That's not it." He shook his head, negating the thought. "It's a matter of privacy. I've shown you my corporation, ValCorp, but I haven't shown you my house, Valadon House."

Miranda was confused. "But I thought Valadon House was the same as ValCorp. What's the difference?"

"ValCorp is my place of business. Valadon House is just that, a home, and only my closest people live there." He smiled affectionately at her. "It's below. Would you like to see it?"

Miranda was more than curious, but she didn't want to step on the toes of his vampires. "If your people would rather I wasn't there—a human," she stared pointedly at him, "I don't want to invade someone's privacy."

"It's my house, my rules," he said reassuringly. "And you're an invited guest." He extended an arm. "Care to join me?"

Miranda wasn't sure this was a good idea, but she felt reasonably safe with him. She was fairly certain he wasn't taking her to the dungeons. She lifted her chin. "All right, show me your house."

Valadon led her to the elevator.

She was entering the private domain of the most powerful vampire in NYC...alone. And she was going somewhere made up entirely of vampires. Not a wise decision. But, as always, when it came to dangerous situations, her curiosity won out over her fear. Was it any wonder Lizandra had nicknamed her *Pandora*? She wasn't sure what she'd find below; but if no other humans were allowed down there, would she be allowed to come back up?

Chapter Twenty-One

When the elevator doors opened to an elaborate living space, Miranda nearly gasped in awe. This was certainly no dungeon. There were white marble columns with gray veins and similarly shaded tiles on the floor. The high ceiling had to be at least fifteen feet tall, and the white brick walls were lit by sconces. But what really illuminated the immense room was the magnificent chandelier in the center of the room.

To the right was an expansive marble fireplace with lion heads carved in the stone on both sides of the hearth. Above that was a theater-size flat screen TV. There were several couches and chairs in lush fabrics. The French doors on the far wall were decorated with burgundy drapes to give the effect of windows. Miranda had to remember they were deep underground.

On the left side of the enormous room were two pool tables and a bar in the corner. As Valadon led her around the elevator to the other side, she saw a kitchen with a huge stainless steel fridge and two stoves—all state of the art in black and chrome. Beyond the spacious granite kitchen nook was an elegant dining area with a long oak table that could easily accommodate twenty people.

Valadon directed her back to the living area. "This is where we come to relax." As she stared at the chandelier, he added, "They're runes—from an old language."

"It's dazzling." Miranda stroked her bracelet and remembered studying Celtic runes in college. She could almost make out some of the symbols.

Valadon pointed down one of the corridors to the right. "That wing leads to the Torians' apartments." He clasped her hand and guided her in the opposite direction. "But this is the wing I wanted you to see."

Miranda was excited at discovering something new, but couldn't help wondering what was behind the doors at the end of the dimly lit hallway. She noted the security camera mounted in the corner. If this was his private keep, and only his most trusted people stayed here, why would he need cameras? The heavy double oak doors had intricate carvings around the edges, and she tried to figure out the lettering above the arched doors. "That sign better not start with, *'Abandon all hope, ye who...'*"

"Not quite." He grinned as he opened the doors. "After you."

It was dark inside, and she hesitated for a moment, but wanted to see what he'd been determined to show her. When Valadon entered behind her, he flicked a switch that illuminated one of the most breathtaking rooms she'd ever seen.

Miranda sighed. Now, she knew what the word above the doors had been: *Archives*.

Having studied first at NYU and then in Paris, she'd been in grand rooms before, but this was sublime. Valadon's libraries consisted of three levels that descended downward from the center of the magnificent room. The floors were parquet with Aubusson carpets. Dark oak paneling with intricately carved designs covered the walls and edges of the bookcases. There were aisles and aisles of books, and if the chandelier in the living room was impressive, the one in the center of this vast space was splendid with several tiers of crystals that were connected by ropes of smaller crystals that shone brightly as diamonds.

But what held her spellbound were the many paintings from different centuries accenting the walls. She smiled in appreciation; Valadon was sharing something special, and the gesture wasn't lost on her. The works of art were magnificent. She stood mesmerized, forgetting to breathe, just taking it all in.

When Valadon came up behind her, he whispered softly, "Welcome, Miranda."

His breath on her skin sent a thrill rushing through her body. She laughed as he held her hand and led her down one of the twin curved staircases with red carpeting to the middle level. She studied the ventilation system and noted the cameras. Paintings and books this old had to be in controlled atmospheres to diminish any threat of decay, and she was sure Valadon utilized the necessary steps to preserve his masterpieces.

"The runes on top of the doorway spell out the word..."

"*Archives*," they spoke simultaneously.

Valadon nodded. "This is where we keep our histories, our art, and...a few personal mementos."

Miranda noticed the gold trinkets in the glass enclosures as she passed by, but went straight to the artwork on the walls. The artist was a master of brushstrokes and his use of intense colors. *Caravaggio*. No, earlier, had to be with the patterns and movements. She grinned. "El Greco." The painting was a version of *The Vision of the Opening of the Fifth Seal*, and the subject's eyes looked like a living flame striving upwards. The use of color, light and movement was extraordinary.

Valadon stood alongside her. "I've been a collector for centuries." He motioned with his arm to the various paintings covering the walls. "Even though his more famous paintings hang in museums, there are several here that have never been publicly displayed."

"Yes, I know. El Greco defied the clergy, and they refused to pay him until he painted certain leaders in a more favorable light." They had objected to his use of Venetian Red in his paintings and made him change the coloring as well as the compositions.

Miranda strolled along the wall, admiring the various paintings. Then, she came to a series of paintings by an artist she'd never heard of: Asanti. One painting was of a striking young woman with long dark hair and emerald eyes. Valadon's eyes. She glanced back at him and tilted her head questioningly. "Mother?"

"My sister, Bianca." Valadon appeared as rapt as she was. "The artist, Asanti, is an old friend of mine. He painted this portrait when we lived in Europe. Bianca was dearer to me than any other relative. She was Nick's mother."

"My student." Nick had taken a few of her classes, and she was very fond of him. Miranda saw the similarities right away: the gentle smile, the easy-going manner, only the color of the eyes was different. Nick's were blue.

"Yes, when he saw you in my offices, he mentioned you were one of his professors. He enjoys your classes very much. There's one more level below. Come, I will show it to you."

Miranda held Valadon's hand and felt a low level hum travel up her arm. The way she was feeling, if he'd invited her into hell, she'd have gone voluntarily to see such works of grandeur. With that epiphany, she realized she was beginning to feel comfortable with Valadon and let him lead her down another flight of stairs. When they reached the last step, she saw that these were his oldest and rarest of antiquities. There were glass enclosures and electronic locks for most of the books and art work.

"This section contains my finest collections and must be properly maintained. We weren't sure they would endure as long as they have, but technology has made it possible for their longevity."

Valadon casually escorted her around the room, pointing out one artifact after another and telling her tales of long ago when he'd lived in Europe. "Before I had my own territory, I belonged to the main vampire court in Paris, but I also worked for several other courts throughout Europe. Some were delightful; others...were a nightmare." He shrugged. "I was financial advisor to some of the world's most *intriguing* leaders. My title was Minister of Finance."

"When the territories opened in America, I petitioned for a court of my own. After many deliberations, they finally granted my petition."

"They didn't want to let you go," she guessed.

"No, they didn't."

Miranda enjoyed hearing his tales of people from different centuries. His melodic voice was soothing. She had many questions for him she still didn't feel comfortable asking, but perhaps in time, she might. For all the majesty of his library, Valadon was even more impressive, and she was developing a reverence for him she didn't think possible. "Thank you for sharing this with me."

Valadon nodded, then accompanied her to the back reading area. There were Tiffany lamps on the end tables where two leather couches faced each other with a coffee table in between. A mahogany fireplace with intricate carvings stood at the far end. A slender man in a butler's outfit, complete with vest, white gloves and serving tray approached. He appeared to be in his sixties with his white hair and neatly trimmed goatee. Smiling pleasantly, he offered the tray to Valadon. On it was a message Valadon read quickly.

"Thank you, Escher."

"Very good, sir. Would you and your lady friend care for a refreshment? Perhaps some wine?"

"We have Turkish tea if you so desire." Valadon winked at her.

Miranda remembered the few times she met her students at the cafes by NYU, and Nick knew she always ordered Turkish tea. "Sure." She let her purse drift off her shoulder and sat on one of the couches, welcoming the reprieve to get off her feet.

Valadon nodded to the butler then sat directly across from her. He crossed one leg over the other. "I must admit I had an ulterior motive for bringing you here."

Intrigued, she asked, "Oh, and what would that be?" then casually removed her heels.

"When my nephew began spouting your accolades and his fondness for art, a thought occurred to me."

"And that was?" Miranda probed.

"All that you see around you..." He exhaled and looked almost pained, nearly embarrassed. "I don't have a catalog."

Miranda's jaw dropped. "How do you keep track of all your possessions?" She leaned forward. All collectors kept catalogs of their fine art; she was amazed a vampire as old as Valadon didn't have one. But she knew vampire memory was considerably sharper than a human's. It would have to be; they lived far longer.

"Until recently, I've never needed one. But, before you answer me, please take the time to consider my offer."

Escher returned with their teas and a few biscotti and set the serving tray on the table between them. "Would there be anything else, sir or madam?"

Valadon looked at Miranda, who shook her head. "No, thank you, Escher."

"Very good, sir."

She sipped her tea and thought this was heaven. What a wonderful archive Valadon had, and she felt fortunate to have had the opportunity to admire it.

Valadon drank his tea, balancing the saucer on his bent knee. After a while, he asked, "How would you like to work for me?"

She nearly choked on her tea. "Doing what?"

Valadon seemed amused at her look of astonishment. "Write my catalog."

Miranda was speechless. Yes, she had her graduate degrees in art history, was two courses shy of a PhD, but there were art historians far more qualified than her. Felicity immediately came to mind. "Valadon, there are people—good people, PhD's—in New York who are far more knowledgeable than me; surely, you'd want one of the top people in the field to complete your catalog."

"I don't grant access to my archives to others, Miranda. The reason I chose you is because I trust you. This is my *private* collection. I believe you will keep it confidential. I would not trust a stranger to keep my confidence, let alone be in the same room with my possessions."

He had a point there. If she had a collection this vast, there were only a few people she'd trust with it. Collectors were a strange lot. Some were very possessive about their works of art and never displayed them. Part of their pleasure was knowing they owned an object of beauty others would never see. And some had acquired their works by dubious means better left uninvestigated. Still, others were more generous and often loaned their art to museums. She sipped her tea then set it on the table and leaned forward.

"What exactly would you require in your catalog?" Was she actually considering his offer? Between her job at the museum, the authentications, and her classes at NYU, she did *not* have time to take on another assignment.

As if reading her mind, Valadon said, "You could make your own hours. I just need a listing of my works with perhaps a page of history for each. These books give the background history for most of them. I could fill you in on the ones that don't have a written account. And...you can hire an assistant." He smiled. "I was thinking of Nick. He knows this collection almost as well as I do. I'm sure he'd love the opportunity to work with you." Valadon sat back and watched the expressions float over her face.

"Miranda, you don't have to decide tonight. I merely wanted you to consider my offer. Take whatever time you need. Come." He rose and extended his hand toward her. "I know this must seem overwhelming, but it doesn't have to be. You can take as long as needed with the project." He caressed her hand. "There are no deadlines."

Miranda was still astounded at the offer and gave it serious thought as they climbed the stairs to the second level. Valadon motioned to a door on the side. When they passed through it, she heard a commotion coming from the end of the hall. So, this was where all the vampires were. It had been too quiet so far. As they walked along, she noticed workout rooms containing weights and other training apparatus.

When they came to a spacious training room lined with blue mats, a fencing match was in progress. Both men were shirtless and barefoot, wearing only dark, loose fitting pants. The Torians were rapt in the match and only a few turned and made eye contact with Valadon, who nodded to his men, not wanting to disturb the match in progress. She immediately recognized Morel with his blond hair and the Torian he was sparring with, Remare.

Morel was stunning with his tall figure and broad shoulders. His muscles bunched and stretched as he moved. He lunged and parried as well as any fencer she'd ever seen. What a beautiful sport, too bad it was a lost art.

However, no one seemed to have mentioned that to Remare, who was the aggressor of the two. Even though Morel had more bulk, Remare's body was made up of striated muscles that moved fluidly when he thrust. He pounded away with strokes and lunges, but it was his footwork that transfixed Miranda. He had the grace of a dancer and the speed of a snake. She heard an onlooker say no one could match him for speed. Tonight, his long black hair was tied back, and a few strands had broken free. Sweat was glistening over his body as he moved in continuous strokes, his nipple ring glinting with the overhead lighting.

Valadon noticed her concern for Morel. "Don't worry. They often spar like this. Morel is quite capable of holding his own."

"Remare is faster."

"Yes, he is," Valadon said with pride. "He's one of the world's leading fencers. He helped coach some of the American Olympians."

She had attended an exhibition in Brooklyn with Cyra about a year ago. Morel had wanted to watch one of the rare times Remare instructed the Olympians, and Cyra wanted female company. Miranda had admired Remare's skill and speed. No one there had come anywhere close to his swiftness or grace. He'd been absolutely relentless when it came to his opponents and never once faltered. After the match, for one brief moment, they had made eye contact, and even then, Miranda had sensed his dark, seductive power.

Someone called time, and the match was over. Morel laughed. "Jesus, don't you ever get tired of winning?" He shook Remare's hand.

Remare smirked. "You play to win, or you don't play at all."

Escher handed them towels to dry off. There was a round of applause for Remare, and the men divided up, talking about different moves and techniques. Miranda felt for her purse and then remembered she'd left it downstairs. "Go, socialize with your men. I left my purse on the couch. I'll just get it and be back in a minute."

"All right."

She watched as Valadon talked with his Torians. They were such an intrinsic group—their camaraderie evident in the way they laughed and joked together. She was happy Valadon had the loyalty and love of his people just as Lizandra had the same love and respect of her clan.

Miranda hurried down the hall and then down the stairs. As she was leaning down for her purse, she sensed the sudden drop in temperature and the violent prickling of her skin as a dark presence entered the room. A very old powerful presence. Her eyes slowly closed. Power like no other she'd ever sensed registered in every nerve ending of her body.

"My, my, whatever do we have here?" His raspy voice was like black oil left in the coldest depths of an ocean far too long, and the pitch Miranda possessed to detect vampires began shrieking like a wraith.

Chapter Twenty-Two

Fear does strange things to a person. Whatever our basic survival instincts were millenniums ago still kick in under extreme circumstances. The fight or flight instinct kicks in so the brain doesn't have to think—just react. But some cognitive impulse in Miranda was misfiring, and childhood memories of the Bronx Zoo surfaced.

She'd been near the tigers' area, hamming it up for the camera until she saw the look of horror on her mother's face. She instinctively knew the tiger had come perilously close to the edge. Miranda had sensed his presence and was terrified...but whatever curiosity she had then to turn and look hadn't diminished over the years.

She slowly turned to see the ancient dressed in a black furred robe. Valadon's law decreed vampires had to mute their powers so as not to harm a human. But this one wasn't; he was giving her the full dose and relishing her pain. Miranda felt like daggers were cutting into her brain until she remembered to raise her internal shields. An empath, she had learned years ago to build walls in her mind to block out the emotions of others, but it seemed to work with vampires too from the startled look on the ancient's face.

Since Miranda could breathe again, she inhaled deeply until the spots in front of her eyes dissipated. Then, she peered at the vampire's face. Cyra had explained when the vampires developed the formula for their sunblock, it didn't work on everyone. That seemed to be the case with this vampire. He was bald and the skin on the left side of his face had the shiny texture of burn victims. But from what she could tell of his bone structure and the right side of his face, he must have been a handsome vampire at one time.

However, it wasn't the scarring that made him hideous; it was the depth of darkness in those soulless eyes.

"Who are you? What are you doing down here?" His icy voice resonated around the room. "No humans are allowed in the archives."

"I thought vampires were supposed to mute their powers in the presence of humans." Miranda gritted out through clenched teeth. "How come you're not?"

"You *dare* to question me?" he snarled. "Any rules *you think* you know don't apply here." The vampire moved closer. "Now answer my question."

Miranda hoped Valadon would soon come looking for her; she didn't like it when others tried to force her hand, and this vampire's attitude was in need of a serious adjustment. "Tell me who you are first."

The burst of pain in her head made her see explosions, and she had to grasp the couch for support or pass out from the agony. "All right, all right! Stop it!" She clutched her forehead. "My name is Miranda Crescent. I work for Valadon. He brought me down here."

He slowly circled her. "Why would he do that?"

She didn't know who this vampire was and wasn't about to disclose any more information than necessary until she knew who he was and what he was doing in Valadon's private domain.

"Answer my question." He sneered at her. "Why did Valadon bring you down here?"

Miranda caught her breath and straightened her spine. "You didn't answer my question."

She shouldn't have pushed him so far. He seemed to consider her. He had to be very old, his scent was more musky and earthy than most vamps, but there was something rank about him. Other vampires smelled like the ground after a hard rain, but this one smelled foul, like something deep beneath the earth's surface that had been buried long ago.

"If you are an acquaintance of Lord Valadon's, as you claim to be, you should know who I am. Otherwise, you are a transgressor."

"Well, I guess you didn't get the memo, then."

He moved so fast Miranda couldn't track his movements. He slashed a line across her cheek with nails sharp as blades. Blood dripped down her face. The bastard stared at her as he licked the blood off his finger and smiled. "Yummy. I think I'll have another taste."

***

"Your foot work has improved since we sparred last." Remare finishing tying his black sleeveless gi.

Morel drank deeply from his water bottle. "But I'm still not as fast as you."

Remare grasped Morel's shoulder. "You will be someday."

Cyra, who'd been in the communications room, rushed to Morel. "Miranda's in trouble! I saw her on the monitors; she's down in the archives with Mulciber."

Remare didn't waste time asking questions and used his vampiric speed to fly down the stairs to where Miranda was faced off with Mulciber. Her cheek was bleeding, and she was trying to stem the flow of blood with her fingers. He met her eyes briefly then pulled her to his side and licked the blood off her face, sealing the wound with his saliva, ensuring it wouldn't scar. Remare could hear Miranda's heart thundering in her chest. He stared at Mulciber, who he wanted to kill for such an attack on a woman.

"Would you care to join me for a tasting?" Mulciber glided closer to Miranda. "We could share her."

Remare swung Miranda behind him, protecting her from Mulciber's reach. His hand flexed for the sword he'd left upstairs. "We could..." He inwardly smiled when Miranda's nails dug into his sides. "But I don't think the lady would welcome such attention." Cocking his head, Remare sensed his eyes turning black. "But more importantly, Valadon would not welcome it."

"Pity. I so hoped for another taste. I don't think the few drops I had were quite enough."

"She's *not* yours." Venom laced Remare's voice as he scrutinized the evil that was Mulciber. "She is Valadon's and not to be touched...by anyone."

Remare felt Miranda's forehead against his back.

"Valadon has taken a human mistress?" Mulciber seemed simultaneously shocked and repulsed.

"She is his." That was all Remare would impart, neither confirming nor denying Mulciber's supposition.

An enraged voice bellowed from the top of the stairs. *"MULCIBER!"*

In a blur of motion, Valadon swooped down upon the scene, followed by Morel, Cyra and the rest of his Torians.

Remare was momentarily reluctant to let Miranda go, but handed her to his lord.

Valadon held her chin in his hand as he examined her face. "Are you all right?" he asked, meeting her eyes.

"Just shaken up," she admitted.

The red rims around Valadon's irises pulsed with rage. "Take her upstairs. Now!"

Determined to follow his lord's commands, Remare nodded, grasped Miranda's arm and led her up the stairs. He spied the action below from the upstairs balcony.

"You should have told me you had a human woman. I wouldn't have touched her." Mulciber's voice grated. "She tastes sweet, like plums rolled in sugar." He then proceeded to make an obscene gesture with his tongue licking the inside of his two splayed fingers. "As I'm sure you know."

Valadon's fangs lengthened, ready to tear Mulciber's throat out. "Professor Crescent is a guest in *my* house." His eyes narrowed as he stared down the ancient. "*My* house, or have you forgotten, Mulciber, by whose permission you are allowed access."

"Perhaps it is you who have forgotten to whom you speak." Mulciber sneered. "You may be lord of this house, but you still answer to the council."

Valadon's voice deepened in the commanding way it did when he needed to assert his supremacy. "I haven't forgotten, but let me remind you that you are in my territory and subject to my laws."

"As an ambassador, I am immune to your ridiculous rules. The woman is human. What care do I have what happens to her?"

He roared, "She is under *my* protection and not to be harmed." Then said in a voice even more threatening, "Be careful, Mulciber. Ambassadors can easily be replaced."

"You think to challenge me? *ME!*" he thundered. "You've been in America far too long if you think your political clout reaches beyond the ocean.

"Perhaps in your advanced years, your brain has become feeble, Mulciber. The council approves of my lordship and the way I run *my* territory."

Mulciber scanned the Torians lining the stairs and balcony. "Perhaps they do, but don't be so confident of your allies. Not everyone is as supportive of you as you think." He clutched the edge of his flowing robe and walked silently through the lower level door to the archives, locking it soundly behind him.

***

Miranda took a few more deep breaths in the elevator. She was glad to have gotten the hell away from Mulciber and knew Valadon's Torians wouldn't let any harm come to their leader. At least, that was what Remare had told her. Repeatedly. "I want to go to the infirmary; this scratch still burns."

Her heart was still hammering as Remare inspected her cheek again, his breath on her neck. He then pressed the button for the infirmary. "My saliva not only sealed your wound, but cleansed it, as well. You have no infection and shouldn't be able to feel anything."

Miranda closed her eyes and exhaled deeply. She regarded her savior. "I suppose...I owe you thanks for closing the wound." Remare stood with his arms folded and his back against the side of the elevator. This close up, without his usual scowl, he seemed less threatening, less dark...almost handsome, and she wondered what he'd look like without the goatee. She touched her cheek and gazed downward. "Thank you," she said softly, then met his eyes.

After a pause, Remare said, "You're welcome," without his usual snark, maintaining the eye contact between them. "It took courage to deal with Mulciber. Most would have given him a wide berth or avoided him altogether."

She broke eye contact first, eyes darting to the level indicator as her breaths evened. She needed Gabriel to examine the wound and a damned mirror to make sure she wasn't maimed. But more important, she was worried about Valadon. "You're sure he can handle himself with Mulciber?"

"Don't be insulting, Mir-randa. Valadon is a Blueblood, the strongest of us all. Of course he can handle himself." He looked at her incredulously. "Do you think I would have left him if I didn't think he could defend himself?"

She heard the anger and frustration in his voice and mirrored him by crossing her arms over her chest. Somehow, she didn't think she made as formidable an impression as he did. "Who is Mulciber and how did he become so scarred?"

Remare remained silent as if contemplating how much he would tell her. "Mulciber is an ambassador to our court." At her perplexed look, he continued, "In America, we refer to them as houses, but all courts across the globe answer to the VHC—our ruling court in Europe."

Her sarcasm returned. "You mean he's a spy for the vampire high court?"

Remare narrowed his eyes and nodded once.

She processed that bit of information. "What happened to him?"

"The sun."

Miranda wasn't going to push for more answers, though she wanted to. When the elevator opened on Gabriel's floor, she hesitated, then said, "I'm safe now. Why don't you go back down to Valadon?" She wanted Valadon to have his strongest Torian with him. "I'll stay with Gabriel."

"Let me make sure he's there. Then, I'll contact Valadon."

"Gabriel?" She called out and was relieved to find him at his desk.

When he glanced up, a warm smile brightened his face. "Miranda."

"I'm glad you're here." Gabriel's presence had a calming effect on her, and right now, she needed some semblance of normalcy.

After she gave him the short version of what happened, Gabriel examined her face. He checked the inside of her cheek, as well. "You're fine, Miranda. There's no trace of any incision or infection." He then turned to Remare. "And you're sure Valadon is all right?"

"Quite."

"Thank God." Miranda exhaled in relief, then met his eyes. "But I still want to see for myself. Do you have a mirror around here?"

She saw the smirk on Remare's face before he hid it. "I'm so pleased you realized we have reflections."

Miranda glared at him ready to say something equally snarky, but she'd had enough of insolent vampires for one night.

"Right in there." Gabriel pointed to the bathroom in the corner of the room and then turned to Remare, who was silently watching them. "How deep was the cut, really?"

"Deep enough." Remare finished texting.

When Remare pocketed his phone, Gabriel asked, "What's going on, Remare? First, we get the attempts on Valadon's life, then girls start turning up dead all over the city with their throats torn out, and now, this."

"Boys, too."

"What?" Gabriel wasn't sure he heard right, but when Remare silently nodded, he muttered, "Christ," and started pacing, running his fingers through his hair.

"Now, you take an interest in vampire affairs? When you're set to leave him in only a few weeks?" Remare tilted his head and stood with his arms crossed over his chest. "Why would you care?"

Gabriel understood Remare's resentment. He'd rarely taken an interest in vampire business, only when Valadon demanded it. He shouldn't care even now. But he did. As far as the ruling vampire of New York went, he knew Valadon regarded his position seriously and did what he could for vampire/human affairs. Admittedly, he was one of the best vampire lords. "I'm not blind, nor deaf, even for a turned vampire. Someone's planning on making a move on Valadon's territory. Who?"

"If you bothered to show up to any of our meetings, you would know that is precisely what we are working on."

"Poison, now?" Gabriel began pacing again. "I spoke with Valadon when I received the results of the compounds in the dart." He knew Remare, above all others, was closest to Valadon. He'd even once believed the rumors that they'd been lovers long ago. "I told him the chemicals wouldn't have killed him. It was meant to paralyze him; he would have been vulnerable for a few moments—enough for someone to get to him."

"If you're so concerned, why don't you make time for him out of your busy schedule, doctor? He just went up against Mulciber to protect the woman in there." Remare gestured to the restroom. "Valadon's going to need all the trusted friends he has in the coming days." He slanted his head. "A united front would work well for him, don't you think?" Remare turned and walked down the hall toward the elevator.

Miranda stood beside Gabriel. "Did he give you any more information?"

Gabriel gently caressed her cheek and realized Miranda was beginning to burrow into his heart. He'd spent the better portion of the day thinking about her. "Not really. This place isn't safe for you. I'll take you home."

"What do you know about Mulciber?"

"Enough to avoid him." Gabriel went back to his desk to get his keys. "He hasn't paid me much attention. Doesn't think I'm important enough, and I prefer it that way. I like to keep a low profile around here." He smiled, even though he knew that might be changing.

When they met Remare, who had changed into a dark suit, by the elevators, he informed them, "Valadon gave me explicit orders to escort Miranda home." He then turned to her. "He said to tell you he would soon be in touch."

Gabriel nodded. "I'll call you later." He watched the elevator doors close and made a decision he'd been thinking about for some time. He'd be leaving ValCorp soon, but before he left, maybe there was more he could do. As if on cue, the other elevator opened in welcome. He entered and pressed the button for the archives. He had used the libraries extensively when he'd first become a vampire, hoping to find the answers he searched for in their histories, then turning to science when history had offered him no solutions.

Exiting the elevator, Gabriel walked quietly to where the group of vampires were talking. Valadon and the Torians looked amazed to see him.

"Heard you had some trouble down here," he said sarcastically as he met Valadon's eyes, and then, probably making the biggest mistake of his life, he added, "What can I do to help?"

Valadon smiled approvingly at his progeny. "Join us."

***

Miranda didn't like feeling she was being handled. Remare was pulling her along with one hand and texting with the other. "Will you stop dragging me? I can walk."

"Then, hurry up. The sooner I get you home, the sooner I can return." He remote started his car—a black Mercedes SUV, M-Class and opened the door for her. Remare's masculine scent was stronger inside. She could almost detect evergreen; it wasn't a bad scent, Miranda admitted as she examined the luxurious black leather interior. Of course, Remare had the coolest gadgets, half of which she had no clue what function they performed.

"Who's Mulciber?" she asked after buckling her seat belt. When he refused to answer as they pulled out of the garage, she asked, "Is Valadon in danger?"

Remare remained quiet until they were on the road then glanced at her. "Valadon can handle himself. This is his territory, and Mulciber insulted him when he cut your face."

"Yeah, I was pretty much insulted, too," she mumbled as she rubbed her cheek.

"You don't understand vampire politics. What Mulciber did could cause a major rift in the détente between the European court and our own. Valadon has always longed for autonomy, and now, they will most likely send an elder to investigate. None of us welcome that idea," he said, watching the other drivers and speeding up the avenue, dodging taxis and pedestrians.

"Why?" Miranda was curious about the politics between the two courts. She had gathered fragments from conversations between Cyra and Morel and just now with Gabriel, but sensed there was much she didn't know.

Remare seemed reluctant to discuss vampire business with a mere mortal.

Miranda decided to use logic. "If Valadon trusts me enough to show me his private archives, don't you think you could, too?" She tilted her head.

Remare appeared pensive. "Perhaps you should know what you're becoming involved in. Mulciber is a very old vampire. He's here to oversee the finances of ValCorp. He periodically checks our records...as if we'd attempt to deceive the high court," he muttered.

"Does he hold jurisdiction over Valadon?"

"Not personally, no. He's here to advise or suggest. He has no authority over Valadon, even though he seems to think so...but he does have very powerful friends in Europe." Remare maneuvered around a cab to beat a light and had to dodge some intrepid pedestrians. "Some have wanted to vex Valadon for many years now."

"Why?" Miranda noted the Mercedes handled very smoothly. Remare was as an adept driver as he was a swordsman.

Remare glanced at her. "Look at all Valadon has; don't you think there are those who covet what is his, what he has worked several human lifetimes to achieve? Through the centuries, there have been many feuds, petty jealousies of certain court members...and worse.

So, Valadon has even more enemies. Miranda gazed out at the city. New York never slept, she thought as people went about their business, even this late at night, grabbing late night snacks, socializing. Dane had sent her some information concerning hate groups and promised more when he returned from his business trip. She missed his handsome face, then thought of another's more hideous features.

"How did his face become disfigured?"

"You're certainly inquisitive tonight." Remare stroked his jaw. "If you're going to survive in our world, there are a few things you should know. ValCorp manufactures a sunblock that enables vampires to tolerate sunlight for a certain amount of time."

"I thought vampires developed immunity to the sun, part of your adaptability over the ages." At least, that was what Cyra had told her.

Remare grimaced. "Not *all* vampires are so lucky. Some have developed partial immunity; some haven't. That's why we created the sunblock. When we did the initial tests, it seemed to work well on a fair amount of vampires, but with Mulciber... Unfortunately, it did not. It had taken years to get the formula right. He was very impatient to be able to go outside during the daylight hours. He refused to wait until we completed more tests. At first, the ointment seemed to be working, but then it quickly deteriorated, and Mulciber had been foolish enough to be in a location where he could not seek shelter swiftly enough. He burned, and the resulting scars changed him." Remare glanced at her. "As you saw tonight. He was not always like that."

Miranda imagined being scarred and how that could alter someone's personality. No wonder the vampire was easy to anger. "What did he look like before the accident?" she wondered aloud.

"There is a painting of him on the lowest level of the library, in the corner on the right. Next time you're there, see for yourself."

Miranda remembered gazing at the different portraits, but couldn't remember which one was his. Vampires were incredibly beautiful. Nature's way of providing for the species, making them attractive to their prey. "He must have been handsome at one time."

"He was," Remare said softly as he turned down her street.

She pointed to her home. "That's my place up on the right."

Remare pulled over and escorted her up the stairs. "Let me have your key. I want to make sure your home is safe."

She wasn't sure that was necessary, but rather than argue, she gave him her key. As they entered her house, he flicked the switch on and began to search through all the rooms. When he finished with the upstairs, he came back down.

"Why don't you have a security alarm system?"

Miranda was stunned by his angry attitude. "Well, until recently...I didn't need one." She cocked a hip and tilted her head.

"You're a single woman living alone in the city. And you think it's wise you don't have a security system?"

She met his stare straight on. "As I said, I never really needed one. Look around here. There's hardly anything worth stealing." Miranda frowned. Her furniture was old, and many of the other furnishings had been her parents she had yet to replace.

Remare looked like he was ready to pop a vessel. "Isn't your personal safety worth something?"

"Fine! I'll consider it. Happy now?" She jutted her chin in his direction.

He glared at her. "I've fulfilled my obligation to Valadon. Good night, Mir-randa."

She watched him turn and leave, liking the way he pronounced her name with the rolling r's, thinking it was one of the few times he'd called her by her first name.

His seductive scent of evening woods clung in the air long after he was gone.

Chapter Twenty-Three

Miranda kicked off her heels, shed her dress and dug out her black jeans and her favorite pair of black leather boots. She felt stronger wearing the boots with the three-inch thick rubber heels that laced up the front. Then, she found a black sleeveless shirt that showed off her toned arms, and just for the fun of it, slid on a pair of long black gloves. Damn, she looked kickass as she gazed in the mirror.

During the cab ride up Central Park West, they passed the Dakota apartment building; the neighborhood was nearly deserted, but Central Park was a different story. Miranda exited the cab and ran through the park until she reached Werehaven. As soon as she entered the club, an eerie feeling crept over her. Scrutinizing the club, she noticed there weren't half the Weres there usually were. She made her way to the VIP lounge and found Brent, Liz's financial advisor, on one of the couches reading from his laptop.

"Miranda, I didn't expect to see you tonight." He rose and kissed her cheek.

Brent was tall, slender and deceptively built—not unlike a certain vampire she knew. Brent sparred with some of Lizandra's guards, and the Were could hold his own. But his true strength was in his intelligent, piercing blue eyes. He could predict the moves of others and attacked or retreated with startling speed.

But Brent only sparred for fun; he didn't have the aggressive demeanor some of the Weres had. With his black hair and finely chiseled cheekbones, he was a looker. And his partner thought so, too.

Quint, Liz's legal advisor, loped up the stairs, grabbed Miranda in a bear hug and kissed her forehead. He seemed perplexed when he sniffed her hair. Where Brent was dark and ponderous, Quint was blond and lighthearted. Together, they made one of the handsomest couples she'd ever seen, straight or gay. "Damn woman, you look hot enough to turn a gay man straight." He laughed. "What brings you here tonight?"

Miranda became uneasy when other people looked at each other in a manner that implied they knew something she didn't.

That was the way Quint was now eying Brent. "Where is everyone? Why is it so empty tonight?"

Quint exhaled softly. "Come sit down."

"Do you want a drink?" Brent shifted his laptop to make room for her.

"Am I going to need one?" She asked with concern. "Where's Lizandra?"

"She's out checking our borders. We had an *incident* at one of the entrances tonight." Quint sat and faced Brent, who continued, "Lately, there've been a few minor altercations. The Red Claws have been encroaching on our borders."

"Has anyone gotten hurt?" Miranda's heart sped up. The Weres were like family to her. She was ready to offer whatever assistance she could. Perhaps she couldn't fight as well as the Weres, but like Gandalf, high up in a tree, she could throw fireballs at their enemies.

"A few minor cuts and bruises." Quint added, "They know the law, yet are trying to test Lizandra's resolve. They think they can manipulate her to open her borders. They obviously don't know her very well." Both men tapped their beer bottles together.

"The Red Claws have been the aggressors," Brent explained. "There are rumors they want to petition the Commissioner of Clans to let all packs have access to the park at night as we are centrally located in the city."

"But that's insane. Liz told me Red Claw has dominion over Riverside Park." A park with awesome views of the Hudson River.

"Right you are. Our commission set forth strict rules about which clan has dominion over which areas, but every few years, Red Claw thinks they can break the treaties." Quint smiled as he sipped his beer and put his hand on Brent's knee.

"Lizandra will never let that happen," Miranda said with certainty.

"She will freeze in hell with the devil himself before she *ever* allows that to happen!" Lizandra, Were Queen of Black Star Clan, bellowed as she majestically ascended the stairs to her lounge. Liz looked regal in her fighting clothes that showed off her muscular physique. Wearing the thick soled boots soldiers wore, she was clearly over six-foot tall. But the presence she commanded was what really defined her. The men and Miranda immediately stood. Liz looked Miranda up and down. "What the hell are you doing here? You're supposed to be in the sack with vamp king."

Both men peered at Miranda with raised eyebrows and then back at their queen. Brent asked, "How'd it go tonight?"

"The usual bullshit. A couple of Red Claws crying they had the right to pass through *my* park to get to work on the East Side. I had to explain the rules to them so they could understand my English."

Gavin, Thalia, Liz's brothers, David and Sam, joined them; each was covered in sweat, and Miranda could swear she saw blood stains on Gavin.

"I think they have a clearer understanding, now." Gavin smirked as a bartender brought a case of beer into the lounge and started passing the bottles around.

Sam and David high fived it and did the knuckle dance with their fists.

"Damned right they do!" Lizandra grabbed Gavin and gave him one of the most heated kisses Miranda had ever seen in public and felt herself getting warm.

"Did anyone get hurt?" Miranda asked.

"Not from my clan, but a few Red Claws will be limping for a while," Liz snickered. "I need a bath. Anyone care to join me?"

Liz didn't have to ask twice. Miranda loved the hot tubs Lizandra had installed in the compound's lower level. The cave was left mostly natural looking with strings of tiny lights along the walls and a huge mural of a Caribbean island with palm trees and the turquoise sea. There were enough Jacuzzis for Lizandra's entourage. Gavin joined Lizandra's, and Brent shared Quint's. Someone turned on the music system, and the female Were, Allende, started singing the sultry Latin songs Lizandra liked. The warm water caused a mist in the room, giving it a dreamlike quality.

Miranda felt soothed by the warm water and was almost comfortable watching the Weres walk around naked. To them, it was a very natural thing; and for a Were, it was. But Miranda was human and averted her eyes, despite the good-natured teasing she received. She was glad to see none of the Weres were wounded.

Lizandra lay back against Gavin's chest, singing a few of the lyrics and smiled at Miranda. With one very long painted fingernail, she pointed at her. "So, girlfriend, are you going to tell me why you're here...and not riding da sex-eh vampire?"

"Sure." Miranda gave the short version of the night...up until Mulciber showed up.

"Shit! Miranda." Liz was impressed. "Are you going to take him up on his offer?"

"I'm thinking about it. But I'll probably turn him down. I'm just too busy with my work at the museum and teaching. I don't see how I'd have the time."

"But he said you could make your own hours," Thalia tossed in.

"I'm considering it." Miranda sank deeper into the hot water, wishing Dane was there to rub her back the way Gavin was massaging Lizandra's. But as she lay back in the gloriously heated tub, letting the soothing warm jets relax the tension in her muscles...another's face surfaced in her mind. And it was his hands she wanted touching her body, his mouth on hers and his scent on her skin. *Eau de Vampire* came to mind, and she burst out laughing.

"What?" Liz asked quickly.

Gavin ordered, "Give!"

"Let's hear it." Thalia leaned forward in the water.

The others splashed her with water when she refused to tell them what she was thinking, which only made her laugh harder.

Lizandra merely narrowed her eyes mischievously. "I will get you for that."

Miranda smiled. "You can *try*."

***

Mulciber laughed with devilish delight as he walked down the hall. This was too delectable not to share with the others. *So, Valadon finally has a weakness. And a human one at that; how delicious! Valadon, don't you ever learn? I would have thought you learned your lesson by now.* He rapped on his daughter's door and entered without waiting for a reply. The scents of opiates and sex assailed him. Brandon and Persephone were sprawled naked on the bed. If Jeremy or Kaylee had been present, he might have joined them. He sat on the edge of the bed as Persephone casually pulled a sheet over them.

"What has put that remarkable grin on your face? Was your last meal *tastier* than you expected?" Brandon quipped as he sat up.

"Oh, better than that, though she was delicious." He smacked his lips in glee. He so enjoyed the blood of youth in his veins. And what a joy it was to taste his delicate flowers' fragrance in her blood. The toxins from his plants had such a desirable effect on humans, illegal, of course, but oh so pleasurable. It was almost as good as when he removed his mask during sex. The poor darlings always thought they were bedding a handsome man, but just as they were peaking, he'd peel off his mask and show them his true face.

He got off on their horror every time. Poor things didn't last long after he drank his share of desire. He was never quite sure if they died from heart failure due to the illicit substance or the shock of his visage. Mulciber shrugged; it didn't matter either way to him. "I found a way to expedite our plans. And one of you...gets to play a major part."

Chapter Twenty-Four

The spectacular bouquet of red roses contained pink orchids in the center. Black and gold ribbons completed the arrangement with a handwritten note from Valadon apologizing for the incident with Mulciber. When the flowers failed to elicit a response, he sent her a pair of Gia Bellini shoes that would've cost a week's paycheck. And then...the jewelry started. Miranda sent them back to him but kept the shoes. She rationalized keeping them because the heels she'd worn the night they went out had given her blisters. He owed her for that.

The next day, Orion, her roommate, laughed and told her there were *ten* more boxes of shoes in the living room, and that she should *"just call the guy already"*. Miranda had been astounded and was going to send the shoes back. Eventually, except for the fine leather boots. She never should've tried them on, but the leather was so smooth and felt like they were molded from her body.

One night after class, Nick stayed late and had a pained expression on his face. He'd been one of her favorite students, even before she'd found out who his resolute uncle was. "Let me guess...Valadon sent you to talk to me."

"He really wants to see you again." Nick blurted out before taking a breath and choosing his words more eloquently. "He just wants you to call him." His boyish smile widened. "I think he's been thinking a lot about you, Professor Crescent."

Oh, this is so not fair, Valadon. You're using a kid to get to me. She looked up into Nick's beautiful blue eyes, saw his pleading and then glimpsed the two small packages he was holding.

"If those are for me, you can tell your uncle to stop sending me jewelry. I won't accept it."

Nick grinned. "These aren't jewelry boxes, Professor Crescent. But they are for you." He quickly left them on her desk and took off before she could stop him.

Next, a few of her female students were waiting to speak to her. "Professor Crescent, are you going to see Orion play tonight?"

She'd forgotten Orion was performing at Oasis, a Midtown club run by Weres. Miranda had promised him several times before she'd come hear him play and had always been too busy. "I'm not sure. What time is the show?"

"He has two sets: one's at nine, and the other is at eleven."

"I can probably make the later one."

That put smiles on their faces. "Okay, we'll see you, then."

Miranda regarded the two little packages on her desk with one eye shut and wondered what Valadon was sending her, now. When she unwrapped the first one, she discovered an iPhone with a note explaining the phone was pre-set to Valadon's private number as well as the numbers of several of his Torians. The embossed black and gold card simply said, "*Please.*"

I'll think about it! Then, she opened the other box and smiled. It was a bag of chili pepper chocolates, her favorite. *Now, how did he know that?* The assortment included smooth, delectable dark chocolates that melted on your tongue as well as creamy milk chocolates that could put a girl in heaven. The enclosed card said, "*Enjoy the sampling, but if you want the whole box, you'll have to come to ValCorp and visit my newly acquired chocolatier, Crescent's Chocolates.*"

The bastard! He went and named his chocolate store after her. She read the last sentence on the card. *Press nine on the phone, and a car will come pick you up.*

She ate the chocolates.

***

Oasis was not as chic as the vampire clubs, but what it lacked in elegance, it made up with ambience. People wore jeans and dressed for comfort. From the oak paneled walls to the black ceiling with the mirror ball, it felt good to just hang out and sample the spicy scents emanating from the kitchen, drink a beer and simply enjoy the music.

Tonight, they had Orion, one of the best male singers Miranda ever heard. And the man was magic on stage, whether he was playing his electric guitar or wowing the mostly female crowd with his soulful ballads on his acoustic.

Miranda made her way through the crowd and noticed all the tables were packed. At the bar she ordered a cranberry and vodka. Sipping her drink, she scanned the crowd for her students and spotted them up close to the stage. When she caught Orion's gaze and broad smile, she raised her drink in greeting. Still searching the crowd, she was surprised to see Nick with the blond student from her class. Damn. Where the hell were his bodyguards? As a Blueblood, Nick wasn't supposed to go out in public alone.

The club was warm, despite the air conditioning, the usual for a Were hangout. The humming in her head warned the place was packed with Weres. There were several humans present, but she couldn't detect any other vampires. Strange, especially for a mixed-race establishment.

Orion finished his song and then switched to his electric guitar. His seductive, enchanting music had the crowd cheering and rapping on the tables. The noise level definitely increased, so did the undercurrents of the place. A couple of Weres encroached on Nick's table. One spilled his drink and then had words with Nick.

Oh shit! This could get ugly fast. She remembered now who the student was with Nick: Cerise, the niece of the clan chief of the Red Claws. *Double damn!* Miranda reached in her purse for the phone Valadon had sent her. There was no way she'd be able to hear with the noise in the club, so she prayed the Torian she sent the message to read his texts. Then, she pocketed the phone and made her way through the crowd.

When she finally reached Nick's table, the Weres were egging him on into a fight. There was some filthy language about vampires, and then, they started in on Nick and what made him think he was good enough for one of their own.

"Well, boys, I see you're having a good time tonight. Think Orion appreciates the outburst during his performance?" Miranda restrained her voice in an effort to calm the belligerent Weres.

"Shut the fuck up, bitch; no one asked for your opinion," one growled. His rolled up shirt sleeve revealed a red claw tattoo.

Great! He was an enforcer, as evidenced by the blood drops off the claw. "Now, gentlemen, there are three of you and only one of him. Do you think that's fair?"

"Butt out, human. This doesn't concern you," sneered the dark haired Were.

"Maybe you should go home," Nick said in a low voice. "I can handle this."

The fuck you can! And where the hell were the bouncers? Each had their backs turned. *Convenient!*

"Actually, I plainly remember you saying you'd give me a lift home, and I'm ready to leave, now." She glanced at Cerise, who appeared equally agitated as Nick. "Cerise, would you like to come with us?"

"She stays with us. She's one of us and doesn't belong with his kind," barked a Were sporting a Mohawk.

"Is that so? Cerise, do you want to stay here?" Miranda kept her tone reserved as Cerise reluctantly nodded.

"C'mon, Nick, I have some friends you might want to meet." Miranda silently warned Nick to keep his mouth shut and willed him to rise behind her as she stared down the three Weres.

When the Weres looked like they were going to move in, Miranda removed the cuff she often wore and showed the Weres her own tattoo, of which they were momentarily startled.

"What's a human doing wearing a clan tattoo?" Red shirt snarled.

"Oh, don't you know who I am?" Miranda summoned the heat to rise in the palms of her hands the way she usually did before she formed a fireball. "I'm blood sister to the pack." She let them feel the heat that poured off her no normal human could ever generate. "Now, if you don't want to start something you can't possibly finish, we'll say goodnight." Miranda pushed Nick in front of her and herded him out of the club.

"Why did you do that?" Nick growled at her. "I could have taken them!"

"Oh, for the love of male pride," she muttered. For an intelligent young man, Nick could be pretty stupid. "Yes, and then, your uncle would've had my hide." She started pacing the curb outside the club. "What the hell were you thinking? Going to a Were club without your guards."

"I can go wherever I want. This is a mixed club, anyway." He pointed up at the sign near the door that indicated all races welcome.

Yeah, right!

At that point, a couple of Weres she didn't recognize started toward them. They were older than the college age morons inside who had tried to intimidate them. And more dangerous, as she sensed they were carrying weapons. "Oh, this just keeps getting better and better," she quipped as her pulse sped up.

"So, you're a friend of Black Star," the one with the dark hair and even darker eyes said. "We didn't know we had an acquaintance of the Were Queen in our establishment. Few members of the other clans visit us."

Right! Got it!—A little late, though. Miranda didn't know who he was and certainly didn't trust him. "And who might you be?"

He smiled pleasantly. "I'm Victor Gren, and this is my club."

If this was his place, he was connected to the leader of the Red Claws, Edgar Renworth. And she had just walked into very dangerous territory. Maybe showing her tattoo hadn't been such a good idea.

"Not all clan members agree on everything, as I'm sure you know. I don't approve of the confrontations our clans have had in the past." He never took his eyes off of her. "I'm a firm believer in boundaries and respecting them as such."

Message received and understood. Miranda nodded at Nick. "He's young and didn't understand the rules." She looked pointedly at Nick. "He won't make the same mistake again."

Victor's gaze drifted to Nick. "See that he doesn't." He turned and left, leaving his two goons behind. Miranda didn't like the way they were watching them, but didn't dare take her eyes off them.

Suddenly, two dark Mercedes SUVs pulled up to the curb in a screeching halt. One license plate said ValCorp 2, and she knew immediately who was driving. Miranda was quickly flanked by Torians who grabbed Nick and escorted him to the car. The other Torians faced off against the Weres until Nick was safe inside, then they turned and got back in their cars.

Remare, who couldn't look any more dangerous in his long black leather coat that just screamed *hidden weapons underneath,* stared down the Weres, daring them to make a move against him. He beheld her for a moment, quirked a smile, saluted her with two fingers to his forehead and got back in his car and drove off as quickly as he had arrived.

Thanks for the lift, Remare! She watched as the taillights grew dim in the distance... *"Really—no problem, I can walk. I only live on the way. Asshole!"* Miranda froze as she felt the Were behind her approaching. She exhaled slowly.

Orion circled his arms around her and whispered, "Can't leave you alone for a minute, can I?"

"This was *so* not my fault." She welcomed his embrace, grateful he'd been there for her.

"I'm sure it wasn't." He narrowed his eyes at the soldier who watched them leave. "Let's go home."

Chapter Twenty-Five

"Professor Crescent, it's urgent I talk to you! Can we meet at the café near the university?"

"Louise, what's this about?" Louise Cameron was one of her most diligent and warm-hearted students, whose mother happened to be the wealthy socialite, Barbara Morley Cameron, but Miranda wasn't sure she wanted to get caught up in her students' social lives,

"I overheard a conversation discussing your picture with Valadon. I can't discuss it over the phone. Please, it's important!"

Miranda considered the messages on her desk. Two were from her boss, reminding her about the upcoming fundraiser. Another was from Dane, stating he'd be back soon. Nothing required her immediate attention. "Give me an hour."

When she arrived at the café near Washington Square Park, Louise was already waiting outside. "I'm glad you came. Could we just walk a little around the park, Professor Crescent?"

"Sure." As they strolled around the park, they passed several older men playing chess and a few kids on skateboards. A cool autumn breeze swept across their path, and the leaves were already falling from the trees. After they'd walked a while in companionable silence, Miranda said, "You sounded a bit anxious on the phone. Want to tell me what's going on?"

She shook with trepidation. "I'm not sure I did the right thing." Louise breathed deep and found her resolve. "When I heard your name mentioned and then saw your picture with the vampire king on social media, I thought maybe I should tell you."

Miranda wondered if Valadon knew people called him *the vampire king*. "My name mentioned about what?" She picked up a red maple leaf and twirled the stem in her hand.

"You know who my mother is, don't you?" Louise frowned. "She's in the society pages a lot."

"Yes. We met at a social function once." When substance abuse had taken its toll on the former model and she had crashed her car while driving in the Hamptons, she'd had to do a stint in rehab. She'd come out of it a changed woman. Rumor had it hubby said she wasn't as much fun once she stopped drinking, and they eventually divorced.

Miranda breathed in the cool air from the park and admired the Washington Arch they were nearing. She glanced at her young companion. "Are you going to tell me what you heard?"

"My mom's not married, now. She said she's through with marriage and all the legal hassles, but she does date. Anyway, she said she was with a guy just hanging out watching TV when they showed your picture with Valadon on one of the entertainment channels, and he said he should talk with you, but he didn't want to get involved." Louise grimaced. "He said he liked flying under Valadon's radar."

"This man your mother was with, is he a vampire, by any chance?"

"Yes." Louise looked pained. "He's a paid escort."

Miranda wasn't sure what embarrassed Louise more, her mother seeing a vampire or that she was paying for sex.

"What's his name?"

Her face was marred with distaste. "Kristoph."

"And did he give any specific reason why he wanted to speak with me?"

"Not to me. But my mother said you need to have a conversation with him." She glanced up at Miranda. "She seemed nervous, Professor Crescent; my mother doesn't get nervous; she's the strongest person I know." Louise steadied her breathing. "And last night, I heard her say that he *had* to speak with you." She dug out his card. "She told me to give you this and make you promise to call him."

Miranda considered the merged sun and moon logo and wondered if Louise knew what it meant. *Professional Escort Service, by Appointment Only.* She noted the phone number and email address. Miranda didn't like the idea of calling a stranger and wondered what she'd find when she Googled him. "Are you sure you didn't overhear anything else? This could be important."

Louise shook her head. "I don't know what's going on. But I don't like seeing my mother this nervous. She likes you, you know. She was thinking of inviting you for lunch or dinner." She shrugged. "Or something."

"Okay." Miranda tried to be reassuring. "You did the right thing. This may turn out to be nothing." However, she didn't think so. "I'll give him a call and see what he has to say."

After Louise disappeared up Fifth Avenue, Miranda fingered the card, wondering if this was a good idea. Probably not, but she dialed his number. When his service answered, she hesitated then left a message. She barely made it across the street when her phone rang.

"Professor Crescent, I've heard interesting things about you. I take it you got my message."

"What's this about, Kristoph? I don't have a lot of time here." She grew testy at the annoying charm in his voice.

"Nor do I, but I think it would be in the best interest of our mutual friend if we met."

"And who would that be?" She already knew, but she wanted to hear him say it.

"I think you already know."

Miranda wanted to meet Kristoph somewhere public with a lot of people, but he adamantly refused, citing he would lose clients if he was seen in her company and insisted she come to his apartment. She deliberated getting Orion to come with her, but as Kristoph said he was free at the moment, she decided to go see him. She quickly texted Orion the address. If he didn't hear from her in an hour, he'd come find her.

She'd keep her phone on during the meet if she felt she was being played.

***

Miranda considered the posh apartment building Kristoph lived in on Park Avenue. With clients like Cameron, he could afford to live well. The doorman nodded as she entered the lobby and went to the elevators. She pressed the button when a familiar voice echoed behind her.

"Professor Crescent. Why is it you keep showing up at the most intriguing places?"

She turned to see Remare impeccably dressed in an elegant, dark blue suit with a European cut that emphasized his trim physique. Despite her distrust of him, she gave him credit in the style department; the man always knew how to dress. She quickly blinked that thought away. "What are you doing here?

"Funny, I was about to ask you the same thing." He tilted his head and watched her scrutinize him.

When the elevator doors opened, Miranda entered and pushed the button for Kristoph's floor. She had a sinking feeling they were both here to see the same person. *Could be a coincidence, but not the way her life worked.* "Are you going to answer my question?" She regarded him as her pulse quickened.

"I'm here to see...someone who may have useful information."

Damn! They were here to see the same person. "What floor is your friend on? You didn't press the button."

"Same as yours. And what brings you here? You don't have your equipment you usually carry for authentications."

Deciding not to play any games, as he would see through any pretenses she could come up with on such short notice, she boldly said, "I'm visiting a male courtesan, who may have information about the attempt on Valadon, but is too chicken shit to meet with him personally."

Remare's head whipped around as he hit the stop button. He stared at her with his arms crossed over his chest. His nostrils flared with his rapid breaths.

Having the ability to surprise him gave Miranda a jolt of satisfaction, and she restrained a smile.

"What do you know of Kristoph?" he asked angrily.

"Not much," she admitted. "But when he saw my picture with Valadon, he sent me an invitation to meet with him."

"I didn't think you would be familiar with someone who provides such services. Not with the Weres you hang out with. Have you ever met him before?"

She ignored his intentional barb. "No. Have you?"

"Perhaps."

Miranda hated his one word answers. She wished she could read his mind as she stared at his dark brown eyes. Eyes of sinfully decadent chocolate.

Remare pressed the button for the elevator to continue and silently watched her. When the elevator doors opened to their floor, he let her exit first.

They walked side by side until they reached Kristoph's door. Miranda knocked and waited. After she'd dropped her bombshell, Remare had been unusually quiet. As hard as she tried to get a bead on his thoughts, his face was impossible to read. All she sensed was wry amusement.

Finally, the door opened, and Miranda was struck speechless, finding herself in a rare situation: She wasn't certain if the person greeting her was male or female. He was of medium height and build, had thick lashes around his dark eyes that seemed to be laughing. If he was male, he had to be the most beautiful male who ever walked the earth with his soft features and fine pale complexion. She could detect no hint of a beard on his smooth face. His wavy mahogany hair reached past his shoulders. He was dressed in black lounge pants, shirtless, except for a short blue robe loosely tied to reveal his hairless chest.

"Miranda. Remare. I see you two know each other." Kristoph's voice had a musical quality she thought charming. He motioned for them to enter.

"Close your mouth, or you'll catch flies that way," Remare whispered as he walked past her into the opulent room.

Kristoph liked Louis XIV furniture, and from his *objects d'art* carefully placed throughout the room, he had distinguished taste. With his delicate hands, he gestured for them to make themselves comfortable in his living room. Hands the size only a male would have. Miranda grinned at herself; he was definitely male with his Adam's apple. She could see how both sexes would be attracted to him.

"Can I get either of you something to drink?" he asked politely. "Remare, a cabernet?"

Remare nodded.

"I'm fine," Miranda said, but when Remare cleared his throat, she quickly added, "I'd like a soft drink." After Kristoph went to get their drinks, she glared at Remare for not preparing her, who smiled in amusement as she sat in one of Kristoph's plush chairs. When Kristoph returned with their drinks, he reclined on the sofa with Remare.

They exchanged a few words in a language she couldn't place. It sounded like a combination of Italian and French, but not quite—maybe one of the Eastern European languages.

"He says you're lovelier than the picture the media posted," Remare remarked as he sipped his wine.

"You called me to meet with you and said you might know something concerning Valadon." Miranda had never been good with small talk and could have kicked herself. She knew vampires liked to socialize first before getting down to business, but didn't have their level of patience.

"Barbara speaks highly of you. She warned me you were a woman who cut to the heart of matters. I can see how you would capture Valadon's interest. Would it be fair to surmise you know the title and artist of every painting in this room?" His voice hinted at something naughty. "I have a private collection you might find stimulating."

"Professor Crescent is not interested," Remare interrupted before Miranda could speak.

"Pity. Some pieces are quite inspirational." Kristoph drank deeply of his wine. "I had thought to speak to you privately. But after you called, Remare informed me he was on his way. I hope you don't mind."

"Remare is Valadon's second. I would think anything you had to tell me would certainly reach him," Miranda murmured, "one way or another."

Kristoph leaned back against his cushions, crossed one leg over the other and slowly rubbed his lips with his fingers. He was making overt sexual motions as if he'd practiced his moves so much over time they were now second nature. His movements weren't really casual, just designed to appear so. Whether it was in the seductive way he moved or the way he fingered the stem of his wine glass, it all suggested sex.

"Barbara said your reputation was above reproach in work and in social customs. When I told her what I overheard with another client, and we saw your picture in the news, she recommended I contact you." He sat forward and spoke directly to her. "You must understand, confidentiality is important in my line of work. But I wasn't comfortable with certain aspects and thought it best to speak to you personally."

Miranda was confused. "Kristoph, if you overheard something regarding Valadon's welfare, why not just call him directly; why call me?"

Remare leaned forward. "Kristoph was once a member of Valadon House." He slanted Kristoph a glance. "He no longer has that status."

She considered the implication and wondered what Kristoph had done to get himself kicked out. She'd let that slide, for now. She looked from one vampire to the other. "Then, why not call you or any of the Torians?"

"Miranda doesn't understand vampire law and the social nuances we have," Remare explained to Kristoph. "However, now that we are both here, why don't you tell us what you overheard?"

"Of course. Last week, one of my clients was in the bathroom on his phone. I only heard part of the conversation, so I don't know who he was talking to. But I did hear him mention something about chemical compounds. It didn't register with me as anything important, so I went to the kitchen to get myself a drink. On my way back to the bedroom, I heard him mention Valadon's name."

"You're certain you didn't hear him mention the other person's name?" Remare questioned.

"Truly, but I did hear him mention the word *'order'.*" Kristoph stared at Remare, and Miranda knew they were silently communicating. She hated when vampires did that, but knew it was their way.

When they stayed quiet, she leaned forward and asked, "As in the Human Order of Light?"

Both males nodded. This news didn't seem to surprise Remare, whose eyes remained fixed on Kristoph, so she figured he'd already suspected they were the organization behind the attack. Dane and she had researched the former hate group, but Miranda thought they had disbanded.

"You should have contacted me sooner." Remare rose. "As soon as you heard this."

"And would my calls have been returned?" Kristoph narrowed his eyes, and then, Remare and he exchanged words in their language. She could only guess the content of their conversation. Kristoph ran a hand through his luxurious mane of hair and nodded in agreement to whatever Remare said.

"We're done here," Remare informed her as he turned to leave. Miranda wasn't so sure and wondered what else Kristoph might tell her if she stayed alone with him, but from the look on Remare's face, now was not the time to push.

"It was a pleasure meeting you." Kristoph stood, took her hand and kissed her knuckles. "I hope we meet again someday," he smiled seductively up at her, "under different circumstances."

As soon as they said their goodbyes and Kristoph closed the door, Miranda felt an odd sensation low in her belly, like butterflies taking flight. She dismissed it, thinking it was due to being in the presence of a vampire who had a lot of sex. Vampires denied they had any special pheromones they used to attract humans, but she often wondered if that was completely true or the vampire version of political correctness.

When they were alone in the elevator, she breathed deep. Her pulse was quicker than normal, and her skin felt clammy. When she glanced down and then at Remare, he was sporting an impressive erection. So, she wasn't the only one affected by the seductive vampire. *Yeah, right, no pheromones!*

When the elevator doors opened, Miranda inhaled the fresh air, and the distance from Kristoph's apartment seemed to help.

"I'm going back to ValCorp. Do you need a lift?"

She wasn't about to get in closed quarters with Remare after what she'd just felt. "I could have used one the other night," she muttered.

Remare narrowed his eyes, stayed silent for a moment, then said, "Suit yourself." When they were out on the street, he turned to her. "I don't have to tell you everything concerned with vampire business is confidential."

"Unnecessary. I won't say anything. As usual." As he walked to his car, Miranda admired the sleek black Mercedes SUV and ran her hand over the hood. The car was chic, elegant and powerful—like its owner. "Tell me something, though." She met his dark eyes as he opened his door. "What did he do?" When Remare just looked at her, she asked, "To lose his status? What did Kristoph do?"

Remare tilted his head and smirked. "He woke up in the wrong bed." He nodded to her, then closed his car door and drove off.

Miranda watched as his car disappeared into traffic and wondered whose bed Kristoph had woken up in. A strange set of erotic images danced in her mind. One particular image was intensely graphic, and she raised her eyebrows in surprise, but dismissed it due to her overactive imagination.

However, the butterflies in her lower belly returned.

And brought their friends.

Chapter Twenty-Six

When Miranda opened the door to her house, she noticed two things: One, *when did we get a new alarm system?* And two, the butterflies in her belly were now dancing to a very erotic beat—one that would not be denied. Orion walked out of the kitchen, eating a sandwich, his long black hair still wet from his shower. Barefoot and shirtless, he was wearing a pair of low riding jeans he hadn't bothered to button at the top. The Were had a six-pack to die for and was throwing off some serious heat.

Orion had been her friend and roommate for years, and she'd never reacted this strongly. *What the hell is going on?* His muscles rippled as he walked toward her then she heard a low growl.

Laughing, Orion set his sandwich down on the hallway table. "Well, that's a first. I can't remember you ever growling—even when you saw me naked at Werehaven."

She tried to keep her face from flushing. "Did you install an alarm system?"

"No, I thought you did." He removed an envelope from his back pocket and handed it to her. "Aiden and Bastien showed up with a work order, saying it was pre-approved and paid in full."

Miranda opened the envelope and read the note. *"A gift for protecting Nick. The city is far too dangerous for a single woman. –R"* It also said if she ever had any trouble, the system would notify ValCorp, then send someone over or notify the human police, her option.

"Is everything all right?"

She glanced at the windows with the silver line of security and the panel to the right of the door. Exhaling deeply, she shrugged. *Too late, now.* But she was going to have a long, serious conversation with Remare.

"Aiden said the system came with a password. It's on a delay, but you usually have only thirty seconds to re-set it or the alarm sounds at ValCorp."

She growled when she read Remare's password. If she wasn't blushing before, she was now. *Twisted son of a bitch, isn't he?*

"Miranda, I need to know the password so I don't trip the system when I come in late." Orion took another bite of his sandwich.

Glaring, she handed him the letter and went to take a long, cold shower. Halfway there, another wave of lust hit her that had her bending over. "Orion, I'm only going to ask this just once...and I would appreciate an honest answer." Keeping one hand on her stomach, she straightened and took a deep breath. "Do you paranorms have pheromones?"

Orion's eyes sparkled as he grinned and then re-set the password. "You've been around us for how long and you're just getting around to asking that, now?"

Miranda narrowed her eyes at him.

"Of course we do." He exhaled, then sobered. "But they only work on members of the same species, not on humans. I thought Lizandra or Dane would've told you that by now." Orion tilted his head then sniffed the air. "Who've you been in contact with?"

Remembering Remare's warning, she chose her words carefully. "A vampire. A very sexy vampire who I think broke one of Valadon's rules." She peered up at him. "What about vampires?"

Orion took a deep breath as he leaned his shoulder against the wall and exhaled slowly. "Well...they *say* they don't, but you know every vampire is different. Each has their own unique gift. I've heard some vampires can seduce humans by scent alone for their blood as well as for sex."

"That's illegal. One of the laws Valadon was adamant about was that vampires couldn't use their powers on unsuspecting humans."

"You and I both know not all vampires obey the laws." Orion appeared thoughtful. "Besides, there are humans who frequent vampire clubs for just that purpose." He ran his hands through his mane of dark hair. "They want to be seduced. I wouldn't exactly call them unsuspecting." His back straightened. "Who tried to seduce you?"

"Have you ever heard of a vampire who lives on the East Side named Kristoph?"

He shook his head. "Never heard of him."

"He's a high-priced escort who caters to both sexes."

"Miranda, what the hell are you doing with a professional?"

"Not what you think." She returned his look of agitation. "I merely went there to follow up on a lead."

"There sure seems to be a lot going on around here. Red Claws poaching on our territory, a vampire kid almost gets mauled by a couple of punks, and you all of a sudden get a new alarm system." He stood with both hands on his hips. "Mind telling me what the fuck's going on."

Miranda wanted to unload all the crap that was going on around her, but she'd given her word to Valadon and Remare she wouldn't speak of vampire politics. She was about to give him a watered down version of events when a blast of heat shot up her spine and had her clutching the wall.

"Oh, that's fucking great! He sexed you up, didn't he?" Orion frowned. "You're going to need sex real soon, Mira. The hunger pains don't stop. They only increase."

"What do you know about it?"

"I know heat when I see it. And right now you're giving off a lot of it."

"Gonna take a cold shower. That should ease it." Miranda turned for her room. Orion was a friend, and friends didn't jump each other's bones. At least not in the *Book of Miranda*. In her book, there were certain lines you didn't cross. Jumping your roomie for a quickie was seriously in the *"Do Not"* column. And if she stayed there any longer with him, she would do precisely that.

"Not really," Orion muttered as he reached for his phone and made a call.

***

Tapping his index finger on the steering wheel, Remare waited in his car, pondering his next move. The investigation was progressing smoothly. Irina was on assignment with an important member of the HOL. Insipid humans may vocally despise vampires, but fucking one didn't seem to be a problem. On the contrary, some humans lusted for vampires, were easily seduced by the very thing they professed to hate. Irina could hide her fangs very well, and her mark would never know he'd been with a vampire. She enjoyed the control factor, liked being on top, playing with her prey before she pounced. His cat—who had very sharp claws.

Tristan was meeting with Zoe one last time to obtain whatever information she had. It was a difficult position Tristan was putting himself in. Dealing with former lovers was never easy. Remare laid his head against the head rest and closed his eyes. He exhaled deeply and allowed the memory of one beautiful, raven-haired vampire to surface. *Vivienna*—the one woman who had nearly brought him to his knees.

Unfortunately, Tristan didn't have Remare's experience and had looked pained at the prospect of meeting with Zoe again, but if there was the slightest chance she knew something about the attempt on Valadon, he had to see it through.

Bastien and Gregori were checking on their sources and putting the heat on Stryder. Remare smiled and considered paying a visit to his former nemesis.

The others were pursuing their leads. In time, someone in the HOL would get sloppy and make a mistake. It seemed they had already made one. How stupid for a prominent member to allow himself to be overheard in a sensitive conversation. Remare would have put a serious hurt on any of his own people if they'd been so careless. He exited his car and crept along the shadows as he entered the apartment building.

"Well, this is a surprise. Two visits in one day." Kristoph, dressed only in a pair of black silk pajama bottoms, opened the door for Remare. When he tried to flick the lights on, Remare stopped him with a hand on his wrist.

Remare inhaled the scents in the room. No humans were present. "Off night for you. I would have thought you'd have had a client this evening."

"My usual canceled at the last moment. Some sort of family emergency. Hard for the wife to sneak out for a quick bite when one of the kids is home sick with a fever." Kristoph grinned as he went to his bar, lit a candle and poured a drink. "Can I get you something? I have a very good merlot here."

Remare nodded as he peered out the window scanning the shadows. "Have you learned anything else since we spoke?"

"It's only been a short while." Kristoph drank his wine as Remare moved silently through his apartment. "I told you as soon as I do, I'll contact you." He handed Remare his drink and reclined on his sofa.

Remare sat across from Kristoph and observed the handsome vampire; his affairs and skill in bed had been legendary. But after seducing a prominent member of the house, Valadon thought he'd outstayed his welcome. At the time, Remare didn't think there were ill feelings on the part of the amatory vampire, but perhaps he'd been wrong. "Do you miss it at all?" When Kristoph cocked his head in question, Remare added, "Belonging to a house."

Kristoph sipped his drink. "I suppose at times, I do," he said quietly. "But I have freedom now I didn't have before. I come and go as I please and bed whoever I choose." He shrugged. "I don't have to answer to anyone, anymore." He made himself comfortable on the couch by tucking one leg under the other and began circulating the wine in his glass. "Why are you asking me this?" He met Remare's eyes. "You didn't come all the way here just to reflect on old times."

Remare smiled and dismissed his doubts. "No, I didn't. I came to ask you about some of your more illustrious associations while you were at Valadon House." He sipped his wine, never taking his eyes off Kristoph. "In particular...Mulciber."

"Mulciber, the old one," Kristoph snorted with a vague disgust. "He's still alive, then? What do you wish to know?"

"Do you remember who he associated with when the European Court last visited?"

"What's the old fool done, now? Of all my former lovers, I detested him the most."

Remare raised an eyebrow. "Why did you sleep with him if you hated him so much?"

Kristoph shrugged. "Like so many, he made promises, empty promises." He sipped his wine. "Ennui seemed to raise its ugly head, and I looked for variety to break the dreaded malaise. Mulciber was a brief interlude, one that I regretted. I can still feel the scars on my back. And other places where he played." Kristoph put his wine down. "Why do you want to know about Mulciber? You were there in the house; don't you remember who he was with?"

Remare remembered much, but he wanted confirmation. "Refresh my memory."

Kristoph leaned his head back and closed his eyes. "There were many. But his favorites included Calisar, Tobias and Merlinder. What of it?"

"I was curious." Remare narrowed his eyes. "And at Valadon House, who was he with the most? Who did he share you with?"

"He enjoyed many in the court, females and males. I don't remember him having a preference. He did enjoy his group sex, though." Kristoph drank more of his wine. "Did you know he procured my services to teach his daughter about sex when Persephone was young and then watched as we fucked?"

Remare wasn't surprised and had his own spies watching the ancient's movements. Mulciber had become too vocal criticizing Valadon's protocols and personal life that closer scrutiny was warranted. "Was there any one person who Mulciber seemed to have more conversations with? Someone he seemed to spend more time with?"

Remare watched as Kristoph searched his face, trying to discern exactly what he was after. He knew Kristoph wanted to taste him, but that was one pleasure currently unavailable. One of Kristoph's faults was that he was attracted to powerful men. A flaw that had cost him dearly.

Kristoph asked, "Why the interest in Mulciber?"

"Let's say...he's become a person of interest."

"I'll say." He smiled at Remare and stretched out on the couch, reclining on his side, giving Remare a good look at his body.

Remare wasn't interested. "One other question. Why did you ask to meet with Miranda Crescent? Anything you had to say to her, you could have said to me."

"Jealous?" Kristoph laughed. "She's intriguing. A human." Kristoph seductively lowered his eyelids. "When I saw her picture with Valadon, I wanted to meet her. Valadon doesn't take many human lovers." He leaned on his elbow and softened his sultry tones. "I was curious. Aren't you?"

Remare's eyes wandered over Kristoph's body and was amused at his meek attempts at seduction. He even considered the possibilities; perhaps that would ease the edginess that had been plaguing him. Kristoph was incredibly handsome; some would say beautiful. In some ways, Kristoph reminded him of Irina. Both could be highly seductive, were talented in the bedroom, but Irina was far more dangerous.

"Professor Crescent works for Valadon. I would not involve her in any more discussions concerning vampire business."

Kristoph glanced at Remare's hard-on. "Is that impressive salute for the human or someone else?"

"I'm sure you already know the answer to that question."

"As you wish. But you have to admit, she's nothing like his former lovers. Having met her in the flesh, I can understand Valadon's attraction to her."

"Leave her out of this; she's Valadon's concern. Not yours." Remare rose to leave.

"But you're interested too." Kristoph added, "You're unusually tense tonight."

"There's been more than usual activity at ValCorp." Remare wondered how much Kristoph knew of the happenings at the compound and if he'd been holding back.

"You could stay. I could...lessen your tension." He glanced down at Remare's crotch.

Remare wondered how much further he would take this flirtation and noticed Kristoph's arousal. "A challenge then?"

"If you want." Kristoph grinned up at him. "For old times' sake."

Remare smiled. Like a cat.

Chapter Twenty-Seven

Orion gazed upon Miranda's nude body and frowned. "Miranda," he said softly as he sat on the bed beside her and stroked her hair. "You don't have to suffer. I called Lizandra; she's sending Gavin over with some meds that'll take the edge off."

Miranda shuddered at Orion's touch. As expected, the cold shower did nothing to lessen the sexual hunger pains, and alone time with a vibrator hadn't decreased the desire; it had only intensified the need. She was aroused and going to stay that way until she found satisfaction.

"I can relieve the pain. It's only sex." Orion's hands fisted. "If I ever find the vampire who did this, I'm going to take a chunk out of that male's hide and show him what damage a Were's fangs can do."

Miranda seriously considered his offer. She gazed into his bright blue eyes, a combination of sympathy and male edginess. Of course, they could have sex. Orion was one of her closest friends and one of the handsomest men she'd ever met. His perfectly sculptured body was a work of art. She shook her head. When it was over she wouldn't be able to face him. "Could you dim the lights? My eyes seem to be more sensitive than usual."

"Sure." When the doorbell rang, Orion threw a sheet over her and left to answer it.

"Hey, Miranda." Gavin entered her bedroom, the scent of her arousal clear to everyone. "Orion said you met a vampire seducer." He grinned whimsically. "The good news is the effects won't last forever."

She smiled up at Gavin. She'd always liked him and considered him a good friend. Lizandra was lucky to have found her red wolf. He was the strongest in the pack and a natural born leader. Together, they presided over a clan that had become her family. "Hi, Gavin. Nice to see you. Now, when can I expect this to pass?" Finally, her hormones subsided, seemingly knowing not to respond to her best friend's lover.

"Depends." He sat on the edge of the bed. "Tell me exactly what the vampire did to you."

Miranda couldn't remember Kristoph pulling on her psyche. Valadon had outlawed mesmerism, but that didn't mean some vampires didn't try.

Gavin glanced at Orion, who stood leaning against the doorway, and then back at her. "Miranda, I hate to ask, but did you sleep with the guy?"

"No way! I just met the vampire. I was only there to ask him some questions."

Offering her comfort, Gavin stroked her arm. However, as soon as he touched her, her hormones spiked, and she groaned. Realizing his mistake, Gavin quickly moved away. "Miranda, this could be dealt with easily," he said encouragingly. "Orion or I could take care of it. We'd be gentle. Won't you let either of us try?"

They were discussing sex with her like they were talking about removing a splinter. She growled. "Not happening! Now, tell me what meds Lizandra sent, and why she didn't come herself." Miranda could have used her best gal pal right about now. If anyone was an expert on sex, it would be Lizandra. Though, Cyra would've been a good choice, too. But she nixed calling her, thinking she'd get Valadon involved, and that was the *last* thing Miranda wanted.

"She's busy with an injured Were, but sent over some tranquilizers she said would knock you out." Gavin sat by her side again. "You have to tell me what the vampire did, though."

"The only thing Kristoph did was kiss my hand when I was leaving." She peered up at them as they straightened their spines. "What?"

"By any chance, did he cut you with one of his fangs?"

"No. But I think he got cute and licked between my fingers." A look passed between the two Weres. "Tell me."

Gavin breathed deep and exhaled. "Vampire saliva is very potent. I think he purposely sexed you up, but what his intent was as you were leaving is beyond me. Obviously, he didn't arouse you for himself. Was anyone else with you at the time?"

She was so going to kill Kristoph the next time she saw him. Vampire games. Some vampires loved to do idiotic little things like this to humans simply because they could. But why he'd want to cause trouble between Remare and Valadon was beyond her. "Leave me," she muttered as she turned over and closed her eyes.

"Okay, I'll leave the tranqs with you and get some water." When Gavin returned, he placed two pills on the end table with the glass of water. "Take these if the pain gets unbearable."

After they left and shut the door, she gritted her teeth as another wave of heat spiked through her. Sweat was already dripping off her face. Lust was a powerful emotion, but even more potent when denied. Liz was going to laugh her head off when Miranda told her she felt like the female equivalent of a male when he had blue balls. *Pink balls!* That's what she had— pink balls. "You are so losing it, girlfriend," she said in a ragged whisper.

"You're losing what, gorgeous?"

Miranda swung around, relieved to see Dane closing the door behind him. She reached up to hug him and gave him a long, thorough kiss. "I thought you were away on a business trip."

"I just got back. Orion told me what happened. You should know better than to hang out with vampires, especially professional escorts," he teased as she pulled him down on the bed.

She was happy to see her California Boy. Some men were drop dead gorgeous, had boyish charm or dripped sexuality. But none possessed the grace of Dane. "Be with me."

"I intend to." He grinned sexily as he undressed, letting his clothes fall to the floor and slid beside her.

Miranda couldn't get enough of seeing him nude. Matisse, an artist famous for his nudes, would've had a field day, she laughed silently. Her hands drifted up his back, delighting in the smooth texture of his skin, then buried her face in his neck and breathed in his luscious masculine scent. A deep purr of female satisfaction escaped her throat.

Dane held her close and kissed her slowly, dancing the dance of tongues. He laughed when she tumbled him beneath her so she could have the top position. Miranda laughed, too, as she held his face and kissed the hell out of him, then her tongue traced circles down his body.

Miranda did things with her tongue to drive him crazy, and she knew the one place where he was especially sensitive. She moved farther down his torso, tracing her movements with her hands and looked up to see his warm smile. It undid her every time. She stroked the muscles of his thighs, then cupped him, and bent down to take him in her mouth, rocking his world.

"Oh, no, you don't. Tonight's about you." Dane lifted her up, flipped their positions and kneaded her breasts, kissed them reverently, and drew circles with his tongue around her nipples.

Miranda made sounds in the back of her throat she wasn't sure she was capable of. Truly, she'd been hanging out with Weres too long; she growled like them, she chuckled. When Dane slid his hand between her thighs, she finally felt some semblance of relief. Then, he positioned himself above and slowly penetrated her, watching her eyes as her breathing became ragged.

She fell apart. God, how she needed this and thought how sex gave people the ability to realize their inner animal, to acknowledge their most basic instincts, to act without cognizance. Sex was raw, primal, something humans retreated from when it got too dark. But with Dane, the connection was there. She moved her hips in sync with his movements, giving and receiving pleasure as his natural heat enveloped her—warming her body and her soul.

Instinctively, she knew why Weres howled. It was an affirmation of being alive. Miranda felt the pressure building, her body winding tighter and tighter until she shouted loud enough she was sure Orion would come running to see what was wrong. A few strokes later, Dane growled in glorious passion, his muscles taut as his shoulders bunched. Before collapsing, he rolled them onto their sides.

"Hey, you're not falling asleep on me, are you?" He smiled down on her.

Miranda smirked. "I was thinking about it."

"Don't. I brought you back a present, but my legs are too tired to move, right now."

She looked at him questioningly.

"You forgot already." He laughed. "The files you wanted on the HOL. I dug a little deeper and found some interesting stuff."

"Oh, that," she muttered as she snuggled closer, thinking Weres made the best blankets. "It can wait."

"Okay, but I want to hear what you've been up to. Incubus vampires are nothing to fool with."

"Not sure he was an incubus. Some vampires have more talent in seduction than others."

Dane lifted up on his elbow. "Why'd you go see him?"

"Information only. Gavin thinks I went there for sex. Ha! So not my type."

"From what I hear, you've been spending a lot of time with the vampires. Especially their leader. What's going on with that?"

"I don't know." She gazed up at him. "I really don't. Valadon likes me. I can't understand why when he has a whole court of beautiful females."

"As if you're not a looker. So, how do you feel about him?"

"I'm not sure. The truth, he scares the hell out of me. He's very powerful." *Too powerful.* "Sometimes, when we're alone and he forgets to mute himself, I can feel ripples of it against my skin." Miranda rubbed her arm. "It almost burns. It's scary knowing someone has that much power and can unleash it, anytime." She saw Dane was listening intently. "He's been kind to me. Hell, he bought me ten pairs of shoes." She laughed. "He even named a chocolate store after me."

"Well, then, it must be love if there's chocolate involved." Dane grinned at her. "You going to see him again?"

Miranda gave him the lowdown on what he missed, ending with Valadon's job offer, and it helped clarify her thoughts.

"I think you're right, and the vampires are dangerous. I'm not liking this Mulciber person very much, and you need to stay away from him. Completely."

"I agree, absolutely. Valadon promised he would take care of him if I returned to ValCorp." She snuggled closer. "So, what do you think, should I take it? He made a very lucrative offer."

"How lucrative?" Dane asked as he played with her hair.

"Very."

He glanced at her. "How badly do you want it?"

"Honestly? Part of me wants to jump at the chance to research his paintings. Dane, it's like a whole undiscovered country down there—a fantastic new world just waiting to be explored. But, part of me feels that if I do, I'll be getting sucked more into the vampire world. I don't know how much deeper I can go."

Dane continued playing with her hair. "Well, if you decide to do it, I think you need to set boundaries. Like making sure you have a guard with you, at all times. Be in constant communication with Cyra or any other vampires there you trust. Make sure you're never left alone. Do phones even work that far down?"

Miranda smiled at Dane's protective streak. "Yes, they do. They have their own communications network and security cameras all over the place." Much of what he was saying had already crossed her mind. She'd mention it the next time she met with Valadon.

"I have some news of my own to share." He tenderly stroked her arm.

She looked up at his solemn brown eyes. "What is it?"

"I'm thinking of relocating back to California. My family's out there, and I could spend more time with them."

Miranda was saddened by his admission, but remembered he'd mentioned moving back once before. She searched Dane's eyes and sensed he had pretty much made up his mind. She'd miss him terribly and had a terrible feeling in her gut he wouldn't be around much longer. "I'll miss you when you're gone." Feeling her skin turning cold, she braced her arms around his back and hugged him tightly, relishing his warmth.

***

Remare watched as Kristoph pretended to sleep. He'd almost been tempted to take Kristoph up on his offer, but when he had entered the bedroom, he'd felt nothing remotely arousing. Kristoph could put up a good façade about being happy in his independence, but Remare knew, once a vampire belonged to a house then found himself on his own, it was a hard life to live—especially for vampires who lived for centuries.

He'd wondered if Kristoph knew more than he'd initially told him about Mulciber and the others in the courts as well as in Valadon House, but he could detect no subterfuge. And Remare was quite good at navigating through various layers of deception. For all of Kristoph's bravado, he *did* want back in Valadon House. The friendships forged between house members were precious and what helped vampires endure very long lives, especially through dark times. Something Gabriel would soon learn.

"You never stop thinking." Kristoph opened his eyes and smiled up at Remare.

"Rarely," he exhaled slowly, "but I do. I have to get going soon."

"You looked tranquil when you were talking before. You always exude such razor sharp intensity, it was good to see you relaxed—even if it was only for a fleeting moment. You inquired if I was content with my decisions, but I never asked you the same question."

"Am I content?" Remare didn't need to think about it. "I'm not discontent. Why do you ask?"

"Because, you're not happy. I can see it in your eyes, hear it in your voice. It's subtle, and you take great pains to hide it, but I see it, and I'm surprised no one else has."

This was a subject Remare wouldn't discuss with him or anyone else. "I think you over-analyze. All vampires who live long enough go through periods of reflection."

Remare made a motion to get up, but Kristoph grasped his arm. "I'm glad you came tonight, and I wanted to tell you that you're welcome in my home. Anytime."

Remare saw the hunger in Kristoph's eyes, a longing he could never answer and felt pity for the once fun-loving vampire who may have experimented far too much with his indulgences. Some vampires became addicted to experiencing new things, new depths. They traversed such far distances they forgot who they were and could never get back to who they once were. He thought Kristoph such a vampire. "I'll be in touch." He rose to leave and walked to the door.

"If I remember anything else, I'll contact you directly." Kristoph strode from the bed and followed him to the door. "Give my regards to Valadon and to Brandon; I hear he's back."

"He is. There will be a party to celebrate his return sometime soon." Both men glanced at each other in mutual understanding: Kristoph would not be receiving an invitation.

Kristoph rubbed his neck. "You asked me about Mulciber and his many flings. I almost forgot about Brandon." He shrugged. "But I guess you already knew about him."

Remare's blood turned to ice. "What did you say?"

"You asked me who else Mulciber brought to our bed. Who was one of Mulciber's favorites. Brandon was one of them."

Chapter Twenty-Eight

"And get the volume on Asanti; I want to learn more about him," Miranda called down from the upper balcony. She had set up her work space on a large oak table near the entrance to the archives. That way, if anyone bothersome showed up, she could make a quick exit. "And the codex on the seventeenth century." She enjoyed researching Valadon's collection, and working with Nick made the work even more pleasurable.

He went through the stacks quickly and thoroughly sorting through the countless volumes. She wondered how many years Nick spent down here learning their history.

Miranda studied the life-sized portrait of his mother and wondered if Bianca had loved art and books as much as she did and that was the reason Valadon had hung her portrait in the archives. Nick resembled her with his dark hair and fair complexion. But it was those bright eyes and gentle smile that bonded the two together. She pondered what kind of woman Bianca had been and if she shared her son's zest for life.

"Found it. I'll be right up." Nick smiled up at her from the first floor. Miranda grinned at his boyish charm. When he got older, he'd have a slew of girlfriends, especially if he resembled his debonair uncle. Even without the family resemblance, Nick was stunning, and the fact that he was totally oblivious to his appeal made him all the more alluring.

Miranda told Valadon she'd work on the third floor, but going down to the first floor was not an option; therefore, Nick was dispatched to run down and locate any items she needed. She had tried to find some of the sources through computer databases, but none of the books she needed were online and, according to Valadon, *"never would be"*. These were his personal treasures and would stay that way.

When Nick came up with the books, he laid them down on the table and watched her work. "Professor Crescent, I don't want to interrupt you, but can I talk to you, for a minute?"

"You're not interrupting me. You know I always have time for you, Nick." She stopped reading and looked up at him. "But, as I've told you before, I'm only Professor Crescent at the university; anywhere else, it's Miranda." She removed her glasses and pointed them at him. "Now, say it."

"I just wanted to ask you a question, Prof—eh, Miranda."

"See, that wasn't so hard."

"Don't you think Valadon's being unfair? Why shouldn't I be allowed to socialize with whoever I want? I'm almost twenty-one, and he associates with all types of people, so I don't know why he got all in my face about it."

Miranda didn't want to get involved in family issues, especially vampiric affairs. The Weres were her friends, but she'd learned never to get involved in clan business, unless they directly asked her opinion. She exhaled. Valadon and she were becoming close, and she didn't want to jeopardize their budding friendship. "Did you talk to him about it?"

"He doesn't listen." Nick rolled his eyes. "He commands." When Nick saw her wry expression, he softened. "All right, he doesn't command. He just sets down the rules like I'm still a child or something."

In the eyes of the older vampires that was exactly what he was—an infant, but a youth on the verge of manhood. But what a man he would be in a few short years. "Then, what you have to do is make him listen," she explained. "Don't go in there all hot-headed; go in with a clear head. Speak to him intelligently and calmly." She smiled knowingly at him. "He might surprise you."

"Okay, I'll try to talk to him, again."

Miranda felt the hairs on her arm raising in awareness of a vampire's presence—one far more powerful than Nick. His pitch distinguishable from all others.

"I see you two are getting along well." Valadon's deep voice penetrated the air as he came beside her. "You've been working for hours. Nick, why don't you take a short break and find the professor something to drink?"

When Nick looked at her, she thought she could use a soda. The climate-controlled area was good for the books, but made her throat dry. "I wouldn't say no to a Pepsi."

"You got it, Miranda." Nick winked at her as he left.

Valadon sat beside her. "How's he doing?"

"He's a kid who got caught being out when he wasn't supposed to be. How would you feel?" Then, a thought entered her mind. "Can you remember that far back?" *Oh, yes, that filter of hers went off duty again.*

"Yes, I can remember that far back." He arched a brow as he smiled. "And I would not have been caught doing something so stupid."

Miranda put her chin in her palm as her elbow anchored the table. "What, you wouldn't do something so dangerous, or you wouldn't have been caught doing it?"

"Both." He laughed. "And, if I did go into dangerous territory, I wouldn't have gone alone, like he did."

She liked that they were becoming friends and felt comfortable in his presence; although, as reassuring as he had been about the lower levels, she still felt inhibited to go down there. "As long as you're here, I was wondering if you could answer a couple of questions regarding a few of the paintings on the lower level."

"Of course, which ones interested you?" He clasped her hand as he led her to the staircase and held it as they descended.

"There's a painting down here of a European court, but I can't figure out who everyone is, despite the volumes and histories Nick explained to me."

Valadon let her go as they reached the second level. "Nick has been well-educated, but I don't think he knows everyone who was associated with the courts of Europe." As they neared the lowest level, he asked, "Which one caught your attention?"

Miranda walked to the wall with paintings of groups of people dressed in fashions of the seventeenth century and stopped in front of the one that had piqued her curiosity. Most of the subjects in the composition they'd been able to identify, but there were a few neither Nick nor she could find information on. "Who's the man with the long blond hair talking to the man seated at the table?" She thought she knew who he was but kept that information to herself.

Valadon eyed the painting. "Oh, you found Guy de Montglat; he was ambassador to the French court in the early part of the seventeenth century. I believe he's in a few of my paintings." He led her to where Montglat was in another painting. This time, his hair was dark and cut short, and his clothing more in fashion of the latter part of the century. In yet another painting, he wore a finely trimmed mustache and beard. "Guy changed his appearance as often as he did his name. He had several that he went by." Valadon paused and ran his forefinger over his lips. "But, if memory serves, he was mostly known by his nickname."

Tilting her head in question, Miranda peered up at him.

"*Le Cameleon.*"

"The Chameleon." Guy was able to change his appearance so meticulously that if she hadn't been studiously examining the paintings for other details, she wouldn't have known it was the same vampire. So, this was who he'd been in a different life, in a different era. Valadon knew him as Montglat, but Miranda knew him simply as...Blu. She'd given her word to Felicity and him that she wouldn't reveal his presence in New York and intended to keep that promise. As long as he posed no threat to Valadon.

"Yes. Even though his title was that of ambassador, he was actually an agent for our monarchy." He murmured, "And a very good one at that. Our leaders only called upon him when the missions were the most dangerous. King Savinien had once called him the best spy the realm ever had."

"What became of him? There's no record of him in any of the books."

"There wouldn't be. His identity was kept secret for political reasons." Valadon seemed to reflect. "Some say he went to ground, to sleep so to speak." When Miranda gazed at him in puzzlement, he said, "Old vampires, such as he, may go through periods of...unease—times of melancholy or ennui after living for centuries—and shut themselves up in seclusion away from the rest of the world." Valadon became pensive. "Others think he was killed on a mission to one of the Eastern Courts. I prefer to think he went under."

Oh, he went under, all right. A lot closer than you think! Miranda finally posed the question she'd been hesitating in asking. "Was he a friend or enemy of yours?"

"That would depend on the century." He smiled at her. "Sometimes, we served the same ruler; in other eras, we served opposing leaders." Valadon seemed lost in his reminiscences. "I don't remember him ever being an adversary, though."

Miranda let out a breath she hadn't realized she'd been holding, relieved to know Blu wasn't Valadon's enemy. As they strolled companionably through the archives, she asked questions about some of the other figures in the paintings, and her comfort level with him increased. Any reservations about being on this level dissipated.

"Have dinner with me, again, Miranda. I enjoyed our last evening out, and I find conversation with you...endearing." He held her eyes as he spoke. "Are you free tomorrow night?"

"Actually, I have a hot date with a very handsome man who plans to do very wicked things with me," Miranda said impishly. When she heard the growl and saw his expression, she laughed. "Jordan, my boss, is making me go to a fundraiser with him. He knows I detest those events and doesn't trust I'll show up on my own. I have to be on my best behavior and *'play nice with the museum's benefactors'*."

"Ah, I see." He looked disappointed. "Perhaps one night next week."

She nodded.

"If it hadn't been for Mulciber, would you be this hesitant with me?"

Miranda was surprised he felt that way about her; she hadn't realized she was being reticent. "We come from different worlds, Valadon. All that you've shown me," she said as she waved her arms around the library, "it's new to me."

"It doesn't have to be. I like sharing my world with you and would like to show you more." He linked their hands and stroked her fingers with his thumb.

She felt the heat rising in the temperature-controlled room, and suddenly, the open space of the library seemed diminished. "You're a wealthy entrepreneur, successful, handsome." She searched his eyes. "You could have any woman you want. Why would you want me?"

"Such innocence," he whispered. "Do you still not know me?" His voice was deep, sensual.

Miranda's heart began throbbing and she started searching for the nearest exit. Things were heating up too fast, and she needed to leave before he overwhelmed her.

Valadon put a hand on her arm to stop her departure. When she pulled away, he let her go. "Why do you flinch at my touch? You know I would never hurt you."

Her breaths intensified. It was impossible not to react this way in close proximity with the most virile, sensuous vampire on the planet. She couldn't look at him; if she did, she'd be sucked into a world she couldn't comprehend and had no business trespassing in. He could possess her, envelop her in a passion that would consume her.

People who thought vampires were just humans with fangs were so wrong. Vampires have an animal magnetism, an instinct that screams primal that humans had never acquired or could hope to possess. Miranda's sensitivity to the pitch vampires vibrated at sang loudly in her ears. Valadon's otherworldly abilities were bleeding through, and she felt like a fly caught in a spider's web.

She knew she shouldn't look. To be captured in a vampire's eyes was the stupidest thing a human could do. She knew better, but God, she wanted to see, needed to see, what was in those turbulent sea green eyes of his. Eyes that held a profundity of knowledge, a dark carnal awareness no human could ever fathom. Miranda was held captive by all that she saw and when he bent to kiss her, she felt herself drifting on his sea of passion and returned his kiss. Lost in a world she knew nothing about with nothing to anchor her. When Valadon lifted her hips on the work table and ground himself between her thighs, she felt her body shuddering in painful awareness. He pulled her closer so she could lock her ankles in the small of his back. The darkness in his eyes was impenetrable. Fathomless. Sensual. Deadly.

"Miranda, we were out of Pepsi, so I brought you a Dr. Pepper," Nick called from outside the door. The veil of shadows that had darkened her desire lifted, and Miranda pushed Valadon off her and sat up, taking deep breaths to steady herself. In a display of power, Valadon raised his hand, then shut and locked the door, effectively keeping Nick out. Miranda was almost alarmed at the speed of his mental command and the effect it had on her body as every hair on her skin rose in caution, her body knowing it was in the presence of a powerful predator. She wondered at the dire possibilities if he ever unsheathed the full scope of his power.

"This isn't over, Miranda," he said as he straightened his clothes, his turbulent eyes never leaving hers.

She was afraid to answer him, knowing she was in over her head. Moments ago, she had been content to walk alongside him, discussing history and art. Now, fear clawed at her. No one should be able to overwhelm another like that.

Passion that strong could destroy a person, and Miranda didn't want to dance with that particular dragon.

Chapter Twenty-Nine

The night of the fundraiser Miranda was tempted to cancel, but Jordan Knox was generous in allowing her flexibility in her work schedule and didn't make too many demands. She hated playing dress up for New York's elite, but for Jordan, she'd endure the tedium and serve as a public relations liaison for the museum. She checked to make sure she had her migraine medicine. Whenever there was a disturbance in atmospheric pressure, she'd suffer from brutal migraines. Lizandra called her a human barometer, able to sense approaching storms.

After what happened in the archives with Valadon, Miranda could still feel his sizzling kiss, she needed some time around humans.

When Jordan arrived in his dark three-piece suit, he looked stunning. He was the epitome of the handsome, sophisticated, mature male. Jordan was tall, in his late fifties, but kept himself fit and was in better shape than many men half his age. Even with his gray hair, he made a formidable sight.

Jordan kissed her temple in greeting, glanced at her ponytail and tried to hide his disapproval. "Have you ever thought of letting your hair down at one of these occasions? You really do have lovely hair."

Miranda smirked at Jordan's disdain for her style. Knox was old school, but basically, he was a decent man and a good friend. "I like my hair up; otherwise, I'm constantly fussing with it." She slanted him a look. "When did you become so interested in my hair? You only ever said I had to *attend* these functions, nothing about my appearance." She knew she could get away with teasing him. Sometimes, she thought, it just clicked between boss and subordinate, and the work environment benefitted. Otherwise, it just flat-out sucked.

"I think I pay you enough for you to have regular visits to the salon," he muttered.

When Miranda reached for her dark-rimmed glasses, he said, "Tell me again why you never wear contacts?"

"You know I'm allergic to contacts. Besides, wearing glasses gives me the impression of being scholarly. You want me there for my intellectual appeal, remember." Miranda laughed at

Knox's frustrated expression as she gathered her wrap and the
tiny purse with the thin shoulder strap. "I'm ready."

Jordan was unusually quiet during the ride to the home of
Mr. and Mrs. George Ormont III, one of the most elegant town
houses on the Upper East Side, with a spectacular view of
Central Park. The floor was a checkerboard of black and white
polished marble. But the centerpiece of the home was the life-
sized portrait of George Ormont I hanging on the wall near the
elaborate staircase. Miranda was familiar with the portrait as
well as several other paintings in the Ormont home.

Celeste Carson Ormont, simply known as Cee Cee, acted as
hostess at some of the museum sponsored luncheons. Tall and
slender, she claimed she never dieted to maintain her svelte
figure. Miranda wondered if that was true, or due to the
handsome man across the room, Dr. Elijah Stevens, one of the
best plastic surgeons in New York. Cee Cee had a gleaming mane
of white hair she kept to just below her shoulders. Some less
than merciful friends said it was to hide the surgical scars.

If all smiles and social niceties were with the wife, George
Ormont was all business. Miranda couldn't remember a time
when Ormont wasn't wearing a scowl. Like his wife, his hair was
white, but thinning, unlike his wife, Ormont needed to lay off the
scotch and see a nutritionist about his growing paunch.

Miranda meandered around the crowd, sampling a canapé
from the servers who circulated throughout the magnificent
home. Observing the fashions of the uber-wealthy, she wondered
if any of the guests were daring enough to wear a Cesare. She
peered down at her Gia Bellini shoes and smiled; only a woman
designer would know how to design comfortable evening shoes.

When Sylvia Rogers signaled to her, Miranda smiled and
went willingly. Sylvia was a no-nonsense woman who was
married to Andrew Smith Rogers, a transportation tycoon. Sylvia
had many idiosyncrasies, one of which was that she didn't feel
the necessity of using a filter to express her opinions. *Sylvie* was
in her seventies and was one of those women who always
grasped your arm when she talked and walked with you. "And
you know we have that beautiful ranch in Scottsdale right near
the golf course Andrew loves so much, and still, he can't find the
time to take a decent vacation."

Miranda thought she was being helpful when she asked,
"Why don't you go yourself?"

Sylvie tossed her head back and laughed. "Andrew would
miss me too much."

She smiled at the older woman, who always had an arcane
intelligence in her gray eyes. Sylvie liked to put on a façade of

being old and feeble, but Miranda knew the woman to be sharp as a stiletto.

"Whatever happened to that nice young man I sent your way?"

Miranda arched a brow. "He already had a partner—a *male* partner."

Sylvie shrugged. "I thought he might know some nice men for you to meet."

As if on cue, a strikingly handsome man made his way toward them. The tall, platinum blond man was one of the most beautiful males she'd ever met and carried himself with the self-assurance of a man who knew he was blessed by the gods. With his high cheekbones, full lips and green eyes, Jason Morgan was a media favorite, often photographed with the most gorgeous women.

But tonight, he seemed to be alone. Always with a perpetual grin, he took his good looks in stride. Miranda had once nicknamed him *Peter Pan*, because of his constant party-going. However, she knew his flamboyant lifestyle was just a cover for an intensely shrewd businessman who worked with his semi-retired father in running the family business.

"Sylvie, you're looking spry as ever." Jason bent and kissed Sylvie's cheek.

"And you're as charming as your father; where is the old fox? I thought he'd have been here by now."

Wilson C. Morgan was one of wealthiest financiers in NYC. Of all the museum's benefactors, Miranda liked the octogenarian the most. Morgan enjoyed intelligent discussions about art, culture and politics. The fact that he was fabulously wealthy didn't seem to detract from the man himself. With others, it was their calling card.

"He had some late calls to deal with, but he mentioned for me to say hello to both Rogers." Jason shifted his eyes. "Miranda, always a pleasure to see you." As Jason hugged her, he whispered, "We need to talk."

Andrew came to collect his wife, and the men discussed business for a while. When she saw Sylvie giving her the eye and nodding at Jason, Miranda rolled her eyes.

"You're not getting any younger, Miranda, and that caboose of yours isn't getting any smaller," she whispered loud enough for all those in the vicinity to hear.

"Thank you for your *astute* observation, Sylvie."

After the Rogers left, Jason smirked and led her to the bar. "Can I get you a drink, Ms. Caboose?"

Miranda stifled a growl and grinned. "Sure, Peter Pan. Any chance you might have a beer in there?" she asked the bartender.

Jason left a hefty tip and said, "Make it two."

They carried their drinks out on the balcony. Even though it was a chilly night, Miranda didn't feel cold. Something she attributed to hanging out with the Weres for so long.

"You're looking handsome as always, Jason." She sipped her drink. "Now, you mind telling me the real reason your father didn't come tonight. He never misses these events."

"Well, when you reach the age of eighty, you never know when a party is going to be your last, so you make sure you attend as many as you can." Jason casually leaned against the side of the building and sipped his beer.

"Is your father all right?" Miranda asked with concern.

"He's fine," Jason said reassuringly. "It really was just business tonight." He tugged a strand of her hair. "You should give him a call. He enjoys discussing art with you and has his eye on a new acquisition."

She chuckled. "Aren't you afraid he'll try to set us up again?"

"I think he's given up on me and the prospect of any grandchildren." A rare look of disappointment surfaced then quickly disappeared. "So, tell me, how did you wind up dating Valadon?"

Miranda grunted. One lousy photograph on social media and the whole world thought she was Valadon's mistress. "We had dinner out." She glanced at him and then up at the night sky. "It really wasn't anything...special." *Why am I explaining myself?* "I authenticate his art; he has quite an impressive collection, you know."

"I'll bet. The media implied romance." He sipped his drink. "Just how involved are you with the vampire leader?"

"You never cared before who I dated; why the sudden interest, now?" An uneasy sensation grew in her gut. Jason was never possessive toward her; if he was asking her these questions, he had a good reason.

"You never dated a vampire before." He seemed pensive. "Do you know what you're getting yourself into?"

Miranda scrutinized his eyes and sensed no jealousy, not that she'd expected any. "It was just one date." *And one incredibly sensual kiss.* "Did your father put you up to this?" One of the reasons she liked the elder Morgan was that, when the vampires came out, he was one of the first to do business with them; images flooded her mind of Morgan and Valadon shaking hands at one function or another. Other images came to mind of corporate leaders who wanted nothing to do with Valadon or his vampires. Their expressions of condemnation had been evident.

"He's concerned about you." Jason's voice sounded whimsical. "You know you occupy a soft spot in his heart."

Miranda agreed. "I know."

"They're not like us, Miranda. Sure, they look like us, but there's something fundamentally different."

She sensed he was holding something back. "I thought you and your father were friends, business acquaintances of the vampires."

"We are. I have nothing personal against them. Many of my business transactions with ValCorp have been very profitable. But, we're not talking about just any vampire. Hell, they call him the vampire king." Jason rubbed the back of his neck then turned her in his arms to face the French doors. "Take a look inside, Miranda. Those men in there, the ones you've done validations for, been to their homes, had lunch with their wives, worked in their offices. Do you think they're happy that you're dating one of their strongest business competitors? A vampire?"

She wondered why the guests had been socially polite but made little or no attempt at conversation. Usually, they tried to impress her with their knowledge of art. If one or several of the board members resented her dating a vampire, they could make serious trouble for her at the museum.

She glanced up at him with concern. "What are you saying?"

"I'm just saying be careful. Know what you're getting into." He pointed at the room with his chin. "There are many people in there who never accepted the vampires. Never will. Sure, they attend many of the same functions, shake hands in public, put up a good façade for the media, but underneath it all..." He shook his head and frowned.

Miranda thought it was time she had a long talk with Knox. If any of the board members had issues with her, he'd know. "I'll consider what you said." She smiled up at Jason. "Tell your father I appreciate his concern. Maybe I'll have lunch with him sometime soon."

"I'm sure he'd like that." Jason peered over her shoulder into the room. "Now, if you'll excuse me, I have to talk to someone." He grinned at her. "It was good seeing you, again, Miranda. Be safe."

She watched him weave his way through the crowd. Then gazing up at the night sky, she breathed deeply. It was soothing being outside inhaling the cool, woodsy scent of Central Park, seeing the trees swaying in the wind. She fondly remembered a line from Whitman's poem, "When I Heard the Learn'd Astronomer," about the night air being mystical and smiled. Whitman had always been a favorite. After a while, Miranda decided to go back inside.

After circulating around the main rooms and nodding to Jordan, who was in his comfort zone discussing business with several of the men, she was ready to call it a night. However, before she left, she wanted one last look at the Ormonts' Van Gogh.

Miranda slipped upstairs for a private viewing of the prized painting and casually wandered the long hallway, admiring the paintings. When she was near the end of the hallway, she paused to study the Van Gogh, admiring the brush strokes and the pigment variations. Something about the painting caught her eye: A trick of the overhead lighting. Van Gogh used variations of gold and burnt sienna colors in his composition. His rich colors were a trademark, but for a moment, one of the golds appeared more yellow in color than what she knew it to be. Must be the lighting; she shrugged.

Then, she heard voices coming from the closed doors of the library. Normally, she'd ignore anything she overheard in the homes of the patrons, but what she heard made her listen closer.

It was a decision that would change her life.

Forever.

Chapter Thirty

"How many of us suffered a major financial hit because his business empire has grown too powerful?" an angry, bitter man asked.

"Some of us more than others," the one next to him sneered.

Another shouted, "My company nearly went bankrupt because of him. I want him dead!"

"When are we going to move on them?" a man asked the people seated around the library—a room where access was granted only to an exclusive group of people, individuals who had great influence and shared similar beliefs. "I warned you this would happen. Years ago! I told you then, if we let him live, he would amass too much. You should have listened to me, then!"

"We *have* moved on him in the past, but our attempts have been thwarted. Don't worry; we have plans already in motion." The person seated behind the mahogany desk spoke in confident tones that hinted of his cultured background. "He won't survive the next attempt." The Regent silently approved of those around him whose ire had risen to where he needed it to be. Alone, he couldn't carry out his vengeance, but with their combined resources, success was attainable.

An older female cried out, "I want something done about the vampire who debased my daughter! Before we move on Valadon, I want assurances he will pay for his impertinence!"

"Your daughter isn't the only one who's been sullied by a vampire. He's of little consequence." When The Regent saw the rising hostility in the woman's eyes, he added, "He will be taken care of; you have my word. As will the others."

"When?" asked the dark figure in the corner.

"Soon. Our spy tells us they've been on high alert since the last assassination attempt, and it's not prudent to act hastily." The Regent rose and put a hand on the woman's shoulder. "But Valadon's days are numbered." He stared into the eyes of the one vampire present, and smiled with a hint of wickedness. "Or should I say nights."

***

Miranda struggled to listen through the solid oak door; she couldn't make out everything being spoken, but what she heard terrified her. *This can't be right.* Maybe a television was playing—anything to not have this be real. She shook her head, waiting for her brain to reconcile what transpired. But in her soul, she recognized the hatred for what it was.

When she realized the meeting was breaking up, she quickly moved to the stairs. Hearing the door opening, she prayed no one had seen her. As she descended the stairs, she felt eyes on her. Someone was at the top of the staircase watching her. *No, don't turn back! Just walk, don't run.*

Miranda made it to the foyer, graciously said good night to a few patrons, and asked a server to get her wrap. She tried to be inconspicuous as she chatted up a few people near the door, glad she'd kept her purse with her. When the server brought her wrap, she casually turned and peered up at the top of the stairs.

Her heart went into her throat.

Jim Scherer was there watching her, and he didn't look happy. Scherer was a bodyguard for one of the patrons; her mind was racing so fast she couldn't remember which one. He'd always made her spine shiver. There was something cruel in the way he smiled. She made eye contact only for a moment but knew, in that instant, he knew she'd been upstairs. She turned and quickly walked out the door.

Miranda flew down the few stairs to the street and then ran to the corner to hail a taxi. This was Fifth Avenue; there should be cabs all over. Of course, the one time she needed one, there were none in sight. She scanned the avenue to see if any were coming and decided not to hang around. Heart pounding, she sprinted to the next block, hoping to see one, but all the cabs driving by had occupants. Then she spotted Scherer's head with his buzz cut, surrounded by two others, and took off.

She thought about running into the park, but since Werehaven was on the west side, if she was overtaken in the park, no one would hear or see until it was too late. Panting now, she put more speed into her strides. When she saw all the lights up ahead, she realized she wasn't far from the Plaza Hotel on Central Park South. There were usually dozens of taxis in the vicinity. She was finally able to hail a cab that was dropping someone off. She rushed in and rapidly told the driver to take her to ValCorp.

The driver asked in a Mid-Eastern accent, "Why go to the vampire building at this time of night? Tourists usually only visit there during the day."

Miranda growled. *"Do I look like a freakin tourist?"* She glanced at his license on the visor, his name was Abraham. "Listen, Abe, there's an extra twenty for you if you can get me there ASAP. I'm late and should have been there hours ago. It's important, okay?"

"Okay, miss." Abraham swiftly swung into traffic, dodging the other cabs and one irate buggy ride driver.

Clutching her stomach, all Miranda could think of was how fast Abraham could get them to ValCorp. She wished the damned horse and driver in front of them would move faster. Miranda liked animals, really, she did, but if it came down to her or the horse... Okay, she wasn't going there. *Nice horsey, but move your damned ass!* Breathing hard, she turned around and tried to spot if anyone was following them, but there were too many cars.

When the cab driver turned south down Seventh Avenue, Miranda yelled, "It's too slow!"

Abraham quickly replied, "There's traffic at Columbus Circle," then he swiftly cut across and headed to the West Side Highway. Miranda held on to the chicken strap as Abraham careened around cars at an alarming speed, and hoped he didn't get them into an accident on the way. When they sped past the Javits Center, she spotted two cars behind them circumventing the traffic the way Abe was. She knew she was in trouble. "Abraham, I have another twenty if you get us there in the next five minutes."

"Not possible, but I get you there in ten." He smiled at her, then hit the accelerator, and they went flying down the highway.

Just get us there in one piece! He flew in and out of the traffic. They passed the exits for the meatpacking district and then she used the phone Valadon had given her and pressed the speed dial for him.

She reached Remare, instead. Her heart was pounding. "Remare, I need to speak to Valadon. Put him on, now."

"Valadon is indisposed, right now, and unavailable to take your call," Remare said in a bored voice.

"Put him on, now!" she screamed. "I'm in a cab on West Side Highway coming to you. There are men in two cars following me. I need to speak to Valadon. It's urgent! I think they're HOL."

Remare sounded incredulous. "And you're bringing them...*to us?*"

She heard him utter an expletive as he hung up. *Son of a bitch!* Was he going to help her or not?

When they passed the sign for the Holland Tunnel she knew they were not far from ValCorp. She checked the rear window again. The cars following them were inching closer. *Fuck!* Her heart hammered in her chest; they might make it to ValCorp, but she was never going to make it up the stairs to the compound. Before the taxi pulled up to ValCorp, Miranda peeled out four twenties and stuck them in the tray. Then, she removed her shoes, thinking she could run faster with them off.

When the cab came to a screaming halt, she jumped out and heard the screeching tires of the cars following them. She didn't bother looking back but sprinted up the stairs and across the front area of the building. She saw Remare's smirk as he stood behind the glass doors.

Goddamnit! He wasn't going to let her in. *I'm so coming back from the grave to haunt your sorry ass.* She glared at him as she felt the men closing in behind her. The bastard was actually going to throw her to the wolves.

At the last moment, Remare opened the door, swung an arm out to catch her, and tossed her behind him. He then sneered at the armed men who had pursued her. Through the glass, he said in a loud, commanding voice, "You are on vampire property. Cease your pursuit and return to your vehicles or your refusal will be seen as an act of aggression."

Scherer and his friends stood their ground, animosity etched deep in their faces. Miranda wasn't waiting for them to open fire and decided to get out Remare's guns. She ran her hands up and down his back and sides.

Remare turned his head slightly back toward her. "Is there a reason why you are feeling me up?"

"Where the hell are your weapons?" Miranda said breathlessly, her heart thundering as she stayed behind him.

"Search lower." He smirked as he pulled her arm around his waist and casually stroked her hand.

Miranda dug her nails in his waist and would have slapped him on the side of his head, but at the moment, he was her shield. She held onto him to steady herself as she put her shoes on, then slowly peered around his shoulder to see what was going on.

"Look up," he said as he gestured outside and caressed her hand. "Who needs weapons...when you have an army?" He tilted his head to glance at her, his lips only a breath away from hers.

The Torians were stationed along the perimeter of the building. There were twenty or thirty guards with weapons drawn. She recognized Morel's voice as he said, "Continued refusal to vacate the premises is in violation of code. Further delay will result in apprehension and detainment for questioning."

Scherer raked her with a scathing look and smirked. Miranda felt the kiss of evil.

The sneer he gave Remare was hardly amused, but Remare tilted his head as if to say, *"Anytime you're ready. Bring it on."* The two of them would fight to the death if they could reach each other. Then, Scherer's men put their weapons away and turned to their cars. Scherer was the last one to turn and mouthed, *"You made a serious mistake. Too bad you won't live long enough to regret it."*

She exhaled a ragged breath. It was too late to think about consequences. There'd only been one decision, anyway.

Remare faced her. "I suppose...you will now have to prove him wrong."

Miranda heard the elevator ding and turned to see Valadon striding quickly to her. She ran to him, grateful he was alive and uninjured. After what she heard tonight, knowing he was safe gave her some semblance of peace. She relaxed into the safety of his arms, breathing calmly as she wrapped her arms around him and let his body cool down her overheated one. When she glanced at Remare, she saw him staring at her with a look she couldn't comprehend...and then, it was quickly gone.

"Let's get her upstairs to my office," Valadon said in his deep authoritative voice.

Remare nodded, turned to briefly confer with Morel, and then escorted them up in the elevator.

Chapter Thirty-One

"I never eavesdrop on conversations when I'm evaluating a work of art. I don't consider it professional. But when I heard your name and the words *'assassination attempt'*..." Miranda exhaled deeply. "I tried to catch as much of what they were saying, but through the oak doors, I was only able to hear bits and pieces."

Remare heard the anxiety in Miranda's voice and poured her a glass of Cabernet. Stealthily, he observed Miranda and Valadon as he cut his index finger with his thumbnail and let a few drops of his blood fall into the wine glass. His blood would soothe her stressed nerves due to the trauma she'd just experienced. And admittedly, he was curious to see what her reaction would be to his blood.

Miranda graciously accepted the drink from Remare, briefly meeting his gaze, before she sank farther into the plush couch. He studied her as she drank the wine.

Valadon rubbed her neck. "Take your time, Miranda." His voice was soothing, hypnotic. "Try to remember anything you think might be important."

"There were several voices—three males and one female; though I think there were more in the room." She gazed at Valadon with a searing concern in her eyes. "There was hostility in all of them; I think that's what made me listen initially. Their anger was palpable."

Remare watched as Miranda rubbed her arms as if her skin had become infected with their rank animosity and finished her wine. "They fear you, Val. They *really* fear you. I heard one of them say you were becoming too powerful." She set her empty glass down on the coffee table. "But overall...I had the impression it wasn't so much that you're a vampire...as it is you're their strongest competitor."

"In any business venture, when one becomes more prominent, there are always a select few who will try to subvert the one who is more successful." Valadon met Remare's eyes. "This isn't the first time enemies have conspired against me."

"You have to do something about this, Valadon. You didn't hear those men." Miranda stood and paced. "Make them understand you're not a threat. Something. They're going to use the fact that you're a vampire against you."

"Oh, we'll do something, Mir-randa," Remare said as he felt his eyes darkening. "We always do." He smiled appreciatively, pleased that the wine had no ill effects on her. He wouldn't tell her how they planned to deal with their enemies or that they already had a good idea who worked against them. His spies were already placed in the organizations that were most suspect. Valadon hadn't risen to his current status by being unprepared for those who would see him vanquished. Miranda would be surprised at the extent he had gone to in the past to protect his people and all that he had built.

"We've survived threats for eons, Miranda," Valadon reassured her. "We'll survive this, as well."

"I've been wracking my brain trying to remember who was missing downstairs." Miranda continued pacing. "There was one voice." She rubbed her forehead as if trying to remember. "He was so arrogant, so calm, where the others were enraged." She stopped pacing and looked back at Valadon. "I think he hates you the most. Whoever he is, he's intelligent, calculating; it came through in his voice. He was playing on their fears, using their animosity to unite them. To use them against you."

Remare scrutinized Miranda as she gracefully paced, analyzing the information she'd overheard. He respected her intense concentration, appreciated the way her mind worked, but what he admired most was her courage. She'd risked her life to inform them of what she'd overheard.

"We'll get a list of all those in attendance tonight." Valadon rose to meet her eyes as he massaged her shoulders. "We'll figure this out and deal with it. For tonight, I want you to stay here. We have plenty of bedrooms below." When she shook her head, he added, "Just for tonight. Until we sort this out."

"No." She was adamant. "It's not necessary. I have an alarm system in my home."

When Miranda gazed in his direction, Remare nodded with a slight glint in his eye. She still hadn't forgiven him for the password.

"I'm not going to hide here like some scared rabbit. I have a life to get back to."

"Miranda, it's for the best." Valadon softened his voice as he stroked her arm in an effort to comfort her. "They know you overheard them and may try to use you to get to me."

"No. I'll be careful. I'm not going to let them make me live in fear."

"It's not fear, Miranda, but caution. I can protect you better here."

"No! If you want to send a couple of guards to watch over me, fine, I'll accept that. But I'm going home tonight. Besides, it's not me they want. *It's you.*"

Remare viewed their interplay with interest. Valadon was correct; she'd be better off here. ValCorp was like a fortress, not only with their private security force, but they had the place electronically wired for any threat. Except for the one flaw in Valadon's office that was now corrected, the place was impenetrable.

Valadon tried to reach out to her. "Miranda, be reasonable."

"No. I'm leaving. You can assign a few of your men to stay at my place. That's the most I will agree to." She squared her shoulders. "I won't live in a cage."

Valadon seemed taken back by her words. ValCorp and Valadon House were anything but cages. She turned to leave. *Stubborn*, Remare thought, *very stubborn.*

"Don't leave without your guards."

"Two. No more."

"Agreed." After she closed the door behind her, Valadon said, "Put Bastien and Gregori on her. Tell them they are to stay with her. She is never to leave their sight until I say otherwise."

Remare texted accordingly; when he was done he rose to stand near his friend. "She's very headstrong."

Valadon grinned. "Like you."

Remare smiled. *Yes, she is.* "Do you think it wise to become any more involved with her?"

"Do you finally trust her? Now, that you've seen how far she's gone to warn me?"

Remare was becoming more confident of Miranda's character, but *trust*? That was not something he gave easily. "I don't think what I feel matters." He sighed. "But you, my friend, now have a vulnerability. And...our enemies are aware of it."

"I know." Valadon exhaled as he perused the city below from the shadows of the window. "Have your people reported in?"

"Yes. The investigation is progressing," he affirmed. "We'll have the information we need shortly. Irina is close to finding out who in the HOL has been plotting against us. She should have a name for us soon. The others have been diligent in securing other aspects of the investigation. Tristan will meet with Zoe one final time, and Bastien and Gregori have their people strategically placed in Nightworld."

"Has Kristoph learned anything further?"

"I was on my way to meet with him again and will do so." Remare turned to leave, but Valadon stopped him.

"Tristan knows this will be the last time he will see Zoe?"

Remare briefly glanced down. "Yes. Yes, he does."

***

When Miranda and her guards reached her place, both vampires surveyed the area up and down the block, checking rooftops and parked cars. Gregori entered her home and checked the rooms as Bastien stayed with her while she reset the alarm, swearing to come up with a new password. She was glad for their presence. Scherer's cruel smirk had gotten to her, even though she recognized the scare tactic for what it was. Bastien seemed a bit uneasy with too much energy to burn. He kept looking at her like he wanted to ask her a question, but then would shake his head and remain silent. Gregori was more reticent, yet she felt relaxed in his presence and sensed both vampires had her protection as a priority.

Orion had left a message saying he would be staying at Maxine's place tonight, and Miranda felt a pang of jealousy that he'd found someone comfortable enough to spend the night with. She was happy for them. But tonight, she'd wanted to talk with Orion and was disappointed he wouldn't be home.

Miranda pointed to end of the hall. "There's a spare bedroom there if either of you want to get some sleep. Bathroom's across the hall." She gestured to the twin couches in her living room. "Or you guys can crash in here."

Gregori said calmly, "We don't sleep when we're on duty."

She nodded. "Kitchen's down there, if you guys get hungry; help yourself to anything you find in the cupboards. I might have some beer in the fridge."

Bastien looked like he was ready to get himself one, but Gregori said, "Thank you, but don't worry about us. Why don't you get some sleep, Professor Crescent? You look like you're about ready to drop."

She was too tired to tell him to call her Miranda, so she said her goodnights and went to her room, where she slumped onto the bed. She wasn't sure she'd be able to sleep as wired as she was, so she took some calming breaths and tried to put faces to the voices she'd overheard at the Ormonts'. But the emotional exhaustion overwhelmed her, and soon, she was asleep.

Miranda didn't get more than a few minutes sleep when she woke with a start. She kept replaying the voices in her head, hoping to make some connection with their faces. Every time she thought she could almost picture their faces, the images dissipated. She rose, went to her computer and pulled up the files Dane and she found on the HOL and started researching key individuals.

After a while, Miranda's stomach growled, and she realized, except for a few *hors d'oeuvres*, she hadn't had dinner, so she decided to check the fridge for leftovers. She paused at her door when she heard how rapt her guards were in the hockey game.

Bastien kept his voice low. "While you're up, get me a beer from the fridge."

When Gregori found the six pack, he took out a couple and joined Bastien on the couch. "Who's winning the Rangers game?"

"Score's tied. Buffalo's playing hard, though." Bastien sipped his beer. "So. What do you think of her?"

"She looks tired."

"I can see that, but what do you think? It's not often Valadon takes an interest in a human female."

Gregori stretched out his legs. "He never takes an interest in female humans."

"He doesn't seem to take an interest in any of the females at ValCorp, either."

"He's busy." Gregori drank his beer.

"He's always busy, but still, he should take some time for himself."

They watched as a skater on the Rangers broke away from the other players, dodged a hip check and skated in for a goal.

"Pass it, pass it to him!"

"No, skate it in. Skate it in!"

"Yes...yes...yes!" Bastien let out a howl as the Rangers scored and the players surrounded the guy, congratulating him as they rubbed his helmet.

"Okay, your turn to check the upstairs," Gregori said. "She's got a rooftop garden, so you might want to check that, as well. I'll text Aiden and give him our status."

Bas nodded and went upstairs.

As Gregori lowered the lights in the living room and peered outside from behind the curtains, she decided to make her presence known. "The Sabres have a tight defense, but the Rangers have a better offense."

Gregori turned to face her. "Our shooters are better, but Buffalo's got a good goalie."

"True, but not as good as ours."

Managing a half smile, Gregori nodded.

Miranda sat in the corner of her couch and wrapped her arms around one of her pillows. "I couldn't sleep. I was researching the HOL and other organizations. You guys have quite a history."

Gregori grunted. "You don't know the half of it."

"I don't understand how you survived through it all." She studied his face. She couldn't say he was handsome, his features were too rough, but he had a masculine confidence she found attractive. Right now, he was scrutinizing her. Probably deciding how much he could trust her.

"We're a strong race. We had to be."

"But how were you able to survive? I mean, for centuries, you stayed hidden. How was that even possible?"

"We adapt to each era we live through. Vampires are great at adjusting to new surroundings. We also chose our leaders wisely: Valadon is one of the best."

Miranda didn't doubt that for a moment.

"We also had great allies." Bastien walked back in the room.

The younger vampire radiated at a higher pitch than his partner. Miranda sensed his curiosity; it emanated just as his hyperawareness of his surroundings did. Even when he was standing still, some part of him was always in motion, whether it was his fingers tapping on his hips or the movement of his eyes. He certainly was handsome with his finely chiseled jaw and high cheekbones. Like his partner, he had dark hair and dark eyes, but his complexion was fairer.

"I bet you did." She tucked her feet in closer to her body so Bastien could sit. "Do you know why Valadon assigned you to me tonight?"

Gregori answered, "He said you were followed by some unfriendlies, and you might receive some unwanted visitors tonight."

Miranda gave them the rundown of the night's events, hoping to earn their trust. These two vampires were putting their lives on the line for her. *Why would they do that? If not for their loyalty to Valadon.* When she finished telling her tale, she saw Bas' breathing had sped up and Gregori's spine had stiffened.

When they remained silent, she asked, "What can you tell me about the HOL?" A look passed between them. She was getting good at knowing when they were conversing silently. "I took a bullet for your boss. Okay, it was a dart. But I did protect him. Can't you share just one bit of information?"

Finally, Gregori relented and leaned forward putting his elbows on his knees. "I'll tell you this much: they were the hatemongers who called for our internment. If they had their way, they would have tried to wipe our race from the planet." He paused to watch her eyes. "We've been living among you for centuries and never caused any harm."

"If harm was done, it was perpetuated by the Rogues, not us," Bas added. "Most vampires are non-violent, but members of the HOL launched their campaign against us, amping up the fear humans already had from reading too much fiction."

"But what about now? I'd have thought those hate groups petered out in the last two decades."

Gregori raised an eyebrow. "After what you overheard tonight, you can ask that?"

Miranda knew there were people who'd use fear as a tool for personal gain. After a moment had passed, she felt guilty for taking them away from their home. Surely, they had friends or family they'd much rather be with than babysit her. They should be at ValCorp.

And the only way that was going to happen was if she went with them.

"We can't tell you more about the HOL because there are still active investigations going on." Gregori walked to the window again and peered out. "You should ask Valadon your questions."

"You don't think we're safe here, do you?" For the first time, she thought coming here was a mistake.

Bas smirked. "Gregori likes to be thorough. You asked how we survived this long," he said as he passed her to join his partner. "We watch each other's backs."

Miranda was charmed by the two vampires, and the guilt kicked at her. "You two should be home with your friends. Not here." She gazed in the direction of her bedroom. "Give me a minute to pack a bag. Let's go back to ValCorp."

Gregori nodded his head in agreement. "That's a good idea. You'd be safer there."

***

As he approached the door, Remare smelled blood—vampire blood. His fangs lengthened in anticipation. He reached inside his jacket and removed his Glock. He sniffed the air and knew humans had been here: two, maybe three from their scents. Nearing the door, he noticed it wasn't completely shut and surveyed both ends of the hall. Slipping inside, he shut the door behind him. The scent of death and bloodshed was overwhelming. He knew before he saw the body that he was dead; the pool of blood beneath him had spread too wide.

The vampire could have healed some of the wounds on his body, but not all of them, not at the same time. Not with all the silver shards implanted in his skin. Whoever had done this had done a thorough job. Remare exhaled deeply as he bent down to hold his friend's head in his lap. There were multiple lacerations on his beautiful face, arms and legs. Remare removed the metal shards from his face, not minding the minor burns on his fingers, and placed them in a handkerchief. The bastards had tortured him before killing him.

Remare growled and vowed he would mete out the same pain to Kristoph's murderers. They would learn just how severe vampire justice could be.

A low groan escaped Kristoph's lips, and Remare quickly cried out his name.

"Hello, old friend." Kristoph's eyes opened, and he managed a somber smile.

"Don't talk. Just drink." Remare attempted to cut his wrist with his thumbnail, but Kristoph stopped him.

"Don't waste your blood. I'm already dead." He barely managed to speak in a hoarse whisper. "My brain is just refusing to follow my body."

Remare considered all the inflicted injuries. "I can remove the silver. With my blood, you could heal the wounds."

"No. The gashes are too severe." Kristoph pushed his robe from the lower half of his body to show what had been done to him. "As powerful as you are, I don't think your blood could heal this."

Remare's spine stiffened at the damage that had been done. With steely eyes, he asked, "Who did this?"

"I'm sorry, I didn't think to ask their names when they started eviscerating me."

"Kristoph." Remare tried to lift him, but Kristoph moaned in pain. "Drink, I can get you to Valadon. His blood will heal you; you can still have a life."

"A life without fucking?" He started coughing. "I'd rather not."

Remare sensed Kristoph's essence slipping away and gripped his hand. He was barely hanging on now as it was. "The men who did this to you. Did you know any of them?"

"No. But they asked a lot of questions." He coughed and still managed a smile. "You can tell Valadon I didn't reveal any of his secrets. That should make him happy."

Remare knew Kristoph wasn't going to last much longer. "Tell me what they looked like."

"Humans, they had dark hair and eyes; one was taller than the others." He coughed again, and blood spilled from his mouth. "No discernable marks. But one had a buzz cut and a sneer that would do our kind well."

Scherer! Remare would hunt the bastard down and make sure he suffered the most.

"They asked...about your lady friend, Miranda."

Remare tensed, and then held Kristoph tighter, willing him to hold on longer. "What did they want to know? What did they want with Miranda?"

Kristoph looked up as a tear escaped his eye. "They asked about her relationship...with Valadon." More coughing as blood poured out of him. "They wanted to know...how long she'd been...spying for him." Kristoph closed his eyes in pain and exhaled, then gazed up at Remare. "Keep her safe." A weak smile. "She's...yours." A last glimmer in his eyes, his words barely audible. "Would Valadon...have truly...taken me back?"

Remare didn't have time to answer him as the light in Kristoph's eyes faded away. He put his hand over Kristoph's eyes and gently closed them. "Yes," he murmured, "he would have. I'd have seen to it." Remare kissed his friend's forehead, then rose to find a blanket to wrap his body in. He would transport Kristoph's body back to ValCorp himself.

But first, he would tear the place apart, looking for any records the humans would have missed. Remare's breath grew cold. Revenge would come swiftly to those who dared to challenge him.

He could be very creative when it came to dispensing pain.

And very patient.

Chapter Thirty-Two

Miranda thought she'd have to fight Gregori for her backpack as he insisted on carrying it. She won the argument by refusing to let go of the strap. It was either let it go or wrench her arm, and that wouldn't go over well with their boss. Once inside ValCorp, both vampires seemed to breathe easier. During the elevator ride, she convinced Bas to let her off at the infirmary because she'd forgotten her migraine medicine.

Gabriel was transfixed in front of his computer. He reminded her of herself when she did chemical analysis of pigments. Both of them became oblivious to the outside world and wouldn't notice if there was some sort of calamity going on. Though in his case, she sighed, that had already happened.

When data surfaced on his monitor and the results were obviously not what he expected, Gabriel howled in anger and looked like he was about to sweep everything off the table in frustration. Miranda decided to make her presence known. "Don't you ever sleep, doc?" She tilted her head and smiled.

Breathing heavily, Gabriel turned and inhaled her scent, as if it were a balm to his aching soul. "What are you doing here?" His golden-brown eyes roamed over her, as if making sure she was unharmed. "Valadon told me what happened. I thought you went home."

"I did." Miranda slid her backpack to the floor. "But I couldn't see making Gregori and Bastien babysit me any longer." She strolled around his lab table, inspecting the contents of his experiments. "Not what you wanted, I take it."

"Not hardly." Gabriel watched her wander around his lab, and Miranda sensed the predator in him was alive and well. "Brave girl to go to Valadon with what you overheard. Another person would have walked away."

"I'm *not* another person." She always detected a restlessness in Gabriel, but underneath his detached persona, she glimpsed a man with a good heart and, at times, even a sense of humor.

"No. No, you're not. But why are you here? Don't get me wrong... I'm glad to see you, but dawn can't be far off."

Miranda sensed his nervousness when she was around and thought him adorable. She continued circling his lab and found an old bookcase with an even older volume of medicine. She showed it to him.

"It's an antique." He shrugged as he ran his hand through his hair. "I don't know why I keep it here."

But she did. It was one more tie to his human life. She opened up the old text and flipped though the faded pages.

Gabriel gently closed the book and replaced it back on the shelf. "This is one volume of a whole set of old medical textbooks." He exhaled and murmured, "From long ago. The rest are downstairs in the archives."

Miranda hadn't seen them when she worked down there, but then again, she hadn't looked for them, either. "I had a terrible headache before. I was hoping you had migraine medicine." She continued meandering around his lab. "I think it's the stress."

"Seriously. I wasn't kidding before when I called you brave." He opened one of his cabinets and retrieved a bottle of tablets. "I think you're incredibly courageous for what you did." He hesitated, then turned. "Thank you for telling Valadon. It will help with the investigation."

Gabriel was a fascinating study in contradictions: At times, he sounded remorseful when he talked about Valadon and being turned vampire. Yet, he still possessed a solid sense of loyalty. She guessed the bond between vampire and progeny was strong. She accepted the pills he offered. "Gabriel, what do you know about the attempts on Valadon's life? Do you know much about the HOL?"

"Sure, every vampire does."

Miranda was surprised at his phrase of words.

"I'm on the periphery of the investigation. If you want to know specifics, you'd have to talk to Remare; he's heading it. As for the HOL," Gabriel shrugged, "they were big about twenty years ago when we first came out. I haven't heard much about them since. You think they're involved? That the men you overheard are part of it?"

"It's possible. The overall sense I had was that it wasn't some impromptu meeting." Miranda concentrated more on her impressions than the men's words. "The group inside the room were familiar with each other. Familiar enough to divulge their hatred."

When she yawned, he led her to one of the beds in the recovery area and sat her down. "You should get some sleep."

"I've tried. It didn't work. I think I need to go over everything first. Rehash everything in my brain so I can just...let it go. Does that make sense?"

Gabriel rubbed his neck. "I'm not sure what makes sense, anymore. Let me get you some water for those pills; it'll help you sleep." He went to the cooler and then handed her a cup of water. Concern etched his face. "Miranda, do you realize how dangerous a situation you may be in, now?" He sat on the bed nearest her.

She swallowed the medicine. "You didn't see the bastard who chased me. I'm well aware I made myself vulnerable." She yawned again, but quieter this time. "But I couldn't just walk away. Valadon had to know." She shifted to her side, thinking maybe she could organize her thoughts better if she was relaxed.

"Yes, he did." Gabriel yawned and leaned against his elbow for support. "Remare won't give up until he's found everyone involved in the assassination attempt. He's very determined."

"Was Valadon able to access the list of attendees at the fundraiser tonight?" she asked as her mind slowly drifted.

"Aiden was working on it earlier."

"What about the poison in the dart?" Miranda's voice was beginning to sound gravelly and felt the medicine taking effect. "Anyone able to trace where the compounds came from?"

"All I can tell you is that they're working on it. I gave the report to Valadon, and he assigned his agents to track it down." After a short silence, he said, "You know...I have my own bed in the back room. You'd probably be more comfortable there."

"Troublemaker." Miranda smirked. *Oh, yeah, that would go over well with Valadon—her in another man's bed, in Valadon's own house!*

"Could be." Gabriel grinned back as her eyelids lowered. *His Angel.* He closed his eyes as he laid back, wondering how big a fool he was to let himself grow fond of her. Of all the women he'd known in the last century, why was she so *damned* easy to be around? He turned to study her and was half determined to scoop her up and put her in his bed, but she hadn't come to him for sex.

He wondered if one day she would.

***

Valadon paced his room, waiting for Miranda. *How damned long did it take to get aspirin?* Bastien should have stayed with her. Valadon thought he'd been plain enough to his Torian that she was to be under constant surveillance. He called his communications room and reached Aiden, who informed him the last they'd seen of her was when Bastien had escorted her to the infirmary.

Fine, he would go himself and see if she was still there. He didn't get very far when he ran into Remare in the hall. From the look on his face the news wouldn't be good.

***

Bastien wrapped a towel around his waist after finishing his shower. Tonight had been interesting in getting to know Valadon's girlfriend. She'd been intriguing, asking questions about their enemies, and he found himself beginning to trust her. Valadon was acutely perceptive and a good judge of character, so...if Valadon trusted her, he would, too.

As he entered his bedroom, he sniffed the air and knew exactly who was between his crimson silk sheets. He turned and said, "Hello, Persephone."

"Hello, Bastien." Persephone dropped the sheet covering her breasts as the towel around his hips fell to the floor. She purred in appreciation as his cock bobbed as he walked toward her.

Persephone was the picture of any man's wet dream with her long blond locks, seductive smile and voracious appetite for sex. With all the energy he'd been building up the last few days, he needed a vent for all that vigor just itching to get out. As if in agreement, his cock jerked upward as if saying, *what are you waiting for? Go!*

It had been too long since he had a woman and he'd have to reconsider how much time he spent in the training facility working his muscles until he was sore. He liked the pain; it made him feel alive. When it came to sex, Persephone also enjoyed a little pain—the giving as well as receiving.

As he climbed on the bed, he pushed the sheet away and covered her body with his. He savored the taste of her lips. She met him stroke for stroke with her tongue and ran her sharp nails down his back. By morning, the scars would heal, and the sheets would have to be changed. When he pulled up from the kiss, her hands slid over his shoulders and down his pecs, drawing thin streaks of blood as she went. When she reached his groin, she massaged him.

Bastien wanted to play, too, and dipped his head to taste her breasts. He would draw his own share of blood with his fangs. He worked one breast, sucking her nipple between his teeth, biting down with just enough pressure to pleasure her. Bastien knew she liked it a little rough and didn't disappoint.

He kissed his way down past her abdomen to where his tongue wanted to be. Bastien hooked her knee over his shoulder as his tongue entered and retreated from her core. His fangs elongated at her intoxicating taste and teased her swollen flesh. When she was cresting, he would sink them into her. He knew no better cocktail than a female's cream and blood mixed together. Bastien couldn't wait to taste the combination.

As Persephone came, she bucked under him, urging his fangs deeper into her. But before Bastien could mount her, she changed their positions and sank her sharp fangs in his pec. Then, her tongue worked its magic on its descent. Persephone knew how to drive a man insane with her stops and starts, and Bastien's breaths became pants. She cupped him then stroked him softly, letting her fingernail trail down the fine line of his balls to his anus. "So, tell me, Bastien, how was your night?"

***

"I want him to have a proper funeral. Even though he was no longer a member of this house, he was loyal to you and gave us vital information." Finally relaxed, Remare rested his ankle on his knee. Holding his wine in one hand, he draped the other across the back of the sofa. He regarded the ebony fireplace intricately carved with Greek figures on either side of the hearth. Valadon liked to decorate in blacks and golds and had a thing for circular couches. Valadon had once said he favored King Arthur's idea of a Round Table, but everyone at ValCorp knew who sat at the head.

"With Brandon's upcoming party, we seem to have our hands filled with ceremonies." Valadon seemed to consider Remare's request.

It wasn't prudent for a ruler to go back on his word, and Valadon was known for never having done so. However, Kristoph had suffered greatly to protect him. Valadon stopped pacing and faced Remare. "Very well, you may have your funeral for him. But only at night on the roof of this building. No place else. What do you plan to do with his ashes?"

"Kristoph liked the sea," Remare reflected quietly. "I thought I would have his ashes scattered over the ocean. I think he would have liked that." Then, his tone hardened. "This business with our enemies has turned ugly." He sipped his wine slowly. "Perhaps, it's time we took the war to them."

Valadon gave him a sharp look. "The ramifications would be costly. On both sides. Walk with me. I want to check on Gabriel and see if he's discovered anything new."

"Good, I want him to look at the metal shards I removed from Kristoph." Remare showed Valadon the pieces of silver he had wrapped in a handkerchief.

"Fine. Maybe he'll turn up something new." As they reached the elevator, Remare updated him on the investigation and the progress of the Torians. When they exited, they walked down the hall to the medical area and stopped when they saw Miranda asleep in one bed and Gabriel lightly snoring in the other. Each was facing the other. Remare heard the low growls emitting from Valadon. He was surprised to find himself smiling because Miranda had chosen Gabriel instead of Valadon.

Valadon turned on his heel and left. Remare retrieved a blanket from one of the other beds and tenderly draped it over Miranda. He admired her serene expression and leaned in to palm her cheek, but pulled away at the last second. He glanced at Gabriel, then quickly went over to the desk and left a message for him to do an analysis on the metal shards ASAP.

He left swiftly without a second look back.

Chapter Thirty-Three

Miranda woke to realize two things: One, she was not in her own bed, not even wearing her favorite T-shirt and shorts, and two, there was a handsome vampire smiling over her.

"Good morning, or should I say afternoon as it's now two o'clock?" Gabriel offered her a cup of coffee.

"Thanks, but I prefer tea as my primary source of caffeine." She sat up slowly, rubbing the stiffness in her neck. *It was two in the afternoon?* She never slept that late. "What was in those pills you gave me last night?"

"It was a mild pain blocker." Gabriel grinned. "I think you were exhausted from last night's events." He narrowed his eyes. "Both mentally and physically." He then went to his lab and opened his mini-fridge. He found a cold bottle of green tea and brought it to her.

She swallowed the cool, refreshing tea. *Oh, yes, the dragon's quiet, now.*

"What are your plans for today?"

Miranda remembered it was Sunday. All she really wanted to do was go home, crawl under the covers and snuggle in her own bed, but the thought of returning home alone held little appeal. "Right now, I just want a hot shower," her stomach growled too loudly for Gabriel not to notice, "and maybe a meal. I'll make more decisions when I'm human, again." Poor choice of words on her part, she realized and murmured, "Sorry."

"It's all right." He smiled and pointed to the room at the back of the lab. "There's a shower in there with some fresh towels. I think we can both do with some food, away from ValCorp. If you want, I can take you out for a late lunch/early dinner?"

"Sounds like a plan." She pushed the blanket off and swallowed the last of the tea. When she rose, she stumbled and fell into Gabriel's arms. For a moment, they stared at each other, and Miranda felt the stirrings, not only in her body, but in his, as well. The longing was clear in his eyes. "Right, shower first. I'll be awake in a few minutes."

In the shower, Miranda marveled at feeling warm, again. She wasn't sure what she'd say to Valadon but knew he was going to have questions, and she felt she owed him an explanation. The hot water was soothing to her aching body and she basked in the glorious heat, wondering what it would feel like if Gabriel joined her. She thought she'd sensed him watching her, but when she turned to the door, no one was there.

When they were both ready to leave, she said, "I need to speak to Valadon before we leave."

"On Sundays, Valadon usually spends time with his people in the subterranean levels. As a Blueblood, his blood is powerful, but he doesn't tolerate the sun as well as others and prefers to wait until sundown to leave the compound. I'll take you to him."

When the elevator doors opened, Miranda and Gabriel met the stares of several of the Torians who were lounging on the couches, watching a game on TV.

Miranda wasn't sure why she felt guilty. She hadn't done anything wrong but she suddenly felt like a kid going to the principal's office.

Cyra got up and hugged her. "If you're looking for Valadon's rooms, they're down there." She pointed down the hall.

When Gabriel moved to walk with her, Miranda said, "I'll only be a moment. It's better if I talk to him alone."

Gabriel seemed hesitant. "I think I should go with you." When she shook her head, he said, "If you're sure," and kissed her forehead.

"I'm sure," Miranda said, totally uncertain what she would say to Valadon.

***

Valadon finished fastening the last buckle on his boot. He was casually dressed in black pants with his favorite black, sleeveless robe that accented his broad chest. His boots gave him an extra two inches to his already impressive height. Valadon looked every inch the king that he was. Gazing at his reflection, he tied his belt across his waist. His arms were muscularly defined as was the rest of his body. He was the most powerful vampire in NYC, not only because of his mental abilities, but also because of his physical prowess. When Valadon heard the knocking, he knew it was Miranda and waited a moment, then went to answer it.

Valadon could hear Miranda's heart speeding up as her eyes met his. She'd never seen him dressed like this before. He always conveyed a more professional appearance, but decided on the sexier image she was now seeing.

"May I come in?"

Valadon smirked with male smugness at the flush on her face. "Of course." He enjoyed his wealth, decorated with taste, and he wanted Miranda to see his bedroom. His bed was a huge mahogany poster bed, complete with canopy. Black velvet curtains with gold trim were pulled back on each of the four posts to reveal a duvet of similar colors. Several Greek and Roman statues decorated his shelves. To the side of the bed was a sitting area with plush couches and a glass coffee table.

"I came back here last night because I thought you were right." Jutting her chin out, Miranda met his dark green eyes. "It's safe here, and I didn't want to keep your Torians occupied with babysitting me when they should be here with you."

"I have plenty of guards, and this place is a veritable fortress. My safety wasn't an issue."

Narrowing her eyes, she said, "I was on my way to see you last night when I told Bastien to let me go to the infirmary. I had a terrible headache and wanted some pain medicine. Gabriel and I started talking, and I thought I'd rest for a few minutes, and...I fell asleep."

Valadon watched her in silence, something primal seething within. When he was content she wasn't hiding anything, he said, "I was concerned for your safety. Deeply."

"I know you were. That's why I'm here." She smiled up at him. "I'm glad you're safe, too."

Valadon paced a few steps with his hands laced behind his back. "Have you reconsidered my offer to stay here?"

Miranda looked away. "Gabriel and I were thinking of going out for lunch, and then...I was thinking of taking him up to Werehaven. I might stay with Lizandra tonight."

"I see." Valadon suppressed the need to ground his molars. He contained his heartache, along with his bitter disappointment, and considered all the things she wasn't saying. He and his progeny were due for a talk. A very long talk. He strode two paces toward her. "I would like it very much if you would stay here...with Gabriel, for lunch. Then, if you wish to leave, you may do so. But I want you to take guards with you."

Miranda's eyes blazed in defiance. "If I'm at Werehaven, I don't need any guards."

Valadon sensed her rising hackles. But there were ways to protect her and Gabriel without her even knowing it; he inwardly smiled. He was a vampire lord who was used to having his way and his people following his orders. Miranda would not be one of them. Not right away, anyway. "Will you at least stay for lunch?"

"Yes."

Miranda felt like she'd been cunningly seduced during lunch and the drinks with the Torians afterward. Everyone was going out of their way to be friendly.

Cyra volunteered, "We have a full staff of chefs, masseuses, salon workers on call." She winked at her. "Say when, and I'll be your tour guide."

Bree, the wife of the Torian, Aiden, said, "We have a pool, and you can use it whenever you want."

When she made eye contact with Gabriel, he nodded in silent agreement that the vampires of House Valadon were unusually attentive. Whenever they were seated, someone always managed to sit between her and Gabriel. When Cyra and Bree pulled her away from the others, ostensibly to show her their rooms, she turned to glance back at Gabriel, who was deep in conversation with Aiden.

And when she regarded Valadon, she saw a look of royal satisfaction on his face. *Always in control, vampire king, aren't you?*

A deeply male, smug voice reverberated in her mind. *"Always."*

Chapter Thirty-Four

"My father liked to watch the model sailboats race in the lake. My sister, Cassie, and I always picked out our favorite boats and would bet each other which boat would win in the races. I always chose the blue one, and Cassie always picked the red boat. This part of Central Park by Bethesda Fountain has always been my favorite." Miranda stood rapt, smiling at the happy memory. Something about the grand fountain always attracted her. Maybe the angel on top. She breathed in deep as if the memories gave her strength. "God, how we used to yell like crazy."

"Did your boat ever win?" Gabriel asked as they continued along the tree-lined trail.

Miranda grinned. "Sometimes. Did you ever come here when you were...?"

"Human? Sure. It's beautiful here." He gazed around the park as if remembering the area and then pointed to the field. "Over there is where we played baseball, and down that trail is the rink where we now play hockey."

"Cool! Vampires on Ice," she teased.

Gabriel smirked. When they passed a section of wild flowers, he read the sign that forbid people from touching them. "I'd pick you some, but with my luck, I'd get arrested."

Miranda chuckled. "I'd bail you out."

Somehow, his arm wound up around her waist. "Thank you."

She smiled up at him. "For what? Letting me rant about my childhood stories?"

"For bringing me here." He kissed her forehead. "And taking me to Werehaven. After everything you've told me about the Were Queen, I'm looking forward to meeting her."

She tilted her head. "C'mon, it's only a little further. It's beneath the overpass."

Miranda grabbed his hand and led him down the trail to the secret underground passageway. When the Were guards tried to stop Gabriel from entering the underground compound, she stepped forward. "He's with me. Where's Lizandra?"

"She's in the sick bay with the new one they brought in last night." Lawrence, a nearly six foot-seven, heavily muscled African-American, gestured to the back of the club. "The girl was in pretty bad shape. Go on back, Lizandra's expecting you."

"Thanks, Lawe."

More enforcers were milling around so she knew something was up. Gabriel looked in awe at the sights of the club: the immense dance floor, the long bar and the VIP lounge at the far end. "Amazing, isn't it?"

"Yes, I never would've imagined all this. But, then again, I'm sure they don't have a clue about our own habitat beneath ValCorp."

When they entered the sickbay, Lizandra was leaning over a sleeping form covered in sheets. The girl's face was covered in vicious bruises.

Miranda sidled up to her friend. "What happened?"

"Our scouts found her out on patrol. She was tossed behind a dumpster on Amsterdam Avenue." Lizandra glanced up at Gabriel. "She was used by more than one of your kind."

Concern etched Gabriel's face. "Shouldn't she be in a hospital?"

Lizandra shook her head. "Everything that could be done has already been done." She patted the girl's hand. "She needs rest now and time to heal." Lizandra stared pointedly at Miranda.

"How do you know there was more than one?" Gabriel considered the young girl, who couldn't be more than twenty. For a Were, she seemed very pale and gaunt.

"Different bite radiuses." She stood and extended a hand. "I'm Lizandra, by the way."

Miranda coughed. "Right! Liz, this is Gabriel."

"I'm honored to finally meet you," he said warmly as he shook her hand. "I'm a medical doctor. Mind if I have a look at her?"

Liz narrowed her eyes. "You'd have to ask her first."

She turned and stroked the girl's hair. "Sasha, there's a doctor here who wants to examine you. Is that okay with you?"

Sasha turned her head toward Lizandra's voice, the haze of the meds evident in her eyes. When she saw the vampire, she started violently squirming.

"Easy. Sasha, he's a doctor. *A doctor.*" Liz tried to reassure her, holding her down on the bed. "He's *not* the one who did this to you. *Listen to me!* Do you understand? He's a *doctor!*"

"He's a vampire!" She started sobbing hysterically. "He's like the ones who did this to me!"

When she turned into Liz's arms, the sheet lowered, and Miranda saw the tattoo on her leg. "Red Claw," she murmured. When Gabriel looked perplexed, she whispered, "Rival pack. Their hunting grounds are on the West Side—Riverside Park. Central Park is Black Star Clan."

Exhaling, Liz said, "You should leave. Your presence is upsetting her."

"Let me try." Gabriel reassured her.

Miranda knew many people feared being mesmerized by a vampire's eyes, but a vampire's voice was also hypnotic, almost narcotic in its effect.

"Sasha," he said in a soft, melodic voice as he sat on the edge of the bed. "I'm not a Rogue. I'm a doctor. I have been for a very long time." When she just stared at him, he soothingly added, "I want these men punished as much as you. I will find them and hunt them down, but I need to see the bite radius."

Her eyes glistened with frightened tears. "Why would you hunt your own kind?"

"They are *not* my kind. They're Rogues." Gabriel tenderly stroked her hand. "I might be a vampire, but I assure you I'm nothing like the ones who hurt you."

Miranda couldn't stand there and do nothing as Sasha struggled. She moved closer to the bed. "Sasha. I'm a friend of Lizandra's. I've known her since I was a teenager. You trust her, right?" She gestured to the Were Queen. "So, if she trusts me, can't you trust Dr. Gabriel? I know him. He's not capable of hurting someone. He's a doctor." She looked back at Gabriel. "And I promise you, he'll be very gentle. He was with me when I was shot."

Sasha's breathing slowed to long drags of deep breaths. "Why do you let vampires like that live? They're monsters."

Gabriel asked her quietly, "And are all Weres fair and honest?"

Sasha gazed up at Lizandra. "Renworth said I was too weak to be in his pack. He *gave* me to them. Said I was a present." The tears fell from her eyes. "He let them fuck me, then feed on me." Sasha broke down and cried at the brutal memory. "I tried to fight, transform into my wolf form, but they had drained me too much. I can still hear their laughter and mocking voices." After a while, her sobs quieted, and she looked directly at Gabriel. "Do you want to see what they did to me?" Bitterly, she ripped the sheet from her body and let them see the multiple wounds and bruises that ravaged her thighs and breasts.

Miranda inwardly cringed. There were so many bite marks it was a wonder she'd survived the attack, at all.

Sasha pulled the sheet back and turned away from them, refusing to answer any more questions. "Go away; just go away."

"Wait for me in my rooms." Lizandra turned back to Sasha.

Miranda nodded and gestured for Gabriel to follow. Once outside, his body shook with silent rage. She suspected he had a damned good idea who was responsible. Probably the same one who killed the girl they found in the alley. She waited until they were inside Lizandra's apartment to turn on him. "Okay, give. You know something."

He turned so fast she couldn't track his movements. "You think I like this! Being part of a race capable of this?"

"Get off the cross, Gabriel." His fury had ignited her own, and she paced the room to burn off her own anger. He couldn't possibly understand the depth of her sympathy for Sasha. "I know you aren't capable of this. I have friends who are vampires, remember? You imagine I think any of Valadon's vampires could do this?" She smacked herself in the head. There was only one she'd met who was capable of this kind of violence.

"This was Mulciber's doing, wasn't it?" She turned to face him. "You've known for some time." She inched closer as the red rims around his golden-brown eyes intensified. "Haven't you?"

"Bastard has immunity! He's an ambassador. Political immunity, he calls it!" He rubbed his face in frustration. "Entitlement, he cites. Says any host country he's in supplies him with *feedlings*; that's the term he uses for the young ones he uses, then discards." Gabriel's face twisted in utter disgust. He looked like he wanted to throw something.

Miranda's stomach wrenched at the frustration and despair she felt radiating from him. "How come Valadon hasn't done something about him?"

"Oh, he's tried." Gabriel ran a hand through his hair. "He's censured him, sent his own representatives to the European Council to try to get him replaced. There isn't much more he can do."

Head bent, eyes closed, Gabriel breathed deeply. Exhaling, he rubbed his neck, then eyed her with understanding. "Vampires can sense emotions, Miranda. You felt more than sympathy for that girl. You empathized." He stared at her. "Most women don't carry knives in their boots or challenge vampires in a dark alley."

Miranda kept her eyes on him. "No, they don't."

Gabriel's voice emanated compassion. "You went through something similar, didn't you? What happened, Miranda?"

"Does it matter?" She didn't like Gabriel's look of pity. Vampires weren't the only ones who were intuitive. When he tried to take her in his arms, she pulled away. Sometimes, strength came from within, not without, and right now, she needed to feel strong. After the silence stretched on, she glanced at Liz's family pictures on the shelf, anything to avoid his penetrating gaze. "It was a long time ago. College. We were young and stupid. There was a bunch of us who wanted to celebrate the semester's end so we went to a club downtown. Someone spiked my drink. Everything went hazy after that.

The hell of it is...I saw when my friends were leaving. I wanted to tell them something was wrong. I tried to signal them, but they thought I was waving goodbye." She turned to look at him. "Liz's people were out searching for one of their own; they found me instead." Exhaling, Miranda thought the years don't always heal, but they do provide distance. "Except for the bite marks, I was pretty much used the way Sasha was." She examined Gabriel's eyes for censure. There was none. She hadn't really expected to see any.

His voice was tender. "Did they find the ones who did that to you?"

"No. They never did. After bringing me back here, Liz hooked me up to an IV that helped push the drugs out of my system." Miranda half smiled. "After a stern lecture on stupidity, she started training me like I was one of her cubs. I got strong. I don't think I've ever gone to another human club after that." Her spine straight, she clasped Gabriel's hand and stared into his golden-brown eyes. "I don't live in that time zone anymore, so I would appreciate it if you don't repeat any of this."

"Miranda." This time when Gabriel pulled her to him, she accepted his embrace. "I'm sorry, Miranda. I'm so sorry."

"It's over. I don't dwell on it." She smirked. "Liz would kick my ass if I did." She broke away from him. "Your turn. You weren't shocked at Sasha's condition. You've seen this before...and not just with the girl we found in the alley. How many have there been?"

Gabriel appeared conflicted, but after a while said, "Too many. But this is the first time I know of that he used a Were."

"It's not the first time." Lizandra stood in the doorway. With her arms crossed over her chest and her spine rigid, she looked every inch a queen. When she walked into her rooms, she carried herself with the lithe grace of only the most agile Weres. She sat in her chair, elegantly draping one long leg over the other and gestured with her tapered hand for them to join her. They did. She tapped her lethally long nails on the arm rest. "We've heard reports about others." She considered Gabriel. "Care to tell me how many?"

He exhaled. "We found several the human police contacted us about. Mostly young females, but there've been a few males, as well. We were also informed that a significantly increased number of youths have gone missing in the city, but as yet, we haven't been able to locate any of them."

"And you know who's been doing this." Lizandra's voice was more statement than question.

Miranda was proud of her friend who could keep a level temper when she knew Liz was seething underneath. When Lizandra was in full queen mode, she carried herself with the aplomb of a monarch. And was just as impressive.

Gabriel looked at both women and seemed to realize he wasn't getting out of there without giving them answers. "At first, we had our suspicions, but no proof it was someone from House Valadon. Though Valadon hardly considers Mulciber a member of his house."

Lizandra continued tapping her nails. "And he's outside of your laws?"

"Valadon is aware of the situation and is doing what he can to oust Mulciber. Up until recently, we suspected his underlings used more discretion in disposing of the bodies."

Lizandra waited to see if he had anything else to add. After a while, she sat forward. "Your ambassador attacks a Were, he becomes an enemy of my clan." She glanced at Miranda. "I'm sure Miranda has told you what we do to enemies of Black Star Clan."

Miranda knew well of Were justice and wondered if Lizandra would take in the young Were. "Will she become pack?"

"I will put it to a vote, but I'm sure my people will agree to adopt her." She gazed pointedly at Gabriel. "It's not safe in this city to be a lone wolf." Lizandra rose and walked with her hands on her hips. "This is not the welcome I'd have imagined for you, vampire. Werehaven has a reputation for treating its guests better than this."

"I understand."

"Do you?" Liz lifted one brow. "Then, you won't mind if I borrow your beautiful companion, for a few moments." She opened the door, and Thalia, one of her bodyguards, stepped inside. "Escort Dr. Gabriel to the lounge. Make sure he's comfortable and get him whatever he wants."

Miranda saw the caution light in Gabriel's eyes. "It's all right. Thalia's cool." She walked to him and tenderly stroked his arm. "I'll come get you in a few minutes."

Gabriel ran a finger down her cheek. "Promise?"

She crossed her heart. "Always."

After he was gone, Lizandra watched her with eyes that often reflected the calm turquoise of the Caribbean, but were now turning a darker shade.

"Oh, will you stop with the look." She knew Lizandra had a dozen questions for her and was just figuring out the order in which she'd ask them. "Gabriel's a good guy. It took guts for him to tell you as much as he did. Valadon will probably rip him a new one when he finds out."

"Ah, speaking of the vampire…" She went to the fridge and returned with two Coronas. "How is the sexy vampire king?"

"You're starting," Miranda said in a singsong voice as she accepted her beer.

Lizandra raised both of her eyebrows in a gesture of *"Well?"*

Miranda wasn't sure how to explain Gabriel's presence. She quaffed down her beer. "It's a long friggen story."

"Goody! My favorite kind." Liz reclined on the couch and patted the cushion next to it. "Come. Tell mama bear all that's been happening since I last saw you." She narrowed her eyes and said sarcastically, "I *bet* it's been interesting."

Miranda knew that tone and realized there'd be no holding back. Instead of being a physician's assistant, Lizandra Wells should have been a prosecuting attorney. She could coax a confession out of anyone. When Miranda was done with the short version, Lizandra sat staring at her with her nails clicking on the sofa. Nails suddenly reminiscent of claws. "You get chased down Fifth Avenue by goons…and you don't think to *call* me?"

"Wasn't time." She swallowed more of her beer. "I was too busy running for my life." Miranda hated being pulled in two directions. "You and Valadon have got to work together. It gets confusing trying to keep what's vampire business separate from Were business."

"What's Valadon going to do about it?"

"He says there's an ongoing investigation and his people are on it. He wanted me to stay with him at ValCorp," she shook her head, "but I found it too confining."

"You'd be safe there." Liz's eyes softened. "He could protect you."

"It would feel too much like a cage." Miranda cracked her neck.

"Then, stay here tonight. I'll assign two of my Weres to escort you home in the morning. You should be reasonably safe at the museum, but come straight here after work."

"I was hoping you'd say that. Thanks."

Chapter Thirty-Five

When Miranda entered the VIP lounge, Gabriel was drinking his beer and munching on the snacks the Weres had provided. He was watching the Weres sensually dance to the driving rhythms of the music. Thalia, or *Tia,* was explaining the history of Werehaven and the differences in Were clans. When he saw Miranda ascending the stairs, his face brightened.

"Sorry it took so long." She smiled up at him. "How are you making out?"

"Fine." He stroked her shoulder. "How about you?"

"Pretty good. Lizandra has a surprise for you. She feels bad you didn't receive the usual hospitality of the Weres, so she has something special planned."

"What?"

"You'll see." She clasped his hand. "C'mon."

Gabriel marveled at the labyrinth of caves and rooms that was Werehaven. When they entered a chamber at the end of the passageway, he seemed amazed at the natural rock formations. "An amphitheater," he murmured. In the front of the massive room was a piano on a raised platform; to the left, seven succeeding tiers rose to the back, each tier about three feet high as it was deep.

She smiled at his look of awe as she led him up the stairs to the top tier. "Welcome to Songhaven. Where all the sirens come to play." The lighting was kept low with just a few wall sconces lit. "When Liz first played a disc of her music, I thought the voice was Adele's, but then, one of the songs became more sultry, steamier. And I knew whose voice it was."

As they sat in the uppermost tier, Liz's most trusted friends filled up the lower ones. Gavin, her lover, had the first tier, of course; not far from him Tia stretched out. Quint and Brent reclined in their usual place up on the right. Her brothers, David and Sam, sprawled out on the left. In all, about twenty Weres lounged on the tiers to listen to their queen belt out songs as no one else could.

Miranda thought Lizandra should've been a professional singer, but Liz had said that wasn't the life she wanted: *"When I sing, I sing for myself, my friends, family and God above—no one else."*

When Lizandra entered, Miranda wasn't surprised she had Sasha placed on the lowest tier. Liz wasn't barbaric in treating her Weres as the Red Claw Clan, but she didn't tolerate self-pity. She'd sympathize but only to a point. If people wanted to be a part of her world, they had to dig deep and find whatever strength they had to prove they belonged. Miranda got why she had Sasha brought in. Liz's voice held power—spiritual power. Few singers could hit the notes or reach five octaves with the piercing clarity she did.

On stage, Lizandra went to the piano. When she played one of her slower songs, Miranda stretched out and closed her eyes. Music has a power of its own. Liz's voice could envelop a person's soul and take it to a different plane of existence. Make people feel things they didn't think they were capable of. A high so profound it was better than any drug.

Liz had once told her, *"The world is full of horrors, and people are capable of horrendous acts of ugliness. Music helps balance out the harshness of the world."* Miranda often thought that was why she filled her own life with images of beauty. Working in a museum, surrounded by great works of art, endowed Miranda with a sense of symmetry.

Gabriel crept behind her and whispered, "Thank you for bringing me here. Her voice is sensational, one of the best I've ever heard."

"Wait." Miranda smiled over her shoulder. "She's just getting started." Miranda welcomed Gabriel's closeness, a soothing balm to her chaotic life. The Weres were known to be affectionate; to them, touching and being touched was a major part of their existence. She wondered if vampires were the same.

When Lizandra started singing one of Miranda's favorite songs by Neko Case, "Look for Me," a soulful ballad that showcased Lizandra's gift, Miranda purred in pleasure. Humans were never meant to communicate with all the technology available, she thought. Not when people had voices like Liz's. The mystical power of the music took her to a place in her soul she rarely went and something primitive wakened.

A few tiers down, a couple wasn't inhibited by the presence of others, and by their combined scents, Miranda knew they'd taken their desire to a higher level. The heat in the room definitely climbed as her body stirred.

Apparently, the sultriness in the air wasn't lost on Gabriel. He watched the Weres become entranced. The more passionate the Were Queen sang, the more Miranda's blood pounded in her veins. When Gabriel leaned closer, she inhaled his scent and her desire deepened.

The Weres were becoming increasingly affectionate. They could get pretty frisky with their passions, but Miranda preferred not to have an audience when the mood struck her hard. As it was now. That was one of the reasons she always chose the last tier, away from the others. Though with the sounds of grunting growing louder below, the others didn't share her predilection.

She glanced back at Gabriel and saw he was as aroused as she was. He slid his hand past her hip to stroke her thigh. She didn't dissuade him; she pulled him closer, enjoying the sensations of his heart beating against her back.

For her last song, Liz chose another one by Case, "Pretty Girls," and Miranda knew she was singing it for Sasha, the message clearly about survival. Howls erupted every time Lizandra sang about the wolves not being allowed in.

Gabriel's lips touched her ear. "What about vampires?"

Miranda welcomed his touch as his breath blew across her face. She liked how his voice became deep and husky and wondered what it would sound like when he made love. She lay on her back and gazed up at his lazy smile as she held his hand to her stomach.

"What about vampires?" She smiled sexily, her own voice deepening seductively.

"Would you let us in?" he asked with heavily lidded eyes, and then softened his voice as he drew circles around her stomach. "Would you, Miranda?"

She didn't think as one knee slowly lifted and then parted.

That was all the invitation Gabriel needed, and he rolled on top of her, carefully keeping his weight on his forearms. He brushed a loose strand of hair from her face and bent to kiss her. His lips brushed over hers as she ran her hands up his chest and around his neck.

She felt his growing desire as she arched her back. She became lost in the sensations of kissing Gabriel and let her hands explore the rigid muscles of his back. His embrace was as magical as the music. She didn't want the kiss to end, but knew if one of them didn't break apart, the Weres wouldn't be the only ones howling. When he finally lifted off her, his breathing had become arduous. There was longing in his eyes. "Come home with me."

Miranda remembered she was bunking there. She wasn't sure if a vampire had ever stayed the night at Werehaven.

But she knew one was going to tonight.

When she didn't immediately answer, Gabriel rubbed himself against her to encourage her decision and smiled when she purred. "Now, you sound like Rexi."

Miranda smirked. "I'm staying here tonight." She slid her hands up his shoulders and down his biceps. "Stay here with me."

Gabriel gave her a crooked smile. "With pleasure," he promised and kissed her with a soul deep passion.

When she finally opened her eyes and turned her head, Lizandra had finished singing and most of the Weres had already left. When she glanced back, Liz gestured to meet her outside.

"Let me speak with her. I'll be right back."

Liz glanced at her as they walked back to her rooms. "I hope you know what you're doing."

"I think so." Miranda smirked. "You okay with a vampire spending the night here?"

"It wouldn't be the first time," Liz growled softly, then slyly smiled. "Just don't sneak out in the morning without your guards."

She'd almost forgotten she needed them. "I won't."

When they reached Liz's apartment, Miranda asked, "Which vampire stayed here before?"

Lizandra smiled seductively and arched her back as she growled sexily and shut the door, leaving Miranda to figure that one out by herself.

***

Miranda showed Gabriel her room and, for a moment, nearly froze. He seemed to sense her hesitancy and appeared worried she'd changed her mind. But when he put his arms around her, she leaned back into him moaning softly.

"Have you ever been with a vampire before?"

She shook her head, relishing his embrace, not wanting to let go.

Gabriel hugged her closer and whispered, "Then, I'll be your first." He turned her in his arms and kissed her.

Miranda felt like she was riding a wave in the ocean, the breezes cooling her too heated flesh. She'd always run a few degrees hotter than the average human, but now, she felt like she was steaming. She backed away, pulled her shirt over her head and tossed it on a chair.

He tore his shirt off and flung it onto the dresser, then toed off his shoes and socks. He watched her with the hunger of a starving man as his pants slid off his hips.

She admired his body. For someone who spent so much time in a lab, Gabriel was seriously built. But she should've known that from the way he handled himself with the Rogues in the alley.

He unhooked her bra, letting it fall to the floor, and then, he undid the snap on her jeans and pushed them down.

Miranda stepped back to the bed, and sitting down, she unzipped her boots, letting them fall to the floor along with her jeans. Once naked, she lay back against the pillows with a seductive grin on her face. She crooked her finger at him, and he was already there, showing her just how fast a vampire could move. When she laughed, he laughed with her.

"I've wanted to do this for a long time."

"Since I first saw you?" she asked.

"Yeah." His voice was deep, seductive. "Since then." He kissed her tenderly and thoroughly, moving his lips to her cheek and then her neck. There, his tongue traced her vein, sending shudders through her. Working his way lower, he kissed her shoulder and then his mouth drifted to her breast.

Miranda relaxed in his embrace, desiring him, needing to explore his body, wanting him to feel as hot as she was, but knew a vampire could never be as warm as a human or a Were. The cool flesh of a vampire was exhilarating, the sharp contrast to her own body arousing. She held his head to her chest, massaging his neck and shoulders as waves of passion rushed through her.

When her body arched off the mattress, he slipped both arms around her. His mouth glided down, and he kissed her stomach, drawing circles with his tongue around her navel and spiraling lower. When he reached her most intimate flesh, he gave one long lick then kissed the inside of her thigh.

Her breathing became harsh as she savored his touch. She couldn't take her eyes off of him, but when he lifted his mouth from her core and began to kiss her inner thighs, she growled in frustration, and her hands fisted in the bedding.

Gabriel smirked. "Be patient. I don't want to rush this."

"Don't rush. Just go back to where you were."

"Here?" He kissed the top of her thigh.

"Not funny."

He laughed as he kissed her inner thigh. "Here?"

When she let out another growl of frustration, he showed mercy and used his thumbs to separate her folds and plunged in with his tongue.

Miranda's head arched back into the pillows as pleasure sang through her body. Her heart pounded as Gabriel brought her to peak, would let her crest, then slow down. He laughed at her frustration then brought her high, again. The third time, she grabbed his head and held him in place.

He pinched her nipple, and the tension in her body reached a crescendo. He sped up his ministrations, using his thumb to stroke her clit as he tongued then sucked at her core.

She knew she was going to explode. When his finger dove into her, her body arched, and her howl echoed off the walls. But Gabriel didn't relent, teasing out the orgasm longer. When she cried out again from the pleasure, he released her and let her sink into the bed. Miranda turned to her side, catching her breath, and for the first time, saw his fangs. "Your fangs are...impressive."

Her acceptance of his being a vampire seemed important to him, and he reached up to kiss her again. "If you think that's impressive..."

When he moved to penetrate her, Miranda slowed him down. "Don't you want me to take care of you...the way you did me?"

Gabriel rubbed himself against her swollen core. "Does this feel like it needs any more foreplay?"

God, she loved it when he smiled. "No, that feels like it's ready to go cave exploring."

"Har, har!" He scanned the cavelike room. When he rose over her again, his eyes darkened with anticipation. Gabriel was careful with her, going slow, pulling back, then going in another inch or two, easing himself in with graceful movements. When he was buried deep inside, his body was covered in a fine sheen of perspiration.

Miranda knew he was holding back and tried to coax him to go faster. "Gabriel. I'm not made of glass. Go faster. I promise I won't break."

He gazed at her flushed expression. "You sure?"

"Yes, God, yes!"

He increased his thrusts and found a mutually satisfying rhythm. When she screamed again, he continued to pound into her until she came again, and only then, did he allow himself to find his pleasure.

With his skin sweat slickened, he collapsed on top of her, then rolled to the side, taking her with him, holding her close. After her breathing finally slowed, he quietly rose from the bed and went to the bathroom and brought back a warm washcloth. He gently cleaned her then let the cloth fall to the floor. He drew the blankets over them and pulled her close to him.

"Good night, angel." He kissed her forehead.

Miranda sleepily murmured, "Night."

Gabriel felt at peace for the first time in nearly a century. Miranda had done that for him. He knew she had entered a dangerous world, her life now jeopardized because of her decision to aid Valadon.

Valadon, his so-called father, a term he'd never used, he thought as he exhaled. Now, there was a conversation he wasn't looking forward to, but right now, none of that mattered. What mattered was Miranda's well-being. She would need someone to watch over her, guard her, and he wanted to be that person. Gabriel held her close, cherishing her warmth, and realized he'd do whatever was necessary to make sure she was not endangered.

As a doctor, he was sworn to protect life, but for Miranda, he'd kill to ensure her safety.

Chapter Thirty-Six

"Do you want the history or the biography?" Nick asked from the second level.

"Just the biography," Miranda called down from the upstairs railing. She was studying Titian's *The Venus de Urbino*, a painting of a striking woman reclining on a couch. Dark red drapes hung in the background. Titian was one of her favorite artists from the High Renaissance in Rome because many of his paintings reflected a sense of balance and serenity. The figure in his painting conveyed her sensuality with an air of confidence Miranda thought mesmerizing. "What a beauty."

"I think so." Valadon's voice echoed behind her. "She's one of my favorites."

The hairs on her arms rose as usual when she became aware of his presence. And probably always would. "Hello, Valadon. Come to help us with your catalog?"

"If need be." He glanced at her computer screen and notes. "How's the catalog coming along?"

Miranda was happy to see him and that surprised her. She'd thought he might pick a fight with her because she'd spent the night with Gabriel. But Valadon didn't address the issue, and for that, she was grateful. "Pretty good. Nick is extremely helpful; if it weren't for him, it would be taking me twice as long. We're about halfway through the sixteenth century."

"I'm glad to hear that." He sat beside her. "I came to ask if you would like some refreshment or if you wanted to take a break."

"I'd like some refreshment." Nick came up the stairs, carrying the books she requested.

Valadon gave his nephew a look. "*You* can help yourself. Miranda may not feel comfortable visiting our kitchen, even though...she is welcome to *anything* we have." The red rims of his irises pulsed.

"Thanks, but I'm not hungry."

Nick turned to make a kitchen run, leaving her alone with his enigmatic uncle.

Valadon appeared to study every nuance of her face. "You look well," he said in his deep resonant voice that never failed to make her shiver.

"I am...for the most part." Miranda was uncertain if she should tell him about the uneasy feeling she had most of the day. "I'm still a little rattled by what happened at the Ormont home."

"As you should be. But we're looking into it." He squeezed her hand reassuringly. "You must trust me, Miranda, to deal with my enemies...as I have for centuries."

A tingle rushed up her arm. When she peered into his dark green eyes, she knew he spoke the truth: He'd been fighting his enemies for hundreds of years. And had endured. She found herself believing in him and trusting his judgment. "I do."

Nick returned with a bottle of green tea for her, she graciously accepted.

"Nick and I would like you to have supper with us one day this week." Valadon glanced at Nick, who looked momentarily surprised, then quickly hid his expression. "My chef is an excellent cook and has been known to take requests."

Miranda bet he did and was charmed at the idea of socializing with them. "Sure, but first, let me check my schedule at work."

Valadon nodded and rose. "Good. I'll wait to hear from you and let you get back to work."

After he left, Miranda realized she missed his presence. On one hand, she was frightened by his inherent power, but at the same time, she felt herself strangely attracted.

"What do you think of him?" Nick asked unassumingly.

She wondered how much of what she said and did was reported back to his uncle. "On or off the record?" she asked mockingly.

"Aw, c'mon, Professor Crescent, what happens in the archives, stays in the archives," he joked.

She grinned. "All right, I'll tell you what I would tell him." She thought for a moment. "I like him. I like what he's done for the city and your people...as well as mine. But..."

Nick frowned. "It's never a good sign when someone uses the 'but' word."

Miranda tried to put into words why she kept her distance. Valadon was important to so many people. He ran this huge organization, ValCorp, was the leader of his people. And his power... It was prodigious, and she feared the full force of it. "We live in different worlds, Nick, and I think he gets pulled in too many directions."

"He'd be good to you."

She glanced at the books he brought up and quickly changed the subject. "Hmmm, I saw another biography on Titian downstairs. Mind escorting me down there? I want to see what else we have."

"Sure thing."

As they descended the stairs, a thought came to her. "Nick, by any chance do you know where the medical books are?"

"Yeah, sure. They're over in the corner." He pointed to the left. "Why do you want to see those? I don't know why we even keep them. They're obsolete."

"I'm a bibliophile. I was just curious. That's all." Miranda loved old books; to her, they were museum pieces, and she remembered Gabriel told her his old medical volumes were down here. From the looks of it, no one had touched the books in years, probably decades. She reached for one and inhaled the old smell.

"God, these go back centuries." She scanned the shelves. Apparently, Gabriel had collected books, as well. Then, she spotted a thinner volume, different from the others in size and shape. Strange, it didn't have the fine coating of dust the others had. She flipped through the leather bound pages, but it was written in Latin, a language she barely knew. But one word stood out—*potio*. Her stomach churned. "Nick, can you read Latin?"

"Unfortunately." He grunted. "Valadon insisted I learn several languages, and Latin was one of them. I don't know why, though." He shrugged. "No one uses it, anymore."

Miranda wasn't so sure. She handed the book to Nick, whose eyes immediately widened.

When she pointed to a word, he peered up at her. "Poisons."

Upstairs, Nick immediately wanted to show it to his uncle.

"Nick, think about it, for a moment," she tried to reason. "This could mean nothing." Though, she didn't think so.

"Really? My uncle gets shot with a poisoned dart, and you call that nothing!"

Actually, she'd been the one who'd been shot, but she wasn't about to get into that. "That's not what I'm saying. Hear me out." Miranda began to pace, knowing she thought better when she was in motion. "Look where we found the book. It may very well be that someone in this house used the book, but we don't know who."

"It was in the section with Gabriel's old stuff," Nick said with one hand on his hip.

She rolled her eyes. "Do you *really* think Gabriel had anything to do with the dart?" She rubbed her butt, reminding him she was the one who'd been hit.

Nick thought about it, and anger saturated his voice. "He never wanted to be a vampire. He blamed Valadon, for years. He could have done it."

"I don't think so, Nick. They brought me down to the infirmary right after I was injured, and Gabriel was already down there working in his lab. I don't see how he could be hanging out of a helicopter, one minute, and in his lab, the next."

Nick seemed to ponder the logistics. "Good point."

Miranda considered who else could have been in the archives researching poisons. "Before we bring this to Valadon, I think we should know more."

"Like what?"

"Help me, Nick," she pleaded reasonably. "Help me understand who would do this. We can find the person or persons responsible. You know the members of your house better than I do." Miranda softened her voice and narrowed her eyes. "Think, Nick. Who would want to harm Valadon?"

Nick rubbed his forehead in anguish and began to pace. After a moment, he stopped and met her eyes. "No one. *Everyone* here is loyal to him. His Torians have been with him since before I was born. Every one of them would die for him. It's not a member of this house. Can't be. It's someone else."

She wasn't so certain and thumbed through the book. When she got to the last page, she inwardly gasped and shut the book. Francis Peralt hadn't been the author as she'd thought from the cover, though the experiments had been his. The book was written by a vampire documenting the information gathered by Peralt, a vampire who was in Valadon's territory—uninvited and without permission. He'd been here all along right under her nose. *Well, hello, Blu*, she thought silently. A picture of Guy de Montglat was drawn on the last page.

She convinced Nick only by knowing how they came up with the chemical compounds in the dart, could they figure out who was behind the attack. Nick hadn't been so sure, but he reluctantly agreed. He'd given his word he wouldn't say anything for twenty-four hours. After that, if she didn't find anything viable, then they would take the book to Valadon.

Miranda started Googling Peralt. The chemist had been a member of some ancient brotherhood in Europe during the Inquisition. Apparently, he had worked for an extremist group that rounded up what they had termed *"demon children"* and experimented on them in the most heinous ways. It always amazed her how far some fanatics went in the name of religion to justify their cruelties. Whether or not the church actually sanctioned these atrocities was unclear. But what was apparent was that Peralt had experimented with different chemical compounds. From the drawings in the book, it was obvious what he called demons had been vampires.

She ran a computer program translating the Peralt text into modern English. After scrutinizing the new version, she wasn't sure the program was interpreting some of the words correctly and made plans to meet with Felicity.

***

When she arrived at the New York Public Library, it was already closed, but the security guard said she had special permission to stay late. He didn't say from whom. Felicity wasn't there to meet her, but an envelope containing the elevator key was. Miranda walked through the dimly lit marble corridors and had an eerie feeling she was being watched.

The elevator doors closed, sealing her in. Miranda exhaled. *This is a bad idea.* She exited on the level where she'd first met Blu. She followed the path Felicity had shown her, keeping her eyes open to any threat that may be lurking in the shadows.

Miranda hesitated when she reached the door. Deciding not to knock, she opened the door and walked in. The room was exactly as it was the first time she'd seen it. *Where are you, Felicity?* She examined every corner of the room.

"Miranda Crescent. How nice to see you again."

She trembled at the sound of Blu's voice, then stiffened her spine and turned to see the youthful looking, blond vampire dressed in a dark gray suit standing behind her. He looked more mature than when she'd first met him, and her skin tingled at his restrained power. "Where's Felicity?"

"She's resting in the other room." He gestured to a door on the other side of the room. "I can wake her, if you wish." Blu moved closer to her. "But I would prefer you let her rest." He strode to a table and poured wine from a decanter. "Would you care for a drink?"

"No. I'm here because I wanted Felicity to translate something I found."

"Yes, she told me," he said without turning around. "I can probably interpret it for you." He turned to face her, smiling pleasantly. "I speak *many* languages."

"I bet you do." Miranda scrutinized his every move, but didn't perceive any dangerous vibes. "I found a book written in

Latin, centuries ago. Perhaps you can tell me what it says." She handed him the tome she'd previously made copies of.

When he stood before her, his nostrils flared. He glanced down at the volume. "So, there it is. I haven't seen this book in centuries. Wherever did you find it?"

Miranda tried to sense his intentions, but Montglat was one of the few beings she couldn't read—no matter how hard she tried. His demeanor wasn't threatening, but she wished her mentor was with them. Felicity, she trusted; Montglat was an unknown. "Your portrait is in the back of the book. You wrote it."

"Yes. Centuries ago." He reclined on the sofa, sipped his wine and gestured for her to join him. "What would you like me to tell you?"

"Why would you write a book on ways to torture and kill vampires, when you yourself are one?"

"You give me far too much credit. I didn't write it initially; I merely compiled notes on a chemist who lived in Luxembourg centuries ago. You must remember, Miranda, I served the leaders of several courts in Europe. We kept guard on many of our enemies. Peralt was one of them. This," he tapped the book, "was my report to my then king."

"Was Peralt accurate in the use of poisons on vampires?"

"Why do you want to know?" he asked facetiously. "Are you planning on torturing a vampire?" He grinned as he drank his wine.

Miranda's stomach roiled at the flippant manner in which he discussed the harm of a vampire. "How could you allow a book like this to survive the centuries? Surely, you must know, if it ever fell into the wrong hands, someone could use it for nefarious reasons."

"I didn't allow anything. I presented it to King Robert, as I was commanded centuries ago, and that was the last I saw of it." Montglat sniffed the air. "Why would Lord Valadon give you such a book?"

"He didn't." She glanced away. "I borrowed it from his archives."

Montglat watched her with eyes old as time. "I see, so he doesn't know you have it in your possession."

Miranda wasn't sure how much she could trust him—if at all. There was no way she was ever going to be able to read him with his impenetrable shields. Dr. Walcott was highly perceptive, but an ancient vampire whose nickname had been the equivalent of a reptile certainly was capable of duplicity. She decided to go for it. See if she could somehow trap him with the truth. "About a week ago, I was in Valadon's office, when an attack occurred; a dart meant for him hit me, instead. It was loaded with poison."

"Yet, you survived." He smiled. "How is that possible?"

"You tell me." She scrutinized him, beginning to feel some semblance of trust. Try as she might, she could detect no malice, only warmth. "Are there poisons that only work on vampire anatomy and don't affect humans?"

"Of course." He eyed her studiously. "You think whoever fired that dart used my book to compile the ingredients to harm Valadon?"

"It makes sense, doesn't it? That book was found misplaced among some old medical volumes at ValCorp. Someone's trying to kill him."

"Valadon is a Blueblood." Guy lifted the book to his lap and perused the pages. "The most anything in this volume would do to him would be to possibly paralyze him—temporarily. But a vampire as old as Valadon would shake off the effects within moments."

Miranda considered the possibilities and didn't like the implications. That shot hadn't meant to kill him; it was to restrain him so someone he trusted could finish the job.

"So, whoever is trying to kill Valadon, it's probably someone in his own organization." Montglat seemed perturbed.

Miranda's eyes narrowed. "Who?"

Exhaling, Montglat replied, "Men as wealthy and powerful as Valadon have many enemies. Someone jealous of his attributes, his accomplishments, of which many are distinguished, or perhaps someone who thinks ValCorp is in need of a change." He studied her. "You're playing on very dangerous ground. I hope you know that, Miranda. Felicity is quite fond of you, and I would hate to see her upset if you were harmed because you were unaware of what you'd gotten yourself into."

Miranda knew she was in over her head. She needed help trying to find Valadon's would-be assassin. "Can you help him?"

"I cannot." He stood and strolled around the room. "Remember, Miranda, I am in his territory illegally. Also, I do not wish to announce my presence here. I took great pains long ago to disappear from our ruling court. I have no wish to alert them," he seemed reflective, "... to my renaissance."

She understood his desire for solitude, but what if Valadon's attackers succeeded in perfecting a drug that could kill him? She couldn't bear the thought.

"Valadon is quite powerful, Miranda. He has good people under him. I'm sure he can handle those who plot against him. This isn't the first time he's had to deal with adversaries. He's quite a formidable foe."

Her anxiety rose as she regarded Montglat. "Will you reconsider your position?"

"No. But...I might be able to do something for you." As he searched one of the drawers of an antique dresser, she heard the door opening.

"Miranda." Felicity stood in the doorway, dressed in a blue nightgown.

She was shocked at how young her mentor looked. The rest had obviously done her good. When Felicity hugged her, Miranda noticed the fine lines around her eyes had faded. Most people grew old with age, but Felicity was growing young. Miranda eyed Montglat, who only smiled and winked at her.

"I heard you talking out here. It's good to see you again." Felicity strode to Montglat and put her arm around him. "I'm sorry Valadon is having trouble over at ValCorp."

"I'm afraid whoever tried to kill him is going to try again." She looked directly at Montglat. "Imminently."

He went back to searching the drawer. "Ah, here it is." He brought over a small box and handed it to her. "It's an amulet, made long ago. By someone of your talents."

Miranda's brow knitted. "What do you mean?"

A knowing look passed between Guy and Felicity. "You have talents, Miranda. Have you never wondered why you are different from other humans?" he asked.

"I've done some research on extra-sensory perceptions. I know I can sense things in other people and that I'm an empath."

Montglat murmured, "I suspect you can do much more than that."

She didn't want to discuss her other abilities with him and instead examined the necklace with an exquisite piece of amber encased in gold. When she held the amber to the light, she saw a dark red substance in the heart of it.

"That's a drop of my blood, Miranda." Montglat placed the necklace around her neck. "Wear it. I cannot help Valadon. But, perhaps, I can help you. If you find yourself in need of assistance," he said, grinning at Felicity, who returned his smile, "call my name...and I will answer." He seemed to pause in thought. "Felicity tells me I acquired the nickname, Blu. I think I rather like it."

Okay, enough weirdness for one day. Miranda was ready to go home and sleep. Tomorrow, she'd return the book to Valadon and let him deal with it.

"That was naughty of you."

"It was." Guy smiled slyly as he handed Felicity his wine. "But it was the least I could do."

Felicity glanced at the door. "Why didn't you tell her the rest?"

"She'll learn soon enough, I'm afraid." He exhaled with a sigh. "It's up to her to decide what she'll do, now."

Chapter Thirty-Seven

"His ashes have now been washed out to sea." The lights kept low, Remare sat quietly in Valadon's office. "I had one of our sages, Victor, preside over the funeral... It was a quiet affair," Remare said softly, and remembered draping the wooden coffin in garlands of red roses and mint leaves, Kristoph's favorites. He'd taken Kristoph's body out to sea, placed it on a wooden pyre, and then solemnly watched as the flames engulfed it. He sighed. "No one from our house attended the service."

Valadon turned from watching the night sky and the city below. "Does that surprise you?"

Remare felt some people from the house should have attended as Kristoph had been a member for centuries before Valadon had requested his departure. Apparently, no one had agreed with him. He understood their decisions. "Surprised? No. Perhaps...mildly disappointed." He glanced down at the old leather book of vampire scriptures, slid his fingers over the gold and purple binding, and remembered the generous words the sage had uttered in memory of Kristoph.

"I did abjure him. The house knew that."

"I know." Remare exhaled a long breath. "Kristoph was many things, some I did not agree with either, but he was a good informant and loyal. Especially at the end."

"Then, this is settled?

Remare rose and walked toward him. "It is settled. Kristoph now sleeps. And I believe we have more pressing matters to attend to."

"Morel and Aiden have been handling all the communications. Those that needed monitoring are being watched. Go home, Remare. Get some rest. You've been working nonstop since the attack."

Remare nodded. He hadn't gotten much sleep, hadn't ever required much to keep his mind alert. Perhaps, he'd visit his home in Sutton Place; it had been a while since he'd been there, and tonight, he wanted solitude. "I will after I return this book to the archives. Victor said it was so long since we had a funeral, he wasn't sure where his copy was, so I borrowed this."

"Good, then I will accompany you down in the elevator."

***

Miranda was halfway home when she decided to return to ValCorp. She wasn't comfortable carrying around a dangerous book such as the Peralt writings and thought she'd return it to the archives before heading home. When she exited the elevator on the subterranean level, all was quiet as she made her way to the archives.

Once inside, she kept the lights low then walked to the balustrade where she fondly gazed over Valadon's collection and down at the vastness of the archives. She was mesmerized at the different world down here. She closed her eyes and deeply inhaled the scent of the old books and smiled. What a history was here, just waiting to be discovered. Valadon had given her an incredible opportunity, one other scholars would have given their eye teeth for. *Pretty heady stuff.*

She considered turning the overhead lights on before descending, but decided she saw pretty well with the low lights. She grinned and thought she was hanging out with the vampires way too much because her night vision seemed to be getting stronger. She'd once told Lizandra hanging out with the Weres had improved her sense of smell to the point where she could identify distinctions she'd never been able to before. Liz had merely laughed and told her when she started turning furry at the full moon then to let her know.

Miranda decided against returning the volume to the shelf where she and Nick had found it. Whoever had consulted the book to harm Valadon was probably done with it, but she wanted to make sure its location was safely hidden. She was halfway to the biographies on the second level when she sensed she wasn't alone. Her spine quickly stiffened, and her heart sped up. She slowly eyed the shadows, searching for whoever might be down there with her.

Suddenly, a dark apparition appeared behind her. Immediately, the hairs on the back of her neck stood up, and she cautiously turned to face her latest nightmare.

"Keeping late hours...aren't you, professor?" The figure stepped out of the shadows to reveal himself.

Startled, Miranda accidentally dropped the book. At first, she thought the scent of the ocean preceded Valadon's presence, but realized it was Remare's sardonic voice she was hearing and exhaled. *What if Remare was the one who had used the book? Was it possible he was the one behind the attack?* When she asked Nick who was next in line to take over ValCorp if something happened to Valadon, he had abashedly admitted the title of lord would pass to him. However, the council would appoint another to manage affairs until he was properly prepared. In the meantime, the responsibilities would fall on Remare's shoulders. *Could he be the one who tried to assassinate Valadon?* He'd certainly benefit if Valadon was out of the picture. She bent to retrieve the book, keeping the cover hidden with the palm of her hand.

"You're here pretty late yourself. Couldn't sleep and needed some late night reading?" she asked sarcastically.

Remare smiled at her bravado, amused she didn't realize he could sense her distrust. He casually crossed his arms over his chest and leaned against the edge of the bookcase. He'd watched from the shadows as she entered the archives and stood rapt; he'd been transfixed by her sense of serenity that seemed to make her face glow. Remare was beginning to understand Valadon's interest in her. Women with her grace were rare; this was a woman who had found profound pleasure in art and history. He pondered if her interest in art history was to avoid her own kind and then wondered why such an idea had entered his mind.

He gestured to the book in her hand. "What has you so captivated that you're here this late?

"I often work late when I want to finish an assignment." She tried to casually conceal it behind her back. "It's nothing, just a volume of research."

Remare's instincts sharpened, and his eyes darkened. "Then, let me see it," he said with all the charm he could muster, never taking his eyes off of her. Miranda was obviously lying, but why would she lie about a book? Valadon had given her free access to the archives; if she wanted to borrow a book, she had permission to do so. Unless...there was something else in the volume she didn't want him to see. As he moved closer to her, she hesitated, then turned and ran.

Remare's predisposition to chase heightened, and within seconds he was on her back, knocking her to the floor. In an effort to free herself, she elbowed him hard enough in the ribs that he loosened his hold on her. Scrambling to her feet, she was almost to the door when he pounced on her again, trying to get the book.

The impact dislodged it from her fingers, and it flew a few feet in front of them. Miranda reached for it, but so did Remare, and his arms were longer than hers, so she tried to head butt him, but missed. Remare could snap her neck with the slightest of efforts, but he wanted answers first. To stop her from getting the book, he wrapped his fist around her hair and pulled, hoping to stop her forward momentum.

Miranda screamed. "Get off me!"

"Tell me why you ran and what's in the book," he demanded as she wriggled under him, trying to get free. The motion aroused him as her ass rubbed against his hardening cock, but he wouldn't allow the distraction to detract him from the book. He reached for it, holding her down, but when she twisted an arm free, the book seemed to gravitate toward her, and she quickly grabbed it then pulled it under her. His fangs elongated, and he brushed them against the side of her neck as he inhaled her scent. In a sinister voice, he said, "Give. Me. The. Book."

"Go to hell!"

Remare slipped his hands under her and pried the book away from her fingers. She struggled and twisted again until she faced him. She fought like an Amazon to get the book back, using her nails and fists to retrieve it, but he pinned both of her wrists above her head with one hand.

When he saw the cover of the book, his eyes narrowed, and his animosity for the human intensified. What a fool he'd been to believe she was a woman of worth. He loathed himself in that moment almost as much as her for even beginning to trust her. "Why would you want a book on poisons, unless you yourself were working with Valadon's enemies?"

"I'm the one who got shot, remember?" Miranda was panting, now. "You're the one who hopes to succeed him. You're the one who ordered the attack."

Remare was aghast that she would *dare* to question his loyalty and wanted to tear her throat out. She had to be the mole working with their enemies. He'd been certain the traitor was someone else. His breaths quickened, and his fangs extended to their full length. He let her taste his rage as he opened his mouth wide enough to let her get a good look at what would rip her to shreds, but as he lowered his head, his nostrils flared, and he was surprised it wasn't only her fear that was aroused. He whispered softly in her ear, "I would never harm Valadon. He's my liege. But you wouldn't understand such a concept as loyalty. Would you?"

Miranda returned his heated look and screamed, *"VALADON!"*

Remare's ears were ringing at the volume of her shriek, and he was beginning to sense something was very wrong with this situation. When he inhaled again, he could sense no duplicity on her part, no betrayal. *What the fuck?* he thought, as he slowly rose over her.

Valadon burst into the room and saw Remare's fangs hovering over Miranda's neck and used his powers to force them apart. Remare went flying into one couch, and Miranda was gently lowered into the other. Valadon's voice reverberated off the walls. "Why is it I always have to separate you two?"

Miranda sat up quickly and urgently said, "Valadon. Stop him! He has the book on poisons. He's the one who tried to kill you!"

Valadon was baffled by her outburst; his expression ripe with incredulity.

"As if that were ever a possibility," Remare murmured. "I found her here with the book in her own hands." He handed the volume to Valadon.

Valadon eyed both of them and was determined to get to the bottom of this.

"I had nothing to do with the attempt. But he did." She gestured toward Remare. "As soon as he saw the book, the guilt was on his face." Miranda breathed deeply. "I saw it, Valadon."

"What guilt? I wanted to kill you for possessing the book."

"I didn't steal it. I only borrowed it." Miranda smacked herself in the forehead for saying the last.

"Settle down. Both of you." Valadon's deep voice resonated. He gestured for them to remain seated. Like two pit bulls that would tear each other to pieces, Valadon thought as he eyed them. He smiled in amusement that each was ready to kill on his behalf. He had to settle this, now, before the situation got out of hand. "Miranda, Remare had nothing to do with the attempts on my life. He would never betray me. He's been with me for centuries and could have killed me numerous times." He smiled at his friend. "And I could have destroyed him ages ago."

"You could have *tried*," Remare said mockingly as he narrowed his eyes and rubbed his sore ribs.

"He's next in line for your throne. Who else would want you dead? Nick's too young to take control of ValCorp, so it has to be him."

Valadon and Remare exchanged a look. "What has Nick to do with this?"

"He was with me when I found the book. We found it in the stacks together, looking at..."

"What were you looking for?" Valadon asked curiously.

"Just books." Miranda answered.

"What books?" Remare sneered sweetly at her.

"Why don't you ask Nick? He was with me, at the time."

Valadon saw the hostility between them and wondered what had caused such animosity. "Nick's on his way down here, now."

"I'm here." Nick descended the stairs. He glanced first at Miranda and then at the barely controlled rage on Remare's face. "What happened?"

"Tell him about the book, Nick," Miranda said. "They don't seem to believe me."

Nick sat beside Miranda and recounted how they found the book, echoing her version of the events. Halfway through, Valadon was pleased to see that Remare began to look at Miranda differently.

"Why did you want to wait to bring me this book?" Valadon leafed through the pages, remembering when his king had asked him to take the book and hide it. He thought he'd kept it in the vault and not out in the stacks. Someone else had moved it; someone in his own house, who would know about its contents from centuries ago, had used the book in hopes of incapacitating him. But why leave it out? Why leave it in the medical section? Unless the party involved wanted suspicion to fall on Gabriel.

"Nick thought Gabriel was involved, and I knew that wasn't possible." Miranda shook her head. "I wanted to run a translation program and learn more about Peralt before bringing it to your attention. I only asked Nick to wait maybe twenty-four hours, tops. Then, we both would have brought it to you."

Nick nodded in agreement.

"I see." Valadon began remembering events long ago. "And what did your translation tell you?"

"More than I ever wanted to know about your enemies," Miranda admitted. "I downloaded a list of the chemicals Peralt used in his experiments and was going to see Gabriel tomorrow to see if any of them matched the substances found in *me*." She glared at Remare.

"He's probably still up," Valadon said. "We can go see if he's still working in his lab."

"Not me, gentlemen. I've had enough excitement for one night. I trust you three can handle everything. I'm going home." Miranda collected herself and searched for her bag.

"I think it would be best if you stayed here tonight."

Miranda's shoulders sagged at the command in Valadon's voice. "No, thanks! I think I'll be more comfortable in my own bed."

"Perhaps. But you will be safer here."

"Perhaps." She imitated Valadon's tone. "But I'm going home."

Valadon exhaled in frustration that she still didn't trust him or feel comfortable enough in his house to stay the night. A corner of his mouth lifted in amusement. "If you leave, you'll take an escort with you."

Miranda stopped short and said, "Fine." And then flinched when Valadon uttered his next words.

"Remare. Make sure Miranda gets home *safely*. I trust you can manage that without harming a single hair on her head."

The look of shock and sheer reproach on Remare's face was enough to make Valadon smile.

Chapter Thirty-Eight

The ride to Miranda's home was a quiet one—except for the mumbled expletives emanating from Remare. She felt like telling him for the third time it wasn't her idea to have *him* drive her home. The last time she'd said that to him, he'd glowered at her with cold, lethal eyes that said, *"I could think of a hundred other things that require my attention more than safeguarding your sorry ass!"*

Miranda simply relaxed back into the comfortable seating of his black Mercedes SUV. His car was luxury and power wrapped all in one, and she liked the smooth ride. Except for its driver, who seemed to be emitting steam from his ears. She'd tried to argue with Valadon for a different guard, but the stubborn vampire king had made up his mind. At least she knew there were two other vampires in the car following them should Remare forget the part of Valadon's orders with the no causing harm component. She rubbed her scalp again, certain she'd lost a chunk of hair when Remare had gripped it.

When they pulled up in front of her home, Remare stayed in the car, surveying the neighborhood, checking out rooftops and the other cars along the street. She felt safe with him, thinking if anything happened to her, he'd have to answer to Valadon. Not like he couldn't care less himself; she smirked. But still, she'd felt his power when he'd tackled her—even before then, and knew he was one of the most powerful vampires at ValCorp and he could protect her. If he wanted to.

When he didn't get out of the car immediately, Miranda figured it was time to talk. "I care about him."

When Remare glared at her, she saw the ice in his eyes hadn't melted. Pieces of conversations she'd had with Cyra and Morel advocating Remare's loyalty surfaced in her mind. If she hadn't been surprised by his unexpected presence in the archives, she'd have remembered what they'd told her. But who could blame her lapse in judgment after reading the journals of Peralt and hearing the deranged viewpoints of the HOL? She breathed deep and exhaled. "Okay, I was wrong to think you plotted against Valadon. I apologize. I was wrong. Happy, now?"

He growled, "Not. Hardly." He got out of the car and climbed the front steps of her brownstone.

Miranda didn't like him having a key to her home, but let it pass, for now. When they were safely inside, he reset the alarm system, and she watched as one corner of his mouth minutely lifted. He sniffed the air, then did a search of her rooms.

Remare's senses, which had been heightened at ValCorp, hadn't diminished. Upstairs, he needed a moment to get control of his emotions. Breathing hard, he still couldn't believe Valadon had given *him* the assignment of guarding Miranda. He was the leader of the Torians; he didn't do missions that were little more than babysitting. Miranda had gotten under his skin since she'd first come to ValCorp. Initially, he hadn't trusted her because too much was unknown about her. Valadon seemed narrow-minded in his interest in the human, and Remare believed Miranda too costly a vulnerability.

How odd she kept showing up at the most inopportune times. First, at ValCorp when Valadon was almost shot, then at Kristoph's apartment, and now, in the archives when a long-forgotten book was unearthed. Who could blame him for his distrust? But the concern she had for Valadon was genuine; Remare could detect no duplicity. And he was impressed with the way she'd fought tooth and nail to get the book away from him when she'd thought, erroneously, he'd been the one trying to kill Valadon.

He shook his head at Valadon's decision to put them together. Valadon had wanted him to realize what his lord had already known: Miranda was sincere in her protectiveness, not just for Valadon, but for Nick and Gabriel as well. *Gabriel,* he snorted. She had traces of his scent on her Valadon must have been aware of. When Remare was done searching her rooms and satisfied there'd been no tampering, he went back downstairs.

Miranda was in the kitchen, making tea. "Would you like a cup?" She dipped the tea bag in her cup, then met his eyes, "or something stronger."

Remare stood staring at her whiskey-colored eyes. He had a thorough investigation done on her and could find no evidence of treachery. There were no hidden bank accounts, here or in other places of the world. She was a woman who lived within her means and paid her bills on time with no outstanding debts that might predispose her to a bribe to betray Valadon. There'd been no secret meetings between her and members of the HOL. He should have remembered that when he'd nearly sunk his fangs into her. If he was honest with himself, he couldn't truthfully say if he'd meant to harm her or not. Her scent of arousal had nearly undone him; it was no wonder he'd reacted so strongly to her.

"Do you have Moroccan Mint?" he finally asked, knowing she kept some in the back of her cupboard.

"Sure, in that cabinet. It's in the white bag in the corner." Miranda prepared his tea, then led him into the living room. "Are you going to be staying the night?"

"No." Remare sipped his tea as she curled up on the couch. "Gregori will stay with you until morning." Eyes on her, he waited for a remark. "Is that all right with you?"

"Fine. I understand Valadon's concern. How long do you think I'll need guarding?"

"I should think it will not be much longer." Remare watched her as he reclined on her sofa and surveyed the simple elegance of her home. The furniture hadn't been replaced in a long time, but it had a welcoming ambience to it.

After a while, Miranda asked, "You've been following key members of the Human Order of Light, haven't you?"

Remare wondered how much of the investigation Valadon had told her. "We've been keeping an eye on many of Valadon's adversaries throughout the years. HOL members are just one component."

"Valadon has a lot of enemies, doesn't he?"

Remare nodded as he drank his tea.

"I've done some research online," she explained at his inquisitive look. "After the attack. I was curious about who might've tried to kill Valadon and hit me instead." She rubbed her hip for emphasis.

Remare eyed the way she stroked herself and casually crossed one leg over the other. He was interested in how far her research had progressed. "What did you discover?"

"Quite a bit, actually. About twenty years ago there were three main players in the organization." Miranda relaxed more into the couch and tucked her legs into the cushions. "Peter Lundquist, William Tolliver and Theodore Walker. Of the three, Lundquist was the most outspoken against your race."

Remare was intrigued she had done her homework on the HOL. "Go on."

"Lundquist organized rallies and support against having your race given legal status. Valadon and the Coalition for Vampire Rights then went on national television and disputed all his claims against vampires. The CVR was made up of businessmen from around the world who had financial interests in ValCorp and wasn't about to let an extremist organization get in the way of their profits. They waged televised debates that proved vampires had been an integral part of our history since time began. Charles Kendrick then produced the documents to show that you fought on the side of the allies in WWI and WWII."

Remare was impressed with her research and her accurate account of events. "True, but the HOL tried to prove we weren't another race, but a complete and different species that wanted to dominate your kind. They tried to instill fear in the masses in hopes of taking over our financial institutions. It was never about the differences in our beings; they saw our wealth and power as a threat. They spread propaganda about what monsters we were. I believe some of the terms they made up are still in use today such as 'the walking dead'?"

Miranda nodded, then continued, "Valadon became involved in politics, civic affairs. Gave a ton of money to human relief causes like hospitals, schools, and libraries. I watched him give some of his speeches at the museum benefits. He's quite impressive."

The beginnings of respect stirred in his gut for her. "Yes, our people worked tirelessly to present a positive image so humans wouldn't live in fear and hunt us as in times past." He thought for a moment. "It took quite a bit of time and effort to make the transition."

"But public acceptance wasn't complete."

"No. There are still members of the HOL who hope to thwart the progress we've made."

Remare had his people closely monitoring those members whose finances were in precarious positions because of ValCorp's success. As he was about to continue his conversation, his phone rang. Gregori had arrived and was parking his car. Remare was now free to leave, and he almost regretted the Torian's arrival. "It seems we will have to continue our discussion another time." He rose to leave. "Gregori is here. He will watch over you until you are ready to go to work in the morning." He felt the envelope in his pocket and handed it to Miranda.

"What's this?" she asked as she opened it.

"An invitation to Brandon's welcome home party." Remare paused on his way out and then turned to face her. "Valadon would like it very much if you would attend."

"I'll check my schedule and get back to him."

Remare nodded and left as Gregori entered.

Miranda felt a pang of disappointment as Remare departed. This was the most conversation she'd had with the vampire. At least when he wasn't trying to kill her; she smirked. Okay, maybe cracking him in the ribs and biting his wrist hadn't been the best of ideas. And accusing him of treason against Valadon *may* have offended him.

He'd sure looked shocked when she'd said as much when he was on top of her. Miranda tried not to concentrate too much on when he'd held her wrists down. The memory was too disconcerting.

Gregori peeked at the invitation and whistled.

She glanced up at him with raised eyebrows. "What?"

"Brandon's welcome home party. It's traditional, not modern."

Chapter Thirty-Nine

Remare grimaced at the text he'd just received from Tristan. He'd told the youngest Torian to wait for him. Remare didn't like that Zoe seemed to be calling the shots. He texted Tristan to wait until he arrived, but knew Tristan wanted some time alone with her. *Spare me young fools in love!* Then, he texted Morel to meet him in Chinatown. He would take Seventh Avenue downtown and cut across Canal Street. He'd already buried one friend and wasn't about to let fate claim another.

You were young once, too, an inner voice reminded him, *and in love*. Yes, he had been and had nearly died because of it. He put his car in gear and sped toward Chinatown.

***

Zoe hadn't worked for Xiang Shu Xhen in some time. His jewelry stores on Canal Street sold the most exquisite jade and gold pieces; so of course, he had to have the proper chemicals to keep such precious pieces in pristine condition. And it had been too easy to smuggle the illegal substances along with the approved compounds. The powerful vampire had deigned to give her an audience, and after much self-effacement, she was finally able to procure the information she needed. But only at a severe cost. That was always the case with Xhen. Nothing came for free, especially information. She waited in the alley on Mott Street, observing the late night tourists while she kept an eye out for Tristan.

Tristan parked his motorcycle on Pell Street then read Remare's text. He contemplated waiting for him as he checked the area. He was breaking protocol, but this would be the last time he'd see Zoe. Remare and Valadon had made that perfectly clear. Glancing at his watch, he decided not to wait.

He walked north on Mott Street, ignoring the pungent scents of Asian cuisine, passing the drunk and loud tourists exiting the bars. Up ahead, he saw Zoe peering out of the alley. He sighed. Saying a final goodbye to her was going to shred his heart.

As soon as he approached, Zoe dragged him into the alley, threw her arms around him and kissed him wildly.

Tristan knew this was goodbye, but wanted to feel what he'd once felt with her. What he'd never felt with anyone else. His passion rose as Zoe's arms tightened around him. Finally, he broke from the kiss. While they were still panting, he asked if she had what he'd come for.

Zoe nodded and handed him a piece of paper.

"What's this?"

She smiled. "Did you think I wouldn't come through for you?"

Tristan quickly glanced at the paper then put it in his jacket pocket. "I can't stay, Zoe." He perused the alley as an uneasy feeling crept up his spine. "We can't meet again." Tristan felt like a heel for the disappointment he saw in her eyes and brushed a strand of hair from her face. "I'm sorry."

"So am I. For so many things." She reached up and embraced him. "I wanted to see you, one last time."

Tristan's heart was breaking. Remare had been right, he shouldn't have come. He'd already said goodbye. Drawing it out again wasn't helping the situation. "I wanted to see you, too, Zoe." He stroked her cheek. "But we can't go back to what once was."

"Oh, such sentimentality from a Torian," Stryder crooned derisively as he appeared out of the shadows, a dozen enforcers flanking him.

When Tristan glanced behind him, there were other vampires blocking the entrance to the alley. Hell, he wasn't getting out of this alive, he thought, as the rush of adrenaline whirred in his brain. He could handle two or three, maybe four. But there was no way he could fight this many and survive. These vampires were straight up killers, Rogues. He stared at Zoe. *"You get that information to Valadon!"*

"Thank you, Zoe. We couldn't have done it without you." Stryder pulled Zoe to his side and kissed her temple, then smiled at Tristan.

Tristan stared at Zoe, who shook her head frantically. "It wasn't me. I didn't know they were here. I swear it!"

For one blinding moment, Tristan wasn't sure if he believed her. "I know you didn't." Turning with all his vampire speed, he used his daggers to slash the necks of the two men closest to Stryder. If Tristan could make it to the entrance, he might have a chance to get to his motorcycle.

Even though he fought as fast as he could, slicing several men behind the knees, across the neck and abdomen, wherever his blades could find flesh, he was soon overpowered. When he stumbled on one knee, they circled him, and multiple fists connected with his jaw and ribs.

Then, one severe kick to his spine had darkness claiming him.

Zoe screamed in horror as Tristan fell.

"He's already dead to you, my sweet dove," Stryder whispered. "Who else will protect you, if not me?" She fought against his hold, but the Rogue leader was too powerful, and she watched tearfully as Tristan's body hit the ground. Even when he was down, they continued to beat him until his face ran with blood.

Xhen appeared with two of his men. He briefly glimpsed the fallen Torian and then faced her. "I believe you have something which belongs to me."

Zoe didn't fear many men, but Xhen terrified her as he stood staring at her. He had no mercy. She could be bleeding out in the alley, and he wouldn't spare her a backward glance.

Remaining silent, she sank into Stryder's arms. When Xhen's men went to search her, she blurted out, "I don't have it." She knew they would torture her to the point of death. "I gave it to him." She never saw the slap that came from one of the men until she flew from Stryder's arms and hit the wall. Blood trickled down the side of her face.

Xhen's bodyguard searched Tristan's unconscious form, then handed the paper to his boss. Xhen carefully folded it and placed it inside his suit jacket pocket.

"And I believe you have something that is mine." Remare stealthily entered the alley. In his hand was his favorite toy—his sword cane. Within the cane was one of the deadliest swords he'd ever fought with, the edges sharp enough to behead a vampire, if necessary. And tonight, it appeared it would be very necessary.

"Look around you, Remare," Xhen said. "Your reputation is well-known, but do you really think you can fight against all of my men?"

With the confidence of a seasoned warrior, Remare scanned his surroundings and then smirked at Xhen. It had been some time since he'd fought against such odds. But these vampires were only a couple of hundred years old, at best, and against his experience and training, they wouldn't last long. "Let's find out."

Remare unleashed his unrivaled speed and severed the heads of three vampires before they even moved. He whirled the heads at his adversaries before spinning lightning-quick and cutting the tendons at the back of the knees of the vampires. More men fell to the ground moaning. The scent of blood rent the air. Before the others could attack, he had sliced the tendons in the arms of two more assailants, nearly amputating an opponent's arm. When he stopped fighting, his breathing had barely increased. He surveyed the carnage and the remaining men whose faces betrayed hesitancy—a lethal flaw in combat. He then smiled. "Don't stop, now; the foreplay was just getting good."

The other men deferred to Xhen, who raised a hand to end the fighting. When he turned to leave, Remare stopped him.

"I believe you owe me for the damage you have done to mine." He nodded to the fallen Tristan.

"We would not have killed him. Only ransomed him to your leader."

Remare pointed with his sword. "I'll take that piece of paper you have in your pocket. Please go slowly. I would hate to have to use this again and ruin your fine suit."

Xhen slowly removed the paper and tried to hand it to Remare, who shook his head.

Remare nodded to Zoe. "Give it to her."

Zoe clutched the paper and handed it to Remare, who quickly secured it in his pocket.

When she backed up, one of Xhen's men came forward and, in a blink, slit her spinal column. There were many wounds a vampire could heal, but a severed spinal column wasn't one of them. Her body crumbled to the ground.

"Now, we have both suffered a loss." Xhen turned with his remaining men and left the alley.

"Well, that didn't go according to plan." Stryder gazed down at Zoe. "I was rather fond of her." He exhaled. "What a waste."

"Stryder." Remare finally addressed the Rogue leader. "You pick interesting people with whom to do business." He turned with his sword, pointing it at Stryder's neck. "You ally yourself with Valadon's enemies, you become one of them."

"I wasn't aware that Xhen was an enemy."

"Of course not." Remare tilted his wrist up and sliced Stryder's chin, the opposite side where he had already given him a scar. "Perhaps, that will remind you to be more careful with whom you choose to associate."

Stryder leapt forward at the insult. "Someday, I'll have the advantage." He touched the small wound then looked at the blood on his fingers. He glared at Remare. "And I'll be sure to return the favor."

As the vampire slithered away in the darkness, Remare quickly turned to Tristan, whose breath was becoming labored. He bit his wrist so the blood could drip into Tristan's mouth. Several centuries older than Tristan, his blood was powerful enough to revive the badly beaten Torian.

When Tristan opened his eyes, he moaned at the elixir healing his body and pulled at Remare's wrist. When he'd taken enough, he sealed the wounds then stared up at Remare. "Zoe?"

Remare shook his head, then gestured to her body. Tristan's shriek sounded like that of a wounded animal discovering its mate had been killed. As there were no words that would offer little more than cold comfort, Remare held onto the grieving Torian. Aware Morel and the other Torians had arrived, he squeezed Tristan's shoulder. They had known Tristan had never completely gotten over Zoe and solemnly retrieved her body.

Morel waited a moment, then came forward. "We have to leave. Some of the tourists are becoming curious." He bent down and put his hand on Tristan's shoulder. "I'm sorry about Zoe."

"Thanks." Tristan muttered as he was pulled up by the Torians and led to a waiting van.

"Morel. About time you showed up," Remare said sarcastically as he cleaned his sword.

"I would have joined you sooner," he smirked, "but you seemed to be having so much fun."

Remare read the paper Zoe had given him and exhaled. "We need to speak with Valadon. He needs to be updated."

***

"Well, you were lucky; your kidneys were badly bruised, but you'll heal with bedrest." Gently, Gabriel finished taping Tristan's cracked ribs. "Try to avoid any strenuous activities for a few days. The Vicodin should help with the pain, but let me know if you need more."

Tristan felt like he was run over by a Hummer. At least, he had stopped pissing blood; that was a sight he could have done without. His bruises were already beginning to fade, but they still hurt like hell. A vampire's skin was tougher than a human's, but given enough punishment, the pain was the same. Normally, he didn't take painkillers, but tonight, yeah, he needed them.

He remembered another time when Gabriel had bandaged him. Almost a century ago. If he hadn't gone back to Gabriel's home, to thank him, he never would've found Gabriel and his family, who'd been slaughtered by Rogues. The abattoir of blood had haunted him, for years. He couldn't imagine the hellish nightmares Gabriel must have had. Tristan remembered wishing he never lost someone he loved as much as Gabriel had loved his family.

And now, he had.

As he lay back on the bed, Gabriel rearranged the medical supplies. Word had been out among the Torians for some time that Gabriel would soon be leaving ValCorp. Tristan was saddened at the prospect. "You're really going to leave us?"

Gabriel seemed to reflect. "I have to. It's my calling. I'm not like you and the rest of the Torians. I remember too well what it was like to be human. It's not something you forget."

Tristan knew Valadon thought of Gabriel as a son. "He'll miss you. We all will."

"As much as I hate to admit it...same. But my grant came through. If I don't leave, now, I never will, and my research is too important to me. Besides, I'll still be in the city, only uptown at Rockefeller University. I'll come back every now and then to check on you guys." He seemed to hesitate. "Do you want to spend the rest of the night here or in your own room?"

One corner of Tristan's mouth lifted. "My bed's more comfortable." He didn't want anyone to know how much pain he was in and wanted some time alone.

"I don't suppose I can talk you into using a wheelchair?"

Tristan gave him a look that had Gabriel shaking his head. No Torian would ever choose to be seen as weakened.

"Okay, I'll help you to your rooms." Gabriel hooked his arm around Tristan and escorted him out of the infirmary. In Tristan's room, Gabriel carefully laid him down on the mattress, and more memories from a century ago surfaced of when he'd been badly hurt by Rogues and Gabriel treating him.

"Did you blame me? All those years ago?" Tristan asked quietly.

Gabriel was confused. "Blame you for what?"

Tristan thought it was time he told him. "When your family...when you nearly died...it was *me* who called Valadon. When he saw you were still breathing, he made the decision to turn you. He said you were too valuable an ally, and a too good friend, to let you die."

Gabriel slowly closed his eyes. "I never blamed you."

Tristan remembered Gabriel's beautiful wife, Kate and his son, Peter, but he especially remembered Karen, Gabriel's young daughter and her ever smiling face. The Rogues had been merciless with her young body. "While you were transitioning, Bastien and I hunted down the Rogues. But when we found them they had already been slaughtered."

"I know. Valadon told me he'd make sure they never did to another human being what they did to my family."

No one had ever spoken of it, but when Bas and he had returned to their mansion, Tristan saw Remare cleaning and sharpening his sword. Remare had merely tilted his head in his direction and gone back to his task. "Valadon ordered their executions."

"So I wouldn't have to." Gabriel sighed, seemingly lost in his memories, and then turned toward Tristan. "You should get some sleep. If you need more meds or anything, call me. I'll be upstairs." He paused momentarily at the door. "I'm sorry for your loss. I never met Zoe, but the rest of the Torians spoke well of her."

"Thank you." Tristan thought for a moment. "Hey, you're still going to play left wing in our annual hockey game, aren't you? Bas says you're one of the best shooters he's ever seen."

"Sure thing." Gabriel grinned as he shut the door. "You guys would lose without me."

After Gabriel left, Tristan limped to his dresser and found an old leather bracelet with stones threaded in the center he'd once bought Zoe. She'd left it behind when she departed from Valadon House. He believed she'd left it for him to remember her. Tristan barely made it to the bed when there was a knock on the door. He knew who it was before the door opened and quickly shoved the bracelet under his pillow before laying down.

"Don't rise. I won't stay long." Remare closed the door behind him, walked over to the edge of the bed and sat. He eyed the contusions covering Tristan's face and sighed. "The bruises will heal. When you're ready, I want you in the gym. I need all my Torians combat ready. Sometimes soldiers suffer a lack of confidence after surviving a defeat. The training will do you good."

"You're going to kick my ass for not waiting?"

"Only if you ever do something as stupid as you did this evening." Remare glanced down. "Valadon has issued a decision regarding your behavior tonight."

Tristan swallowed audibly. For a moment, he feared he too would be kicked out of Valadon's service. But if that were the case, Valadon would have come himself. "What is it?"

Remare smiled reassuringly. "He was not pleased you left without backup, again, and had contact with Zoe, even though her information was valuable to us."

Tristan nodded. At least, she didn't die in vain. Zoe would've hated that. "What did she find out? I never had a chance to read it."

"A name." Remare sighed. "The name of a very powerful man who may have ordered the hit on Valadon and a list of chemicals bought and paid for. We're working on it now." He exhaled. "Valadon is not in a position to let his laws go unpunished, especially those rules designed for your protection, as well as that of all the Torians." When Tristan rose his hand in a gesture of explanation, Remare quieted him. "Before you ask, know this, Valadon has his reasons for the decisions he makes and doesn't always make me privy to them." His voice softened. "Understand there are wheels in motion I cannot discuss. That being said, Valadon wants you in seclusion."

Tristan wondered what Remare wasn't telling him. "How long?"

"One month." Remare rose and strolled around the bedroom. "You can do that."

Seclusion. Tristan would be in seclusion for a month away from the Torians. In times past, the isolation would have been bitterly painful for some vampires, but with all his electronic toys, the penalty of seclusion didn't have the same bite it once had. Valadon had been merciful. According to their laws, Tristan would not be able to talk with others, share a meal with them or be in their presence. But he could text them. A month, now, was nothing compared to the seclusions other vampires had endured in the past. Some had suffered in far worse surroundings for far longer durations.

"Where?" Tristan swallowed loudly, again. A month away from his friends would be agonizing, but he'd endure it. The Torians were his family, and he'd miss them. He never understood the stories he'd been told about the ancients who voluntarily went into seclusion; to him, it was just another form of death. But he guessed at Valadon's reasoning. He'd screwed up tonight and almost died because of it. Valadon wanted him to reflect on that.

"For now, you'll stay in this room. Meals will be brought to you, and Gabriel will say when you're ready to travel. You will not be allowed to attend Brandon's welcome home party. In a few days I'll transport you to one of my homes." When Remare saw Tristan's jaw drop, he smirked. "I'm sure you'll find the accommodations acceptable." When Remare neared the door, he stopped and slowly turned to face Tristan. "I am sorry...about Zoe. I know you had feelings for her."

After Remare left, Tristan let his head fall back on the pillow. Remare had several homes throughout the world, but he hoped he'd be stationed in Remare's Sutton Place town house. He didn't want to be far from ValCorp; Valadon needed all his Torians near him. He'd been looking forward to Brandon's party, but even if he hadn't been secluded, he'd probably be on bedrest anyway with his cracked ribs.

At least that's what he told himself as the painkillers kicked in and sleep finally claimed him.

Chapter Forty

"And you're *sure* there's nothing else I need to know about traditional parties?" Miranda slipped into the dress Cyra insisted she try on.

Laying on her bed, Cyra threw her head back and laughed. "I already told you the difference is in the fashions. *Mostly*. It's sort of like a masquerade, but not really. Oh, and *no* electronic devices are allowed. Even the music will be live. Rarely do we celebrate in the old ways, but Brandon insisted on it, and sometimes, it's just plain fun dressing up in the old styles." She rose to adjust Miranda's dress. "Brandon feels we sometimes forget who we are or where we come from, like we could ever forget." Cyra rolled her eyes. "He likes to party in the old traditional ways. Oh, and one last thing. No one *ever* wears red at these parties." She smiled, revealing her fangs. "For obvious reasons."

"Good to know." Miranda stood in front of the full-length mirror, admiring the long black gown.

Cyra tied the thin gold straps that crisscrossed beneath Miranda's breasts and went around her back. Some of the other vampire gowns were risqué, more daring than Miranda would ever consider wearing, but Cyra promised this dress would look good on her.

"Wow, he's really going to love you in that gown."

"Not sure about these slits, though." Miranda showed her leg where the slits went up nearly to her hip. "I think I can wear a really nice pair of black leggings with this."

"Don't you *dare!*" Cyra was outraged. "That gown was designed to show off your assets."

"But I'd feel more comfortable with something else underneath." Miranda walked around, checking to see how much was revealed when she moved.

"I'm glad you accepted the position Valadon offered you. He seems happy, more content, than I've seen in years past." Cyra became sullen. "He's been alone for too long."

Before Miranda could answer, Morel appeared dressed in a tan tunic that showed off his powerful biceps, which were adorned with gold cuffs, and dark brown leather pants and boots.

"Whoa, what have we here?" He walked in and gave his wife a hug. "Miranda, you look marvelous." He eyed the dress and the way it draped over her figure.

"Not too shabby yourself. My God! Morel, you could pass for a god of times past." She winked at Cyra.

"Who says I wasn't?" He laughed as he circled his arms around his wife.

Cyra and Morel were wearing the same colors, and it wasn't lost on her that she was wearing Valadon's colors of black and gold. *Not too subtle, Valadon.* She wondered what colors Gabriel would be wearing.

***

"She wouldn't admit to it, but I'm positive she knows of Mulciber's activities." Bastien sat in the wingback chair in Valadon's room and reported on Mulciber's and Persephone's movements. "The little sex kitten thought to elicit information from me. She had no clue I was the one playing her."

Valadon stood back and considered Bastien. With his dark hair and eyes and sculptured cheekbones, Bastien could easily have been a Hollywood actor, but his real talents lay elsewhere. As a spy, he was one of the best, using his intelligence and good looks to accomplish the most difficult of assignments. Valadon had known both of his parents in Europe. But if Persephone was aware of her father's illicit activities, he had to know. Unlike her father, who had diplomatic immunities, Persephone could be punished for criminal activities. "Did she tell you anything else?" Valadon asked as Bastien squirmed for a comfortable position in the chair.

"No, but she did try to weasel out of me your involvement with Miranda Crescent. She asked several questions about her." Bastien shifted to one side in the chair.

Valadon suspected Mulciber had set Persephone upon his Torians. Of all his guards, she seemed to focus her sights on Bastien the most. He had instructed the handsome Torian to feed her information innocuous enough to keep her coming back. Bastien had been able to convince her he was pliable, even though he'd always been fiercely loyal to Valadon. "What did you tell her?"

Bastien appeared mildly surprised at the question. "Only what I know: she's here to validate your art collection. That's common knowledge enough."

"Did she believe you?"

"Not hardly." He grimaced as he shifted again. "She kept digging, hoping I would tell her more."

There was a knock on his door. Remare entered, immediately noticing the pain Bastien was in. "The party seems to be going well. The others are out there, enjoying themselves." His oldest friend chided him. "You do plan to make an appearance at your own brother's welcome home party?"

"Of course. But I thought I'd let Brandon enjoy himself a little longer before I join them. He seems to like the attention in the court, especially from the ladies." Valadon's voice lowered. "Has Mulciber made an appearance?"

"Not that I've seen, but I've only just arrived." Remare smirked at Bastien. "Tristan left his motorcycle in Chinatown. Do you feel up to retrieving it for him?"

Bastien narrowed his eyes, and Valadon nearly laughed, knowing Remare was having fun at Bastien's behalf. It was common knowledge among the Torians that Persephone liked her sex games with an edge, often inflicting pain.

"I'm sure our people have already returned it."

Valadon grinned at the thought of Bastien going anywhere near a motorcycle with his sore balls.

"Ah, of course they have," Remare said in a mocking tone. "Whatever was I thinking?"

"How's Tristan doing?" Bastien asked. "When I went to visit him, I saw the seclusion warning on his door. Is he going to be all right?"

"He's going to be fine," Valadon answered. "Gabriel reported he's healing very well." He slanted a look at Remare. "In another night or two, he'll be able to travel."

Concern marred Bastien's face.

"It won't be that long a while." Valadon exhaled. "We'll have him back soon enough."

Bastien rose, bowed, and then left, closing the door behind him.

"How are the others taking the news of Tristan's punishment?" Valadon asked.

"They understand." Remare folded his arms over his chest and stroked his goatee with his thumb. "As you know, Tristan is the house favorite."

Tristan was well-liked because of his quick wit and sense of humor. He would be missed, but it would only be for a short time. And no one in the house besides Remare and he would know where Tristan was secluded. "What have your spies learned?"

Remare smiled as he relayed his latest intel. "Irina has been very successful with a member of the HOL. It appears our friends have a celebration of their own planned at an estate on Long Island. Several members of the HOL will be there as well as our own people. I was thinking of bringing Aiden in on the investigation, let him access their computers and get the proof we need those involved willfully and knowingly conspired to murder you."

Valadon sighed. Irina was one of their best operatives. She'd been coldly trained by her Russian handlers and knew well the art of seduction. But it was her affinity for pain that concerned him. "Very well, but wait until after the party to inform him." Aiden, along with his wife, Bree, were the best at information retrieval. But tonight was for socializing, and Valadon wanted his people to have one night of enjoyment before they set out on their missions. "Now, if you don't mind, I wish to get ready for Brandon's party."

Remare walked down the corridor to his own rooms and grinned at the thought of them all in formal dress tonight. Usually they held celebrations in the upper floor banquet rooms. The view of the Hudson River was spectacular, but Brandon had wanted the lower level for his party. Valadon's brother had always been a traditionalist, and that concerned him. Remare ground his molars. The news his spies had sent him was less than encouraging; some of their European cousins still participated in rituals most modern vampires considered archaic and distasteful. Brandon had gleefully taken part in some of those blood parties. Even more disturbing were the reports that the Council thought Valadon was becoming too modern in his associations with humans. Didn't they know Valadon was first and foremost a vampire—a leader amongst their people?

However, when Valadon wore the robes of ancient times, he truly did look like a king. Even his voice deepened and assumed a tone of supreme authority. The only thing missing was a crown. But that was where Valadon drew a line. He'd once said he would never wear a crown. And he never had. Everyone revered Valadon and was loyal to their leader who had worked long and hard for their freedom. *Well, almost everyone.* Remare frowned. Soon, those who had conspired against Valadon would be unveiled.

And then...there would be no mercy for any of them.

Chapter Forty-One

When the elevator doors opened, the dimly lit main room was nearly deserted. Following the sounds of laughter and music, Miranda walked down the corridor to the banquet hall. On one wall was a life-size painting of Brandon with a sash across it, *"Welcome Home!"* She studied the curve of his lips and the look in his eyes, and immediately, the hairs on the back of her neck tingled. *What canaries have you swallowed?* This was a man who held many secrets, she was sure of it.

She gazed around the crowded room; a dais with ornate chairs was at the far end. She had a pretty good idea who'd be sitting there tonight. Most of the people were dressed in gowns and outfits from ancient times, as per Brandon's request. Conversations continued as she strolled in. Barely anyone glanced her way. Except for one.

Miranda grinned at Cyra's mock horrified expression at her choice of footwear with the elegant gown. Miranda thought she looked pretty damned badass herself, but perhaps at such a formal gathering, the boots may not have been the best choice. The leggings felt like a second layer of skin under the revealing dress. So what if no other females were wearing leather boots? Miranda wasn't a vampire and didn't have to dress like everyone else. Right?

Cyra playfully glared as she embraced her. "I see you made it and took my advice."

"But the main point is that I did make it." Miranda laughed as she hugged her friend and admired her tan dress that covered one shoulder and left the other bare. With Cyra's red hair up in curls and draped down her back, she could give Venus a run for the money in the looks department.

"You look stunning."

"So do you." Miranda adored Cyra and was in awe of her elflike visage with her fair complexion, pointed chin and small nose. It just didn't seem fair that vampires appeared more attractive than humans. *Were we out sick the day they gave out the best features?* Although she knew when she applied makeup for special occasions, her features came alive. She accentuated her eyes with liner and mascara to full effect and made sure her already high cheekbones were accented as well. Vampires weren't the only ones who could play dress up.

Miranda glanced around the room and recognized many of the vampires she'd met when Gabriel and she had visited House Valadon, but didn't see her favorite assistant. "Is Nick here?"

"I saw him earlier, and he said he had other plans. Morel's making sure everything's running right in the communications room and will join us later." Cyra then introduced her to a few vampires who worked for Valadon Miranda hadn't met before.

As Miranda circulated the banquet hall, Aiden and Bree strode toward her, and she saw how handsome the vampires of Valadon House truly were. Tall and of slender build, Aiden was a looker. With his dark hair and dark blue eyes, he was striking, as was his wife who had similar aspects.

"We never got the chance to thank you for saving Valadon's life." Bree said quietly, "You were very brave."

Bravery had nothing to do with it; she'd just reacted on instinct. Jumping on top of a powerful vampire to protect him may not have been the smartest decision she'd ever made but she was glad she had.

Aiden smiled. "Bree is right. We should have done something to show our gratitude to you for saving Valadon's life."

"Not at all." Miranda shook her head. "From what I've heard, he'd gladly have done the same for me or any of you." She scanned the room. "Where is he?"

"He's still meeting with his Torians." Morel joined them and hugged his wife. "I see you went with the boots." He grinned.

"Everyone's a critic," Miranda muttered, forgetting how acute vampire hearing was.

"Hey, I like them. I think they look great on you." Morel coughed as Cyra elbowed him.

"So, this is the charming woman who saved Valadon's life." A vampire who was almost as tall as Morel joined them. Like everyone else, he was dressed in clothes suitable at an ancient Roman celebration, though his accent sounded Scandinavian. Like Morel, he was blond, but kept his platinum locks long and wavy. He was incredibly handsome and smiled as he kissed her hand, never taking his aquamarine eyes off of her.

Miranda felt the tingle of vibrations she usually felt in the presence of vampires and instinctively knew he was an older vampire who was currently dimming his power.

"Miranda, this is Arik. He's the leader of the vampires on Long Island," Morel said. "Arik, Miranda Crescent, Valadon's guest tonight."

"Good evening." Most vampires knew how to hide their fangs when they smiled, but Miranda had the distinct feeling he was baring his for her perusal.

"Well, I will say Valadon has good taste in women. It's a pleasure meeting you, Miranda. I hope we'll get a chance to speak more later." He bowed, then left to talk with another vampire.

"Arik has been an ally of ours, for a long time, but doesn't always attend our parties," Morel remarked. "I'm surprised he made it tonight. I didn't think he was all that friendly with Brandon."

"Court politics." Aiden explained, "They both have mutual friends in our high court. I hear Arik's been spending considerable time visiting with them."

When they looked at each other in a manner that suggested silent communication, Miranda wondered what Aiden and Morel were discussing and sensed their camaraderie. Vampires weren't so different from Weres. This was Valadon's family: His Torians were his brothers and sisters, and like the Weres, they were fiercely protective of each other. All of the Torians she spoke with had a good vibe, and she could sense their loyalty.

Miranda continued circulating and spotted Gregori, who stood off in one corner, looking uncomfortable in his tight leather pants. *My God*, the vampire was seriously built with more muscles than any other vampire there. His biceps were huge! Noting the tattoos on his forearm, she wondered what language the words were in. "Hello, Gregori."

Gregori nodded, admiring her dress. "Hello, Miranda. Interesting concept for a party, huh?"

"You know, I kind of like it." She smiled. *Interesting, yes.*

"Miranda, I'm glad you made it."

As she turned, the hairs on her neck rose. She recognized Bastien's voice, but not the young woman on his arm. With her long blond hair and penetrating blue eyes, she was beautiful. As Bastien talked with Gregori, Miranda's sense of vibration sharpened. She barely heard Bastien's introduction as she stared at the woman whose eyes became dark as midnight. Miranda knew to keep her mental shields up, but with this vampire, it seemed imperative. She could feel a wave of energy trying to mentally grasp her mind—something highly illegal. After a moment, it receded, and she was grateful the woman moved on. After they excused themselves to talk to others, Miranda took one step and froze.

Strange how memory is affected by the sense of smell. She would've thought it was something people saw that triggered memories, or perhaps, a sound woke the brain up to a distant memory that had been sleeping. But tonight it had been the whiff of perfume that jogged her memory.

Remare observed the guests at the party and spotted Miranda talking with Gregori. He smiled when he saw Gregori keep shifting his gaze toward Irina. Then, Miranda turned in his direction and stopped dead in her tracks. Something had affected her that made her stand rapt. Remare silently made his way toward her, noticing how her dress accentuated her feminine curves, which he was becoming annoyingly attracted to. With the slits nearly to her hips and the dark leggings caressing her legs along with the leather boots, she looked captivating, like a warrior woman. Remare wondered how she'd look wearing only the boots and felt himself grow hard. He immediately cleared his head and concentrated on her face, her expression growing more pensive.

"Mir-randa," he said softly to get her attention.

She peered up at him, and a plea escaped her throat. "Remare."

When Remare heard her plaintive cry and saw the pained look in her eyes, every instinct he had fired up to take her in his arms and protect her from whatever was affecting her so adversely. He stared into her eyes, willing her to confide in him.

In a voice that was barely a whisper, she said, "I know."

Remare heard her heart beating rapidly and knew what she'd remembered was crucial. He pulled her closer and whispered, "School your face. Or everyone else in the room will know, as well."

Miranda tried to avert her expression by taking deep breaths. "I can't," she whispered as she lowered her head.

"Try harder." He tenderly lifted her chin. "Concentrate." He stroked her cheek with his thumb and moved in closer. "Breathe."

Miranda curled her fingers around his forearm, and Remare felt her becoming focused. He led her to the exit, and when they were in the hallway, she said, "I remembered."

"Not here," Remare said in a low voice. There wasn't anyone nearby, but vampire hearing was acute, and he wasn't going to take any chances of being overheard. He pulled her down the hall until they reached the main living area and the set of French doors that opened to a balcony. This far down, the only view was of the cave lit up by tiny lights. He pushed her outside, making sure no one saw them, and closed the doors behind them.

Miranda's eyes were mesmerizing in their intensity, and Remare reminded himself he was here for information, not to be captivated by her beauty, even though she was having a drugging effect on him. He stepped closer. "Tell me."

She nodded. "It was the scent of her perfume that triggered the memory," she finally whispered. "At the time, I didn't think anything of it, but..."

Remare narrowed his eyes. "What perfume?"

"It's called, *The Stars at Night*, by Rimini, one of your designers, I think. Cyra gave me it for Christmas one year and explained the scent is different on vampires than on humans or Weres." She gazed up at him. "I recognized the scent tonight, Remare."

"Who was wearing it?"

"She was with Bastien...Persephone."

Remare stepped back, giving her the space she needed to organize her thoughts. "Go on."

"The night of the attack, I was walking down the hall to Valadon's office when I smelled this perfume." Miranda met his eyes. "Remare, I don't know how...but hanging out with the Weres, my sense of smell has become sharper than it used to be—more precise. I know the scent."

He believed her and wanted to hear more. "Tell me."

She walked the few steps to the end of the balcony and placed her hands on the smooth stone. "I saw a shadow in the hall outside Valadon's office, but thought nothing of it. Perhaps, someone had worked late, I thought. I wasn't paying attention. God! I can't believe I'm just remembering this, now." She stared at him. "Persephone was there. The night Valadon was in his office, and I was shot. I'm sure of it."

Remare had wondered who was in the vicinity when Valadon was supposed to be incapacitated. Those drugs in the dart were never meant to kill him, just paralyze him so another could finish the job. A growl rose up in his throat. He never believed it was one of his Torians, but everyone else in the building had left or been accounted for. There was no reason for Persephone to be there that late.

"Did she see your expression when you remembered?" Remare needed to know.

"No. She was already turned from me when I caught the scent."

"Be sure, Mir-randa." He gently caressed her arms. "This is important. If she thinks for a moment you remembered something from that night, you could be in danger."

"No. Bastien and Persephone were already turning to talk to someone else when the scent hit me."

"You're certain?"

"Yes." Miranda nodded. "We need to tell Valadon."

"I want you to go straight to his rooms. But walk casually, don't attract attention." His eyes narrowed. "Do you know where they are?"

"Yes. I've been to them." When he arched a brow, she rolled her eyes and added, "As well as the living quarters of the Torians. Bree and Cyra showed me around when Valadon invited Gabriel and me for lunch." She shrugged nonchalantly.

One corner of Remare's mouth rose. "Thank you for telling me. Tell Valadon everything. I'll join you in a few minutes. It's better if we leave separately and are not seen going to him together."

Miranda nodded and turned to leave, then looked back. "Who is she? Persephone?"

"Besides Bastien's sometime lover," Remare smiled one of his trademark smirks, "she's Mulciber's daughter."

Well, that would explain the burning sensation Miranda had felt going up her arms when she met the female vampire. She had known something was wrong as soon as she sensed the vampire slithering behind her. Something evil. Miranda knew it as she walked down the hall to Valadon's room. And if Mulciber was her father, the apple didn't fall far from the tree.

Her body shuddering, Miranda paused, then turned and thought of Remare on the balcony. He'd looked dangerously sexy dressed in black leather. She'd known he was muscular from the time she'd seen him spar with Morel, but hadn't realized how sensually attractive Remare was until she found herself standing only a breath away with his hands on her, his thumbs tenderly caressing her skin. She remembered his masculine scent and how she'd been drawn to him. Remare's energy level was intense, but for some reason, it didn't affect her the way other vampires did. Unlike the burning sensation she felt with other vampires, Remare's vibration hummed against hers.

Continuing down the hall, Miranda hesitated outside Valadon's door, not sure if she should knock or just enter his private quarters. She'd been checking behind her to make sure she wasn't followed. Instead of waiting any longer with the chance she might be seen, she opened the door and slipped inside.

Remare waited a few minutes before leaving the balcony. He needed to collect his thoughts. He was becoming attracted to Valadon's woman and needed to back off. Miranda was truly as dangerous as he'd first surmised when he'd pounced on her in Valadon's office when he believed her to be an assassin. But it wasn't just Valadon she was becoming a threat to. Remare's hunger for her was growing, and he'd nearly pushed her up against the wall to have her. His first and only loyalty was to Valadon, so why was he wanting her? He needed to get her scent out of his mind, and that was the real reason he'd stayed behind.

When Remare saw his erection was still hard, he sighed and willed himself to soften. Centuries ago, he'd been trained by the council elders, as many vampires of his age had been, to seduce and be seduced. Through the harshest of training, he'd learned to control his emotions and his body's reactions.

But tonight, his training was failing him. He grimaced sarcastically; it was a good thing he'd chosen the long vest that covered his groin.

Chapter Forty-Two

Miranda took a deep breath, then another, and another. What a sight Valadon made as he finished pulling on his black leather pants over his long, muscular thighs and curved butt. Lizandra would've said, *"Definitely bitable,"* and Miranda wondered if she had.

Valadon had been standing at an angle when she opened the door, and she couldn't miss seeing how well-endowed the vampire king was. *My God!* The vampire was blessed in the male parts department. And she thought male Weres had won that lottery. Her eyes drifted over his tight abs to his pecs. Valadon was built, but until she'd seen him nearly naked, she had no idea just how finely sculpted his body was. She knew she should say something, but couldn't utter a syllable as she beheld his magnificent form. "I...I..."

"I'm glad to see you too, Miranda." Valadon smirked, amused by her reaction. He slowly finished tying the laces of his fly so that her attention was focused on his groin. "Are you enjoying...the party?"

Miranda found it difficult to breathe, but managed to utter, "Hi."

Valadon had just finished his shower, and the moisture was still slick on his skin. When he lifted his arms up to smooth back his hair, Miranda got a good look at his broad chest. His hair was still wet and wavy as he ran his hands through it. *Holy smokes!* Her heart sped up, the vampire was a god with his body. She appraised his whole appearance and inhaled his clean night ocean scent. All the female hormones in her body started raising their hands saying, *Ready now, pick me, pick me!*

With sensual prowess, Valadon strode toward her. Gripping her arms with his hands, he inhaled her scent. A low growl of male satisfaction erupted, and he bent his head, his breath brushing against her neck just below her ear. When she whimpered, his tongue caressed the vein from the base of her neck to her ear.

Miranda's knees buckled. She held on to him, knowing she'd melt to the floor if he wasn't holding her up. She shouldn't be doing this, she knew it, but for the life of her, she couldn't remember why. When his lips met hers, the ability to think vanished. Miranda was riding a wave of sensual desire as he held her in his muscular arms. His wonderful male scent sang across her skin, giving her a profound sense of womanhood.

Valadon had to be experiencing similar sensations because he rubbed himself against her, and then, she heard the sound of purring deep in her throat. He lifted her in his arms and brought her to his bed. Miranda's dress fell by the sides of her legs. He caressed her thigh with his hand, bringing her knee up and out so that he could fit inside the cradle of her thighs. He kissed her sternum and worked his way up her throat to her jaw and mouth.

Miranda was drowning in sensuality, wanting, craving his touch and inhaling his scent that endowed her with the ability to grasp new heights of pleasure. One knee rose as Valadon fit himself against her core, but there were too many clothes in the way. Both of them should be naked, this wonderful energy between them stroking them senseless. Her hands roamed his back, enjoying the sensations of his muscles rippling under her touch.

Valadon lowered the top of her gown down with his fangs, gently pulling the material off her shoulder, letting his tongue travel around her breast.

"Valadon, did Miranda finish telling you what she remembered?" Remare's voice cut through the sensual haze, and Valadon roared at the interruption. When Valadon glared at him, there was fire in his eyes, the red rims around his irises widening and glowing with sparks. Remare stood silently against the door, watching as Valadon took deep breaths and got hold of himself.

Miranda righted herself and pushed Valadon off as she slipped from the bed. It took her a minute to realize what the hell had just happened, and she evened her breathing as she held Remare's scrutinizing glance.

"Doesn't anyone knock in this place?" Valadon shifted off the bed and reached for his sleeveless robe. After tightening the gold belt around his waist, he stroked one hand down Miranda's arm before he turned to face his second. "Why are you here?"

"I do believe I told Miranda I would be joining you a few moments ago," Remare said matter-of-factly, then perceived her flushed face. "Isn't that correct?"

Miranda nodded, went to the bar and grabbed a bottle of cold water. After she swallowed a few gulps and her hormones swam back to the depths of her consciousness, she was able to speak again. "I needed to *talk* to you. That's why I came here."

When she finished telling her tale, Valadon stood rapt with his fists on his hips, his body vibrating with rage.

Finally, Remare moved from his stance by the door to stand by Valadon. "If Persephone is involved, you know she was acting on orders from her father." He gripped Valadon's shoulder. "She doesn't have the resources to pull off something like this by herself."

Valadon regarded Miranda so intently she thought she'd turn to stone if she didn't move. "You're absolutely certain it was Persephone's scent you caught that night?" His deep authoritative voice made her skin prickle.

Miranda nodded and turned away. She wasn't about to tell him it wasn't the scent alone that convinced her. How could she explain that she sensed a vampire's natural vibration and pitch? Each was like a signature—unique. That wasn't information she wanted anyone else to know. She turned back. "Liz says that it's my time spent with the Weres that's increased my ability to discern nuances in smell. Whatever! Valadon, I'm sure it was her. Every instinct in my body tells me so."

Valadon brushed a strand of hair off her face. "I can't have her punished on instinct alone." Then, he turned to Remare. "I didn't want to believe he'd go this far. And there's something else: Mulciber's been skimming on the tithe to our council. Reese, in accounting, showed me the financials. I should have confronted him, then. I didn't think Mulciber had the balls to plot an assassination attempt against me. It makes no sense; he cannot be lord of this territory." He paced his room like the ruler he was, barely reining in his temper. "Unless he hopes to cause concerns in the council and has already chosen my replacement." He eyed Remare with wrath and disdain. "Who'd be fool enough to challenge me?"

Miranda and Remare exchanged a look as they felt Valadon's energy escalating. She glanced at the walls and wondered if they were beginning to tremble with the force of Valadon's power. "Wait a minute. I thought it was the HOL who were conspiring against you?" She met Valadon's eyes. "You think he was allying himself with your enemies?"

Remare stared at her with a sarcastic gleam in his eye. "The enemy of my enemy is my friend."

"Jesus, Valadon, you have a lot of enemies." She remembered reading the tales of Peralt in the archives and his atrocious experiments on vampires. She quickly shook off the memory. "But what about Persephone; will you call her in for questioning?"

"Even if we did, she'd lie through her teeth. Her father is ambassador to our ruling court in Europe. I can't make an accusation without proof."

"So, get it." Miranda didn't have a full grasp of vampire politics, so when both heads turned in her direction, she said, "You can't make a move against Mulciber without evidence. So, get it from her."

"I'm the one who set forth the laws governing vampire powers. I can't very well invade her mind." He sneered. "It's possible I would destroy her before she admitted to any wrongdoing."

Miranda knew from Mulciber's pitch and energy levels he was far older than Valadon. She didn't want to contemplate what a confrontation between the two vampires would be like. "But you're the king; couldn't you confront him about his daughter?"

Remare stepped forward. "You don't understand vampire politics, Mir-randa. To make such an accusation without proof is tantamount to accusing a high-ranking member of our ruling court of treason." He crossed his arms in front of his chest and breathed out. "Bastien has been keeping a keen eye on her movements, for some time, and he has not been able to gather the evidence we need."

"So, you've suspected her before this?"

"We like to keep an eye on those we don't fully trust," he smirked at her, "and have a pretty good idea of her loyalties." Remare glanced up at Valadon. "She hasn't yet mastered the art of subtlety."

When there was a knock at the door, all heads turned as Valadon said, "Come in."

Gabriel walked in and seemed surprised to see Miranda. His face brightened. "I checked on Tristan. He's resting well. I also have the report you wanted on the other matter." He handed a folded piece of paper to Valadon, who briefly glanced at it then tossed it on the table. When Gabriel eyed Valadon in bewilderment, Valadon gestured for Remare to tell him what they discussed.

Valadon watched as Miranda kept her eyes on Gabriel. It was not lost on him the glances they gave each other or the way she casually positioned her body near his progeny.

Gabriel frowned when Remare finished his version of events. "What does Mulciber hope to gain from all this? He can't become king; he's not a Blueblood."

"Any number of things," Valadon said. "If he gets someone else in more accommodating to his...indulgences, he can benefit financially and gain more power."

"How?" Miranda asked.

"If he helps a rival member in the court become king, he would expect certain allowances in return. With money comes power."

Miranda was confused. "To do what? He still wouldn't be king."

"Mulciber has never been one to follow Valadon's laws and has been known to use his powers to lure others to his way of thinking." Remare stared at Valadon and shared an image in his mind. "He doesn't think our liege is traditional enough and would like to see a return to more archaic ways. Especially in the procuring of, what's the term the Rogues use now, *feedlings*. Apparently, our blood banks don't appeal to him."

Miranda shuddered and rubbed her cheek.

Valadon decided it was time she left before she learned anymore about their history. "Gabriel, take Miranda home with you to the apartment you keep. Keep her safe and away from ValCorp. With Persephone here, I don't want to take any chances."

Gabriel nodded and put his arm around Miranda, who looked back at Valadon one last time. When Valadon saw Gabriel's face, he knew there was something else his progeny wanted to discuss with him, but now was not the time. There was much Gabriel and Miranda didn't understand about vampire protocols or what measures he and Remare would take to ensure their safety.

Once they were alone, Remare asked, "Are you certain you want her with him?"

Valadon stayed silent for a moment and then glared at him. "He's already sleeping with her."

"Ah, I thought you sensed the heat between them. Would you like me to eviscerate him for you?" Remare asked casually.

Valadon gave him a sly look. "He's still my fledgling."

"Then, why send her to him?"

"Gabriel cares about her. Deeply." Valadon paced with his hands behind his back. "Gabriel's stronger than he lets on. He'll protect her. She'll be safe with him for the time being." Valadon breathed deeply then turned to face Remare. "It's time we ended Mulciber. The report Gabriel gave me," he tilted his head toward his desk, "proves that the bite radius on the victims are Mulciber's. He's repeatedly broken my laws and shown depraved indifference to human life. I've already alerted our allies in the high court of his behaviors."

"And so it begins." Remare warned, "He won't go easily."

Valadon looked at him from the depths of the darkest part of his soul. "Who said I would make it easy for him?"

Chapter Forty-Three

"It's all right, Tristan." Katya locked the door and put the tray down. "Remare sent me to make sure you had enough to eat. With the party going on, there's a lot of food."

Tristan sat up and glanced over the tray. His bruises hurt, but not as before. "I didn't think I'd be having any more visitors." He watched her move around his room. "Gabriel was just here." When his stomach growled, he started picking at the meal.

"I'm more than a visitor." Katya stood near his bed and slid her hands over the spike of his footboard. "I'm going to be your handler." She smiled down at him as she ran her fingers along the corner post.

"Handler?" he asked, suddenly curious.

"Certain aspects of the investigation are progressing faster than expected. Remare is going to be busier than anticipated and wants me to transport you, then check on you from time to time…to make sure your needs are met." She continued to stroke the post with her fingers. "I thought I'd tell you this, now, so you wouldn't be surprised later on."

Tristan didn't think he'd heard her right and wondered *how* she would meet his needs. Valadon and Remare couldn't be that generous, *could they?* "Am I worse off than they're telling me?"

Katya laughed. "Hardly." She walked sensuously around the bed and sat by his side. "They want to make sure you don't get too bored and do something rash." She raised an eyebrow. "Like maybe sneak out at night."

"I'd never do that." His eyes held sincerity, aghast anyone would even consider otherwise.

"Damned straight!" Katya glanced down, then sobered. "I'm sorry about Zoe."

"Thanks," Tristan mumbled as he continued eating the Veal Marsala, which was smothered in mushrooms and wondered if Katya had known it was one of his favorites. He studied her features; most of the males thought Irina was more beautiful, but he'd always believed Katya was more attractive with her shimmering dark hair and eyes. "How often will you be checking on me?"

"As often as needed." She smiled seductively, and this time, Tristan had no second thoughts about her meaning. When he finished his meal, she retrieved the tray and turned to leave. Her fingers barely brushed the doorknob when she faced him. "It was pretty stupid of you to go out without backup."

He rubbed his sore ribs. "Tell me about it."

Katya hesitated for a moment. "When Remare told me he needed someone to care for you, I volunteered." His eyes met hers. "I thought you should know that."

Tristan regarded her with understanding and nodded in appreciation. "I won't disappoint you. I'll obey the rules of seclusion."

"You'd better," she purred. "I know well how to punish little boys who misbehave." She winked as she closed the door behind her.

For the first time since he was informed of his punishment, Tristan was looking forward to getting away, for a while. *As needed, huh?* He drifted back on the pillows and grinned. "I can deal."

***

"I'm glad you came home with me tonight," Gabriel moaned sexily as he lay naked on his side. Miranda caressed his hand as they listened to Enya's enchanting music. He liked her exploring his body, and nearly purred in male satisfaction. Even Rexi seemed content on the bookshelf watching them. When they had first entered his apartment, there'd been one brief moment of awkwardness, but when their eyes had met, their mutual desire had surged. He'd caressed her face with both hands and kissed her senseless. It hadn't taken long for them to find their way to his bed.

"Me, too." She lazily gazed up into his eyes.

"You're an amazing lover, Miranda." Gabriel kissed her shoulder. "But do you realize sometimes, you get this look as if you're someplace else."

"Oh, sorry," she said apologetically. "With all that's happening at ValCorp, it's hard to keep my mind clear."

Gabriel beheld her eyes as a little growl escaped his lips.

"I will say this for you." Miranda smiled. "You have the most incredible ability to make me forget the rest of the world."

"Then, why do you get that faraway look in your eyes?"

"My mind drifts. Liz just throws things at me when I zone out. My parents told me it was something I did even as a child." She kissed his arm reassuringly. "Gabriel, I'm here with you, and

I can't think of any other place I'd rather be. Sometimes, it's hard for me to key down." She brushed his jaw with her thumb. "Maybe I just think too much."

Gabriel didn't allow himself to become close with many others, but Miranda had nestled into his heart, and he hoped she felt the same way about him. "You're a remarkable woman." He stroked her arm with the tips of his fingers. "I like having you here. With me."

She tucked her head under his chin and breathed in his scent. "Do you have any idea how good this feels?" She sighed in pleasure as she wrapped her arms around him. "You're easy to be with, Gabriel. Too easy."

"Am I?" He smiled as she curled her body around his.

Miranda massaged his smattering of chest hairs. "Um-hmm." She peered up at him with shadowed eyes. "But I've been having this bad feeling something terribly wrong is going to happen."

"With Valadon, you mean?"

Her eyes narrowed as if deep in thought. Again, she seemed to drift to a place where he couldn't reach her. "I'm not sure. I just have this vague, nagging feeling other things are in motion. As if something is out of balance." She shook herself of whatever was affecting her. "Do you think Valadon will be able to handle everything with Mulciber?"

"He's over a thousand years old. He didn't survive this long by being careless. And he has his Torians; they'll protect him with their lives, if need be."

"He's that old?" Miranda appeared surprised. "What do you think he's planning to do concerning Mulciber?"

"I suppose he'll be in contact with the ruling court in Europe." Gabriel then asked what he'd been thinking for a while, "You have feelings for him, don't you?"

She studied his eyes. "I'm not sure how to explain this, but I think you should know something."

"Go on." Gabriel didn't want to admit he was envious of Valadon, but he was.

"Some women are attracted to power, wealth and status. There are a lot of human women who see him as a Hollywood star and crave the attention, the limelight."

Gabriel had seen how the women in ValCorp jockeyed for position with their leader. Many would've given their left fang for just one night with him. He knew Valadon was interested in Miranda and had hired her to work in his archives. He had to have trusted her completely, and Gabriel suspected Valadon's interest was more than professional. "And you?"

She exhaled, her breath brushing along his chest hairs. "I'm not like most women. I neither crave nor enjoy the spotlight. But, I like his policies of détente between the races. Who wouldn't love him for all he's done for the city?"

Gabriel could think of one or two. He continued to stroke her hair as he asked quietly, "Do you?"

Miranda kissed his palm. "Truth is...I'm more comfortable with you." When she saw his relaxed smile she added, "He did kiss me, but you should know what I thought at the time."

Gabriel didn't like the idea of her kissing Valadon, but right now, he was more curious about her thoughts.

"Some women are attracted to powerful men, men who hold high levels of authority, status. They like the feeling of being enveloped and protected. I never understood women who drooled over men in influential positions. I've worked for some powerful men whose wives seem to be *shadow-walkers*—women who seem happy to live in the shadows of their more prominent spouses. That's not me."

Gabriel gazed at Miranda and didn't believe she'd be with him if she were like the women she was describing. "But you don't."

"No. I don't. I find it overpowering. Stifling." She narrowed her eyes. "That's not who I am. I don't like being someone's shadow. I *like* who I am."

Gabriel appreciated her honesty and his heart warmed. "I like who you are, too." He bent down and kissed her and felt her arms tighten around him. Yes, this was what he wanted, her body curled around his, her warmth heating his flesh. His very soul. "I want to make love to you again," he whispered huskily.

Miranda snaked one leg up and around him so that she was straddling him. "Let me do the honors, this time." She playfully nipped his chin.

His cock slid into her heated flesh as his head blissfully arched into the pillows. Being with her made him feel like a man—human or vampire, it didn't matter any longer. Having someone to belong to made him feel more complete than he ever imagined. He restrained his urge for her to move faster as he held her waist. Never taking his eyes off hers, he let her set the pace of their lovemaking.

He breathed deep as she threw her head back in joy as she rode him, leaning back her hands grasped his thighs. Gabriel's fangs elongated, and he fought the desire to plunge them into her neck. Every instinct he had was screaming to reverse their positions and dominate her, speed up the pace, and control the fucking. But he fought the beast within and let her ride him, their bodies glistening as she quickened her strokes. When her body shuddered and her inner muscles clutched him hard, a roar escaped his mouth as his own climax shot up his spine.

Gabriel held her tenderly in his arms, never wanting to let her go. Sleep would claim them soon, and he would finally experience a sense of peace he hadn't known for nearly a century.

***

Miranda woke just before dawn, time to head home. She smirked at her outfit; her dress was definitely something worn when the sun was down, not shining on the horizon. She was probably going to get sneers from strangers, but didn't care. She looked one last time at Gabriel, who was serenely sleeping that she didn't have the heart to wake him. She brushed his hair and jaw with the barest of touches and decided to leave him a note. "You take care of him, Rexi," she said as the cat jumped on the bed and curled up on the pillow she'd slept on. "He's a good man." Rexi purred in agreement.

She'd been moved by the longing in his eyes. When Gabriel was aroused, his scent became stronger and the intensity in his eyes darkened, but he didn't make her feel vulnerable the way Valadon had. He didn't consume or overwhelm her with his hunger, but stirred her own desire.

On the way home in the cab, Miranda felt a rare sense of contentment and smiled at the dawning light. There were moments in her life when she felt special—blessed. And that if she touched the sky, she could feel a presence more powerful than anything on earth. This magical part of the night just before dawn, she could sense the earth's vibration as if it was humming along with her happiness. She was content to be a part of the universe, and for one shining moment, all was right with the world.

But Miranda should have known whenever she felt the kiss of grace, a dark veil of shadows, with its ensuing cruelty, would fall on her afterward.

Chapter Forty-Four

During the cab ride home, a childhood memory of Miranda's surfaced. They were driving through the French countryside. She was sitting in the back of the car with her sister; her parents were in the front listening to Tiseira singing about going home. She'd loved the sun on her face as the mountains and trees passed by; she thought nature beautiful, magical. She had believed herself graced, kissed by the sun, moments before the car driving on the wrong side of the highway forced them off the road and down a cliff that led to her family's demise.

Miranda shook off the haunting memory, paid the cab driver, and ascended the stairs to her home.

As soon as she unlocked the door, the uneasiness she'd felt earlier returned. Miranda called out "Orion," as an eerie feeling crawled up her spine and burrowed deeply in her mind. She quickly entered the security code, cursed Remare again, and reached out with her senses to see if there was anyone else in the house. Her empathy had always been strongest at sunrise and sunset. When nothing stirred her instincts, she tossed her purse on the table, and noticed the gift box with her name on it. She sighed. *No more shoes, Valadon.* But if it was the luscious chocolates he'd sent before, those she would keep.

When Miranda opened the box, she stood frozen and thought the brain an interesting organ. When a sight so far out of our comfort zone, so far from the reaches of our imagination as to what we perceived as normal, the mind takes a time-out to catch up with what the eyes see. But she had gone temporarily blind and couldn't see anything. She gazed at the mirror on the wall, and everything went hazy, her reflection growing grotesque, and she couldn't remember making a fist and smashing the mirror. When she looked down at her hand covered in blood...it was as if it wasn't her hand.

Sensations of disassociation invaded her psyche, and she wondered what the loud buzzing was that she heard.

When a shard of reality finally penetrated the haze of unreality, she realized she'd been screaming until her voice couldn't utter any more sounds. In shades of gray, reality crept into her consciousness, and Miranda reached for the box. Her breathing sped up as her body vibrated with dark emotions.

Dane had been one of the handsomest men she'd ever known with his beautiful, long blond hair and California tan. His charming smile had been one of the things that had first attracted her to the benevolent Were. Dane had a great job waiting for him in California and a family who loved him. He was going to have a great life living on the West Coast...if they could ever figure out how to reattach his head to his body. Miranda's knees buckled under her, and she crumbled to the floor. She tried to stand, but the darkness dragged her down. Crawling across the carpet, she sat with her back against the wall.

Miranda didn't know how long she sat there, covered in shadows. Every now and then, she'd glance at her hand and wonder why it was red. Why was the room so dark? she wondered, and what was the name of the music playing in her head? Minutes passed by, or was it hours, she had no clue. Time meant nothing for the dead—why should it matter to the living? Wasn't there something she should be doing? Yes, she was supposed to be doing something, but Miranda couldn't remember what it was. She sat on the floor, admiring her boots. *Cyra doesn't like my boots*; she laughed. Too bad, Miranda liked them fine. More darkness covered her until she didn't know if it was day or night.

When the shadows finally lifted enough so that she could deal with a fragment of reality, she reached for her phone and called Lizandra.

Someone else answered, and Miranda told the person to get Lizandra. The voice said she was busy in a meeting and could take no calls. She screamed, "Put. Lizandra. On. The. Phone. NOW!"

Miranda tried to slow her breathing, watched the candles in the wall sconces glow bright and dim, glow brighter, then dimmer and realized the pulses of energy were emanating from her hand. She knew, if she didn't gain control over her powers, she could burn the house down and focused her energy on dimming the pulsing flames until they were completely extinguished.

She heard talking on the phone and recognized the voice. "Lizandra."

"Miranda, this had better be important. I'm in a meeting. Another one of the Weres was attacked last night, and we're dealing with members of Red Claw encroaching on our borders."

When there was only silence on the line, Lizandra's voice sounded cautious. "Miranda?"

Trembling, Miranda couldn't get the words out. She tried again...and failed.

Liz asked, "What's wrong?"

Finally, able to shake off the immobilizing haze, Miranda murmured, "They killed him."

"Who?" Liz bellowed into the phone as fear echoed in her voice. "Where are you? Are you in danger?"

"Dane's dead." Miranda's voice was hoarse, so she could barely utter a whisper. "They killed him."

"Where are you?" Liz asked frantically. "Are you home?"

"I'm home. Could you come over?" That was the last thing Miranda remembered as she slid down the wall, her head crashing onto the carpet, the shadows finally claiming her.

***

Still in shock, Miranda's senses began to wake when the Weres arrived. She vaguely remembered giving Liz an extra key. As soon as they entered her home, Liz's nostrils flared, and then the Were Queen peered in the box at what was left of Dane. A tormented howl tore out of Liz's throat that reverberated off the walls and could be heard blocks away. Enraged, she immediately ordered her people to search the premises. When Liz spotted Miranda, she reached down and forced her to sit up. Miranda heard her, but couldn't respond. When Liz could get no response from her, either by shaking her or calling her name, she slapped her. Hard.

"Owww! That fucking hurt!" Miranda rubbed her cheek as the scent of her friend comforted her.

"Good! It was fucking meant to!" When the Weres came down and shook their heads that no one else was in the house, Lizandra asked, "What the hell happened?"

"I don't know. I came home and found the box." Miranda's tears began falling again and she thought she was going to retch; she had to hold her stomach and take deep breaths. "They killed him, Lizandra." Her voice was barely recognizable to herself. "The bastards killed him."

"Who did this?" Lizandra's voice was edged with a murderous darkness Miranda rarely heard.

"I don't know. At first I thought it was another gift from Valadon." She shook off the vestiges of shock. "I think I blacked out."

"Pack a bag. You're coming with us to Werehaven." Liz straightened and pulled Miranda to her feet. She swayed with vertigo. Liz brought her into her bedroom and sat her on the bed.

The Were Queen then snatched a backpack and grabbed some clothes from the closet.

Miranda glanced down at her bloodstained hand. "Do I have time to take a shower?"

"Make it a quick one. I want us out of here."

"I will." Miranda turned the faucets to the hottest setting allowing the water to wash away the remaining tendrils of fog from her brain. When she stepped out, she towel-dried her hair and dressed in the jeans and sweater Liz had left on the vanity. She tried to put makeup on but her hands were shaking too much so she just grabbed a few bottles and shoved them in her bag. "I'm ready."

Miranda glanced at the table and noticed the box was already gone, then saw the broken mirror. "Did I do that?" She rubbed her hand and knew that she had.

"C'mon. You can tell us more at Werehaven."

"Wait." Miranda went back to her bedroom and found what she was looking for. "Let's go."

***

Miranda stood in the back of the conference room at Werehaven in awe of Lizandra. When the two of them got together, there was always plenty of laughter and good times...and cake, she smiled. It was rare to see Lizandra lose her temper. If anyone crossed her, she'd calmly wait until the other party felt safe and, only then, would she pounce. She believed in coolly plotting her revenge. Miranda could easily see her as the head of her own corporation in a power suit with killer heels, running a meeting with all heads turned her way. The woman commanded respect, and it was never more evident than tonight.

Lizandra and her most loyal Weres were reviewing the files on the large screen from the flash drive Dane had given Miranda. Dane had dug far deeper into the individuals associated with the hate group than she'd imagined. Leaders who had been suspiciously neutral during the human/vampire debates had made hefty donations to sister organizations of the HOL. How Dane had been able to dig that deep had Miranda shaking her head. Unfortunately, he must have tripped some alarm somewhere. And they came looking for him.

She hoped Dane hadn't been tortured at the hands of the HOL's henchmen, tried to imagine a quick death, but no matter how many times she tried to convince herself—she knew it for the lie it was. God, how he must have suffered. If they had decapitated him, she tried not to think what else they might have been done to his body before they eventually killed him. She closed her eyes, knowing the images in her mind would forever haunt her.

"This will be a Were operation. No one else is to be involved, understood?" Liz's voice rang out from the head of the table, and her eyes settled on Miranda.

"Valadon should be given a copy of the files." Miranda spoke softly as the Weres watched her. "It was his life they wanted."

"Agreed. But not until after Were justice has been served." With an arched brow, Lizandra gazed at Miranda. "ValCorp currently has their own problems to deal with. No one there will be informed of our plans."

Miranda disagreed with Lizandra, but wouldn't question her decisions in front of her own people.

"Since we're coming up on the Lupinar, no actions will be taken until the full moon wanes." Weres changed into their wolf form during the nights before, during, and after the full moon. No humans were allowed in the park after dark, but especially during the full moon because Weres became too feral in their wolf form.

Miranda closed her eyes, her mind drifting on a wave of oblivion until the meeting ended and she was left alone with the Were Queen. She let the silence linger before speaking.

"They don't say a word." Miranda's head hung low as she paced with her hands on her hips. "But they blame me for Dane's death."

"*No one* here blames you for his death." Lizandra swiveled in her chair.

Miranda choked back a laugh. "Oh, really, did you see their faces?"

"Stop feeling guilty, Miranda." Lizandra pointed one of her lethally long nails at her. "It will fuck you up in the head more than anything."

"Too late. Mea culpa." Miranda's voice rose in anguish. "I was the one who asked for his help." She gestured to the screen with the image of one particular member of the HOL staring at them. "All this research he did—he did because of me." She continued pacing. "Dane never would've done any of this if I hadn't asked him."

Lizandra watched as Miranda vented the pain and guilt that was tearing her apart. "And I'm the one who sent him to you, if you remember." The Were Queen narrowed her eyes as she tapped her nails on the table. "Do you think I should feel guilty for that, as well?"

Miranda stopped pacing and looked at her friend.

"Choose your words *carefully*, Miranda, before your body hits that wall," Liz said decisively as she eyed her and glanced at the wall. When the silence lingered between them, Liz finally spoke. "You're not the one who killed him."

Miranda objected, "But…"

"No buts! *No fucking but*s!" Lizandra's fist banged the table as she rose to her full height. "You didn't kill him!" Her voice shook the walls as her long braids went flying. Slowly, she reached across the table, laying her hands flat as her nails dug into the wood. "You're not the one who abducted him, held him against his will and murdered him, are you?" When Miranda remained quiet, Liz joined her friend in pacing, crossing her arms over her chest, her fingers massaging the muscles in her arms.

"No," Miranda softly murmured.

"No!" Liz pointed at the screen. "But those fuckers did! And they *will* taste Were justice."

Miranda trembled at what the Were Queen was devising in the way of retribution. There were details Lizandra refused to discuss with her. Liz rarely left her out of business matters so Miranda knew what she was planning was going to be extremely violent. And very illegal.

As if reading her mind, Lizandra asked, "You don't approve of Were justice?"

"I didn't say that." Miranda shook her head; there would be no going to human authorities for any type of justice. The men and women Dane had investigated were some of the most powerful people in New York City. Each was connected politically and socially. Human law couldn't or wouldn't touch any of them. But Lizandra could…and would. Were justice bordered on biblical proportions; an eye for an eye, etc. There would be no lengthy trials, expensive teams of lawyers or plea bargains. The HOL members believed themselves untouchable. And, now, their lives were finite.

Miranda glanced up at the screen, again. She'd been wracking her brain, trying to put faces to the voices she heard at the Ormont home, but it had been a lesson in futility. "How do we know who actually did the killing?"

Lizandra smirked. "Persuasion."

Miranda never wanted to know what they did with the Weres who trespassed on their territory or hurt the Black Star Weres in fights that had turned ugly. But she had a pretty good idea of what Lizandra was capable of. Weres were incredibly territorial. In the Were community, mercy was seen as a weakness. If Lizandra was ever thought of as anything less than lethal, she would have the other clan chiefs taking a piece of her and her people. Something Lizandra would never permit to happen.

"Dane was a clan favorite. Do you remember when David needed help barbecuing? Dane came from the volleyball tournament and helped out. Whenever I needed assistance with any number of tasks, Dane always volunteered to help. I will not allow his murder to go unpunished. No one, but no one touches my Weres. Blood will pour over this."

"Valadon needs to know about this," Miranda finally said.

"Valadon has many fine attributes, but I will not allow any interference in my operation. After we've dealt justice, he will be notified."

"No," Miranda said in a calm voice. "These monsters will try again. Do you want to take the chance they make another attempt on his life? What if they succeed, this time?"

Lizandra seemed to consider Miranda's words. She went to the computer, retrieved the flash drive, and started tossing it in the air and catching it. "If you give Valadon this information, he can't know about our plans."

"Agreed." Miranda had been prepared to argue. "I won't tell him." She pointed to the screen, again. "But this...he has to know."

Lizandra smiled. "All right, then." She tossed the flash drive to Miranda who caught it swiftly with a tight grip. "Let the vampire king know who his enemies are. He probably has his own intel, anyway." She smiled darkly at Miranda. "Leaders should always be aware of those who plot against them."

***

Miranda rode in the back of the van Lizandra had insisted on. Along with the two Weres she provided as escorts. After the gift the HOL members had sent her way, Liz wasn't taking any chances with Miranda's life. Miranda told them to wait for her in the van and that she'd be perfectly safe inside ValCorp. They had escorted her to the door, anyway.

During the drive to ValCorp, Miranda's mind was flooded with images of bloodshed and violence. Wave after wave of horrors haunted her, one image uglier than the next. The more she tried to fight against imagining Dane's last hours, the more those images fought to be a part of her consciousness. As the Chimera of evil invaded her psyche, her temper increased at the injustice of it all, and she channeled all her guilt, all her pain into a burning desire for vengeance.

Miranda sensed the darkness in her soul rising. A gray veil had descended over her vision, and everything became murkier. She knew this was a dangerous time for her, and she'd have to rein in her emotions if she was to control her powers.

Taking deep breaths, Miranda's energy slowly increased as she rode the elevator to Valadon's penthouse.

Chapter Forty-Five

"Our people are in place for the operation. Morel and I worked out each assignment with precision. Irina was able to acquire the necessary documents we needed and everything is going according to our plan," Remare said as Valadon viewed the evening sky and the city below. He felt more secure knowing the windows were now bulletproofed, but still didn't like the idea of Valadon pacing in front of them and was glad when he resumed his seat behind his desk.

"Irina came to me this week. She attempted to seduce me." Valadon raised an eyebrow at Remare.

Remare inwardly smiled. He'd seen the subtle looks on Irina's face whenever Valadon walked into a room. Irina had always been attracted to powerful men, even when she'd been a member of Ivan's court. Until she picked the wrong man to seduce, and Remare had to rescue her from an untenable situation. A classic beauty, her talents in seduction were unparalleled. Though, in Valadon's case, her desires would go unanswered. "Was she successful?"

Before Valadon could answer, a blast of energy blew through the door. Miranda entered on a current of air that carried her into the room. Remare could hear her blood pounding in her veins. She stormed over to where Valadon was rising from his desk, barely acknowledging Remare's presence.

"I need to talk to you. Now!" Miranda was being aggressive and dangerously so with the powerful vampires in the room, but the stoked emotions boiling beneath her skin would not abate.

Valadon had never seen her so enraged; her entire body was vibrating. "Miranda, what's wrong?"

"I need to talk to you." She glanced at Remare with contempt. "Alone."

Seeing the animosity in her eyes, Remare said, "Whatever you have to say to Valadon, you can also say to me."

Miranda turned to face Valadon. He seemed darker to her, but then, everything did through the obscure veil. "Alone." She knew she looked like she had murder on her mind and didn't care.

Valadon peered at his friend, who was standing, stubbornly refusing to leave him alone, and at her. "Miranda, anything you tell me, I will, in time, tell Remare. He's my oldest and most trusted friend."

Miranda moved her head slowly in Remare's direction, who lifted his chin as he studied her. With his narrowed eyes, he looked as if he was ready to leap upon her if she threatened Valadon in any way.

Anger was like a drug. It diluted any other sensations a person might be feeling. No wonder people gave in to their rage so easily. There was no pain, no sorrow, no hurting. The anger blocked out everything else that was rational; it was the best painkiller available. The fury fed her, now, and she welcomed every drop of it. "Very well." She shed her coat and threw it over the chair, her voice a ragged whisper. "Guess what I got as a present today."

Valadon's eyes darkened as if sensing her unrelenting pain. "I have no idea," he said quietly as he held her gaze and came around his desk to hold her in his arms.

It wasn't his fault. He hadn't known she'd asked Dane to investigate the HOL. This was her fault, Miranda reminded herself. Perhaps if she hadn't been so taken with the powerful vampire, she'd have let her curiosity of the HOL go and never would have involved Dane. She shook her head. Even if Valadon wasn't such an enigma, she would've researched them. She leaned her head against his chest, then peered up at him with tearful eyes. "Dane. They killed him."

Remare rose, went to the bar and poured her a drink. Briefly meeting his eyes, she accepted it.

"What happened?" Valadon asked.

Miranda didn't have the strength to relay everything, but after a few sips of the wine, she did her best. When she finished her story, she handed him the flash drive. "You need to view this."

They swiftly read the information on the computer screen. She couldn't watch it, again. Didn't have to. She had it all memorized. Miranda studied the room as they were glued to the monitor. The window had been replaced, and a new Roman statue stood where the old one had been. After a while, she closed her eyes and breathed deeply while she heard their grunts and comments. When they finished reading the file, she glanced up to see the incensed looks on both their faces. Good, she thought. They needed to be aware of the information Dane had paid for with his life.

"Lizandra is going after the men who murdered Dane."

"This is a vampire matter," Remare snorted.

Miranda grabbed her coat and was about to leave. "Yeah? Well, you tell her that."

"Miranda." Valadon's voice was calm as she neared the door. "We already have plans in motion."

"According to Lizandra, Dane was a Were. And they take care of their own."

"What do you know of their plans?" Remare asked.

"Not much. It's Were business, so she wouldn't tell me." She regarded both of them. "Be happy I gave you the information. Lizandra didn't want me to until after she dispensed Were justice." She turned to leave. "I thought differently."

"Tell your friend to back off. I'm not going to have a vengeful wolf fuck up my plans."

Something in Remare's tone completely set her off, and all the rage she thought she'd banked surfaced with a vengeance. Enraged, she turned and, before she knew what she was doing, threw a fireball at Remare's head.

Quickly deflecting the ball of fire, Remare was up and on her before her hand ever touched the doorknob. He slammed her body into the door and growled in her ear. *"Don't. You. EVER. Throw. A. Fireball. At. Me. Again!"*

"Remare!" Valadon thundered as he put out the fire that had burned his carpet.

Miranda watched Remare's dark eyes and knew she shouldn't have thrown her power at him. The red rims around his irises were glowing with rage. His exhalations were coming as hard and fast as hers were, and she felt his breaths brush across her skin. She knew she should apologize, but something else always took over whenever she was in close proximity to the dangerous vampire. Her caution and fear mixed with other dark emotions she didn't want to examine too closely.

When he released her and returned to Valadon's side, both vampires stood staring at her, waiting for an explanation. *Shit!* Now, they both knew. *And why was it neither of them looked particularly surprised she had that kind of power? Damn! They'd already known.*

Valadon guided them into his reception area. The sunken circular area was more spacious and less formal with its plush couches.

"Miranda," Valadon said softly. "How long have you had that power?"

She gazed down and didn't feel comfortable discussing her abilities. She had never wanted anyone else to know besides Lizandra. She'd been stupid throwing it at Remare. Stupid and impetuous; she knew better. But she'd been walking a fine edge since finding the box and had finally exploded. Miranda rubbed her hand, making the itch that accompanied her power dissipate. "Lizandra calls me an *Elemental*. I only have limited influence over the elements." Miranda continued massaging her hand. "Not really sure when they kicked in." She glanced up at Remare. "But I've always been able to start a fire, since I was a little girl."

"The other elements?" Valadon asked curiously, sitting next to her, soothing her with his deep melodic voice.

Miranda wasn't sure why she was confessing to him. "If I can concentrate hard enough, I can call the winds. Just a slight breeze, though." She smiled up at him. "Once, I think I made it rain, but the sky was already overcast so...maybe not." Though, Miranda was pretty sure it was only raining in the one area where she needed it most—her rooftop garden.

Valadon spoke silently with Remare. *"It's rare, but there are humans who have extrasensory abilities. In the Middle Ages, they burned innocent women for practicing their gifts."*

Remare answered him. *"Modern scientists suspect people with Mir-randa's gifts are able to tap into the part of the brain dormant in the majority of the human population. Experts still argue whether humans have abilities such as telepathy and telekinesis. The only thing they agreed on was that there was a part of the brain they were uncertain about. Most humans only use a portion of their brain; evidently, Miranda uses more."*

Setting her half-empty glass down, Miranda exhaled. "Lizandra gave me two Were escorts. They're waiting for me outside."

Valadon wanted her to stay with him but knew she was safer with the Weres, for now. Dane's death had been a warning. The last thing he wanted was another attempt on her life because of her involvement with him.

"I'll be in touch with Lizandra," Valadon said softly as he led her to the door. "We'll come to an accord." He kissed her temple and stroked her cheek with his knuckle. "Thank you for bringing me the information." He smiled warmly. "We'll deal with this. We always do."

After she left, Remare, keeping his back to Valadon, exhaled deeply and finished drinking the wine Miranda had left behind. "We have a vital mission in place." He turned toward Valadon. "I don't want the Weres fucking it up."

"I know." Valadon walked back to his desk. "I'll contact the Were Queen. She'll work with us. She wants the same thing we do."

"Irina has given us the logistics we needed. I'll be attending a very private party of HOL members this weekend." Ice coated Remare's voice. "We'll finally have them where we want them."

"Old friend," Valadon smiled at Remare, "whatever will you do when all our enemies have been defeated?"

Remare smirked at him. "Do you truly believe that day will ever come?"

***

Miranda checked her messages. One was from Louise Cameron, her student who had given her the information on Kristoph. Growing weary of vampires and their enemies and wanting to distance herself from it all, Miranda exhaled as she tapped the phone with her index finger. Uncertainty gnawed at her, but she gave in to her curiosity. She'd only been mildly surprised to discover it was Louise's mother who'd requested a meeting.

Barbara Morley Cameron lived very well in her Upper East Side apartment, surrounded by the best that affluence afforded. She'd been married a few times and, with each succeeding divorce, had accumulated more wealth. Barbara carried herself with the confidence only women of privilege possessed. Nearly fifty, her figure was svelte, and her beautiful face with her white blond hair and piercing blue eyes still commanded attention.

"I'm glad you came." Barbara led Miranda into the living room with a spectacular view of Central Park. The walls, couches and rugs were creams, golds and softer tones of beige in the most expensive fabrics. Feminine, yet sophisticated. Miranda felt comfortable in Barbara's home, even if it was a bit too posh for her taste. "I've been beside myself, for days." Hesitation marring her movements, Barbara reclined on one of the couches and waited for Miranda to sit. "It's been a long time."

"It has." Miranda merely smiled, refusing to answer her unasked question.

"I won't waste either of our time with social niceties, then. There's a reason I had Louise call you." She lit a cigarette and inhaled deeply. "By the way, she loves your class."

"I'm glad that she does."

"You know about Kristoph and me." Barbara exhaled and managed to look both elegant and nervous, at the same time. "I was afraid to contact you directly, afraid you wouldn't come. That's why I had Louise contact you."

Miranda's curiosity was spiked before she entered the woman's home and wanted the older woman to get to the point. Remembering Remare's phrase, she said, "Tell me."

"As you know, I'm divorced, and sometimes, my ex-husband, Robert, and I spend time together with our daughter. The psychologist said it would be beneficial for Louise." Barbara inhaled a long drag of her cigarette. "When I was in his apartment, I wanted to leave a note for Louise, and I went into his desk to get some writing paper, and I came across a file. A very disturbing file."

Miranda narrowed her eyes. "What was in the file?"

"It was a list of chemicals. At first, I simply thought it was something he brought home from the office. But, then, I flipped to the next page, and I saw some other documents." Barbara angrily stubbed out her cigarette. "The bastard is a member of the HOL. Do you know who they are?"

Miranda nodded.

"Of course, you know who they are." She waved a well-manicured hand in the air. "You're dating Valadon." Barbara's voice was stern. "I swear to you, now, I had no idea he'd been a member of that despicable organization when I married him. Sure, he talked trash about the vampires when they first came out. Many did, but I never thought he was the type of man to join that awful group. That wasn't like him. At least not the perception I had of him." Barbara clasped her arms. "He's proved me wrong in many ways."

Miranda had no interest in Cameron's marital woes. "Ms. Cameron, what was in the documents?"

"Dreadful things. Meetings, dates, appointments with men who shared their hatred of Valadon." Tears glistened in her eyes. "They killed him, the monsters. They killed him! My beloved Kristoph." Cameron breathed deeply and continued. "Somehow, Robert found out I was having an affair with a vampire, and it enraged him. Even though we've been divorced for some time now, he always felt proprietary where I'm concerned."

Miranda's head was spinning. "Barbara, what are you talking about? I saw Kristoph a week ago; he was fine."

"He's dead!" Cameron tilted her head. "Didn't you know? I went to his apartment when he failed to show for one of our evenings." She closed her eyes as if in pain. "There was blood on the carpet. A lot of it." She looked directly at Miranda. "When I had my people investigate his disappearance, all I was told was that Kristoph wasn't coming back. The only one who would give us any information was that arrogant vampire from ValCorp. They wouldn't even admit to me he was dead. But I knew. Kristoph would never leave without saying goodbye or telling me of his plans."

Miranda wondered why Remare hadn't told her of Kristoph's death. "I can find out, if that's what you want?"

"Oh, don't bother. I already know he's dead." Her hand trembled as it brushed a loose strand of hair back into place. "Robert still goes to those parties." Barbara rose to stare out the window, the fading sun highlighting her face. "You know which ones I'm talking about."

One night in the home of one of the museum patrons, Miranda had foolishly stumbled into a room where a highly stylized orgy was in progress. She had quietly stepped back, closing the door behind her, unsure if anyone had seen her.

"They're having another one of their soirees this weekend. Out on Long Island. Robert even thought to invite me." She laughed with quiet rage. "As if I would attend," she murmured. "I know he had something to do with Kristoph's death." She glanced at Miranda. "I thought you should know as you're now involved with Valadon."

Miranda ignored her last comment. "Can you remember any other names, places, anything else you might have seen?"

Barbara gave Miranda one of her viper smiles. "You bet I can." Inside her trouser pocket she retrieved a folded piece of paper and handed it to Miranda. "I think you'll recognize some of the names. If I'd had my phone on me, I would have photographed the information for you to give to Valadon. I wrote down what I could remember." She breathed out. "They're all going to be at the party this weekend at the West Gate Estate. You know who owns it, don't you?"

Miranda knew exactly who owned it and to whom she'd be giving this data. "Ms. Cameron, thank you for this information. Maybe some lives could be saved because of this."

"Actually, I was hoping some lives would be lost." She laughed when she saw the look on Miranda's face. "My ex-husband, for one."

Miranda collected her purse and rose to leave.

"I never apologized for what happened all those years ago."

Miranda stopped, but didn't turn around. "I was very young, then. And stupid."

"Weren't we all?" Barbara sighed. "Wasn't it Shakespeare who said it was a pity youth was wasted on the young?"

Yes, it was a pity...and a crime. "Save your apologies for Terese. I hear she still suffers from acute anxiety." After Miranda shut the door behind her, she closed her eyes and leaned against it. Memories of the club where someone had spiked her drink surfaced. Terese, a fellow student, and she had been the only ones left and, somehow, had wound up with Barbara who was celebrating a birthday. *"Do you want to go to another club, something a bit more risky?"* Terese had been more drunk than Miranda and agreed when Barbara said it was downstairs.

What Barbara hadn't told them was that it was a dimly lit sex club where participants were in glass enclosures like the animals at the Natural History Museum. Only these people were in the throes of various sex acts. Miranda had drunk heavily before and had always been able to shake off the effects, but this time had been different. It had been like a waking dream. Once downstairs, Barbara had gone off with some guy, and Terese and she had gone exploring. It was as if they had been moving in slow motion. On the other side of the glass enclosures, there was a stage with a live sex scene going on. It all seemed so surreal.

Miranda had been transfixed by the amount of heat in the audience as well as the performers. She knew she should have left, but she'd never seen sex with other people and stood mesmerized by the eroticism. Everything was so dreamlike, and Miranda's awareness of time and place had become shadowed. She remembered a handsome dark haired man smiling at her as he approached. She had smiled back. He whispered something in her ear, then clasped her hand and led her to a door painted black. Glancing behind up at the stage, she'd seen Terese had joined the performance.

Miranda shook herself of the memory. Even now, she couldn't remember what the handsome man had whispered.

Chapter Forty-Six

Needing to clear her head, Miranda walked along the Hudson River Park at dusk, the river breezes cooling her too-heated skin. The air was cleaner here, and she felt more relaxed. When she reached Teardrop Park; she sighed. *Apropos.* She missed Dane, and now with the news that Kristoph was dead, too, her heart felt heavy.

She sat on the park bench and watched the waves made by the tourist boats. She could make out Lady Liberty in the bay as the calm of twilight permeated her soul.

The Weres wouldn't rest until Dane's death was avenged. Orion, Dane's best friend, had been devastated by the news, but even he wanted blood spilt. Miranda wasn't sure she could go through with what had to be done, but knew when the time came, she'd find the courage.

Her thoughts drifted to Kristoph and Remare and their friendship. She wondered if the vampire with such cold eyes was feeling regret, as well. Damn, she could've killed him when she'd thrown the fireball at him. Studying her right hand, Miranda flexed her fingers. She'd never wanted to use her powers to hurt someone...and nearly had.

Miranda observed the waves lapping at the shore and held up her hand. She closed her eyes and focused her concentration. When she peered out at the water, the waves had responded to her mental command by rising and falling to the cadence of her breaths. When she made a fist, the waves resumed their normal rhythm. The sun was almost completely down, and soon, there'd be a full moon. Her powers would be strongest, then.

She sensed someone behind her. She didn't need to turn to know who. "Shouldn't you be at Werehaven?"

"Nah. I don't have to be there until later." Max, Orion's gamine of a girlfriend, quietly sat next to her. "Tonight's the Lupinar; we won't change until midnight, anyway."

Miranda slanted her a look. "Did Lizandra ask you to keep an eye on me?"

"We've actually been following you, for a while now."

Miranda liked Black Star's youngest member. At barely five foot-two, Maxine was smaller than most Weres, but with

Lizandra's guidance—*"If you can't fight clean and win...fight dirty"*—Max had trained hard and became strong. Just as Miranda had once...long ago.

"Lizandra asked if you wanted a couple of her brother's friends from the police force to stay with you or if you were going to hang with the vampires."

"Thanks, Max, but I've got it covered." Miranda hadn't made up her mind where she'd go, but Werehaven was out with the Lupinar, and she didn't want to go back to ValCorp. Maybe Gabriel's.

After the silence lingered, Max stretched out her feet, which were covered in plaid sneakers. "She's worried about you. We all are."

Miranda knew Orion was concerned about her. It was Orion who'd introduced Dane to her. The two Weres had loved playing volleyball in the park. Orion always said Dane had a fine voice and should join him sometime on tour. Now...he never would.

A mock laugh escaped Miranda's mouth. "I would think the Weres would be happy if I never returned."

"How can you say that?" Max leapt up. "You're family. Why would you even *say* something like that?" With both hands on her hips, she faced Miranda, her feet clearly dug in. Lizandra called it her Peter Pan pose.

"I'm sure there are some Weres who blame me for Dane's death. It's my fault."

Max tilted her head, tears forming in her eyes. "That's not true! *No one* in Black Star blames you."

"I do. I blame me. I'm the one who asked him to help."

"But you shouldn't." Max bent down in front of Miranda and held her hands. "Even if you hadn't asked him, he would have followed up, anyway. Dane was like that. He was curious about everything. That's why he was such a great researcher." Max smiled. "Lizandra, Gavin, and Orion blame the HOL; everyone does. Lizandra's meeting with her advisors, and they're already planning strategies."

"How can you be so forgiving?" Miranda clutched Max's hand.

"There's nothing to forgive, Mira."

Miranda had once called her Maxi, and was told, in no uncertain terms, Max never wanted to be nicknamed after a feminine product and *never* to call her that, again. But she figured if she called her Max, she could call her Mira.

"C'mon. We're close to ValCorp. We can escort you there and then report in."

Miranda rose and gazed over the river one last time. "This is going to get bloody, isn't it?"

Max smirked. "Lizandra wouldn't have it any other way."

Miranda wasn't allowed to be involved in Were justice. But she had relayed the information Cameron had given her to Lizandra so she had a pretty good idea where and when the vengeance would take place.

She walked with Max to ValCorp. It figured she'd wind up there. But Miranda wouldn't stay. After Max reported in, she'd grab a cab and go to Gabriel's.

Chapter Forty-Seven

Saturday night came quicker than Miranda thought it would. After much argument, she persuaded Lizandra to let her come along to the West Gate Mansion. The plan was for her to wander through the party, wearing the tiny ear bud, and alert the Weres to any trouble. It had taken Miranda some time to come to terms with walking nearly naked around in the mansion, *Hey, it was a human thing.* But, for Dane, she'd do it.

Tonight, everyone would be dressed only in capes and masks, each person's assets on full display. Entrance wouldn't be a problem as Barbara had given Miranda the password and invitation. Liz had instructed her people to abduct key members of the HOL to be *"questioned"* by the Were Queen and her enforcers.

Since Dane's death and the territorial disputes with the Red Claws, the Weres had been wired for violence.

Lizandra would stay in the van and monitor the Weres' progress. Her brother, Sam, a private security consultant, made sure Liz was outfitted with the best equipment.

When Miranda gave the butler her invitation and the password, *"oligarchy"*, she entered the grand foyer and heard the classical music by Revel. As she walked past the main entrance, she tried not to gasp. This truly was a scene right out of a Stanley Kubrick film and felt as Tom Cruise must have felt in the movie. People were dressed in black capes and masks that were fashioned from centuries past, while others had elected the simpler black silk masks.

Miranda knew what to expect from the stories Barbara told her. Nothing was off limits. There'd be specialty rooms for multiple partners: M/F, M/M, F/F and any and all combinations, Doms/subs, bondage, etc. Miranda wasn't a prude; she enjoyed sex, especially with Gabriel, however, she felt pity for the individuals who frequented these parties. There was no real passion, no warmth, and no humanity. What they attained in terms of variety and excitement, they lost in intimacy. They believed they benefitted from the diversity; she found them lacking.

Barbara told her many of the guests thought straight sex was too common—something reserved for the lower classes. From time immemorial, monarchs had multiple partners, and the city's wealthy believed they were entitled to the same indulgences. As far as Barbara knew, these types of parties had been going on for decades, if not centuries.

Miranda didn't make it past the grand foyer when an arm suddenly reached out, grabbed her and dragged her into a darkened alcove. "What the *hell* are you doing here?"

Her breathing rapidly increased from the close contact with the one vampire who vexed her more than any other. His sylvan, masculine scent pervaded her being, and when his body pushed up against hers, she realized he was as naked under his cape as she was under hers. Her heart thundered but she steadied her breaths. "I could ask you the same thing. I thought your tastes were more the fang type."

Remare lifted his mask and stared at her with eyes of ice. The tension in his hands gripping her flesh tightened. The attraction between them simmered. "I didn't realize you had such sophisticated tastes, Mir-randa. Does your lover know you're here, or did the good doctor accompany you here, as well?" When he saw her eyes narrowing in indignation, he added, "We have a critical mission in progress, and I don't want you fucking it up."

Startled, Miranda wondered how he'd found out about the party, but with ValCorp's resources, it shouldn't have surprised her. "What mission?" she asked cautiously.

"Something we've been working on for a long time. Go home, Mir-randa. You don't belong here. Things can turn ugly fast, and you shouldn't be here."

"Can't." Miranda considered her next words carefully, trying not to be affected by the way he pronounced her name. "You're not the only one here with a purpose other than sex."

Remare scrutinized her eyes and then inhaled her scent. "Fuck! You brought the wolves, didn't you?"

She heard Lizandra's voice in her ear. *"Tell Remare to fuck off! This is a Were operation."* One look at Remare, and she knew he'd heard it, as well.

"Tell them to back off, right now." Remare's fingers dug into her shoulders.

"Maybe it's you who should back off." Her voice turned to ice as she stared the vampire down. "It was a Were who was killed. Remember?"

Frustration and something else Miranda couldn't identify etched Remare's face. "I don't have time for this. If you or any of your friends get burned in this operation, don't come crying to me, again."

"I'm not the one who's going to get fried," she hissed as he turned and bled into the shadows.

Miranda made her way through the main room with the throng of people already in the throes of various sexual acts on couches, chairs, and carpets with the voyeurs looking on. The magnetic energy in the room affected her. When people fucked, the natural vibrations in the air increased, and she could feel it intensifying. The scents of sex were also increasing, and she just wanted to be away from all the glistening, moaning bodies.

She hoped her casual stroll would go unnoticed and that no one would choose her as a partner. Walking neither fast nor slow, she nearly made it to the back hall of the mansion when another arm reached out and pushed her into a corner. A voice she was sure she knew whispered, "Leave now, Miranda. You're in danger. You should never have come here tonight."

Was that Jordan's voice? The figure disappeared into the crowd. *Definitely not something you ever wanted to learn about your boss.* She quickened her steps and was nearly to the servants' entrance when two men appeared, blocking her exit. The one on the left said, "Come with us."

Miranda's heart sped up and she considered making a run for it, but she didn't think she'd get past them. She prayed Lizandra heard them. They led her down a hall to a dimly lit security room rife with men at computers and surveillance equipment displaying the various rooms and hallways where people were fucking. At the far end of the security room was a large, rectangular window that looked into another area resembling a police interrogation room.

"So good of you to join us," a man said as he took her mask, then her arm, and steered her forward. Miranda didn't like being handled and pulled away. Like the other people in the room, he had his mask and black cape on.

"Thank you, Greer. That will be all."

Both guards turned and left.

"I was delighted to see you attend our party, Ms. Crescent. If I had known your proclivities ran to the exotic I would have invited you long ago."

Miranda tried to place the voice, but failed. Some of the men seemed to be waiting for something to happen in the other room. The others were glued to the monitors watching the evening's entertainment as if it was a sporting event. And to them, she supposed, it was. She turned to the one who'd spoken to her. "How did you know it was me?"

"We've been observing your movements, for some time. Ever since you became involved with Valadon."

Her heart rate doubled, but she remained calm, knowing her friends were in the mansion. *Please be hearing all this*, she prayed as she lightly touched her ear.

"Oh, I'm sorry. Due to the private nature of tonight's activities, we have all transmissions blocked." He held out his hand. "Please hand over your device."

Miranda hesitated, but when she regarded the men who waited on her, she removed it and handed it to her captor.

"I see you have our guest of distinction already in hand," another man said as he entered and closed the door behind him. Unlike the others, he removed his mask, and Miranda gasped at Emerson Whitney, one of the wealthiest denizens of the city. From Dane's research, she remembered he had stayed neutral during the debates concerning vampire rights. However, his company had taken a major hit when ValCorp had branched out into communications. After him, one by one, half the men took off their masks, and a sinking feeling made her stomach twitch. She'd had a chance as long as they kept their masks on. Now, if Lizandra's Weres didn't come rescue her, she wasn't leaving the room alive.

Miranda recognized several of the men. Besides Whitney, Cyrus Langhorn eyed her with contempt, and Walter Pettigrew looked like he couldn't wait to ruthlessly fuck her. As they talked among themselves, their voices came back to her in a flourish. These were the men who'd been behind closed doors in the Ormont home. *Oh God, help me!* Her pulse spiked. When another man suddenly joined the group, the temperature in the room dropped significantly and the voices quieted. But instead of wearing a black cape like the others, his was maroon. Unlike the others, he kept his mask on. He briefly glanced at her, then went directly to the window.

Three men in masks and capes entered the other room and brought a prisoner in chains. Her startled gasp was noticed by those around her. Remare had been captured, and they'd bound him in silver chains. From the burns on his arms and torso, Remare was averse to the metal, and the chains were digging into his flesh, leaving blood trails and grooves in his skin.

"Are you insane? Do you know who he is?" Miranda's heart thudded painfully in her chest, her breaths rushing out. She tore her eyes from Remare to the men in the room. "Do you *want* to start a war with the vampires? Valadon will kill you for this!"

"Valadon is too much of a negotiator to start a war," one of the men said.

Oh, really! They so didn't know who the vampire lord was and what he was capable of.

A voice from behind a mask uttered in disgust, "What are you afraid of, my dear? Even if Valadon did order a strike against us, the human sympathizers he has garnered over the years would see him for the monster he is."

They bent Remare over the table. He glanced up at the window and his eyes seemed fixed on hers. Frantic, she tried to reason with the men. "You've got to stop this! He's Valadon's second. Valadon will destroy all of you! Don't you understand?"

None of the men responded to her warning. But the man in the maroon cape nodded to her, then turned and left with two others.

When one of the men started whipping Remare's back with the silver chain, Miranda screamed. *"Stop this! You can't do this!"*

The man who had handled her pushed her up close to the window. "Watch carefully what we do to vampires like that bastard gigolo who dared to touch one of our own."

She realized they were the ones who had killed Kristoph, as well as Dane, and her rage intensified. She knew her emotions ignited her powers and tried desperately to gain control by breathing deeply. If she started a fire in this enclosed room, they would all die.

Miranda witnessed the bastard who whipped Remare cruelly smirk and lean back for another strike. She couldn't watch anymore and surveyed the room full of faces who were enjoying the torture of another being. How could humans be this depraved to witness such a horrible sight and do nothing to stop it? Their ugly comments nearly made her retch.

The two angels who always guided Miranda in her choices warred in her mind at her indecision. Finally, the angel of light slowly turned her back and bent her head as a tear fell from her eye. The dark angel arched her brow and smiled wickedly with delight.

God forgive me for what I am about to do. Miranda's energy pulsed in her hand and she laid it on the computer closest to her. Then, she quickly glanced up at the camera in the corner of the room and the overhead sprinkler. If the men in this room wouldn't stop the torture, she would. Closing her eyes, she let the current in her body flow into the computer down into the wires that spread quickly to the other computers and monitors. She faced the door and concentrated harder than she ever had before and felt the blood dripping from her eyes. She was causing a brain bleed by forcing too much power, but she went ahead and melted the door lock and then the overhead sprinkler.

And then...the fires erupted.

Miranda turned to see Remare's face twisted in pain, the blood pouring off his back, and placed her hand on the window. *"Hang on,"* she whispered. She glanced at the man standing next to her and knew she'd be haunted by his terrified gray eyes. The men started screaming *fire* and ran for the door, a door that would never be unlocked. They whipped off their capes and tried to fight the blazes, but the fires burned too hot, and their capes were quickly consumed by the flames. Like madmen, they beat at the door. One by one, they fell to the floor in fits of choking and coughing. Miranda closed her eyes, said goodbye to her own humanity, and let the fires jump to the men. The screams and scent of burning flesh would forever invade her dreams.

Using her powers to keep the flames away and the air around her clear enough for her to breathe, Miranda watched them die in horrific agony, then turned and raised her hand to the window.

***

Remare had one moment to mind-speak with Irina, who was assigned the task of information retrieval from a member of the HOL's computer. *"I've already depleted the contents of the safe, and Aiden has returned to ValCorp with the documents proving the duplicity of those trying to kill Valadon. Meet me at the transport when you are done. Hurry!"* Suddenly, the mirror exploded in a rush of shards that blanketed the entire room. Dagger-like fragments of glass sliced the throats of the men who had tortured him, leaving wide gashes of blood spurting out. None of the shards touched him.

Miranda climbed through the opening with her cape clutched about her. They looked down at the man who had tortured him: Scherer, the goon who had followed Miranda to ValCorp, was drowning in his own blood and still managed to convey his hatred of her in his last gaze. Remare wished him a speedy trip to hell.

Remare had wanted the pleasure of killing the bastard himself. He watched the blood dripping from Miranda's eyes as the links in his chains splintered and fell from his body. She pulled the rest away from his flesh and handed him his cape. He threw it around his shoulders and wiped the blood from her cheeks with his thumbs as he caressed her face. Then, he grabbed her hand and pulled her through the door.

The mansion was in chaos with the alarms ringing and the flames spreading to other rooms. People were running in all directions to get out as fast as they could. The exits blocked by the frantic mob, Remare dragged Miranda out a rear window. He landed on his bloodied back, making sure Miranda suffered no injury.

He ran with her toward the woods where he knew his people were waiting for him in the SUV. As soon as they were in, the driver tore out of there. Within moments, Miranda had passed out and he held her tightly during the entire ride back to ValCorp.

Chapter Forty-Eight

Miranda woke up in the infirmary. Gabriel was asleep in the chair beside her. She heard a deep masculine voice say, "She's awake."

Instantly, Gabriel woke and took her in his arms, kissing her forehead and the side of her head. "My God, Miranda, what the hell happened?"

She welcomed his embrace. She felt weak and barely remembered what had happened. Then, she peered up at Valadon and tried to sense what he was feeling. He exhaled slowly. She realized he was relieved to see her and smiled up at him. "How's Remare? He was hurt tonight."

"He's resting in his room. He refused to come to the medical unit. Even after I ordered him." Valadon's melodic voice was a welcome sound. "His wounds are deep, but healing."

"What happened tonight?" Valadon asked.

"Somehow, they recognized me. I'm not sure how."

"What were you doing there to begin with?"

"I was helping Lizandra. She wanted to *interview* some of the HOL members about Dane's death. I don't know if she was able to detain the ones she wanted."

Gabriel caressed her hand. "You're safe, now." He slanted a look at Valadon, and Miranda could only guess at their silent conversation.

"My phone has been ringing non-stop from the Were Queen checking on your progress. When you didn't return with her Weres, she was livid her men left you behind until I confirmed what one of her Weres saw: You came back to ValCorp with my team."

Miranda sat up. "Sounds like Liz."

"You should rest. Miranda, you were bleeding from your eyes." Gabriel gently stroked her hair. "The only thing to cause that is a brain bleed." He sounded concerned. "I don't think you should get out of bed until I run more tests."

Miranda glanced at Valadon, an accord silently reached. "I'll be fine. What I want more than anything is a shower." She sniffed her hair and was suddenly nauseous. "I can't stand the scent of smoke on me." She tried to rise, but Gabriel kept his hands on her shoulders.

"I don't think that's a good idea. You should rest more."

"I'll rest better if I'm clean." She swung both legs over the bed, pulled the sheet around her, and made her way to Gabriel's bathroom.

In the shower, the water fell gloriously down her back and head, washing away the awful smell of smoke and the scent of death. Bracing herself, she placed both hands on the tiles in front of her and wondered if she'd ever feel clean, again. She knew she had lost part of her soul tonight and shuddered at the thought of what she had done. *Deal with it! Just deal with it.* Then, she grabbed the bottle of shampoo and washed her hair twice to make sure the scent of smoke was completely gone and began to wash the rest of her body when she felt Gabriel's hands tenderly stroking her shoulders.

"I nearly had a heart attack when I saw them bringing you in," he whispered. "I feared you were taken from me."

Miranda leaned back into Gabriel's chest, welcoming his soothing touch. His hands drifted forward to wash her stomach and then reached up to do her breasts, his thumbs brushing across her stiffened nipples.

She turned to cup Gabriel's face and kissed him. When she rubbed her cheek against his chest, she saw through the steam Valadon watching them, his eyes a mask of emotion. Then he slowly turned and walked away. Closing her eyes, she put her arms around Gabriel's waist and held him. Another time, their naked bodies would have sung in pleasure, but tonight, Miranda needed tenderness, a reminder that there was still good in the world.

When the water began to cool, Gabriel shut it off. He helped her dry her back and then grabbed another towel for himself. As Miranda didn't have any clothes, she asked Gabriel for a robe, and he handed her the dark gray one hanging on the hook.

"You need sleep," he said softly.

"I will." She smiled at him and touched his cheek. "But I need to talk with Valadon, first. There are things he needs to be made aware of." She reached up to kiss him, again. "Stay here and wait for me. I shouldn't be long."

Miranda tied the robe around her waist and made her way down to Valadon's bedroom. Now that her mind had cleared, she could remember better. This time, she knocked when she reached his door and waited for his invitation before entering.

Valadon saw the glow was back in Miranda's face. "You're feeling better?"

"Yes, much. Thank you. We need to talk." Miranda moved farther into his room. "I thought you might want a more thorough account of tonight."

Does she have any idea how much it delights me to have her here in my bedroom? From what Remare had told him, he was able to surmise most of what had happened tonight, but there were still some pieces missing. "Join me." He gestured to his sitting area. Miranda accepted his hand as they walked to his couch.

"I guess Remare told you what happened tonight?"

Valadon nodded as he sat beside her and twisted his body to face her, immediately regretting letting go of her hand. "Not everything." He couldn't remember the last time his second had been injured on a mission. It was only after they talked, his second confessed he let them take him to give Irina extra time to complete her task. "Perhaps, Gabriel is right and you should be resting?"

"I will. But I thought you should know everything that happened." Miranda seemed comfortable sitting next to him and filled him in on the Were operation. She tried to give him as many names as she could remember and the number of the men in the room with her. By her count, she'd killed eleven men tonight.

Valadon was aggrieved she'd been at one of the more notorious human parties known for its debauchery. The thought that any of those HOL members could put their hands on her infuriated him. But he'd been pleased with the documents his people confiscated; even now, Morel and Aiden were sorting through them. "You're an amazing woman, Miranda." He smiled. "But, then, I've always thought so." He'd hoped their relationship would blossom into something more, but from what he saw of her and Gabriel in the shower, he knew that wouldn't be happening anytime soon.

She rose to pace in front of his fireplace. "I'm not sure I'd use the word amazing."

"Power is not something to be frightened of, Miranda." He watched as she continued pacing. "It's neither good nor bad, only the person who wields it makes that determination."

Miranda snorted. "So, does that make me good or evil?"

Valadon grinned at the despair in her voice. "Well, for me and Remare, I'd say it makes you *very* good." He stood to face her and smirked. "The HOL members might think otherwise, but if you want a definition of evil, I believe it is spelled H-O-L."

Miranda rubbed her neck. "I'm not even sure what I think, other than what a freak I am."

"Your powers are a gift, Miranda." Valadon massaged her shoulders and gently rubbed his thumbs along her collarbone. "You're not a freak. Over my long centuries, there have been various humans with your abilities. There are others now who possess the powers you have. You're not alone."

"Oh, God, how is it you know the right thing to say to me?"

"Because I care about you. Greatly." He pulled her to his chest and gently wrapped his arms around her.

Miranda returned his embrace. "I care about you, too, Valadon." She peered up at him with soulful eyes. "But I'm involved with Gabriel."

"I know." He silently sighed, keeping his emotions guarded. "I'm not blind. I've seen the way you two look at each other. I won't lie and say I'm not disappointed," he said as he stroked her hair, "but I understand your attraction to Gabriel. You both deserve happiness. Especially Gabriel. He's suffered for many years. It's good to see him happy for a change." Valadon surprised himself with his last admission and realized it was true.

"You're not angry?"

Not with you! "How could I be? Your happiness and well-being are important to me. Do you understand?"

Miranda smiled up at him with such a serene expression Valadon thought his heart would break. "I think so."

"Will you still work for me? In my archives? I very much want you and Nick to continue to work together." It was imperative to him she remained in his house; he was already taking steps to improve her status.

She cocked her head. "You still want me to?"

"Of course." He smiled at her. "It's the only way I can make sure Nick is thoroughly involved in something productive."

When Miranda left Valadon, she intended to go back to Gabriel's quarters, but ran into Katya in the hall. She'd never spoken to the female vampire, but recognized her as one of Remare's women from the pictures on social media. As Katya approached, Miranda asked, "Do you know where Remare's quarters are?"

Katya appeared to scrutinize her as she was studying the vampire. When Katya inhaled deeply, Miranda wondered whose scent was more prominent—Gabriel's or Valadon's. She knew the vampires of Valadon House were curious about her and observed Katya's expression grow warm. "He's resting, now, but if you want to see him, his room is down at the end of the hall. Last door."

Miranda continued down the corridor and knocked gently on the door. When a voice answered, she entered the dimly lit room and scanned his living area and bedroom. His Oriental décor suited him—especially the twin swords mounted on the wall. She climbed the two stairs to his bedroom and sat on the chair facing his bed. He was sprawled on his stomach with his back covered in bandages. Her stomach tightened at the memory of his brutal torture and felt a twinge of guilt for not coming to his rescue sooner.

Surprise seemed to flicker across his face. "What are you doing here?" he asked in a raspy voice as he stiffly rose to his elbows.

"I just wanted to check on you." Miranda wasn't sure why she'd entered his private domain. She just knew she wouldn't be able to sleep tonight if she didn't know he was all right.

Remare stared at her as if she was some sort of apparition. "Gabriel says the wounds should heal." His voice was still groggy from the painkillers Gabriel had given him. "Vampires recuperate from injuries far faster than humans."

Miranda knew that, but the pain etched in his dark eyes summoned her empathy. Along with other emotions she couldn't easily identify. Gabriel had told her Remare's wounds contained liquid silver and had burned deeply into his flesh. "How are you feeling?" It was a stupid question people asked others who were hurt. *Of course, they felt like shit—they were injured!* But she couldn't come up with anything else. And she really wanted to know if he was okay, but why she cared so deeply was a mystery to her. Guilt, she supposed.

"Like I've been whipped with chains dipped in liquid silver," he said caustically.

"I know," she said, lowering her eyes, and wondered if she should leave, but her legs refused to move. He continued staring at her, the red rims around his eyes glowing. Her heartbeats steadily increased. When the silence dragged on between them, she thought she should just go. "I'll leave and let you get your rest."

As she was turning to go, Remare reached out and grabbed her arm so that she tumbled onto the bed with him. In one swift movement, he had her under him and her robe had opened. He breathed in her scent, and that seemed to calm him, though it scared the hell out of her. "What *really* brings you to my room this late, Mir-randa? I'm sure Gabriel could tell you the extent of my wounds *far* better than I can."

Miranda's heart was hammering against her rib cage. Clutching his biceps, she stared into his turbulent eyes. A moment ago, she'd been sitting in the chair talking to him, and the next, she was under his hard male body. Remare's masculine scent was intoxicating and doing strange things to her senses. His pitch vibrated at his usual frequency and hummed along her skin. And that just confused her more. Remare's words were harsh, and his actions brutal, but that was not what she was sensing. "I told you." She gritted her teeth as her fingers dug into his arms. "I came to check on you."

"And so you have." His fangs lengthened as he opened her robe even more and placed his hand over her heart. "But do you notice you have not made any attempt to leave my bed now that you are under my body." He rotated his hips and rubbed seductively at her core.

Nothing cleared the haze from her brain faster than his challenging words. "Ease up, Remare." She narrowed her eyes even as her heart thundered. "I killed eleven men for you tonight."

Remare did rise up from her a little at her words. "Yes, you certainly did, robbing me of my vengeance. I had every intention of killing the bastards myself." He gazed down at her bared breasts. "Perhaps, you have come here to offer your body as penance."

Miranda had enough of his antagonistic attitude. She'd felt guilty for not acting quickly enough to spare him the horrific torture, and instead of being grateful...he was being an asshole, trying to shock her with his aggression. Returning his glare, she said, "You know nothing about me, Remare, or why I came here tonight."

Seeing something in her eyes that obviously set him off, he tossed her to the side of his bed. "Save your pity for someone else. I neither want nor need it."

Miranda tumbled off his bed and on to her feet. *You are such a jerk.* She fought back the burgeoning tears forming behind her eyes. "It wasn't pity, Remare. It was compassion. Even a vampire should be able to figure out the difference." She left without looking back, closing the door behind her.

Remare fisted his hands, wringing the sheets. *What the hell just happened?* His breaths came hard and fast. When she had first entered his rooms, he'd thought he was dreaming; he'd never reacted well to painkillers and was unsure of what to say so he just watched her as he inhaled her wonderful scent. He could smell Gabriel's scent on her, as well. As a human, she would be attracted to the fair doctor who was more like her human nature.

He wasn't sure why he'd turned on her the way he had. Was his ego so weak he couldn't bear for her to see his scarred body? The last thing he wanted was to have her see him weakened, and his male pride had kicked in. Her scent under the robe had driven him crazy, and he hadn't wanted her to leave. Surprisingly, he could detect no real fear. Curiosity, caution, but no fear. And that had just aroused him more.

But what he did detect, the one thing he hated more than anything, was the look of sympathy he'd seen in her eyes. The monster within him chose that moment to raise its ugly head, and he had turned on her.

It didn't matter. She was with Gabriel, and even if she wasn't, Valadon had made his intentions known, so Remare should have no interest in her whatsoever. The only concern he had was her Elemental abilities and how he could use them, nothing else.

At least, that was what he told himself as exhaustion and sleep claimed him.

***

Miranda made her way up to Gabriel's room and stood panting, unaware of why she'd let a vampire like Remare get to her. He was a jerk, a complete asshole, who had no regard for human kindness. Men like him were in love with themselves more than anyone else and couldn't understand who she was.

Never would, either, she reminded herself as Gabriel turned in bed to warmly smile up at her.

But there were good men who walked the earth—humans, Weres and vampires. And the one looking up at her had captured her heart with his crooked smile and kindness. The lamp from the end table made his blond highlights more prominent, and the gold in his eyes was glowing. She could feel the vibrations between them begin to swirl and smiled. But more importantly, he *knew* her. He *got* who she was—flaws and all. And now more than ever, she needed to feel his acceptance of her.

"Move over." The robe fell from her shoulders as she climbed into bed with him. "There's some things I have to tell you. Things you should know about me." Miranda told him the ugly details of what really happened tonight. But instead of recriminations and disgust, Gabriel gazed at her with soulful understanding. He never once interrupted her, but let her finish what she had to say.

"I understand, Miranda." He tenderly stroked her arm. "Believe me, I've seen the ugliness the HOL has inflicted on vampires and, tonight, what they did to Remare. I don't even want to imagine what else they could have done." He glanced downward then met her eyes. "You did what you had to do. They surely would have killed Remare after torturing him, and God only knows what they would've done to you."

"You once told me you save lives, not take them." Miranda wasn't looking for approval. She knew the Weres would applaud her actions, but she needed Gabriel to understand who she was.

"I did. But I've also seen the victims in this war. Some were even children." Gabriel gazed into her eyes, and she knew he sensed her confusion and guilt. "The guilt you feel is not necessary, Miranda. It only proves you have a conscience." He kissed her forehead. "You're still you."

Tears threatened to fall, but she fought them back and sank into his arms. "I think I just needed to hear that." Sleep soon claimed them, but Miranda couldn't help feeling something fundamental about her *had* changed.

She just didn't know what.

Chapter Forty-Nine

Remare lay on his side, thinking about the mission...and Miranda. As far as the operation went, they'd been successful. None of his people had been injured, so in his eyes, it had been a complete success, despite the pain he'd endured. Had he known his chains would be dipped in silver, he'd never have allowed the torture to progress so far.

During the ride back to ValCorp, Irina had watched him with cold eyes as he'd held Miranda in his arms. He would deal with her soon enough, he thought as Valadon quietly entered his room.

"How are you feeling?" He sat in the seat Miranda had vacated.

Remare didn't turn around but answered softly, "The wounds would have healed, by now, if not for the silver." He paused for a breath. "Gabriel says they'll heal in time, but it'll take longer because fragments of silver became imbedded in my flesh."

"Take my blood, Remare; it will speed your recovery." Valadon lay down beside him and curled his arm around Remare so he wouldn't have to sit up to feed.

Remare could heal his wounds, but he didn't want any scars, any reminders. Valadon's blood was stronger than his and would heal him faster. Still, he hesitated, then elongated his fangs and pierced Valadon's wrist. The powerful nourishment flowed through his body. He tried not to make mewing noises, but the blood was rich in the much needed nutrients his body craved, and the soft sounds escaped his throat before he could silence them. After Remare finished feeding, he sealed his bite marks.

Valadon said, "I want to examine your back."

Remare remained quiet as Valadon pulled back the blankets and undid the bandages. He heard Valadon's curses and didn't want to imagine what his back looked like. When he glanced up at Valadon, his friend pierced his wrist with his fangs and let the blood fall on Remare's injuries. With the lightest of touches, Valadon spread the blood with his fingers to make sure each whip mark was coated, then moved the comforter to see how far the scars went. He heard Valadon's sharp inhale when he saw that his lower back and the tops of his buttocks were also scarred. Valadon's hand drifted lower to spread his blood to the affected area.

"Is there anything else I should know about?" Valadon asked.

"I'm not sure how far the silver leaked down when I bled. You're in a better position to see than I am." Remare didn't have any issue being naked on a bed with another male. Long ago, they'd been forced to share a bed, and neither had felt his masculinity had been threatened. In fact, if the elders had thought to harm their friendship, the opposite had been attained, and a bond between the two vampires had been forged. Remare breathed deeply at the memory and didn't mind Valadon exploring his most sensitive flesh. He didn't believe any of his vital parts were injured, but the fear still remained there might be a slight possibility he may have been damaged.

Remare felt Valadon's blood flowing downward as his fingers gently massaged him, ensuring any wounds he suffered would heal. Remare tried to steady his breathing as Valadon barely brushed his tender flesh.

After Valadon finished treating Remare's sensitive skin, he exhaled. "There's no permanent damage. I think you're as virile as ever, Remare, and have nothing to fear." Valadon rose and went to the bathroom to wash the blood from his hand.

Remare gave a silent prayer to the heavens and knew he'd finally find the sleep that had evaded him. Strangely enough, one of his first thoughts was that he should find Miranda and apologize for his rude remarks. "Stay for a few minutes." He figured if Valadon was with him, he wouldn't do something foolish as seeking Miranda out.

"I wasn't planning on leaving you, not just yet, anyway." Valadon shut off the light in the bathroom and joined Remare. He pulled his robe over his legs and sat on the bed, his back against the headboard and sniffed the air. "Is that Miranda's scent I smell in here?"

"She came to check on me," Remare said in a groggy voice. "I asked her to leave after a few minutes."

"Has your opinion of her changed?"

"Somewhat." Remare didn't want to linger on thoughts better left unexplored. "She wears Gabriel's scent." He gazed up at Valadon, aware of his liege's feelings for Miranda. "Do you regret your earlier decision?"

Valadon leaned back and closed his eyes as he stretched out his long legs. "No. Miranda needs protecting. Her safety is a priority and always will be." He had no other choice. At least not until things settled with the HOL. He all but pushed Miranda and Gabriel together, but if there were any other HOL members who thought to use Miranda to get to him, they would see she was with Gabriel and not him. He'd endure the distance for as long as necessary.

Remare searched Valadon's face. "You look tired. You should get some rest."

"Look who's talking." Valadon smiled, then leaned his head against the headboard and pondered his next move. There was still the unresolved issue of the mole in his organization. Something he would address very soon. He closed his eyes, for a moment, then shifted to pull the blankets over his body. He surveyed Remare's room and noted the Oriental décor. He'd lost Remare once to an Asian high lord and had no desire to repeat that mistake.

When he glanced down at Remare, he saw that his blood was already healing the scars. Placing his hand on Remare's shoulder, he willed him to sleep. He'd watch over his second to make sure he healed completely.

***

The next morning, Miranda found her clothes on a bed in the infirmary, neatly piled along with her purse and a note from Cyra stating that Lizandra had her people drop off Miranda's things. She also found a note from Nick requesting she meet him in the archives; he'd found something interesting he wanted to show her. She smiled at the thought of Nick alone in the archives doing research. Miranda quickly dressed as her stomach growled. She wasn't sure she could keep much food down, but she needed sustenance. Reaching inside her jeans pocket, she found the amber necklace Blu had given her and put it on. Then, she went in search of food.

Valadon had said to treat his home as if it was her own and she was welcome to anything in the kitchen. When she had first seen the initials of **V** and **H** on each side of the stainless steel fridge, she'd thought they stood for Valadon House, but found one side contained bagged blood for vampires and the other side had human food. She poured herself some orange juice, then noticed someone had left out a bag of chocolate chip cookies— her favorite. Nick, probably, she grinned. After munching a few and rinsing out the empty glass, she went in search of her young assistant.

***

Gabriel didn't notice until late afternoon that Miranda had left her purse on one of the infirmary's chairs. He'd tried to call her on the cell phone, but only heard it ring in her purse. He figured when she realized she left her bag behind, she'd contact him so he went to work in the lab, quickly losing track of time. When she didn't call him, he began to worry and went to her apartment. When there was no answer, he called ValCorp, asking if anyone knew how to get in touch with her friend, the Were Queen.

***

Valadon shut his phone and grimaced. A sick feeling clawed at his stomach. After speaking with Lizandra and having her confirm she hadn't seen Miranda since the night before, he began to worry. He reviewed the security tapes. Miranda had never left his building. Only one person could have her: Mulciber. He ordered a search, but no one reported seeing her. When Remare joined him, he too reviewed the tapes and said the last account of Miranda was in the kitchen and then her proceeding to the archives.

After that, there was no record of her.

It wasn't until Valadon had called a meeting with his Torians that a message was delivered. He and all members of his house were invited to a ritual of old in the subterranean area below Valadon House. For very old vampires like Mulciber, the darkest parts of the earth were their natural habitat. The lowest levels were where they housed relics from ancient times. Even Valadon rarely visited there. At the time, he'd seen no reason to deny Mulciber access to the level his Torians had nicknamed *Caina*, the lowest section of hell.

Now, he regretted ever letting the primordial vampire in his territory.

Explicit directions were given for them to dress in the fashions of old and would be searched for weapons. Any refusal to meet Mulciber's demands would result in Miranda's painful and bloody death. Mulciber had his army of Rogues seal off ValCorp from any visitors so there would be no assistance from any of Valadon's allies. After reading the rest of Mulciber's letter to his Torians, he dismissed his people to prepare for the night's ceremony.

When all had left except for his elite Torians, it was Gregori who spoke up, first. "Do we know for a fact he has her?"

Valadon held up a lock of Miranda's hair, and Gabriel uttered a groan that had the others sympathizing. Morel squeezed Cyra's hand. Of all the vampires in the room, Cyra had known Miranda the longest, and Valadon felt her concern. In fact, all the vampires had expressed their regard for Miranda and her positive influence on him, even if it had become apparent she was Gabriel's.

Cyra and Bree offered to double check areas. The only ones who didn't express outright concern were Remare's two women, Irina and Katya. But as Remare was heading the investigation into Miranda's disappearance, they'd shown themselves to be active, if not enthusiastic, participants in her search.

"Mulciber has envied you from the very beginning, but I never thought he would go this far," Aiden offered.

Morel added, "He's overindulged in bloodlust."

"What will our high council do if we eliminate this walking anathema?" Katya surprised everyone by asking, making them wonder if she'd had any misdealings with the ancient.

"Mulciber has long sought a way to take over ValCorp. He was the one behind the attacks. He thinks to undermine me by proving to everyone in ValCorp my inability to protect one of my own," Valadon said in a deep authoritative voice. "He will not succeed."

No one was surprised it had been Mulciber who'd attempted to murder Valadon.

"Even if Mulciber were to gain control of ValCorp, he could never succeed you, so what does he hope to accomplish?" Cyra asked.

"No. It is true he cannot succeed me as lord, but I'm sure he has already picked out a prospect he believes he can control more readily."

"Who?" Violence edged Morel's voice.

When Valadon finished appraising his beloved Torians, he addressed them. "One of our own. I'm afraid."

A moment of shocked silence was then eclipsed by a storm of protest. Voices rang out in horror and amazement.

"No one here would ever betray you!" Morel exclaimed.

Gregori added, "You're our king—we would *never* betray you."

"Each vampire here would gladly die for you," Bastien emphasized.

Aiden asked, "You cannot suspect that anyone here would ever seek to replace you?"

"Tell us who the traitor is, and we will take his head!" Gregori demanded.

The rants went on for a few moments longer then Valadon raised his hand to silence them.

"My Torians. I did not say it was anyone in this room. Be content that no one here has betrayed me," Valadon said reassuringly.

Irina finally spoke up. "Then, who, my lord?"

"You should know best, Irina." Valadon's eyes turned to ice. "You spoke to him the most at the party."

All heads turned in her direction. When she stared at him with a puzzled expression, Valadon said, "Remare," and gestured he should address the group.

"The evidence is indisputable. When I first had my suspicions, I did not voice my concerns as I knew it would bring pain and grief to all of us." Remare nodded to Valadon. "I had Aiden position cameras in sensitive areas without anyone's knowledge. I felt, if few people knew about the equipment, there was less of a chance of our mole finding out." He flicked the remote, and the screen showed Mulciber's lair and a figure entering and leaving: Brandon, Valadon's younger brother.

"It can't be," Aiden whispered.

"But Brandon wasn't here when the attack happened," Irina added.

"Wasn't he?" Valadon asked with a raised eyebrow. "I've been in contact with our people in Europe, who confirm that the dates Brandon was supposed to be in Europe do not coincide with the dates he filed here." He then gestured for another of his men to speak. "Gabriel."

"Remare had me investigate the deaths of young humans whose bodies were drained and left in alleys. The bite marks on their bodies match, not only those of Mulciber, but that of Brandon, as well." Gabriel glanced up at Valadon. "As well as others not yet identified."

A hush fell over them. Each knew violating one of Valadon's prime directives meant certain death. None of the vampires present would ever drain someone dry or share that human with multiple vampires. Valadon then nodded to another Torian.

"Persephone, Mulciber's daughter is also involved. She tried to lure me to her father's campaign against Valadon; when her seductive charms failed," Bastien smirked, "she tried to take a bite out of me." He crossed his legs with a grimace.

"Maybe you should be more careful where you stick your dick," Gregori murmured, loud enough for everyone to hear.

"It wasn't my dick she tried to bite off," he muttered back.

"Miranda remembered Persephone's scent the night of the attack," Valadon continued. "She was to finish me off after the dart had incapacitated me. Unfortunate for them, it was Miranda who was hit." He smiled at the memory of a mortal protecting a vampire lord. "It wasn't until she met Persephone at the party that she remembered her scent. I believe we have Cyra to thank for giving Miranda a bottle of Rimini's perfume so that she could recognize the scent." Valadon smiled at Cyra, who held a fond place in his heart.

"What do we do, now?" Bree asked.

"We attend Mulciber's gathering as planned. Let him think he has the upper hand, for now. If he thinks he can subvert me so easily, he will be *bitterly* disappointed," Valadon's voice was coated with venom.

A chorus of approval rose from the Torians, warming Valadon's heart. He looked carefully at his beloved Torians. "But not before we exchange the blood vow."

The blood vow, considered the oldest and most revered ceremony, was sacred to all vampires. Each Torian would kneel before their lord, extend their arm and swear oaths of honor and fealty. Valadon would then offer his blood from a golden chalice and his sworn protection. The resulting bond was said to be unbreakable.

Valadon heard the oaths as each one came before him:

Bastien swore, "Your life before mine," as did Morel and Cyra.

"My service is yours until the last breath my body utters," pledged Gregori.

Aiden and Bree vowed, "The House of Valadon will forever flourish."

Irina and Katya said, "My blood, my love and my loyalty are yours, always and forever."

"Always and forever." Valadon repeated when the last Torian accepted Valadon's blood. After they retired to their own rooms and Remare and Gabriel were left with him, he asked Remare, "Has anyone been in contact with Nick?"

"No. He slipped his guards again. We think he went to meet with the female Were, again. We've already alerted our Were allies."

"He's getting too goddamned good at that." Valadon sighed deeply, rubbing his thumbnails under his chin and hoping Nick stayed away long enough not to witness the ugliness that tonight promised.

Heartsick, Gabriel said, "I've seen the results of Mulciber's handiwork. Do you believe Miranda's still alive?"

"I know she is." Valadon met his gaze as dark tones invaded his voice. "And we will get her back." He saw the vulnerability in Gabriel's eyes and felt sympathy for his progeny.

"Whatever you need me to do to safeguard Miranda's return, I will do." At Valadon's nod, Gabriel turned and left the room.

"Mulciber hasn't harmed her, yet." Remare's enmity was palpable. "He'll wait until we're all assembled before him."

"I know." To destroy an ancient vampire of Mulciber's terrible power, Valadon, even as a high-born Blueblood, couldn't defeat him alone. He would need to borrow power from his Torians, leaving them vulnerable.

It was the only way to stop a mad vampire such as Mulciber.

Chapter Fifty

Miranda woke, not knowing how long she'd been in her cell. She rubbed at the stiffness in her body and realized she was naked. *Great!* Sometime after she'd lost consciousness, they had removed her clothes. Frantically, she searched her body for bite marks and sighed in relief when she found none. Grimacing, she remembered Mulciber's awful touch as he'd stroked her skin and mocked her before throwing her in the cell, locking her in darkness. The only light barely illuminating her room was from the one-inch gap underneath the door.

But it wasn't the darkness that had her heart in a panic. It was imagining what Mulciber planned to do with her. Miranda was certain he was using her to get to Valadon—leading him into some sort of trap. She paced around the cell not knowing if it was day or night. Sensing the earth's vibration, Miranda pressed her palms to the cold ground. This deep, the vibrations were strong, and she could feel the magnetic pull.

She crept along the walls, searching for pipes or cracks, anything that would enable her to escape or call for help, but there was nothing. She banged her fists against the stones and slid down in frustration. Someone would come for her; sooner or later, someone would come for her. She just hoped it would be Valadon and not Mulciber.

***

Nick knew he shouldn't be in Central Park after sunset, but he was with Cerise, and she was a Were, so he was safe. He adored watching her ride the carousel, seeing her happy. Lately, she seemed preoccupied, so when she'd suggested they get out and go for a walk in the park, he'd agreed. He was so rapt watching her, he didn't detect the Weres behind him.

"Vampires should know better than to be in Were territory after dark," one growled.

Nick now regretted ditching his guards, but turned to face the pack of five Weres, who were dressed in leather jackets and sported various tattoos and piercings. Each Were was tall and muscularly built. But these guys weren't typical Weres. They were dangerously feral, their aggression tangible.

Nick stood up to the group, refusing to show any fear. "The carousel and the zoo are open for all kinds."

"Not this late, vampire," the dark-haired Were with the nose ring sneered.

Another snorted. "Pretty stupid of you to come here alone."

"I think we should teach the bloodsucker something about boundaries," the Were with tribal tattoos on his face taunted. "What do you say, boys?"

As Nick prepared to defend himself and Cerise, he heard more snarling behind him and sensed the presence of at least a dozen more Weres.

"The only teaching you'll be doing is back in your den." A tall, redheaded Were strode up to the group. "You're on Black Star territory, Red Claw." He stared down each of the Red Claws, his powerful muscles rippling across his back and shoulders. "You have no business here and are invited to leave." The new band of Weres lined up on his sides, casually displaying their fire power. "Any refusal and we'll be happy to escort you out."

"He's a vampire and doesn't belong on Were territory this time of night." Nose Ring growled as he eyed Black Star's men.

"Maybe. But that's not your call. Is it?" The leader of the Black Star moved forward. His voice turned icy. "Now, turn and leave or we will remove you from our territory."

"You're the Were Queen's second, Gavin the Red. The color suits you." Tattoo Were snarled, "Give the bitch a message from Red Claw. Tell her...her days are numbered. Red Claw is going to claim these lands right out from under her."

Gavin laughed. "Ever hear of treaties? The commission signed it. You'll never get a piece of it. Now, leave, before we get ugly on you."

"Ugly would be an improvement," one of Gavin's men snickered.

The Red Claw Weres looked at each other and, not liking the odds, decided to leave, but Nose Ring pointed behind them. "We'll go, but she comes with us."

Cerise had quietly joined the group and rubbed against Nick. "I better go with them." She then reached up to kiss his cheek and whispered in his ear, "I'll call you, soon."

"Are you sure you'll be okay?" Nick glanced at the Red Claws and wasn't thrilled with her leaving with them.

"Yeah, they're pack. We take care of our own."

Nick and Gavin watched as they disappeared up the hill.

"Nick Valadon! Does your uncle know about your preferences?" Gavin raised an eyebrow and smirked as he assessed the young vampire.

"Thanks." Nick lifted his backpack, prepared to leave, and then turned to Gavin. "How'd you know who I was?"

"Our queen knows many people. She's extended an invitation to meet you."

When Nick didn't say anything, Gavin offered, "That means you're coming with us. No one refuses an invitation from Lizandra."

"—and lives to tell the tale," one of the men added as he moved to Nick's side.

Gavin gave him a reassuring smile as he moved to Nick's other side. "I believe we have some mutual friends."

***

Hearing the guards approaching, Miranda backed into a corner. She would've loved to attack them, but didn't think a water bottle would be much of a weapon. One vampire, she might have had a chance with, but she wasn't strong enough to overcome two Rogues.

As they unlocked the door, one sneered, "Get out."

Momentarily blinded by the light, she placed a hand to shield her eyes and squinted to see. Apparently, she didn't move fast enough because one of the guards dragged her out by her arm. Once in the hall, Miranda used one arm to shield her breasts and the other to cover her crotch and marched between them, wishing they'd give her a shirt to cover up. She was led into a large cave and remembered seeing a similar cavern when she'd been on the balcony with Remare.

Mulciber, dressed in dark flowing robes, was surrounded by his army of vampires. Panic replaced curiosity when she saw a long stake in the ground with wood piled high around it.

"Ah, so our guest of honor has finally arrived." Mulciber's eyes seemed to glow, and he smirked as he came toward her.

Miranda wanted to lash out at him, but he could eviscerate her with one flick of his wrist. She remembered him slashing her face and how Remare had healed her. She wished the cantankerous vampire was here with her, now. Mulciber was making no attempt to defuse his power, and she felt as if fire ants were crawling up her arms.

"Charming." Mulciber stroked a strand of her hair and watched her shudder. "You will be pleased to know your paramour will soon be joining us." Then, he signaled to his men. "Tie her to the stake."

"No! You can't do this!" Miranda struggled against their hold, refusing to go quietly to her death. If they were going to kill her, she was going to go kicking and screaming every inch of the way and not make it easy for them. Until one of them slapped her hard enough that her teeth rattled.

"Oh, but, my dear, I can do a great many things. As you soon shall see." Mulciber sighed with exaggerated concern, then turned to his men with a commanding voice, "See to it that all the torches are lit. I want Valadon to get a good look at our captive. As she dies slowly and painfully before his eyes."

Miranda stared at Mulciber in horror. His red-rimmed eyes were void of anything human, only a monster prevailed.

"But, Father, you promised me a taste," Persephone pouted as she walked in on Brandon's arm.

"And you shall have one." He stroked his daughter's cheek with fatherly adoration. "But not before the festivities begin."

"Brandon, stop this!" Miranda pleaded, hoping the younger vampire still had some semblance of humanity left. "You're Valadon's brother!"

"I'm afraid what's begun...cannot be undone," Brandon mocked in false sympathy. "Besides, why would I want to stop it? Valadon's reign is over. It's a new dawn for us. Pity you won't be around to see it, but then again...neither will he."

Miranda couldn't believe Brandon's callousness. *How could one brother be so different from the other?* There was nothing behind Mulciber's soulless eyes that could be reasoned with, but with Brandon, she saw a glimmer of humanity. "Brandon, your brother loves you! You don't have to do this!"

"Oh, but I do. I've waited long enough for him to step down. His love for your kind has weakened him. He no longer puts the needs of our own kind, first. That will change under my rule."

Persephone hooked her arm around him and smiled slyly. Then, something caught her eye. She climbed the pyre to examine Miranda's necklace. "I see they didn't completely strip you. I thought you might be wearing a yellow diamond, but I see it's only a piece of amber."

Miranda's heart sped up. The last thing she wanted was for Persephone to touch Blu's gift. "Let me keep it. Please! You've already taken everything else. It was a gift from my father." Miranda thought the last would resonate with the deranged daughter, but instead, Persephone reached up to rip the necklace off. "I'm going to die soon! Please, let me keep it," Miranda screamed out in frustration and despair.

"Let her keep it, Persephone. I will buy you diamonds. You don't need a worthless piece of amber," Brandon huffed in boredom.

Persephone shrugged and smiled at Brandon. "I'd rather have diamonds, anyway." She descended the pyre and stood by his side.

Miranda tried to break free of the binds that held her, but the only damage she did was to scrape her wrists raw. She heard the sounds of several footsteps approaching from the ridge above her.

Valadon's Torians were marched in with their hands bound in silver behind their backs. She saw relief and then dread in Gabriel's eyes as he gauged Mulciber's army. When he tried to lean forward to get to her, a guard shoved him ruthlessly back. They were all shirtless, but at least they had the privilege of wearing leather pants. Cyra, Irina and Bree were also wearing leather halter tops and Miranda had a fleeting thought she'd rather not be naked in front of all the members of Valadon House. But all things considered, that was the least of her problems.

When Valadon was marched in last, he quickly made note of all the entrances to the cave, including the balcony high above that opened to his living area. Then, his heart ached when he saw the plea in Miranda's eyes, and his resolve strengthened. He willed her to understand he would free her and end this debacle Mulciber had instigated. Valadon stood proud as the ruler he was and bellowed, "Let her go, Mulciber! There's no need for her to suffer." He eyed his brother with anger and regret. "Brandon, tell him to let her go. She's of no importance here."

"Oh, but my dear brother, on that point, you are mistaken. She is very important." Brandon stepped forward and spoke directly to Valadon. "Perhaps, if you'd spent more time paying attention to business, rather than eyeing the human, you might have noticed things were amiss in your own house."

Mulciber, impatient to get on with the sacrificial ceremony, said, "Enough with the talk. Valadon! Lord of New York, abdicate your rule here in America or watch as we torch your love." Mulciber said the last with glee, believing he'd found the one thing to hold sway over him. Valadon would not give him the satisfaction he so dearly desired.

The full measure of Mulciber's madness was evident in the tableau, but Valadon wouldn't allow himself to be a part of the ancient's insanity. "I will never abandon my people, and you are a fool if you think you'd be appointed my replacement! The High Court would never approve your false claim to the throne."

"Oh, but there you are wrong, again." Mulciber grinned wickedly. "We've already been in covert meetings with several of the High Court officials. You'd be surprised how many would like to see you stripped of your titles here. You should have been paying more attention. Your brother is right about you." Mulciber glanced at Miranda. "You've been too distracted as of late."

Valadon's temper rose at Miranda's look of despair. He could feel Gabriel's pain and fear as his progeny tried to loosen the bonds around his wrists.

Remare's animosity toward Brandon for his treachery was evident. Valadon knew his war strategist believed dividing Brandon from Mulciber was the only way to weaken them. "Even if you did manage to subjugate Valadon, none of us would ever serve you!" Remare's acerbic voice echoed throughout the cave. "You would not keep long that which you seek to possess. You've been played for a fool, Brandon."

"Valadon's second. How very devoted of you to stand up for your king. Tell me, would you take a strike for him?" Mulciber sent a stream of power in Remare's direction, slamming him against the cave's wall. The blast so powerful everyone in the cave heard Remare's bones cracking before his unconscious body slid to the ground.

Gabriel immediately went to him, even though a guard tried to hold him back. When the others saw Remare was still alive, they stood together and banded their strength in a show of support for their king.

"My people will never follow you!" Valadon's voice thundered over the throng of watchers. "Give it up, Mulciber! There's no way you could ever rule New York!"

"Oh, you might be surprised who my followers are," Mulciber hissed at him. "Besides, your brother, Brandon, is quite the financial advisor in his own right and tired of being in your shadow. It's time he assumed his rightful position as head of ValCorp."

"Right? By what right do you *dare* challenge me? *YOU HAVE NO RIGHT!*" Valadon's enraged voice reverberated off the walls. He despised Mulciber for this insurrection and endangering his people. How could Brandon ally himself with this monster?

"Right? I have every right. I am an ancient, far older than you, and should have had this territory. It's *you* who has no right." Mulciber sneered. "If you hadn't been the favorite of a High Court official, this territory would have been mine. I will give you one chance to abdicate. Decline your status as ruler, here and now, and I will spare your human."

"*Never!*" Valadon roared as he bared his fangs and accepted the vitality his people willingly gave him, letting his combined power spew out over Mulciber, who appeared momentarily stunned, then quickly answered with a blast of his own energy.

The two combatants refused to back down or back away from the fight, each sending out streams of current meant to destroy the other. Everyone in the cave sought cover from the exploding rock fragments. The Torians quickly undid their bindings as Valadon battled Mulciber.

In their recorded history no vampire lord had *ever* won a contest against an ancient.

Chapter Fifty-One

Nick found himself in Lizandra's VIP lounge surrounded by people who were as curious about him as he was about them. A pretty, but shy Were stayed in the corner by Gavin, refusing to come any closer. He'd heard stories of Werehaven, but never imagined it to be as astounding as it was, but then, he supposed the Weres would be even more impressed if they ever saw Valadon House.

Lizandra saw Nick eyeing the Were beauty. "Sasha was recently attacked by Rogue vampires and is just finishing recuperating. That's why she stays in the shadows."

Nick's eyes glowed. "My uncle has outlawed the Rogues and set forth rules restricting their activities. We've heard reports certain vampires have broken those laws, and I know we have people investigating them." At first hesitant to join them in their underground lair, Nick was immediately curious about the Were Queen after Gavin informed him Miranda was her best friend.

"I should hope so." Lizandra studied him. "We have been allies with your uncle for generations and are sworn to protect his as we would expect him to protect one of ours."

The Black Star Weres were incredibly polite by offering him food and drink and asking him all types of questions. Some, he could answer, and others, he just shook his head. Gavin had been the most talkative, explaining the differences in clans and territories as set forth by the commission. Nick liked these Weres, especially Gavin. When Orion joined them and told Nick he was Miranda's roommate, he was even more impressed.

"I take it your uncle isn't aware you're involved with a member of Red Claw?" Lizandra's voice held censure. "I must say that's not the brightest of ideas."

"Who I choose to be with is my concern and no one else's."

"Perhaps." The Were Queen crossed her long legs and casually relaxed into her chair. "But, surely, Valadon would assign guards to his only nephew."

Nick didn't want to admit he'd stupidly ditched his guards earlier tonight and ducked his head.

"I see." Lizandra smiled. "You do realize we have to notify him of your presence here. Either we will escort you back to ValCorp or he will send his own people to retrieve you."

One of the Weres strode up the stairs to the lounge and handed Lizandra a piece of paper with a message on it as Nick felt a terrible piercing pain in his side and nearly doubled over. The pain was more excruciating than anything he'd ever felt.

"What is it?" Lizandra asked with concern as she steadied him. "What's wrong?"

At first, Nick didn't know what was happening and had to fight to breathe. He seemed in a stupor, for a moment, as his eyes glazed over, then muttered with teeth gritted, "My uncle...he's in trouble." Nick coughed a few times from the pain. "Help him! Please!"

***

Valadon developed a deep gash across his arm. His Torians were battling Mulciber's vampires, and blood now stained the cave floor. Proud of his people, he watched as Gabriel fought alongside the Torians. Even with the help of his people, after repeated strikes against Mulciber, his energy faltered. His heart ached as Miranda struggled against her bonds. He wanted to free her, but one moment of distraction could be fatal.

Mulciber seemed to waver under the pressure, but so far, he'd managed to avoid any damaging wounds. He continued to blast Valadon with his power strikes. Valadon knew if he didn't throw a killing blast soon, eventually, his reserves would become depleted. From the corner of his eye, he watched Persephone, who had apparently felt her father weaken, unsheathe one of her daggers and stab Miranda in the thigh. Valadon knew, by feeding, Persephone increased her own energy and would lend strength to her father.

When Miranda's screams echoed against the cave walls, Valadon hesitated for only a second to check on her, and that was all Mulciber needed. He struck Valadon with a deadly bolt of energy. A lethal slash across Valadon's chest had rivulets of blood dripping down his body. But sensing his injury, the Torians threw more power his way.

Mulciber's frustration became volatile, and he cruelly directed a stream of power at the Torians, leaving them covered with lacerations. Valadon couldn't help them and fight Mulciber at the same time.

Mulciber sneered as he smelled victory close at hand.

"Give it up, Mulciber! You cannot win this fight! You're too old, and your powers wane," Valadon bellowed as a new wave of energy combined with his own. Another had entered his house and was making his way toward Valadon.

"Lord Valadon, you have been away too long from combat. It is you who weakens." Mulciber could sense the increase in Valadon's power, but knew his weakness. "Watch now, how one of your favorites dies!" Mulciber sent a fatal current of energy at one of the women who went down immediately from the blast, her torso mangled by a gaping whole.

"Cyra!" Morel screamed in horror as he raced to his wife and gathered her in his arms. He frantically tried to stem the flow of blood. His body taut with pain, he howled in rage at the savage slaughter.

"My love," Cyra whispered as the last breath left her lips. Morel roared at the injustice, swearing vengeance. He glared at Mulciber and unleashed his own power directly at him.

Valadon vibrated with the dual pain of the death of one of his own and Morel's despair. His wrath increased beyond memory. "*Coward!* You attack women and innocents. You are no leader and never will be!" He seared Mulciber with another energy bolt that appeared to injure the ancient, and then, Mulciber tapped into stores of power Valadon had no knowledge of.

Valadon continued to pelt away at Mulciber, who seemed to be gaining in power. One after one, his Torians faltered. But Mulciber didn't know one of Valadon's Torians was also a Blueblood, even though he had renounced his origins long ago. His blood was pure, and his Torian fed Valadon with the power of the strongest vampires on the planet.

"I will attack anyone who stands in my way." Mulciber glanced at his daughter. "Persephone, roast the woman," he said in glee as he faced off again against Valadon.

"No!" Gabriel screamed as he fought off one of his attackers.

Mulciber saw Gabriel making his way to Miranda. "You should have been dead by now, Doctor." He sent a stream of power that brutally flung Gabriel against the wall.

Miranda shrieked at Persephone, who laughed as she threw the torch on the pyre. Miranda tried desperately to control her emotions and keep the flames away from her body, but her attempts at halting the fire just increased it. As she glanced down, she saw the blood amber and remembered what Blu had told her. He couldn't save Valadon, but he might be able to help her. She screamed in despair, *"BLU! I need help!"*

***

Guy was enjoying his bath with the almond milk Felicity liked. As he relaxed, his companion massaged his shoulders. He was singing a song by Tiseira when his body suddenly went rigid. Sensing his vexation, Felicity asked, "Guy, what's wrong?"

Guy blinked then looked at her as if noticing her for the first time. "Miranda's in trouble." He stepped out of the bath and threw a towel around his hips. He marched into his living room and slid a hand over the antique mirror. Swirls of grays revolved within the frame. "*Miranda! Open your eyes. Let me see what is going on. Now!*"

"*Help me, Blu! You promised you would help me!*" Miranda's voice raged in pain and fear.

"*I will help you if you let me see what is going on. I can't help you until I see what is happening. OPEN YOUR EYES! NOW!*"

***

Remare woke from hearing Gabriel's body slam into the wall beside him. He crawled to the ledge and peered down at the carnage. His pain was nearly unbearable, but he had suffered worse in battle and knew how to command his body under duress. What he saw enraged him. There were vampires dead or injured on the ground from both sides. When he realized Brandon was feeding his power to Mulciber, Remare bared his fangs. For that alone, Brandon would die. Having fed from Valadon when he'd been injured in the confrontation with the HOL, the power of a Blueblood coursed through his veins. At nearly a thousand years old, his own power was strong, but with the combination, he was lethal.

He threw his power at Brandon, slamming him to the ground, cutting the bond between him and Mulciber, leaving the ancient vulnerable to Valadon. A slice then opened up Mulciber's chest, and blood streamed down his body. Remare sneered with all the pent up revulsion he felt toward Brandon, who hissed in pain and then turned and fled. *Coward!*

Remare wanted to follow, but he heard Miranda's anguished screams as the flames licked at her legs and made his way to her.

***

Blu's cool power rushed through Miranda and she was able to make the flames abate beneath her. She exhaled in relief.

"Use your power, Miranda. Help Valadon! He needs you."

"How? I can barely feel it!"

"Let down your shields. You must! Trust me this once, woman. I'm trying to help you!"

"Trust him, Miranda." Felicity's voice whispered in her head. *"Please. He will help you,"*

Miranda concentrated hard to let down her shields. She'd become so used to keeping them up she'd forgotten how to lower them. Finally, when they went down, a gush of power stronger than anything she'd ever felt suffused her body. With eyes that glowed white, she saw Valadon go down on one knee. In another moment, Mulciber would destroy him. She used her ability to channel Blu's power and directed it at Valadon, who rose in the air and sent a fatal stream of energy at Mulciber and his men in a blinding arc of lightning.

When the light dissipated, Mulciber was dead on the ground. Valadon searched for his traitorous brother. But Brandon was nowhere in sight; he'd fled as soon as he'd seen Mulciber go down. Breathing hard, Valadon immediately went to Cyra, hoping he could mend the damage Mulciber had caused, but it was too late; there was nothing he could do. Cyra was dead, and Morel looked like his heart had been crushed as he peered up at Valadon with glistening eyes. Valadon gently placed his hand on Morel's shoulder. "I'm so sorry."

After checking on his other Torians, who were breathless and exhausted from the fight, Valadon marched over to where Mulciber's body lay shattered with a gaping hole where his black heart should have been and kicked at the corpse to make sure the ancient was dead.

Behind him a Rogue silently crept up with a long dagger pointed at Valadon's nape.

"Get down!" Three shots were heard in rapid succession, and everyone ducked at the loud reverberations. Mulciber's man lay dead at Valadon's feet. Valadon turned to see Katya and Tristan on the balcony with his sniper's rifle. Tristan nodded, saluted his liege, then jumped down the railing onto the rocks and joined him. Valadon smiled. Through his blood bond with the young Torian, he'd been able to send a message releasing him from his seclusion.

Remare wanted Brandon to pay for his betrayal, but knew the coward would eventually surface. And he'd be there when he did. But now, he smelled Miranda's blood. Brandon's punishment could wait. Miranda's predicament was more urgent. He dragged his injured body to where she lay crumpled on the ground. He looked down at her face. She'd bled from her eyes, nose and mouth. When he brushed back her hair, he saw that her ears had bled, as well. He gathered her into his arms and called her name softly, but she was blissfully unconscious. He placed his hand over her heart to make sure it was her heartbeats he was hearing and not just his own, then sighed in relief that she was still alive.

Observing carefully that no one saw him, Remare bit his wrist and let a few drops drip into Miranda's mouth. He then bent his head low and kissed her, his breath forcing the blood down her throat, knowing it would help heal her injuries. When he lifted his mouth, her taste lingered on his lips. "You cannot die, Mir-randa. I will not let you." He tenderly stroked her face with his fingers, wiping away the blood. "You have become far too precious to me."

Remare peered up as Valadon walked to them. "She's alive. But she's in urgent need of medical attention."

Valadon grimaced when he saw her face. "Gabriel was hurt, as well." He glanced over at his unconscious progeny as Tristan lifted him. "I've already made arrangements for his replacement. Dr. Amira will be joining us, now." He then leaned down and gently lifted Miranda up. Remare stumbled, then stood. They watched the Torians rise, one by one. Almost all. A solitary blood stained tear crept down Valadon's cheek.

When Remare glanced up, again, he saw the surviving Rogues who'd fought with Mulciber had their hands folded behind their heads in surrender. Several Weres stood behind them with guns at their backs.

Gavin stepped forward, nodded, and spoke directly to the vampire king, "Lizandra sends her regards."

Chapter Fifty-Two

Three days later.

Remare watched from the shadows as Miranda lay on her stomach in the infirmary in a coma. Her lower legs were elevated by egg crate cushions to help lessen the pain from the burns. He agreed with Gabriel, who'd refused to leave her side despite his own injuries, that there was no need for Miranda to be conscious while her body repaired itself. He was pleased her vital signs were good; she was recovering at a remarkable pace for a human, however, some scarring was inevitable.

They'd been worried about the brain bleed, but the tests had come back negative for an aneurism or brain trauma. No one could explain how Miranda suffered from such an intense brain bleed or how she'd been able to get down from the pyre.

Gabriel glanced up as Valadon entered the medical suite.

"How is she?" Valadon stood alongside Miranda's bed.

"The same." Gabriel brushed a lock of her hair. "Miranda's strong; she'll wake when her body has had time to heal itself."

"She is strong. Stronger than any of us ever imagined. And a fighter."

"Your men are recuperating." Gabriel smiled at Valadon. "I've checked on all of them, and they're progressing well."

"Not all," Valadon commented. "But he will. In time." The vampire lord turned and walked quietly out of the medical suite.

Remare waited until Gabriel had left to see Miranda. It was late and the lights were low. Making sure no one noticed him, he checked the chart near the edge of the bed and noted the last entry. Even in a hospital gown, Miranda was quite lovely. Pity she'd been pulled so deeply into vampire politics. He grimaced. Valadon had been foolish to have become involved with a human. He brushed one finger down her arm. What he was about to do went against the laws of Valadon House. Humans were never to know of the healing abilities of vampire blood. Otherwise, they'd be ruthlessly drained of their life's sustenance.

He opened the case that housed the syringe and the tiny bottle. He then inserted the needle into the rubber tipped bottle and let the syringe fill with his blood. When Remare was satisfied he had enough, he lifted the hospital gown and looked down at the small scar Miranda had from taking the dart in her hip. He smirked at the irony of a human woman protecting a vampire king. He then bent down and injected her with his blood. She'd still have scars, but now, they would be far less noticeable.

"Sleep well, Mir-randa." He leaned over and kissed her temple, inhaling her scent deep into his very being. "There will come a time and place," he whispered, "but not yet, precious."

Miranda heard movement around her. The voices seemed like thousands of miles away. Floating was just so comfortable, she didn't want to wake. Every time it felt like she might, something seemed to pull her further into the shadows. When she did open her eyes, she saw Gabriel trying to get comfortable in the chair by her bed. When he lifted a solitary lid, she said, "We've got to stop meeting like this."

"You're awake." He smiled, but his voice sounded hoarse. "How do you feel?"

She stretched. "A little stiff in places. How long have I been out?"

"A few days." He shone a light in her eyes, then took her pulse. "You have no idea how glad I am to see you awake."

"Undo me." Miranda gestured to all the tubes and wires connecting her to machines.

"I thought I already had." Gabriel smiled and then started disconnecting the wires. "You had me undone from the moment I met you."

Miranda's insides melted. Gabriel was a good man. His concern and his love for her was evident in the way he looked and spoke to her. He knew she wasn't perfect, had done things most men would have walked away from. But he'd stayed with her, had been there for her when she needed him most. He'd even called her precious and that had warmed her heart.

***

Two Weeks Later

"Are you sure you don't want to attend his coronation? I know I've asked before, but I thought one of us should go." Miranda listened on her phone to Gabriel's reasons. She'd hoped he'd change his mind, but he'd been resolute about not going. She suspected, if Valadon had more time alone with Gabriel, he might've been able to dissuade him from leaving. And that was the real reason Gabriel had stayed away.

Miranda walked into the large banquet room on one of the upper floors of ValCorp. She was happy they had decided on modern dress instead of the traditional garb. Everyone was in formal attire to celebrate Valadon's elevation from lord to high lord. Evidently, while she'd been in a coma, there'd been a preliminary investigation into Mulciber's illicit activities by the ruling court of the vampires, and it had been decided Valadon had acted within his rights to protect his people and his territory from the mad vampire.

An ambassador from the European court, Serikhan, had conducted the investigation. Apparently, there'd been talk in Europe that Mulciber had been losing it for some time, but no one had known how far he had devolved. Valadon had liked the African representative to the court and had invited her to stay in his territory. She had politely declined, but assured him she'd visit sometime in the future.

There'd been no sign of Brandon. Many believed he'd gone to ground and would remain under until his part in his brother's assassination attempts were a memory. No one believed that was the last they'd seen of Brandon. Rumor had it Remare was behind the investigation and wouldn't stop until he tracked down the traitor.

Judgment had been passed down on Persephone. Her duplicity could have cost her life, but Valadon had decided on mercy and decreed she'd be in isolation for an extended period of time. Many felt that was a punishment worse than death. Isolation could drive a vampire to the brink of insanity. Some felt that was what Valadon intended so he'd be justified in passing down the execution order.

When the elder ascended the podium and addressed the crowd, Miranda smiled. From what the vampires had told her, it was quite an honor being presented to Valadon. There were representatives from all over to congratulate him on his elevated status. She found it difficult following the elder's words as she scanned the crowd, trying to figure out who everyone was, and wished Cyra was there to explain everything to her. They'd had the funeral rites for her while Miranda was still unconscious. Her ghost, as well as Dane's, would haunt her for some time to come.

When they announced Valadon's arrival, everyone in the room bowed on their knees. Miranda kept to the back of the room as she was an invited guest and not one of Valadon's people. Suddenly, a hand grabbed her and pulled her down as a small embroidered pillow appeared to cushion her knee before it hit the floor. She looked sideways to see Remare smiling.

"If you're going to attend our ceremonies, you should observe our customs."

"But I'm not a vampire," Miranda whispered.

"No, but you're a guest in our house." One corner of Remare's mouth lifted. "Perhaps the day will come when you will choose to be."

Not in your lifetime, buddy. She was so involved in talking to Remare, she nearly missed the speech Valadon was giving. He thanked all those who had supported him and graciously accepted the title of high lord and then met her eyes. "And as high lord of this territory, I want to bestow the title of 'Friend of the Court' on someone who has proven her loyalty and friendship to me, as well as my court—Miranda Crescent."

Applause rang out that had her stunned; everyone smiled and clapped their hands in her direction.

"Welcome to our house, Mir-randa." Remare's eyes glinted as he smirked at her.

Miranda's brow furrowed, sensing something sultry in his voice, then turned to face Valadon. "Thank you. I graciously accept your gift."

"Don't you want to know what responsibilities and obligations go along with that title, before you accept?" Remare had the Grinch's smile plastered across his face.

It worried her. A lot.

"What obligations?" she asked cautiously.

Remare only shook his head and seemed to be laughing as he disappeared into the crowd.

After the party wound down, Miranda joined Valadon in his penthouse. He'd said he had a gift for her he wanted to give her in private. She entered his suite, admiring the view of the city at night as she first had when she'd left her purse in his office. It all seemed so long ago, now. The view of the city at night still made her breathless, especially this high up. After pausing a moment longer and making sure she didn't scent any strange perfume, she continued on her way.

When she arrived at his office, the door was open, and he was gazing out the window. Only this time, it was bulletproof. "So. Do I call you High Lord Valadon, now?" Miranda joked as she leaned against the doorway.

Valadon turned and smiled at her. "If you like," he said in his deep, melodic voice. "But I can think of several other names I'd rather hear you call me."

Miranda grinned. The vampire king looked better than she'd ever seen him. He was glowing with power and contentment, and she was happy for him. He had the love of his people, his status as high lord was secure, and he deserved all his happiness. She felt pride for the vampire who ruled over an empire. "Oh, yeah? Name one." She hugged him when he came around his desk to embrace her.

"Thank you for attending my celebration tonight." He kissed her forehead.

"Of course. I'm sorry about Gabriel." She gazed into his eyes. "He said you'd understand."

Valadon shook his head. "I knew he wouldn't come. It's all right." Valadon moved to his desk, lifted a black velvet box and handed it to Miranda. "This is something I wanted you to have. It belonged to my sister, Bianca...a long time ago."

Miranda opened the box with the clicking noise only jewelry boxes made and was stunned by the necklace. Black square diamonds. A lot of them. Surrounded by smaller black diamonds in various cuts and sizes. "Valadon. I can't accept this. It's too exquisite," she whispered breathlessly.

"You've earned it. You nearly died helping me and my people." He secured the necklace around her neck. Standing behind her, he held her back to his front.

Miranda felt Valadon's rush of power and became lightheaded. She breathed deep and tried to quiet her pounding heart. Vampires had to have pheromones, because her body was responding fiercely to Valadon, more intensely than she ever had before. Vampires resolutely denied possessing the pheromones capable of seducing a human, but she could feel her knees weakening. She turned to face him.

Valadon kissed her passionately as the world seemed to slip away. He deepened the kiss, thrusting his tongue sensually into her mouth.

Miranda, overcome with hunger, returned the kiss. The euphoria of being enveloped in Valadon's scent was intoxicating. She nearly missed seeing his arm reaching back to clear everything off his desk. In one swift motion, he had her laid out and her knees by his hips as he pushed her boots to the corners of his desk and fit himself between her thighs.

She couldn't breathe as she began drowning in sensations of ecstasy. *Think*, she kept telling herself. *Something's wrong here.* Something she was supposed to remember: Gabriel. She was with Gabriel and shouldn't be doing this. Kissing Valadon once in gratitude for the gift was one thing—but the kiss had quickly spun out of control.

And she'd let it.

She had to stop Valadon, who was now kissing her face and neck. When he started to lap at her vein and then suck at it,

Miranda's eyes rolled back in her head. She felt his erection rub against her core, and tears nearly formed in her eyes. It was too much heat, too much passion—she should never have let it get this far. In a ragged voice, she said, "Valadon...you have to stop."

Miranda had to fight through the haze, the seductive, dark veil of shadows that was blinding her. If she let it go on any further, she would cross lines she couldn't live with. "Stop, Valadon, just stop!"

She quickly rolled off his desk into a crouch and then stood. She stared at the shocked look on his face, as if he too had been caught in a vortex of desire. Without a word, Miranda made for the door and ran to the outer office, flung open that door and quickly closed it behind her. Breathing hard, she needed a moment to gather herself.

When she opened her eyes and her panting had slowed, Remare stood in front of her with a questioning expression on his face. When his eyes lit on the necklace and widened, then met her gaze, Miranda hesitated for a moment. Not understanding his look, she tore off down the hall. When she burst through the entrance to ValCorp, she immediately ran to Gabriel who was waiting for her by his car. She didn't dare look up at the windows.

Remare surveyed the items on the floor of Valadon's office and inhaled the scents in the air. He then understood the harried look on Miranda's face. Valadon stood with his arms crossed, gazing out into the night's sky. His body was still, but Remare sensed the underlying emotions he was barely containing. "I take it things didn't go well with the professor?"

Valadon didn't bother turning around. "No. They...did not."

Remare held back by the doorway as he observed Valadon and said softly, "You gave her Bianca's necklace." Even Valadon didn't know it had been Remare who had given the necklace to Bianca centuries ago.

Valadon sighed. "They weren't doing any good sitting in the back of the vault all these years."

Remare nodded and joined him by the window, watching the lights of the city. "You knew she had become involved with Gabriel. If I remember correctly, you even pushed her in his direction."

Valadon growled as he contemplated the night sky. "I was so sure..."

Remare sensed Valadon's frustration and considered his next words carefully. "Her relationship with Gabriel will not...last long." He exhaled slowly. "A man who is not content with himself cannot be content with anyone else." He turned to gaze at Valadon.

"It is only fair. Once I took something precious from him—his humanity. He's now taken something I hold dear to my heart."

They peered down to watch as Miranda flew into Gabriel's waiting arms. For a brief instant, Gabriel looked up and mouthed, "Thank you, Father."

Solemnly, Valadon placed his palm on the window. "That was the first time Gabriel has ever called me Father."

Chapter Fifty-Three

Remare entered the archives from the lowest level and walked over to the sitting area where he inhaled Miranda's scent. He'd become used to her scent and discovered he missed it. He looked around at the vast collection of art and books. This was her world down here. The library hosted a wealth of knowledge not to be found anywhere else in the world. In time, her curiosity would win over stubborn pride. He smiled at the prospect of her return as he ascended the stairs. She would finish the work she'd started with Nick. *Nick,* Remare laughed to himself. Valadon didn't realize how valuable Nick would be in getting Miranda to return.

Remare had stealthily watched the two of them working together down here and the bond that had formed between them.

When Remare reached Miranda's work area, he slid his hand over her work table. Let her enjoy her time with Gabriel. She would need time to get over her fear of vampires and the ugliness she'd seen. In time she would see another side of vampires.

A voice in the darkness whispered, "You look content, Remare."

"I am content. Who wouldn't be, Irina?" He faced his sometime lover who was studying him. "We defeated a powerful enemy, and Valadon's status is secure."

"Then, we should celebrate." Irina slid down the straps of her dress until it fell to the floor. She stood naked before him as she leaned her hips against the work table.

Remare pointed to the overhead cameras. "There would be an audience."

"I've never minded watchers before...and neither have you." Irina arched her back, letting her magnificent mane of blond hair fall to the table beneath her.

Remare had always thought Irina one of the most stunning women he'd ever met and one of the best lovers he'd ever taken. As well as one of the shrewdest. She would have to be dealt with very carefully.

But tonight, he did, indeed, feel like celebrating, even though his mind was on another. He stroked one finger down the center of Irina's chest. "Well...if you don't mind." When he saw her seductive smile, Remare laughed and bent Irina over the table and celebrated in the way he knew best.

Epilogue

Terese Laines didn't want to make a bad impression with her new boss and made sure everything on his desk was perfect. It had been dreadful losing three senior vice presidents at one time. That fire out on Long Island had claimed the lives of some of their leading people, and everyone at Ehrlich Industries was shaken by their loss. She checked again to make sure there was fresh coffee brewing and the files he requested were carefully laid out on his desk. The financial reports were already on his computer screen, and all was as he'd requested.

She smoothed down her skirt and patted her hair to make sure everything was perfect. Terese scanned the collection of old books that had been delivered and made sure the rare books were lined up on the shelves. She tried to read the titles but didn't recognize the language. Why anyone would want old books was a mystery to her. Must be a collector; she shrugged.

When the new head of Research and Development walked down the hall, everyone in the outer offices nodded to him, and he politely smiled back. The whispers already began about how handsome and debonair he was in his dark gray suit and maroon tie. The gossip was that he used the private gym early mornings before work and kept himself fit.

When he walked into his office, he asked, "Terese, the files I asked you to pull?"

"Yes, sir, they're laid out on your desk as you requested."

"And the financials?"

"On your computer screen, sir."

"Thank you, Terese, but please stop calling me sir and call me by my name.

"Yes, sir. Would you like some coffee? There's a fresh pot brewing." When he continued to stare at her from under his eyebrows, Terese tried nervously to remember his name. She could smack herself in the head for not remembering.

The new vice president smiled at her. "It's Frank, Terese. Frank Peralt."

***

Blu lay awake in his bed, his thoughts turning in his head. He glanced at Felicity's sleeping form and smiled, then rose and entered his living quarters. He considered pouring himself a glass of wine, but instead strode to his antique mirror and brushed his hand across it. A figure swirled then came into focus. "My king."

"I was wondering when I'd hear from you," King Robert muttered. "With the current state of affairs, this had better be good news, Montglat. Your last report was less than satisfactory."

Blu smiled. "Oh, it is, it is... I've found another."

Author's Note
If you enjoyed this novel, please leave a review at the vendor of your choice.

Enjoy an excerpt from *The Blue Veil*

"Welcome to Nightshade, Mir-randa," Remare whispered seductively as he came up behind her. His breath blew strands of her hair across her cheek.

Miranda smiled. "Hello, Remare."

"What has you so rapt tonight that you look so preoccupied?" Remare was pleased that Miranda seemed to welcome his presence. He slipped an arm around her waist and pulled her close to his chest so that he could inhale her scent and feel the warmth of her body flush against his.

"I was just remembering the last time I was here. I met Cyra and Lizandra for drinks over there." Miranda pointed to the couches where they had all once hung out. "I asked Gavin to get me a drink, but he got me a soft drink instead because he could smell the painkillers Gabriel had given me *because*...I had gotten shot protecting your boss, Valadon." Miranda then turned in his arms to face him and he felt her heart immediately speed up and that pleased him even more.

Remare grinned at the memory. "At the time, I thought you culpable in the assassination attempt." He pulled her closer, noting the vampires in the club had wisely given them a wide berth—obviously sensing a vampire in their midst far older than most of the vampires who frequented the club. "I've since...remedied my perceptions."

"Um-hmm. Like the haircut?" Miranda asked as she turned once again in his arms so that her back faced his front.

"Ah, are you still angry with me, Mir-randa?" Remare asked as he inhaled her wonderful female scent. "You know I would never intentionally harm you."

Miranda sighed. "I trust you, Remare. Not sure about the vampire over there with the petite human in his embrace." She pointed with her chin in the direction of an incredibly handsome vampire dressed in a dark shirt whose head was nuzzling the neck of the brunette in his arms.

Remare moved Miranda's hair out of the way to closely inspect her flesh. "Your neck has no scars. Did Gabriel never bite you in all the time you were with him?" He slid both hands around her waist and hooked one hand over his wrist securing her within his hold.

Miranda smiled at his sign of affection and slid her hands over his forearms. "Gabriel didn't like showing his fangs to me, let alone using them. I once asked him if I could touch them and he looked as if I asked him to stick his hand in a pot of boiling water."

"Gabriel denies his very being. For a vampire to withhold using his fangs with a loved one is something no vampire would ever willingly do."

Miranda gestured to the amorous couple across the club from them. "I don't think that vampire is going to deny himself anything." Miranda turned her head sideways and whispered, "Isn't that illegal?"

"Perhaps." Remare shrugged. "There are privacy rooms in the back. But no one here seems to be complaining." Content to hold her in his arms, Remare felt Miranda stiffen as she watched the other couple. "Does the prospect of being bitten *frighten* you, Miranda?"

Miranda turned her head to the side and raised an eyebrow. "You said no vampire would ever deny himself. Why not?"

Remare could not believe this was something Gabriel had never shared with her. "To a vampire, part of the pleasure comes from knowing his partner would willingly share something precious—rich with the very nutrients a vampire craves most."

Miranda shook her head. "Then why have the blood banks at ValCorp?"

Remare laughed. "When you are hungry for a meal, do you always go out to restaurants or do you sometimes go to a grocery shop for your food?

Miranda smiled. "I see. So the blood banks are for storage?"

"In a manner of speaking." Remare looked up at the couple across the balcony and watched as the male playfully ran his fangs up the woman's throat. He could stop it, but he wanted Miranda to watch. "Why does doing what is natural to us, so upsetting to you?" he asked seductively.

"I'm not upset," Miranda said as she stroked his arm. "It just doesn't strike me as a fair deal."

"How do you mean that?" Remare looked around the club and its clientele. "The humans who frequent this establishment know it is a vampire club. They come here and offer themselves willingly—no one here is coerced or forced. To be inside a vampire's embrace is something they welcome—to feel wanted, desired. They trade their blood for the embrace, the sensation of desire, the yearning to be desired...the need to feel beautiful."

"You and I see things very differently, Remare." She tilted her head to his side. "I see a predator sighting prey. He desires her blood—*his food.* He uses his allure to pull her in, seducing her. But what does she get in return? A neck with holes in it! I've seen women like her before in these clubs. They're needy.

Not as beautiful as the female vampires here—perhaps not even as attractive as the humans she associates with. I see the longing of a desperately lonely woman. She wants illusion, magic...and he gives it to her. But it's not real, not lasting. Tonight, after he's sated himself with her blood, she will go home alone and still...be alone." Miranda whimsically turned to face Remare and grinned. "Want a drink?" she asked sardonically.

Remare smirked. "If you're offering."

He led her to the corner of the bar where the vampires left to give them room. When the female blond bartender neared them, Miranda said, "Vodka and cranberry juice on the rocks. "What would you like?"

Oh, a great many things, Remare thought as he looked at her neck. "Merlot, please."

When their drinks arrived, Miranda met his eyes and raising her drink said, "Cheers."

Remare considered the woman who had fought courageously against him in the archives, had taken a poisoned dart for his vampire lord, and had fought against Rogues in a dark alley. Miranda was one of the bravest women he'd ever met. Yet the thought of being bitten terrified her. "Did a vampire hurt you, Mir-randa? Is that why you flinch at the thought of being bitten?" If so, he would hunt down the vampire and tear him limb from limb.

"No, I've never been bitten. That's not it. I just don't want to be someone's food." Ironically, Remare heard her stomach growling. "Remember, you're talking to a woman who's never had her ears pierced, so yeah, being perforated doesn't appeal to me. I like my blood right where it is: In my veins."

Remare looked at her ears and smiled. Miranda was as stubborn as he once believed and...in denial. He would change that. And soon. "That sounds much like fear, Miranda."

"Not really." Miranda shrugged. "I'll grant you this: If you or Nick were hungry and needed blood, I would offer you my wrist." Miranda lifted her arm for emphasis. "I just don't want to be seduced for it."

Remare considered her words then nodded. "We have business to discuss. Come to the office and we can discuss it privately." Placing his hand on her lower back, he led her to Rosalyn's office.

When Remare flicked on the low lights, Miranda noted the feminine touches in the room from the pink cascade fabric on the couches to the pink and beige Aubusson rugs. A table was set up in the middle of the room with an elegant meal prepared. She turned to look at the vampire in question.

Remare grinned. "I thought you might want...a bite."

Miranda laughed. "Yes, yes I would."

When Remare took the lids off the meal, he said, "Chateau Briand—cooked medium to your liking. Assorted vegetables in a light Hollandaise sauce."

"What? No dessert?"

Remare gave her a smoldering look. "That comes later." He pulled out her chair. "Care to join me?"

Miranda prayed her stomach wouldn't growl again. "Oh yeah. It looks marvelous. Thank you."

"My pleasure." After seating her, Remare lowered the lights more and then joined her.

Miranda felt her breath catching. She sensed Remare's presence even with her eyes closed. Lately, her senses were sharper than usual, seemingly becoming more hyper-alert whenever she was in close proximity to the one vampire who sent shivers up her spine. Miranda found his scent of evening woods soothing.

When they had watched the other vampire with the seductive music playing, and the fact that they were in dark shadows, apart from all the others, Miranda knew she was on dangerous ground. But she wouldn't run from it—not this time, not like before when she had run from ValCorp and its *two* dominant vampires: Valadon had intimidated her; Remare had intrigued her...and that had scared her even more.

After dinner, Miranda went to the large window behind the desk and looked down on the dance floor and watched the vampires and humans dancing. The server cleared away their table while Remare spoke to one of his Torians on the phone. Remare was a fine conversationalist and she'd enjoyed having dinner with him. A lot.

When Remare ended his call, he joined her by the window. "The club's patrons can't see in, but with the lights turned down all they might catch is a glimmer of a shadow."

"I like the lights low, after staring at a computer screen all day my eyes welcome the soft light," Miranda said without turning around.

Remare stood beside her. "How does Nightshade compare with your chosen club, Werehaven? Morel once told me you preferred it there."

Miranda smiled at the mention of a man's name who had always teased her and welcomed her into his and Cyra's home. "He did, did he? What else did he tell you?"

"Simply that you, Lizandra and his wife were great friends who liked to dance, but that you always chose to go to Werehaven."

"I've known Liz for a long time; Werehaven is like a second home to me." God, I miss Cyra, Miranda thought. "Your club is impressive, too. It's just that...I know most of the Weres at Werehaven and except for Cyra and Morel, I don't know anyone down there."

"Are the Weres so very different from vampires?"

Miranda smiled as Remare's arms circled her waist as she continued watching the dancers below. The Weres ran much warmer than humans and often danced shirtless and more provocatively. "The Weres are my friends."

"Are not the vampires, also?" Remare turned Miranda in his arms. "Am I not...your friend?"

Miranda's heart was hammering in her chest as she peered into his eyes. There was a time when Remare terrified her—now, he scared her for other reasons. Her body seemed to have a mind of its own as one hand drifted up his arm to go around his neck and the other stroked up his chest to cup his cheek. "Are you?"

Remare pulled her closer so that her body was flush against his and brushed his arousal against the apex of her thighs. Twining his hand in her hair, he took her lips in a heated kiss and she felt her body molding to his. Her body became electric at his touch, fully sensitized to his hunger for her. When he deepened the kiss, she became aware that his fangs had elongated.

Miranda felt the world drifting away and tightened her hold on him—rapt in the passion that was Remare. Vampires were cold-blooded, but the heat he was throwing off warmed her very soul. She broke from his mouth to kiss his cheek and jaw, then some insane, primitive part of her commanded she kiss his neck, thoroughly enjoying the spicy taste of him. Miranda moved his collar out of the way, relishing his masculine scent and ran her tongue slowly up his vein from shoulder to ear. Remare's groans s only encouraged her more to explore his body. His neck fascinated her to the point where she felt if she had fangs she would bite him.

"Do it, Miranda," Remare said as he tightened his grip on her. "Do it."

Miranda knew what Remare wanted, what he needed. She just wasn't sure she could give it to him. His sylvan masculine scent was intoxicating and she was getting drunk on his essence. Miranda wanted to give him what her senses were telling her he needed, but she knew vampire blood could be lethal to a human.

Miranda didn't want to admit it, but the thought of having a vampire sink his fangs into her flesh both repulsed and attracted her.

"You don't have to draw blood, Mir-randa. Close your lips and teeth over my skin and I swear I will show you pleasure you have never known before or ever imagined."

As if waiting for those very words, Miranda opened her mouth to take him in and sucked on his flesh, enjoying the taste of him. When she felt his body begin to shudder, she slowly closed her teeth over his skin and bit down.

Remare made sounds deep in his throat that woke something primal in her.

The fear of the unknown had Miranda slowly removing her lips and teeth from Remare's neck as a semblance of sanity returned. Just a hint of blood showed in her teeth marks. She used her tongue to brush against her mark. Her breath ragged, she said, "well...that was a first."

"And not the last." Remare kissed her forehead, then took her hand and led her to the couch. His eyes smoldering, he positioned Miranda on top of him, her legs splayed on either side of his. She slid forward so that her core was directly over his groin enjoying the sensation of his rock hard cock beneath her over-sensitive flesh.

Miranda always knew Remare was handsome, sexy. But the erotic, hungry way he was looking at her now transcended everything she had ever imagined. Her breathing matched the cadence of his breaths and she threw her head back as she rubbed her core over him—imitating the dance of sex.

Remare wrapped her hair around his fist and demanded, "Ride me, Miranda. Ride me," as he lifted her hips in rhythmic ecstasy to his own thrusts against her.

Miranda loved seeing Remare roused and wanted to dance with him in the way of vampires. She wanted to give him the pleasure his eyes were pleading for—a high so profound they could swim in it, enjoy the sensations drifting over them, through them.

Remare gripped her waist, his fingers nearly bruising her flesh, to slow down her pace. He held her eyes for a moment before kissing her again.

Available Now

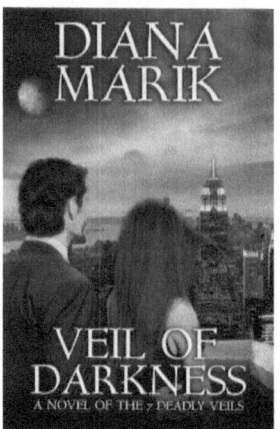

Veil of Darkness
Seven Deadly Veils, **Book Three**

When Nickolas Valadon, nephew of the High Lord of New York, goes missing amidst other vampire abductions by the Human Order of Light, the task of finding Nick goes to Remare. Known as a ruthless, but sexy investigator, Remare contacts the Elemental, his former lover, Miranda Crescent, to assist in the hunt. As they work together, his desire increases to the point where he will defy the devil himself to have her—despite the punishment that will be meted out, death.

Having been forsaken because of Remare's fealty for High Lord Valadon, Miranda distrusts the dashing vampire she once fell for, even though she still yearns for his sensual touch. During their search, Miranda will discover secrets about her Elemental origins and ancestry that may threaten her status at House Valadon.

However, burning desire is not easily denied and feelings long buried intensify to searing heights. In a world turned chaotic by the HOL, Miranda and Remare will risk the vengeance of the High Lord to be together and discover a world of passion neither has ever known before. But passion comes with a price and secrets, no matter how well-guarded, never stay hidden for long.

Available Now

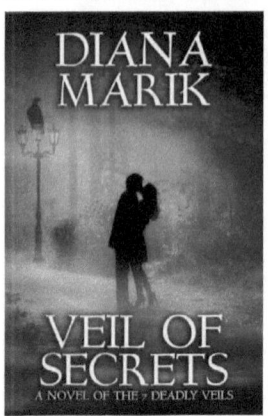

Veil of Secrets
Seven Deadly Veils, **Book Four**

Caught in Queen Magritte's snare and forced to wed someone he loathes, Lord Valadon, King of the vampires in New York, enlists the aid of two of his most powerful allies to thwart the plans of the Queen of All Vampires. Learning that his son survived, but unable to ascertain his whereabouts, he will call upon his trusted friends to locate the one person who can stop his upcoming marriage.

Meanwhile, Remare's return is hardly what Miranda has been dreaming about. With her association with Guy de Montglat revealed, her relationships with Remare and Valadon become strained. If she wants to keep her dreams alive, she will have to choose who to give her oath of loyalty—to her own bloodline or to the vampire who holds her heart.

Everyone has secrets, right? Remare knows this, but the secrets Miranda has been keeping threaten to tear them apart. Only through trust can their love survive. Now he must find a way to earn her trust or risk losing her forever. A situation that will not bode well for House Valadon.

March 2019

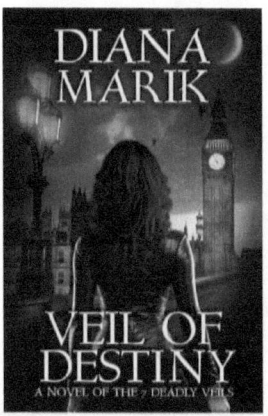

Veil of Destiny
Seven Deadly Veils, Book Five

While vacationing in London, Miranda and Remare learn of an old book that may contain clues to the destiny of Others, *The Book of Origins*. Encountering allies as well as adversaries, their search will take them from ancient libraries to London's darker and more sinister sections. And to an old castle whose eccentric inhabitants may know more than they are willing to impart.

Haunted by dreams of a mysterious woman, Miranda has long yearned to discover her *Elemental* heritage and uncover truths concerning her abilities. However, some secrets are never meant to be unveiled and may destroy what she holds sacred. Remare agrees to help Miranda, but fears their search may arouse the interest of an old enemy bent on revenge.

They will try to keep each other protected from the forces trying to drive them apart. But the fates may have different plans: A destiny neither one of them never imagined...nor desired.

Diana Marik is the author of the Seven Deadly Veils Vampire Series. She grew up in New York City and has her MA in English Literature from Hofstra University. Before becoming an author, Diana worked as an educator, mental health therapist, yoga instructor and camp counselor.

Among Diana's passions, traveling is her favorite. One of her favorite places to visit is the American Southwest and her home away from home, New Orleans. When not writing, Diana loves discovering museums. In her leisure time, she enjoys going to the movies and hanging out with her friends.

Diana is currently at work on her latest novel in the Veilverse and would love to hear from her fans. She can be contacted at www.dianamark.com